LADY AND THE SEA

A Novel Based on a True Story

Oceans of blessings,
Sharon Leaf

Sharon Leaf

WESTBOW
PRESS
A DIVISION OF THOMAS NELSON

WestBow Press books may be ordered through booksellers or by contacting:

WestBow Press
A Division of Thomas Nelson   -
1663 Liberty Drive
Bloomington, IN 47403
www.westbowpress.comw
1-(866) 928-1240

ISBN: 978-1-4497-2270-8 (sc)
ISBN: 978-1-4497-2271-5 (hc)
ISBN: 978-1-4497-2269-2 (e)

Library of Congress Control Number: 2011914905

WestBow Press rev. date: 9/27/2011

For my husband, Rob . . . you are my everything.
My family . . . you warm my heart.
Pastor Ulf and Birgitta Ekman . . . you are my heroes.
The crew and volunteers on the World War II ship . . .
you are in my memory, and in God's heart.

May the legacy of the MS Restoration live on

ACKNOWLEDGMENTS

First of all, I thank the Lord for his love, patience, and grace—you got me to where I am today. Thank you, Mom and Dad, for faithfully taking me to church, where I met Jesus as Savior and best friend at the age of eight. Dad, your humor still amazes me at your young age of eighty-nine; and Mom, I can hear you singing *When I Survey the Wondrous Cross* up there at heaven's gate.

To the Tega Cay Writer's Group—your support has kept me hangin' on. To Roxanne Hannah, my editor and friend, for believing in my story.

And for all of you who read this novel, may the message encourage you to shake off all fear, lose sight of your shore, and take a leap of faith into a new ocean. I love y'all! Shalom.

Lady and the Sea ... the journey

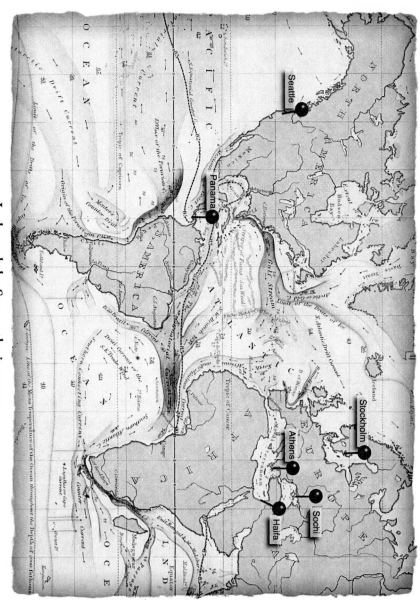

1

July 1995

Within minutes of the MS *Restoration*'s entering the Haifa harbor, an Israeli gunboat sped from the port and circled the World War II vessel. As two soldiers aimed their deck-mounted machine guns at the ship, another shouted instructions in Hebrew through a loudspeaker.

The captain of the MS *Restoration* responded over the ship's radio, "Please, speak to us in English!"

Rosie grabbed the rail. "Do they think we're terrorists?"

Jesse touched her arm. "Rosie, calm down."

"Do they think we're pirates?"

"Just calm down," her husband repeated, holding out his hand.

"Will they make us jump overboard? I don't have my life jacket," she spoke, fighting back her fear of water that was trying to surface once more.

"Rosie, you must get hold of yourself."

Her mind raced as she gazed up at the man who'd brought her on this unpredictable journey. *Jesse's right. What's come over me?* Rosie asked herself, all the time wishing she didn't have to go to the bathroom. She didn't dare leave his side.

The ship, her fellow crew members, and their special passengers—the Russian Jews—had finally reached their destination. No more troubled waters. No more hurricanes. No more delays. On this hot July morning, they were home free—or so they thought.

Rosie looked at the crew, poised as if they were ready to hit the deck. "Isn't this ironic? We've traveled halfway around the world, and this is the welcome we get."

"Stop your engine!" the soldier shouted.

Within seconds, they were dead in the water.

Rosie's stomach churned. She hung her head over the side of the ship and let it rip. After wiping her mouth with a hankie, she grabbed hold of Jesse's arm. She'd heard stories about people who'd experienced close calls. Her seventy-year-old father once told her about the time his ship almost went down in the China Sea during the war. "At that moment, my whole life passed before me," Talmage said.

Now feeling lightheaded as the Israeli soldiers glared at the *Restoration* through their binoculars, Rosie wondered if this was her moment.

1

PART ONE
Beginnings

You cannot discover new oceans until you are willing to lose sight of the shore

2

World War II raged across the Atlantic and throughout Europe. Ships were needed to transport war materials, and so, in 1945, the US Navy commissioned a Georgia construction company to build two hundred cargo ships. Ships in the larger fleet were called liberty ships; those in the smaller fleet were knot ships. Miss Knot was built as a sturdy 338-foot-long ship, weighing in at 5032 tons. Young and inexperienced, transporting cargo would be a safe task for her. She was a lady with a purpose, and she didn't hesitate to strut her stuff.

After he graduated from high school, Talmage Cook left his home in Tennessee and moved to California. Like his ancestor, Captain James Cook, his love for adventure and his sense of wanderlust led him to enlist in the military. He had his heart set on sailing the seas in the Navy, but he was drafted in to the US Air Force and was soon stationed in South Carolina.

The young men at Shaw Air Force Base had nothing better to do with their nights than hang out at the local canteen to drink beer and look at the pretty girls. It was a warm, humid, southern night when Private Cook's eyes fell upon the prettiest girl in the room. One look, and he was a goner. He moved toward the petite redhead through the smoke-filled haze and then stuttered, "Would you like to dance?"

Katherine answered with a smile as she placed her hand in his. As Talmage guided her across the dance floor, her intoxicating Tweed cologne lured him even closer.

The young lovers danced their nights away to the music of Frank Sinatra, and within a few weeks, Talmage proposed. They were married three weeks later.

Nine months to the day, Katherine gave birth to their baby girl. She was fragile like her mother, and had her father's dark hair and olive complexion.

"She's as delicate as a rose," Talmage said as he sat next to Katherine's hospital bed.

"You're quite poetic for a California boy," Katherine teased as she held their daughter.

"I'm a southern boy from Tennessee, remember?" He touched his firstborn's tiny hand. "And this is our little *southern* rose."

"Then we'll name her Rose," Katherine said.

A few months later Katherine was hanging pictures in their one-room apartment when Talmage burst through the door waving a piece of paper. "Let's sit down; I have some wonderful news."

He led Katherine to the tattered loveseat that her sister, Eunice, had given them.

"You got a raise! Now we can buy a new sofa!"

"No raise yet, but something even better." He paused, then smiled. "I'm going to be stationed in California."

Katherine's face turned white. She sat motionless.

"We're moving!"

"Moving?" she asked, her brown eyes flashing. "We've never talked about moving, but maybe we should have."

"Where did you think we were going to live?"

"In Sumter, of course. I've never traveled more than fifty miles from here, and I've never been away from my family for more than a week." She stood in the middle of the living room. "I might as well be moving to Siberia!"

Although Talmage had grown to love the southern hospitality and the miles of tree-lined highways of South Carolina, he couldn't imagine settling down anywhere but in California. All he had to do was convince his wife that she would soon be living in paradise.

"You'll love California—orange groves are everywhere, and the summers aren't sticky. We'll live close to the beach so we can go swimming anytime."

Staring at him, one thing she knew for sure. "I'll never swim in the Pacific Ocean!"

"That's okay, hon, you don't have to. I'll take Rose swimming while you lie on the sand." He held up a small white envelope. "And look! I bought tickets to California on the Atlantic Coastline Railroad, so we'll see the United States like real tourists."

"Okay, darlin', I'll go, but you must promise me that if I don't like California, we'll move back to Sumter."

"I promise. But once we're settled, I guarantee you'll never want to leave the golden state."

Katherine walked over to the corner of the living room and lifted Rose out of their borrowed bassinet. "It looks like you're going to be our little *southern California* rose."

Within a month, they were settled in their two-bedroom duplex in Long Beach, California. One night as Katherine stood at the stove attempting to cook one of her southern meals, her face began to turn the color of the grits she was stirring.

Talmage had noticed that she was spending a lot of time in the bathroom. "Hon, are you okay?" he asked.

Katherine figured this was as good a time as any to make her announcement. "I'm pregnant." She dashed to the bathroom, leaving Private Cook standing in the kitchen, stirring grits and wondering how they were going to make ends meet.

Katherine had finished baking Philip's first birthday cake when Talmage walked through the front door waving a piece of paper. Katherine sat down and positioned herself for another wild announcement.

"Don't look at me like that, Katherine. You're going to love my news! I've been promoted to sergeant. We can afford to buy a house!"

She jumped up and ran into his arms. "Now, that's the kind of news I like to hear."

A few weeks later, they found a two-bedroom bungalow in a new housing tract in the midst of dairy farms and cow pastures. "Downey is the perfect town to raise a family," Talmage stated proudly.

"And look—two bedrooms, a bathroom large enough to turn around in, and a kitchen big enough for a table and four chairs. But can we afford it?" Katherine asked as she stood admiring the black and white linoleum kitchen floor.

"Five thousand dollars is a lot of money, but I'm sure we can swing a fifty dollars a month house payment," Talmage assured his war bride.

The new home erased all signs of homesickness for Katherine. When Rose and Philip napped, she sewed kitchen curtains on her used Singer sewing machine, and in the evenings she cooked recipes from her new *Betty Crocker Cookbook*.

Three years later, Talmage came home carrying a large manila envelope. He placed it on the kitchen counter, and then after dinner, he turned to Rose. "Take Philip in the bedroom to play."

Sending the kids to their room was a sign that a serious discussion was to follow. Katherine stood at the sink, waiting. "What's going on?" she asked.

"The Navy is recruiting, so I enlisted."

Katherine breathed a sigh of relief. "Is that all? I'm sure the Air Force will miss you but—."

"I already received my orders," he interrupted.

Katherine took her hands out of the sudsy water and dried them with a red and white checked dish towel. "Orders?"

"I'm going to be stationed overseas in Japan and Korea—for a year."

She sat down in the kitchen chair across from Talmage.

He watched her face closely. "Are you okay? You're turning white. Are you pregnant again?" He sat, waiting, fearing her answer.

"No, I'm not pregnant, but I might faint anyway. I never imagined I'd be left alone with two children—for a year."

"You won't be alone. Now that Mom and Dad are settled in Elsinore, you'll be able to spend some time with them. The kids love the ranch."

A month later, Katherine held back tears as Talmage gathered her in his arms. "We'll write every day. The time will go by fast."

"I guess sometimes dreams are interrupted when real life comes knocking on your dream-house door," Katherine sighed.

3

In the fifties tension grew in the Pacific, so smaller ships were needed to maneuver in and out of the islands along the Pacific Rim. After the National Defense Reserve Fleet transferred Miss Knot to transport troops, she experienced her first makeover. Bunk beds were set up in the holds below, and small fans were mounted to move as much air as possible in the stuffy rooms. Showers, sinks, and toilets were installed, and an extra galley and troop's mess was added.

Troops carrying duffle bags over their shoulders invaded Miss Knot's gangway, headed for Korea. Pictures of wives, children, and lovers were taped to the metal bunks, where endless letters were written. The China Sea was harsh, sending the off-duty soldiers to their bunks, but Miss Knot stayed true to her course. When appetites returned, the men made their way to the troop's mess. They enjoyed coming together to boast of their sweethearts who waited for them back home. Concerns of war were overshadowed by the love that was in the air. One soldier boasted that when he returned home to California, he was going to take his kids to the San Diego Zoo.

Weathering a typhoon on the China Sea proved Miss Knot seaworthy as she forged through fourteen-foot gales. She stayed true to her course, and when the war was over, the young ship resolved to give her valuable cargo a safe journey home across the Pacific. Afterward, the troop carrier sat in port, wondering what her future held. She had heard dreadful stories of the fate of ships that were of no further use to the government. Many were sold to the ship-breaking graveyards, where they were scrapped for a price—a fate the young ship dreaded. With only a comparatively few running hours, her engine still had a song of its own, so surely they wouldn't send her there.

A year later, Rose was awakened by someone gently nudging her shoulder. A deep, familiar voice whispered, "Rose, wake up, Daddy's home."

She slowly opened her eyes. In the glow of her night-light, a tanned, handsome man was kneeling next to her bed. *Am I dreaming?* she wondered. The uniform made him look like one of those movie stars she had seen on their black and white television. The soldier took his daughter in his arms, and she clung to her daddy until her brother leaped out of bed.

"Daddy! Daddy!" Philip cheered as he jumped into his father's arms. "Daddy, now we can play Geepo!" Talmage loved hiding in closets and then running out with arms waving, yelling, "Geepo is going to get you!" Daddy and Philip could run through the house laughing and screaming for hours. Rose didn't like the frightful game one bit.

"We'll play Geepo tomorrow, and next week we're all going to the San Diego Zoo."

Finally, Katherine said, "It's late; Daddy needs his rest." Rose caught her mother winking at her father, but she was too young to understand their secret message.

Rose loved spending summers at her grandparents' ranch. As soon as Philip's feet hit the dirt driveway, he was nowhere to be seen, which was the way Rose liked it. She loved picking strawberries with her grandmother in the warm sun. Afterward, they would sit in the porch swing while Ga-Ga read Rosie's favorite Golden book, *The Little Train Who Could*. She never tired of the story about the brave little train.

This particular day, Rose shared a little secret. "Someday I'm going to do something brave," Rose told her grandmother.

Ga-Ga smiled. "I'm sure you will, little Rose, and do you know why?"

"Why?" Rose asked.

"Because you're the bravest little girl I know."

Philip changed into his swimming trunks and jumped up and down until Talmage walked him down to the pond. "Come on, Nosey-Rosie, let's go swimming!" Philip yelled, holding his towel in one hand and his father's hand in the other. Rose answered him by sticking out her tongue.

"Rosie's a scaredy-cat, just like Mommy!" Philip teased.

She hated it when he called her Nosey-Rosie, a nickname the neighborhood boys gave her last summer. She wanted to haul off and punch their lights out—but instead, she ignored them.

"Come with us, Rose. I'll teach you how to swim," Talmage said.

She moaned, "Do I have to?"

Talmage thought a minute. "I'll make you a deal. Instead of swimming lessons, I'll teach you how to float on your back."

She mumbled, "Oh, okay," but as she walked down to the pond, her mind was made up: she would never learn how to swim, no matter how many names her brother's friends called her. For now, she figured she was plenty brave just to learn how to float.

Every Sunday the Cook family piled in their four-door 1950 Chrysler and drove to the little Baptist church a mile down the road. Rose never completely understood the pastor's sermons, but one Sunday night when she was nine years old, counting the minutes until they would go home to watch Elvis Presley on the *Ed Sullivan Show*, she saw a light.

She sat mesmerized as Miss Blankenship, a missionary from Africa, told the story of how she walked hours down muddy roads to visit the small villages. "I helped feed the hungry children, and then I shared about God's love."

Rose wondered why anyone would leave their home to walk down muddy roads in a faraway country. She was turning to look at the wall clock when her eyes locked with the missionary.

"I was never afraid because I didn't go to Africa alone. God went with me," Miss Blankenship shared. "If you ask Jesus into your heart, he'll travel with you wherever you go."

Then Miss Blankenship looked straight at the small congregation, who barely had enough money to pay their bills, much less buy an airplane ticket to travel to a foreign country, and asked, "Who would like to travel for the Lord?"

Rose began squirming in her seat. She felt as if the missionary was talking directly to her.

"What's wrong, Rose? Do you have to go to the bathroom?" her mother asked.

"I want to go forward," was the only explanation Rose could give. That was enough for Katherine. She grabbed her daughter's hand and led her down the aisle. When Rose reached the altar, she repeated after the pastor, "Lord, I love you; please come into my heart." Then she added, "And someday I would like to travel the world with you."

Rose didn't fully understand what happened to her that night, but right away she invited her neighbor and best friend, Priscilla, to Sunday school.

4

The US government did not scrap Miss Knot. Instead, they sent her to a storage port near San Francisco, where she sat, reminiscing of days gone by, thinking her glory days were over. Miss Knot heard about the transport ship, Henry Gibbons *that President Roosevelt had commissioned to bring one thousand refugees from Italy to the United States. Perhaps she could be used for such a mission.*

The retired World War II veteran's heart raced when he read about the troop carrier. Could this be the ship of his dreams? His hands shook as he turned the steering wheel of his '61 Ford toward the dock. At first glance, his instinct told him to turn around and head for home. The ship's outward appearance showed signs of aging, but hadn't he acquired a few wrinkles himself since retiring?

Two years later, the ship was still for sale. Since the old war vet wasn't planning on making her seaworthy, he figured he could afford her. He took out a G.I. loan, and then moved on board and began converting her into a military museum. The task brought a surge of energy to the vet's ailing body. The project caught the interest of other local war veterans, and they began donating old military objects suitable for such a ship museum—some of value, most of none.

Rose hung up her Mickey Mouse ears, grabbed her faithful dancing partner, the closet doorknob, and danced her afternoons away to Dick Clark's *American Bandstand,* all the while begging her best friend to go to Sunday school with her. Finally, Priscilla made it clear that she didn't have time for church; but the truth was, Priscilla was boy crazy and she'd rather spend her Sundays at the beach with her older sister, flirting with the surfer boys. Rose knew her friend was annoyed with her constant Sunday morning invitations, but she continued asking anyway.

Priscilla's dream was to one day become a famous hairstylist to the Hollywood movie studios, so she'd spend hours in Rose's bedroom, practicing. She teased and styled until every hair flipped on the ends. Rose loved having her hair coifed in the latest fashions.

One Saturday night as Elvis crooned "Don't Be Cruel" in the background, Priscilla announced, "Okay, I'll go to Sunday school with you on one condition."

"Name it," Rose said.

Priscilla placed her comb on the dresser. "You have to give me some of your rock-n-roll records."

Rose looked at her friend in disbelief. "You know I won't give you my records, so why would you even ask?"

"My dad told me now that you're saved, you won't be allowed to listen to rock-n-roll music or go to dances or wear makeup."

"Your dad is so wrong," Rose replied matter-of-factly. "Saved or not, I will never part with my forty-five RPM records. Well, maybe I will if I decide to go to Bible college someday. But here, I'll give you "Love Me Tender." I bought one, and then my Aunt Eunice sent me one for Christmas."

Rose continued to listen to Elvis, went to all the school dances, and wore the latest shades of Coty's frosted pink lipstick. She proved Priscilla's dad wrong.

It had been four years since Rose and her family had driven three thousand miles for a Carolina vacation. She overheard her mother admit that she would never move back to Sumter—California was her home now—but in the spring of Rose's sophomore year, Talmage noticed Katherine moping around the house.

"What's wrong?" he asked his wife after dinner.

"I miss my family," she said, holding back tears. "So I thought we could spend our two-week summer vacation with Eunice at their beach house in Surfside."

"I'd love to, but I need to stay home and work. Remember, there are bills to pay."

Tears welled up in Katherine's eyes. Talmage hated to see his wife cry, so the next night after dinner, he turned to Rose. "Take Philip outside for awhile." He caught Rose rolling her eyes, so he added with a wink, "Come back in thirty minutes, and we'll have ice cream." Rose quickly led her brother to the back door.

"I have a great idea," Talmage said with a twinkle in his eyes. "Why don't you and the kids take the Greyhound bus to South Carolina for the summer?"

Katherine's eyes widened. She began wringing her hands. "I've never gone on a trip alone with the kids. I've never been on a trip alone, period."

Talmage took her hands. "You'll be fine. The bus driver will watch out for you. It'll be an adventure."

"I don't like adventures!"

"How much do you miss your family?"

It was settled. Katherine, Rose, and Philip would take a Greyhound bus from Los Angeles to Surfside, South Carolina.

Rose dreaded going away for the summer and leaving Priscilla with all the cute surfer boys. She argued with her mother for days, begging to let her stay home.

"I'll fix dinners for Dad, and I'll do his ironing," she pleaded.

"Rose, you hate to cook, and you've never ironed a day in your life. You're going to Surfside, so I don't want to hear another word about it," Katherine said as Rose threw her blue one-piece swimsuit into her suitcase.

Later that night, Rose called Priscilla, hoping for some consoling words.

"Don't worry about me, Rosie, I'll try not to have *too* much fun without you," Priscilla teased.

First it was Philip, then the neighborhood boys, and *now* her best friend had nicknamed her Rosie without asking permission.

"Okay, I won't worry, and I'll do my best to have fun without you, Miss Prissy," she said. "And don't call me Rosie." From that moment, Rose had tagged her friend.

Katherine and Philip found two seats directly behind the bus driver, leaving Rose to sit next to a big black woman in the seat behind them.

"Hello, sweetie, I'm Miss Hart. Is this the first time y'all have ridden a Greyhound? I travel to Atlanta every summer to visit my daughter and her family. Would you like to sit next to the window?"

Rose nodded, exchanged seats with Miss Hart, and then pulled a *Photoplay* magazine out of her straw purse—anything to keep from talking to Miss Hart. Rose read her movie star magazine from cover to cover, and made it a point to stare out the window of the stuffy bus as they crossed the Arizona desert.

Rose pulled Katherine aside at the Phoenix bus station. "Mom, you have to trade places with me. You love to talk, and I'll go crazy if I have to listen to that lady for one more state!"

"Her name is Miss Hart, and you'll be fine, Rose," Katherine said as she handed her a pack of peanut-butter-and-cracker Nabs.

Rose sat back down next to Miss Hart and then muttered, "This is going to be a long trip; I'm going to take a nap."

"What did you say, darlin'?" Miss Hart asked.

"Uh, I said, here, have some Nabs," she said, handing her a pack.

Driving through the New Mexico desert, the air-conditioned bus couldn't keep Miss Hart's thick, musty cologne from making Rose feel ill, preventing her from eating the rest of her Nabs. And she couldn't sleep due to Miss Hart's monotone voice rattling through the night.

"I'm so blessed to be a teacher so I can spend summers with my family. Did you like your teachers last year?"

11

To keep from answering, Rose pretended to be asleep.

The big Greyhound finally drove out of the Texas plains and into the lush southern state of Louisiana.

Rose gasped as she stepped off the bus in Shreveport. "This must be what a sauna feels like."

"You better get used to it, sweetie," Miss Hart said, grinning. "Humidity is what the south is famous for."

As the bus passed through the small towns of Mississippi, all Rose could think about were the lazy days of summer she had left behind in California.

"It's taking forever to get to Surfside," Rose murmured, not realizing that Miss Hart had overheard.

"It's a long trip, sweetie, but it's worth every mile to be close to the people who love you."

Rose had no other choice than to listen as Miss Hart talked about the importance of God and family. As the bus pulled into the Montgomery station, Miss Hart gathered her purse. "Lord, my mouth is dry!"

Rose was thirsty too, so she followed Miss Hart to a nearby drinking fountain. She noticed brown stains on the basin as she gulped down the warm water.

Katherine pulled her daughter away. "Rose, don't drink from that fountain," she said, directing her daughter to the other side of the bus station.

"Why does this water taste colder?" Rose asked Katherine after sipping from the clean faucet, but her mother didn't answer. Rose glanced over her shoulder to watch Miss Hart bending over, drinking the warm water as if it were straight from an ice-cold stream. Above Miss Hart's head was a sign Rose had never seen before. It read, *Negroes Only*.

For the remaining hours, Rose decided to spend more time listening to Miss Hart and less time reading, so Rose handed her mother the *Photoplay* magazine opened to page thirty-two. "Elizabeth Taylor and Rock Hudson are filming a movie together in Texas . . . something about a giant."

When they arrived at the Atlanta bus station, Miss Hart gathered her purse and jacket, then looked at Rose, her eyes twinkling. "Bye, sweetie. Have a wonderful time with your family, and I hope this is your best summer ever."

Miss Hart swayed down the aisle of the bus, then turned and waved as she made her way down the bus steps. Rose decided to heed Miss Hart's request. She was going to have the best summer ever.

Aunt Eunice's son, Buddy, wanted to show off his California cousin to all his friends. Buddy dropped Rose's suitcase in the guest bedroom and then offered to drive her to the pier in his new red jeep. She was out the door and sitting in the jeep before he had a chance to finish his Coca-Cola.

Buddy drove down Surfside Drive and then swerved left on Ocean Road. "Aren't we going to the pier?" Rose asked.

"Later," Buddy said as he pulled the jeep in front of one of the smaller beach cottages. "I met a guy from Texas who's visiting his sister for the summer."

"So?"

"Well, cuz, I think you should meet him."

"I don't want to go on a blind date, especially with a Texan."

"And why's that?"

"I hear that Texans talk all the time, and they exaggerate," she argued as he offered his hand to help her out of the jeep. She jumped down, ignoring his hand.

"Let's make a deal. If you don't like him, just wink, and we'll leave," he said as they walked up the gravel path. "I sort of promised that I'd fix him up with my California cousin," Buddy said as he knocked on the screen door.

"Buddy!" Rose yelled, but it was too late.

"Howdy, I'm Ken," the six-foot boy said as he opened the door. Black hair, green eyes, tan . . . no, bronze. Rose was so busy staring at the gorgeous Texan that she forgot to give her name.

Buddy obliged. "This is my cousin, Rose."

As if he didn't know, she thought.

While they sat at the kitchen table talking about the upcoming stock car races at the Darlington Race Track, Ken and Rose took turns stealing glances at each other. It was her turn when their eyes locked. Embarrassed, she grabbed her sweet tea and took a gulp.

"Let's go to the races Friday night," Buddy said.

"Do you want to come with us, Rosie?" Ken asked.

She was having a hard time resisting those piercing green eyes. *What did he call me?*

"Can I call you Rosie?"

"Uh, yes, of course." She couldn't think straight. "I have plans with my cousin, Judy Ann, on Friday."

Then he smiled that brilliant Texas smile.

"But I'm sure I can change them," she said, blushing.

Those were the two quickest decisions she had made since she could remember. One, to go to the races. And two, forever to be called Rosie.

"Just one look, that's all it took," she hummed softly in between dainty sips of sweet tea.

Rosie suffered through an hour of listening to Buddy and Ken talk about stock car racing. She pretended to be interested, but all she wanted was to be alone with Ken.

At last, Buddy looked at his watch. "Do y'all wanna drive down to the pier?"

Rosie looked at her cousin, as if to say, *what do you think?*

He got the hint. "I'll come back in an hour."

Days turned into weeks. Ken played volleyball on the beach while Rosie watched, basking in the hot, humid sunshine. She learned to tolerate the flies and mosquitoes to watch Ken move about like a bronze Texas god.

Each day, after playing several games of volleyball, he'd yell, "Hey, Rosie, let's go for a swim!"

Rosie would always smile, "Not today." Ken never asked why she refused to join him in the warm Atlantic. *Good Texas southern hospitality,* she thought. Then for a brief moment her fear of water faded. *Maybe I should ask Ken to teach me to swim.* Just thinking of how it would feel having Ken's hands on her body while she was trying to dog paddle for her life in the warm Atlantic Ocean sent a much-needed chill up and down her spine.

In the afternoons they sipped Coca-Colas at the pier café while the jukebox played "Stuck on You" by Elvis. And oh, those hot southern nights of making out on mosquito-infested sand dunes. Rosie had never felt like this before. *This must be love,* she concluded as she scratched yet another welt on her right thigh.

Then all too soon, summer ended. Ken and Rosie kissed good-bye at the bus station and promised to write every day.

"I love you, Rosie," Ken whispered.

She held back her tears, stood tall, and then responded, "I love you too."

As the Greyhound bus pulled away from the Myrtle Beach Bus Depot, Philip teased, "Rosie has a boyfriend!"

Rosie ignored her brother and smiled as she remembered Miss Hart's words. *Yes, Miss Hart, I did have the best summer ever.*

As summer turned to winter, passionate love letters replaced their steamy nights on the Atlantic shore, but eventually Ken's football and Rosie's dancing took the place of pen and paper.

Two years later, Talmage thought a trip to Surfside would be the perfect high school graduation gift for Rosie.

"Isn't Mom coming?"

"Not this trip. This is your special graduation present," Talmage said, beaming.

"You'll let me travel alone?" Rosie asked, her heart pounding.

"You'll be fine, Rose."

"Dad, remember? It's *Rosie.*"

"Yes, of course . . . Rosie. It's been two years, and I still forget. As I was saying, Rosie, sit close to the bus driver, and if anyone approaches you, whack them over the head with your purse and then go to the nearest employee and report them."

Rosie loved her dad's optimism about life. Listening to him give serious yet humorous instructions erased all traces of fear. Besides, Prissy had a new romance, and Rosie's on-again-off-again boyfriend, Bob, casually told her that he was going to spend a few weeks at his parents' summer house in Lake Arrowhead. A summer in Surfside sounded like the perfect escape.

On a warm June night, Prissy watched Rosie neatly pack her yellow polka-dot bikini. "I can't believe your dad talked your scaredy-cat mom into letting you go to South Carolina, on a bus—alone!"

"Mom's trying not to worry. When I asked her if I could stop in Texas for a night to see Ken, do you know what she said?"

"She said no, of course."

"She said *yes,* of course," Rosie said, smiling as she tucked her new silk bra and panties into the corner of her suitcase.

Prissy's mouth dropped.

"But she gave me a what-not-to-do warning list," Rosie added.

"A warning list?"

"'Rose,' she said, 'it's been two years since you've seen Ken. Now, I was young once, so remember, it only takes one drop of—'"

"Eeek! What did you say to that?" Prissy asked, cringing.

"I told her, 'Mom, I'm a big girl. I know all about the birds and the bees. Besides, I'm doing what my Sunday schoolteacher told us: I'm saving myself for the one I marry.'"

"Me too!" Prissy declared.

The girls laughed as Rosie finished packing.

So in the summer of '63, Rosie boarded a Greyhound bus for Surfside, South Carolina, alone.

The next afternoon, Rosie stepped off the bus on one of the hottest days in Texas, wondering what Ken would look like, sound like—feel like—after two years. Would he still be able to make her melt every time she looked into his eyes? All doubt diminished as he walked toward her and took her in his arms.

"Rosie, you're even prettier than I remember," he said in his slow Texas drawl. "Let's go somewhere where we can cool off and be alone."

She was hypnotized by his dreamy voice, but the spell was broken when he said, "But first, let's get something to eat."

Typical man, she thought. Food was the last thing on her mind.

They talked for hours as they dined at the Lubbock Bar and Grill. Later that night, in a small air-conditioned motel, Rosie spent a Texas hot-one-night-stand with her first love. Making out—kissing and hugging—was now replaced with petting—a bit more touchy-feely. They were taking it to the next level, but Rosie was still determined to save herself for the man she would one day marry—and hearing her mother's voice in the background, she knew just when to stop the action.

"I guess I'm old-fashioned," she said, panting.

"That's one reason I love you," he said, breathing heavily as he wiped the sweat off his forehead.

Texans have much more respect for girls than those crazy California boys, Rosie thought as she watched Ken gather his shirt off the floor. He kissed her goodnight and whispered, "I'll pick you up at seven for breakfast."

The next morning as the bus pulled away from the curb, Rosie waved good-bye to Ken through a smudged window. She pulled a hankie out of her purse and wiped her tears. The scene brought back painful memories of another summer past.

As the Greyhound made its way through the south, Rosie wondered if she would ever see her handsome Texas gentleman again. This time there were no promises of love letters.

Rosie's southern family helped take her mind off of Ken. She drove Buddy's jeep up the coast to Myrtle Beach and down the coast to Garden City. She shrimped at dawn in the muddy waters off Murrells Inlet with her uncle, and fished off the Surfside Pier with Aunt Eunice. The humid nights wrapped around Rosie like a security blanket as she danced in the moonlight with the fireflies. Then all too soon, summer was over.

Rosie was sipping sweet tea in her favorite rocking chair on Aunt Eunice's screened porch, listening to the crickets' serenade, lost in thought, when the screen door screeched open.

"Are you all right, darlin'?" her aunt asked as she sat in the rocking chair next to Rosie.

"I'm going to miss all this," Rosie said, looking around. "Why did Mom and Dad move to California?"

Aunt Eunice smiled. "Your daddy was stationed in Sumter, but when he got his orders for California, your mama chose to follow him."

"But Mom's a southern lady at heart."

"It wasn't easy for your mama to pick up and move three thousand miles away, but someday, when you meet the right man, you might be asked to follow him to some even stranger places than California." Eunice reached over and wrapped her sweaty arms around Rosie. "But until then, you're always welcome here."

"I'll be back next summer," Rosie promised.

5

Surrounded by so many old museum objects, Miss Knot was starting to feel somewhat ancient herself.

Rosie didn't want her summer in Surfside to end, but by September, she needed to return home to begin making plans for her future. She had always talked about going to college with Prissy, but now a full-time job seemed inevitable. Her parents had no savings, much less money for college. A week after arriving home, Rosie answered a want ad in the *Los Angeles Examiner* for a stenographer position at the Pacific Telephone Company in downtown Los Angeles. After the second interview Rosie thought it was only fair to talk to Prissy about her plans, so on a cool autumn evening, she asked Prissy to meet her at Stox Café.

After chatting awhile, Rosie took a deep breath and then casually mentioned, "I need a job before I can pay for my journalism courses."

Prissy put her coffee down. "But we talked about going to college together, remember?"

"I know how much a performing arts degree means to you, and I don't want to stand in your way."

"Maybe this is a sign. I interviewed at Autonetics Aircraft yesterday and if they offer me a position, I'll be able to buy a car. I'm getting tired of borrowing my dad's old Ford."

Rosie stared at Prissy. "When were you going to tell me?"

"I was going to call you tomorrow. I'm taking two evening drama classes a week at Fullerton Community College."

"Well, since you mentioned cars, the phone company pays good, so I'm going to buy a Mustang with a great stereo system."

"That'll make that crazy commute to L.A. a little more tolerable."

Rosie raised her coffee cup. "Here's to our future!"

Even with their forty-hour workweek schedules, Rosie and Prissy always found the energy to dance their Saturday nights away at the Cinnamon Cinder Dance Club for the sophisticated over-eighteen crowd. Until Ken finished his fall and winter classes and could write more, Rosie was happy to hang out with her fun-loving friend.

But no matter what time Rosie came home, Katherine always woke her early on Sunday mornings to go to church. "Rose, if you can go out dancing on Saturday nights, then you can give God an hour on Sunday."

And each Lord's day, Rosie pulled herself out of bed and headed for the shower, mumbling under her breath, "Yes, Mother."

After months of dancing to the Beatles, Rosie wanted to do something more useful with her time, so she talked Prissy into going on a week-end mission trip to Tijuana, Mexico with the young adult group from church.

"How did I let you talk me into coming?" Prissy asked late Friday night as they walked down a dirt road to the children's orphanage. As they spread their sleeping bags on the cold concrete floor, Prissy glared at Rosie. "You owe me!"

By Saturday afternoon, Prissy and Rosie sat on the concrete orphanage floor laughing as they taught the dark-skinned girls how to play jacks.

Late Sunday night as the rented school bus crossed the Mexican border into California, Prissy turned to Rosie. "Promise me we'll come back next year."

Yawning, Rosie recalled the joy of being surrounded by the sweet Mexican girls giggling as they played jacks on the cold orphanage floor.

"It's a promise."

Spring of '65 was exceptionally hot, so Prissy didn't have to ask Rosie twice to play hooky from work. Within an hour, they arrived at the beach and strategically claimed their territory next to the Huntington Beach pier. They passed the time sunbathing and flirting with the cute surfer boys. Out came the baby oil, mixed with a touch of iodine. Within minutes, beads of sweat were shimmering all over their oil-soaked bodies.

"Let's go in the water," Prissy said as she glistened her way toward the water's edge.

Rosie didn't swim, but she was ready to take a quick dip in the knee-deep waves close to the shoreline. She was splashing her way back to dry land when she bumped into a slim blond guy staggering out of the water carrying a surfboard. He was breathing heavily and looked dazed, so Rosie's first instinct was to reach out to him. He smiled, trying to give the impression of a cool surfer, but she could see that he was embarrassed.

A stocky guy came running out of the water toward him. "Hey, dude! You survived a riptide!"

Rosie couldn't take her eyes off of the survivor.

"He's cute, but he looks too young for you," Prissy said and then sank beneath the water.

Rosie continued watching the surfer as she thoughtlessly waded into waist-high water, colliding with a little girl.

"Hey, lady, watch where you're going!"

Too late—glub, glub. Rosie drank in what seemed like gallons of saltwater as she fell underneath a wave. Arms waving, she tried to touch bottom with her feet.

Prissy called out, "Rosie, you can stand up in the water!"

Embarrassed, she stood up as the little girl ran crying to her mother.

"Lady, you need to learn how to swim," the mother yelled.

Prissy shook her head. "You really do need to take swimming lessons, girlfriend."

"Not on your life," Rosie muttered as she limped across the hot sand.

California was experiencing the hottest Fourth of July in years. After a long day at the beach, Rosie was looking forward to showering and watching fireworks in the backyard with her family. That is, until Prissy came up with one of her bright ideas.

"Let's go to Disneyland tonight."

Prissy pulled her Volkswagen into the driveway, then turned to Rosie. "Why are you hesitating?"

"Ken's supposed to call . . . but he told me that the other night."

"And the night before," Prissy added. "We're just going to have a little innocent fun."

"Okay, I'll go, but only if you come over early and style my hair."

"It's a deal!"

Black hair piled high around her new hairpiece and skin kissed from the sun, Rosie was feeling giddy as they strolled down Main Street, until a female employee asked her to put her sweater on. "Sorry, no midriffs are allowed to show," she said as she politely pointed to Rosie's tanned tummy.

"Oops, sorry . . . I forgot the new Disneyland rule," Rosie replied as she placed one arm, then the other, in her new ice pink cardigan.

As soon as they turned into Frontier Land, Rosie stripped off the lightweight sweater and then stuffed it in her purse.

"That's the craziest rule I've ever heard of!" Prissy said.

"I didn't buy this new crop top to cover it up," Rosie added with an attitude.

The nine o'clock fireworks no sooner began when, out of nowhere, her rear was the recipient of a pinch, the kind women brag about upon their return from vacationing in Italy.

Without a thought, she turned around and slapped the young man on his cheek.

"Cheek-to-cheek," the good-looking guy said, smiling as he rubbed his tanned face.

Out of nowhere, Rosie's own personal fireworks began.

"It was an automatic reaction," she said in defense.

"I apologize," he slurred. "I think I had one too many beers before I came to the happiest place on earth." He laughed, as did his friend.

"Rosie, lighten up," Prissy joined in. "They look like nice, fun-lovin' guys!"

"I'm Paul, and this is my friend—"

Before he could finish, Prissy asked, "How old are you, Paul?"

Rosie felt her face turning crimson. Why did Prissy always have to act like a big sister?

"Twenty-one," Paul answered.

Prissy shook his hand, then took his friend's hand and headed for the Matterhorn.

"I'm Rosie . . . and I'm nineteen."

Paul and Rosie laughed as they strode towards the Matterhorn and later stared into each other's eyes as they danced under the stars to the Beach Boys' "Little Surfer Girl."

By midnight, Rosie's heart was racing to Annette Funicello's "Tall Paul," so when he asked for her phone number, she didn't hesitate. She dug in her purse for a pen and paper.

"Topaz 8-6974. Here, let me write it down for you."

A few dates later, Rosie found herself in a most awkward position while making out with Paul on his living room sofa. It was too soon to be in this place of passion, but as the fireworks began to build, the hairpins holding Rosie's hairpiece began to fall to the floor.

"I think we should stop," Rosie said, panting.

No reply—only heavy breathing.

As Rosie continued to struggle, the hairpiece Prissy had perfectly placed on her head earlier that evening began to slip off. Paul thought every hair on Rosie's head was hers, so she held her fake twisted braid with her right hand while she tried to push Paul's heaving body away with her left.

"Paul, we better stop!"

But Paul had gone temporarily deaf—*guys do that when their fireworks are about to ignite.* As Rosie held onto her hairpiece for dear life, she could hear her mother's voice resonating, *Rose, save yourself for the man you marry.*

I'm trying, Mom, honest!

And remember, it only takes one drop of—

Too late. Within seconds, the fireworks were over. Rosie pulled up her capris and then staggered down the hall to the bathroom. As she looked in the mirror—hairpiece dangling from two hairpins—she knew they had passed the point of no return, false braid and all. After pinning the hairpiece properly around her natural hair, she made her way back to the living room.

"Why are you so quiet?" Paul asked as he turned on the television.

"When I was in the bathroom, a thought crossed my mind."

"What thought?"

"I was thinking . . . what if I'm pregnant?"

"I doubt it, but if you are, I'll marry you," he replied, as if she had asked him to ride the Matterhorn one more time.

Rosie didn't remember driving home, and as soon as she closed her bedroom door, her knees hit the floor.

"Oh God, I know I've messed up. Please forgive me," Rosie cried. She had been taught in church about God's forgiveness. Rosie was sure he forgave her, but she was much harder on herself.

For days, Rosie tried to bargain with God, which never works, but she tried anyway. "Lord, if I'm not pregnant, I promise I'll do everything right for the rest of my life."

I'm just overreacting to the situation. One quick encounter, a tiny little sperm, couldn't produce another life—could it? Of course not.

Rosie had almost convinced herself, until two weeks later when she started throwing up morning, noon, and night. She had to fight the urge to fall asleep while typing at her desk, and she spent lunch hours sleeping in the ladies' lounge. Each night she fell asleep on Paul's sofa while he watched TV.

Two weeks later, and still no period, she made the dreadful appointment with her family doctor. He took one look into her fear-filled eyes and then smiled and patted her right cheek. "Rose, it's the nice girls who get caught, but we'll take a pregnancy test anyway." She was sure his remark was supposed to make her feel better, but it didn't.

A week later, while vacationing with her family at Lake Arrowhead, Rosie walked to the village pay phone to make the dreaded call to Dr. Drews' office. The test results rang in her ears: her greatest fear had come to pass—she had conceived.

Rosie couldn't remember walking back to the cabin. She headed straight for the bathroom to throw up, but before she could close the door, Katherine tried to pop her head in the door.

"Rose, do you want a slice of this delicious sausage and cheese pizza?"

"No, Mom. I have to go to the bathroom."

Slam. Barf.

Rosie wiped her mouth and then sat on the side of the tub. "Lord, I can't bear to disappoint Mom and Dad, but I don't know how I'm going to keep this a secret," she prayed as she rubbed her tummy.

The next day Rosie drove down the mountain, straight into the arms of the father of her child. The TV was blaring as Paul led her into the living room. She sat next to him on the all-too-familiar sofa.

"Paul, I have something to tell you."

He lifted his arm. "In a minute; I'm listening to the news."

Aside from Paul's flippant remark on the night of conception when Rosie suggested she might be pregnant, they had never talked about marriage. They barely knew each other. He wasn't ready to get married. His divorce wasn't final—the divorce Paul just happened to mention to her a week earlier during an Old Spice TV commercial.

Rosie made her way to the bathroom and threw up while the TV blared something about deadly riots taking place in East Los Angeles.

An hour later, Rosie walked out of Paul's apartment with her secret, while Paul stayed glued to the TV, watching policemen yelling and striking hundreds of black men.

Rosie spent weeks carrying the sex-before-marriage guilt. Her mind worked overtime, causing nagging headaches. One night she stopped at a pay phone on the way home from work and called Prissy. "Can you meet me at Stox Café in an hour? I need to talk."

Over untouched coffee, Rosie spilled her secret.

"Is that why you're not drinking your coffee?"

Rosie nodded, pushed her cold coffee aside, and then continued, "I'll find a home for unwed mothers."

"Do you really want to give your baby away?"

Rosie started wringing her hands. "No I don't! Do you think they'll make me give my baby up for adoption?"

"You're nineteen years old; no one can force you to do anything," Prissy said, trying to console her friend. But Rosie's mind was already going further down a dark path.

"Abortion would solve all my problems. I can go away . . . you can drive me . . . no one will ever know."

Prissy's eyes widened and then filled with tears. Before Prissy could respond, Rosie slammed her fist on the table, almost knocking over her cup.

Prissy jumped.

"Wait! What am I talking about? This is crazy! This life growing inside of me has every right to live." As Rosie placed her hand on her belly, something deep inside brought her back to the light. "Yes, I made a mistake, but this little one shouldn't have to pay with its life," she said as she handed her handkerchief to Prissy.

"Why won't Paul marry you?" Prissy asked, wiping her eyes.

"We haven't talked marriage." Rosie took a deep breath. "But it doesn't matter; I'm going to trust God that everything will work out."

"You have to tell your mom," Prissy said.

"No! I mean, I will tell her, but not yet." Rosie reached for Prissy's hand. "Prissy, it's our secret."

"Of course . . . our secret."

"Thanks for being here for me. You're a true friend."

Prissy squeezed Rosie's hand. "Isn't that what friends are for?"

As Rosie drove home, she figured she had no other option: she would become a statistic, one of the sixties' minorities—an unwed mother.

The next evening when Rosie told Paul she was pregnant, he turned the TV volume down. "Don't worry," he said casually, "I'll marry you as soon as my divorce is final."

"When is that?" Rosie asked, concerned about the timing.

"I'll call my lawyer tomorrow."

"I'd like a small wedding at my parents' house."

"Sure, whatever you want."

The next thing Rosie knew, the volume was blaring again, so she didn't bother telling her future husband that she felt too guilty to have a church wedding.

Later that night Rosie told her mom about the wedding plans.

"What about Ken?" Katherine asked.

"He was just a summer romance, Mom." All of Ken's unopened letters might prove her wrong, but it was too late now.

Katherine glanced at Rosie's tummy. "Why don't you want a church wedding?"

"Paul and I want a small ceremony at home. Besides, it'll save you lots of money."

"Rose, are you pregnant?" Katherine asked.

Why do mothers know so much? Rosie thought as she sucked in her belly underneath her loose-fitting blouse.

"No, Mom, I'm not pregnant," Rosie lied as she walked toward her bedroom.

Rosie and Paul exchanged wedding vows on a cold November afternoon and spent their honeymoon night at the Disneyland Hotel. Thanks to the Maidenform girdle she purchased at Sears and Roebuck a few weeks earlier, only Paul, God, and Prissy knew that Rosie was four months pregnant.

That night in their hotel room, Rosie ripped off the stretched-out girdle and threw it in the bathroom trash can. Free at last.

She placed her hand on her swollen belly. "Well, little one, it doesn't look like there will be any mission trips or summer holidays in our immediate future."

6

Two years into the museum project, the upkeep for the vessel proved too much for the old war veteran, so he put her up for sale and prayed, "Lord, may the future owners of this ship use her for your purposes." His request was heard.

A month later Rosie was still happily setting up house in their apartment in the San Fernando Valley. She was sitting at the small kitchen table, thumbing through her latest *House and Gardens Magazine* looking for ideas to decorate their nursery, when Paul came home from his daily afternoon motorcycle ride. He looked relaxed as he walked toward the kitchen. When he patted her belly, he asked, "Have you thought about a name for a boy?"

"You're quite sure we're going to have a boy, aren't you?" she asked.

"Yep."

"I was thinking about naming him Elvis," Rosie said.

"You are not naming our son Elvis," he said as he headed for the shower.

Thirty minutes later, she walked in the bedroom as Paul was fastening the last button on his new shirt. "I have a name for a girl . . . in remembrance of Elvis's hometown," Rosie said, smiling.

He looked up. "You want to name her Memphis?"

"No, silly," she said, chuckling.

"You're not considering naming our daughter Tennessee, are you?"

"You really don't trust me, do you?"

"Okay, I give up," he said, brushing his hair.

"In memory of Graceland."

He put the brush on the dresser. "Rosie, Graceland is not a proper name."

"Oh, I know. That's why we'll call her Grace."

"You've put some serious thought into this," he said, glancing in the mirror. "Grace is pretty . . . graceful . . . . I like it." He glanced at his watch and then kissed Rosie on the cheek. "I'm meeting the guys for a drink at seven; I'll be back in an hour."

Paul's watch must have stopped. An hour came at daybreak.

Grace was born in April. Motherhood came natural for Rosie; she was learning how to cook, she enjoyed cleaning their apartment, and she loved taking Grace for her morning walks.

Rosie was living the *Ozzie and Harriet* dream, but to her disappointment, Paul was not an *Ozzie and Harriet* fan. He lived life the same way he made babies—fast and without thinking. He thought it was the norm to mix married life with his carefree single friends, and often forgot to come home until dawn. By Grace's first birthday, reality was sinking in.

"Aren't you going to stay for the party?" Rosie asked Paul as he pulled up in front of her parents' house.

"Grace won't remember her first birthday," Paul said as he revved the engine of his new Chevy pickup truck. "I'll be back in an hour."

Afternoon turned to late night. Rosie's tears fell on Grace's porta-crib as she watched their daughter sleep. Paul loved Grace, but it was obvious he was not ready to give up his freedom. Married at eighteen, a father at nineteen, divorced at twenty-one, and married again at twenty-two. Too much, too soon, Rosie surmised.

After too many times of Paul staying out all night, Rosie's raw emotions couldn't handle Paul's unpredictable lifestyle. Talmage and Katherine opened their home to Rosie as a place of refuge. Prissy and her boyfriend helped with the move.

"I'm never getting married," Prissy vowed as she loaded her boyfriend's pickup with baby furniture.

"Don't say that. Marriage can be wonderful. My parents are a perfect example," Rosie said. But the next moment she was thinking, *but you can be sure I'll never get married again.*

A few weeks later, sitting in the small, disarrayed office of a lawyer she had found in the yellow pages, Rosie tried to hold her fingers steady as she signed her name to the foreign-looking divorce documents. Afterward, still dazed, Rosie lost track of time as she walked the back parking lot searching for her red Mustang. Exhausted, she drove home feeling like a real loser.

Eventually, Paul stopped picking up Grace for his weekend visitations. *I don't know how to take care of a one-year-old* was his reasoning. By day Rosie was a nine-to-five working girl; by night she was a tired-yet-dedicated mom. Saturdays were filled with cleaning, laundry, and marketing, and every Sunday Rosie drove Grace to the little Baptist church around the corner.

On a hot July Sunday, Rosie wished she was at the beach rather than in the small, stuffy sanctuary. She recalled a night long ago when she was nine years old. "Lord, I remember that night. I still want to travel with you someday. A girl can still dream, can't she?"

That afternoon Prissy stopped by on her way home from the beach. She was crawling on the living room floor with Grace when she asked, "Why don't you call your old Texas flame and see what he's up to?"

"Prissy, stop playing Cupid!" Rosie answered. Why did Prissy have to bring up the green-eyed Texan of long ago? But later that evening, on a whim, Rosie dialed a Texas information operator. Surprisingly, the operator gave her Ken's phone number. She took a deep breath, dialed, and at the sound of Ken's voice, she blurted, "You probably don't remember me . . ."

He had remembered, and two weeks later, Ken was driving to California. *Handsome and forgiving,* Rosie smiled.

Rosie took a few days off work and Katherine offered to babysit the week Ken was in town. Katherine had always liked Ken, perhaps because she was partial to southern boys.

"Let's drive to the beach," Ken suggested when Rosie picked him up at a nearby motel. His dreamy, southern drawl brought flashbacks of hot southern nights. She headed her Mustang toward Beach Boulevard.

Thirty minutes later Ken spread a blanket on the sand like he had done some three thousand miles away. Petting was now replaced with taking-it-to-the-limit. And so it went for five days, until it was time for Ken to return to Texas Tech.

"Will you wait for me to finish college?" Ken asked Rosie on their last night together. "I'll come back in June and then we'll make plans."

"Yes, I'll wait."

And she did—for three months.

Rosie later blamed it on the October harvest moon, but as she sat brushing her shoulder-length hair at her dresser, she threw her brush across the room. The walls of the house where she had grown up were beginning to close in. Ken's phone calls were becoming more sporadic due to his homework and late-night studies, so he said.

She stared at her reflection in the mirror. "Well, girl, so much for traveling the world."

Rosie turned the whirring fan toward her as she finished rolling the last pink plastic curler in her wet hair, a chore she dreaded. Talmage and Katherine were at Sunday night church, Grace was asleep, and she was contemplating ripping the curlers out of her hair and chopping off her dark locks, when the phone rang. She hoped it was Prissy so she could cry on her shoulder.

"Hi, Rose. Remember me?" She wasn't in the mood for guessing games. No one had called her Rose since high school. She was ready to hang up when a familiar Elvis drawl rang through the receiver.

"Bob?"

"Hey, you remember!"

"How could I forget that voice? That Elvis twang is what attracted me to you so many years ago! Prissy told me you were in Viet Nam. When did you get back?"

"Five days ago."

"How did you know I was living at home?"

"I heard Prissy talking about you last night at my welcome home party."

Bad news travels fast, she thought as she sat down in front of the fan. Bob's voice brought back memories of nights of making out in the backseat of his '61 black Volkswagen. *A former high school boyfriend wanting to date the divorcee,* she figured.

"I bought a new car the other day, so I called to see if you'd like to go for a drive."

Rosie stood and glanced in the mirror at a head full of plastic curlers—not a way to impress a guy who's been in the jungle for a year.

"My hair is loaded with hot pink curlers," Rosie said, hoping he'd be detoured for another night. But he'd been in the jungle too long.

"That's okay, I like hot—I mean, *pink.*"

Bob and Rosie were sitting on the front porch steps, strolling down memory lane, when she remembered why they broke up. When he became a big high school football star in his sophomore year, he started sneaking around with one of his former girlfriends. He had been two-timing for several weeks when Rosie got wind of the whole affair from Prissy. *Break up with him now! He doesn't deserve you,* Prissy had warned. She did and never spoke to him again, until tonight.

People can change, she thought.

Katherine recognized Bob as soon as she walked up the sidewalk. Talmage mumbled a hello and walked into the house. He never liked two-timers. By the conversation Katherine was having with Bob, she was more forgiving.

Rosie stood up. "Mom, Grace is asleep so we're going for a drive. I'll get my purse."

Katherine followed Rosie into the living room. "Isn't Ken supposed to call tonight?" she asked.

Rosie grabbed her purse. "Yeah; he was supposed to call last night too, and the night before. But I'm not sitting by the phone again tonight—I'm going for a drive!"

As they walked toward Bob's new car, Rosie turned around and caught Bob looking her over from head to toe—a good sign for a girl with a head full of plastic.

What started as a blasé Sunday night drive ended with a marriage proposal four weeks later. It happened so fast Rosie didn't take time to think it through, but she knew a few things to be true: Bob wanted to take Grace everywhere, a definite sign that he was good father material. And they loved each other. She needed a new beginning. Not later. Now. So she accepted his proposal.

She felt obliged to write Ken a short Dear John letter. She didn't want to hurt him, so she scribbled, *you deserve better . . . I'm sorry for any pain I've caused you.*

The letter she received from Ken a week later wasn't as considerate. *I hope you know what you're doing . . . you're a very mixed-up girl . . . I hope you find what you're looking for.*

Mixed-up? She crumbled Ken's letter and threw it in the trash, along with her own doubts. She was too busy making wedding plans to care about what an old flame thought.

A month later, an impatient twenty-one-year-old divorcee and an eager twenty-one-year-old sergeant made their way to the altar. The year was 1967, the summer of love.

7

The San Francisco port was beginning to close in on Miss Knot. Then one day another ex-serviceman came aboard. After inspecting her from bow to stern, Private Peters discovered the ship's veins were full of cosmoline—a good sign. He took out a loan, bought her, and then towed her to Seattle, Washington to begin converting her into a fishing boat. His goal was to give fishing instructions to young adults while sailing across the Pacific Rim. A fishing boat wasn't the image Miss Knot had in mind, but having young people on board would bring excitement to her age-defying veins.

After months of toiling over his finances, Private Peters couldn't come up with the full amount to convert the ship, so he would have to sell her. And once again, Miss Knot sat.

The seventies ushered in the women's movement. Liberation was at their doorstep. New opportunities were opening in the workforce.

"Why should we stay at home when we can have a family *and* successful careers?" Prissy asked one afternoon while talking with Rosie on the phone. "I want to make enough money to buy what I want, when I want."

"Prissy, you sound so different . . . so worldly. I think you've been hanging out with that local theater group too long."

Prissy ignored Rosie. "We can even burn our bras! So many choices—we can have it all."

Rosie laughed. "Don't you think you're going a little overboard on this women's movement craze?"

"Maybe, but it's definitely something to consider."

Rosie thought about it and decided she was content to be a stay-at-home mom, which left her no time to burn anything, except for a few dinners now and then.

Rosie had a full life. She volunteered as a Girl Scout leader, she wrote two novels that collected dust on a closet shelf, and she was an avid runner with a few hard-earned medals shoved in the back of a drawer. For Rosie, that's what liberation was about—having time to discover her talents while first giving herself to being a full-time wife and mother.

Meanwhile, Bob was trying to find his own liberation. Alcohol and drugs were his remedy to erase the nightmares of Viet Nam. Their marriage was on the eve of destruction when another movement came on the scene.

The Jesus Movement spread across America, radically changing the lives of thousands. One Saturday night before Bob had a chance to pop open his second can of beer, Rosie asked, "Why don't we go see what all of the fuss is about?"

Bob reluctantly agreed, so the next morning they drove to Calvary Chapel in Costa Mesa.

"I feel like I'm going to a circus," Bob said as they walked into the large tent that was set up in a dirt lot next to a small chapel.

"I read in the newspaper that they outgrew their building, thus the circus tent," Rosie said.

An hour later, before the pastor finished giving the invitation to accept Christ, Bob was halfway down the aisle, leaving Rosie standing alone. She was reminded of the night so many years ago when she was nine years old.

Bob didn't completely understand what happened that Sunday morning, but their rocky marriage slowly found solid ground. Bob lost his desire for alcohol and drugs, and the horse races were set aside for weekly Bible studies. They planned a mission trip to Mexico with a local Baptist church. After Paul moved to Utah, he consented to Rosie's request for Bob to legally adopt Grace.

So, with everything going so great, why was Rosie feeling so nauseous? She hadn't felt like this in seven years, since she lost her hairpiece and her virginity all in one night. Rosie had to know so she made an appointment.

Rosie and Bob sat in Dr. Drews' office, staring at his smiling face. "After five years, it looks like your miracle has come."

"What are you saying?" Rosie asked.

"You're going to have a baby," Dr. Drews replied.

"You're going to have a baby!" Bob yelled in Rosie's ear.

Rosie yelled back, "We're going to have a baby!"

Eight months later, their son was born. Holding Presley in her arms, she whispered, "It looks like the mission trips will have to wait awhile longer."

8

Miss Knot's future didn't look promising, but she wanted to believe there was more for her beyond Seattle's safe harbor.

Sixteen years into their marriage, Rosie was caught off guard. Or had she chosen to ignore the writing on the wall? Lately, Bob's six-pack of Coors appeared and disappeared regularly, and too many glasses of wine caused embarrassing moments with friends. Weekly gambling nights with the boys began cutting into their date nights and already-limited budget. And there were Bob's excuses to skip Sunday church. But it was his mood swings and edginess that alarmed her. When Rosie's life began reading like one of those soap operas she never had time to watch, she asked Prissy to meet her at Stox Café.

"When did this craziness creep in?" Prissy asked.

"A few months ago. Like tonight—he's playing poker at a friend's house."

"That doesn't sound like the Bob I know," Prissy said.

"Especially the night before Mother's Day. We're planning to go to his parents' after church for a big celebration."

"Is he going through that midlife thing?"

"Of course not. Thirty-eight is too young for that."

"Whatever it is, you'll work it out. You and Bob are the perfect couple," Prissy said as she grabbed the check. "I have to go; my dress rehearsal starts in an hour."

Rosie was relieved to change the subject. "Have you found anything interesting backstage lately?" she teased. She was happy her friend had found solace in the local theater, but she was hoping Prissy might find true love in the midst of the scene changes.

Prissy chuckled. "Are you kidding? They're all gay. But they make wonderful friends."

The next morning, Rosie was gathering her Bible and purse for church when Bob moaned from their bed, "I don't feel good."

Funny, he'd been well enough to spend the last two nights out gambling with his friends, Rosie thought. But an illness of this sort had been appearing out of nowhere lately.

"You stay home and rest," Rosie replied sympathetically.

Nodding, Bob turned to face the wall. Rosie tucked him in and then headed to church.

"What's wrong with Daddy?" Presley asked.

"Your dad needs his rest. It's Mother's Day, so by the time we get home, he'll be hungry for your grandma's home cooking."

Bob was still in bed when they returned home. "Maybe it's something you ate—or drank—last night," Rosie said as she felt his forehead for a fever. "I'll take the kids to your Mom's, but we'll be home early."

Bob grunted a faint okay.

They returned home that evening to a dark house.

"How are you feeling?" she asked as she turned on the dresser lamp.

"I'm still sick."

She straightened the covers. He'd obviously been tossing and turning.

"Can I bring you something to eat?"

"No, I need to be left alone."

She turned off the light and then walked out, closing the bedroom door.

Rosie was in the family room watching TV with Grace and Presley when the phone rang. She ran to the kitchen to pick up the phone, hoping not to disturb Bob. At the same moment, he picked up the phone next to the bed. *He must be feeling better.* But before she could say hello, Bob mumbled into the receiver a soft hello. Rosie listened, feeling like a spy in her own home as a young female voice whispered on the other end of the receiver.

"I miss you. When can we meet?" a young, eager woman asked.

For a brief moment, Rosie was stranded in time. She felt no heartbeat.

"Give me twenty minutes," he whispered, not wanting to be heard. Too late.

By the time Bob finished giving rendezvous instructions, her heart began to pound. She placed the phone on a dish towel and then marched toward the bedroom. She abruptly opened the door, flipped on the switch to the overhead chandelier, and then stormed to the sickbed. Bob looked as if he had seen a ghost. Rosie was sure he would have welcomed any unfamiliar presence at that moment rather than the monster that was glaring down at him.

"Who are you talking to?" she asked, her eyes glaring.

"I have to go now," he whispered in the receiver.

"Does your mistress know you're married?" Rosie blurted, loud enough for his Jezebel to hear.

"I'll see you later," he said.

Her husband's pale face told Rosie he was wishing to be anywhere but on his possibly soon-to-be deathbed. He stammered his words, but she interrupted him.

"You get out of bed, get dressed, and hit the road—and don't you come back!"

Bob quickly dressed and dashed for the bedroom door, thankful to still be alive.

"Can't I come back later? I'll sleep on the couch."

Rosie laughed nervously. "Come back? You must be kidding!"

"But where will I sleep?"

How dare he try to push her sympathy button! It usually worked, but not this time.

"I don't care where you sleep. You can sleep in one of those big, green dumpsters behind your favorite liquor store for all I care. Now leave!"

The message was loud and clear—no sympathy tonight. Bob walked out into the darkness, started his truck, and drove to his rendezvous, leaving Rosie behind, numb and sinking fast. Later, after Presley and Grace went to bed, alone in the darkness, she crumbled.

A few weeks later, after countless discussions and counseling sessions, reality hit. Bob chose the younger woman—seventeen years younger, to be exact.

When Rosie broke the news to Prissy on the phone, her friend was dumbfounded.

"I can't believe this is happening to you. This is what TV miniseries and sleazy novels are made of, or the latest gossip about the crazy couple next door," Prissy cried. "This is not the story about the all-American, picture-perfect couple I know."

"*Knew*," Rosie corrected. "And Prissy, stop being so dramatic. This is reality; it can happen to anyone. Right now, I have to think about Grace and Presley."

"That's right! You will not go under in this storm! Dog paddle if you have to, but you will make it through. Oh, sorry . . . forgot . . . no drama. Just know that I'm here for you."

A week later, tired from a full day of job interviews, Rosie pulled in the driveway to find a Buick with a Remax Realtors sign glued to the car door. Bob was showing a thin, pale man through the house when she entered the back door.

"What's going on?" Rosie asked, staring at Bob.

The realtor backed away.

"We're selling the house," Bob replied.

"We're what?"

"Excuse me; I'll be outside," the realtor said, and then made a beeline to the back door.

"Perhaps you have a love nest to crash in with your lover, but where do you think I'll go with Presley and Grace?" By now, she was tapping her right foot.

"I need the money."

"I bet you do! Is your little bimbo draining you dry?"

Rosie felt a sense of relief to finally yell at Bob, but she didn't have the energy to argue with his irrational thinking.

"The house is on the market, so you'll need to find a place to live," he said as he opened the back door. The phone rang, so he stopped to answer it.

"Don't touch that phone!" she said, pointing to the door. "Get out!"

Bob scurried out the door. She took a deep breath, trying to calm herself. It was probably Grace calling to say she'd be home from school before Presley got home. She watched Bob pull out of the driveway as she reached for the phone.

"Rose, can you come to the hospital now?" a shaky voice asked.

"Dad, what's wrong?"

"Your mother isn't feeling well, so Dr. Drews is taking some tests."

Katherine had been recuperating from a recent heart attack when, out of nowhere, she began suffering dizzy spells at the shopping mall, the beauty shop, while watching TV. She sometimes slurred her words and often forgot the simplest things. After she fell in the bathtub, Talmage called 911.

Rosie sat in the waiting room with her father, holding his hand, while Dr. Drews gave them the test results. "Mr. Cook, the tests show that your wife has multiple sclerosis."

The doctor continued to explain the disease, but Rosie didn't hear his words. She wanted to give in to her emotions and break down in the office, but she needed to stay strong for her father.

"I'll retire from my job at Douglas and take care of her," she heard him tell Dr. Drews.

"Mr. Cook, I don't think that would be wise. If you try to care for her, you could end up in a bed next to her," Dr. Drews explained.

As Rosie held his shaking hands, she watched as her father made the hardest decision of his life. The handsome, yet aging, sergeant would place his southern bride in a full-care nursing home.

Those same gentle hands that once reached out to hold Rosie so many years ago the night he returned from the war were now shaking regularly. She held them tighter, trying to give him the comfort he desperately needed, not knowing that in a matter of months, he would be diagnosed with Parkinson's disease.

It was after midnight before she collapsed in her bed. She stared at the ceiling. "Lord, I need your help. I'm thirty-eight, divorced, with two children, looking for a job and a place to call home. Mom's lying in a nursing home and Dad is calling out for moral support. This year has been my worst ever, and the future doesn't look too promising."

As the last tear fell onto her pillow, she drifted off, believing there had to be better days.

9

The Alaskan sea captain and his wife had been talking for years about buying a ship to establish a Bible school on board. Stuart Lang knew they would find the right vessel in God's time. When he read the article about the knot ship, he flew to Seattle. One look told him he had made a mistake to come. Time had taken its toll on the old ship, but as Stuart walked through the superstructure, he looked beyond her forty-something years of neglect and saw her inner beauty. One thing about Stuart: he knew his ships. He entered the engine room and inhaled the aroma of diesel as if it were a rare perfume. Perhaps Miss Knot might have a future after all.

In time, Grace and Presley adjusted to the divorce. Grace attended Cypress College by day and worked part-time at Buffums Department Store on weekends. Joint custody seemed to be the most successful solution, so Presley spent every other weekend with Bob, giving Rosie time to spend with her dad, who had moved to the local southern California mountain town of Big Bear to be near his brother and wife.

Saturday morning, as they were having breakfast in his rented cottage, Rosie noticed her father's hands shaking more than usual. Coffee spilled as he brought the cup to his mouth.

"Are you okay, Dad?"

"I'm fine," he said, wiping coffee off his sweater with a napkin. Embarrassed, he changed the subject. "I've been thinking. Since your house has sold and I'm living up here, why don't you and the kids move into my house?"

When Rosie started seventh grade, Talmage had added an extra bedroom to the two-bedroom bungalow. She had been grateful to finally have her own space back then. Now it was an answer to her prayers.

Rosie poured her dad a cup of lukewarm coffee. "Presley and Grace have always loved your place. And as you recall, this isn't the first time that you've opened your home to me. Thanks, Dad."

With shaking hands, he lifted his cup. "Here's to us—again!"

Prissy and her new friend, Roger, helped Rosie with the big move. Rosie noticed how the two laughed and joked around like friends. But friends didn't touch where Roger touched Prissy. Rosie smiled and pretended as if she hadn't seen a thing.

"By the way, you look gorgeous with short hair," Rosie said while stacking her clothes in the backseat of Prissy's car.

"Thanks, but I'm letting it grow. Roger likes long hair," she said, brushing a blond strand off her forehead.

"Are you and Roger serious?"

"No! I mean, Roger is, but I'm never getting married, remember?"

Rosie glanced at Roger's lean torso as he lifted a nightstand into his pickup truck. "He seems like a great guy . . . and he looks good too."

Prissy smiled. "Well, if you must know, I'm *thinking* about marriage—but that's all!" She picked up another box, noticing the contents. "I can't believe you still have these Elvis records. They must be worth a lot of money. Would you consider selling them?"

"Never!" Rosie said, closing the box top. "Elvis will follow me wherever I go."

Rosie was happy, maybe even a little jealous, when Prissy called a few weeks later to announce that she and Roger had eloped to Las Vegas. "We decided on a whim. That's the only way I could get up enough nerve."

"I'm happy for you, Prissy. You've found your man."

Rosie wasn't as fortunate. Even when she wasn't looking, creeps always seemed to cross her path, looking good and saying just the right words. After being married for sixteen years and then brushed aside for a much younger woman, almost anything looked good. There was the office Casanova, who wined and dined her; and the young hunk of a neighbor who showed up at her door at least once a week, begging for a cup of sugar. Rosie found them more entertaining than the books she was reading, but not nearly as safe. Her inner clock was way beyond the ticking point, but other parts were still in good running order.

Three years of looking for love in all the wrong places found Rosie restless and feeling empty. Her hormones needed a quick, safe outlet, so instead of wasting time going out with losers, she laced up her old jogging shoes and took off running, pushing herself to run three miles a night. A strong heart and lungs, more energy, and slim legs were a few benefits to her new regimen. Running was her answer to those long, lonely nights.

But one lonely night, after a three-mile run and a long cold shower, Rosie tossed in her bed, not able to sleep.

"Lord, I need your help. I'm forty-one and I don't seem to be going anywhere. Could you please steer me in the right direction?" Rosie asked, yawning.

Prayer always seemed to help.

Fighting the freeway traffic from Downey to Torrance was worth the frustration for Rosie to spend time with her mother. Through the years, Katherine had given her daughter the spiritual strength that helped sustain her through some tough times. Now, as Rosie sat on her hospital bed, Katherine kept Rosie in touch with her childhood memories and her spiritual heritage.

"Mom, you're my hero," Rosie would tell her over and over, but Katherine was too insecure for such talk—she would change the subject back to the good old days until Katherine would dismiss her. "Rose, it's getting late; you can go now."

The past weeks revealed to Rosie that her visits were numbered. Katherine grew weaker with each passing day, and she looked twenty years older than her sixty-six years.

One evening, as Rosie leaned over to kiss her mother good night, her heart became heavy. Now small and frail, Katherine's brown eyes still held their glimmer. *Can this be the same woman who selflessly gave her shoulder for me to lean on for so many years?* Rosie thought as she kissed her mother's cheek. "Mom, you're my beautiful southern belle."

Rosie knew it was time to release her mother to her heavenly home. Their tears blended as they prayed. God must have been ready too, because as Rosie held her mother close, Katherine was already halfway there. "Dad will come see you tomorrow."

Two nights later, Rosie was awakened at three in the morning by the ringing of the telephone. A nurse politely said, "I'm sorry to inform you that your mother passed in her sleep."

Rosie sat on the bed and looked heavenward. "Mom, you're home at last."

Through the night, the one who had been temporarily separated from his father as he hung on a cross so many years ago gave Rosie comfort.

"We'll all be together one day."

Talmage eventually moved back home. He told Rosie that mountain life was lonely, but she knew the drive up and down the winding roads was beginning to wear on him. Rosie welcomed his presence around the house. They sat over coffee, reminiscing about the days at the Lake Elsinore ranch, and after dinner, they often slow-danced to the music of Frank Sinatra. But once he joined the local seniors' club, he was gone more than he was home. There were field outings, Saturday dances, and Tuesday bingo. And his eyes twinkled when he mentioned the charming widow. The medication for his Parkinson's helped his shaking hands, but it was Doris who filled his heart with joy. "You can't put *that* in a bottle," Talmage said as he told Rosie of their plans to travel to Spain with the *Have Seniors, Will Travel* senior group.

Rosie was delighted with her father's news, and at the same time wondered if her turn would ever come to travel the world with someone special.

Talmage interrupted her thoughts. "Rose, your day to travel with someone special will come, so don't give up." He could see the doubt in her eyes, so he walked over to the stereo. "Now, let's dance around the living room for a while."

Several months later, Rosie had a dream that she was walking the streets in Jerusalem, and oddly, a tall, handsome man was leading her by the hand. She woke, confused. "Lord, you know I want to travel, but I don't know if I'm ready to trust a man again."

Silence.

"I don't even know if I can trust you, so please help me here."

Silence.

"Well, okay, I *might* be ready, but I've grown accustomed to living on my own. For example, if I choose, the laundry can wait another day. So I'm not sure if I'm ready for someone to invade my liberated lifestyle." Rosie took a deep breath. "And the big question is, am I ready to take on someone else's laundry?"

Rosie glanced upward. "Lord, I have a proposal. If I am to have someone in my life, I want to find him on your timetable, not mine." She smiled. "See? Patience is becoming one of my virtues."

She took her journal and a pen off her nightstand. "And, Lord, *if* the time comes, I do have a few requests. You do want me to be specific, right?"

Silence was her cue to write.

"Here's my wish list. Emotionally, I would like someone who has gone through similar experiences, both the good and the bad."

More silence. She continued writing.

"On the spiritual side, I want someone who will walk side by side with me, not one having to pull the other along."

Still, more silence.

"*And*, on a physical note—as selfish as it may sound—I'd like someone who is *nice* to look at. What I'm saying is . . . I trust you."

After the seemingly one-way conversation, Rosie dotted the *i* after writing the word *nice,* turned off the light, and left the future in God's hands.

The silence would soon be broken.

A few nights later, tired from a hard day's work, Rosie was tempted to skip her evening run. Then she glanced in the hall mirror. "Okay, girl, remember . . . strong heart, powerful lungs, and more energy." But who was she kidding? It was the svelte body that kept her hitting the road every evening after a long day of sitting at a desk.

After her three-mile run and a cold shower, Rosie fixed herself a peanut-butter-and-banana sandwich and plopped down in her easy chair to read her latest adventure novel. She was sunbathing at a seaside village in Greece when the phone rang.

Rosie often let the phone ring and then would check the message machine later, rather than listen to a salesman give his long-winded speech. But tonight she decided to pull herself away from sunbathing long enough to pick up. It was Prissy.

"I'm calling to invite you to go with me to a new Christian singles' ministry tomorrow night." Prissy had loved being married, but Roger hadn't, so he filed for a quick divorce, leaving Prissy alone and depressed. Months after Roger left, Prissy informed Rosie, "I'm not dating anymore. Men will say anything to get you into bed, and I'm not into that scene."

"Yeah, I guess they're just not into us as much as we'd like to think," Rosie admitted.

Prissy was ready to meet Mr. Right, so lately she had been spending her Sundays visiting large evangelical churches to see what they had to offer in the way of eligible men. Prissy knew Rosie was not into the singles' scene—or any scene, for that matter—so she plunged right in with her poor-Prissy pitch.

"I don't want to go to the singles' meeting alone," Rosie's no-nonsense friend moaned. "So you *have* to go with me tomorrow night. I need a word from God."

"No, Priscilla, what you *need* is a man," Rosie teased. "Okay, I'll go this time, but you *owe* me."

When Grace came home an hour later, Rosie gave her daughter the poor-Rosie pitch. "Prissy invited me to go with her tomorrow night to a Christian singles' gathering, so I'm inviting you to come along."

"Why are you going?" Grace asked.

"I need a man—I mean, I need a word from God."

"A Freudian slip, Mom?" Grace asked, chuckling. "Okay, I'll go, but you owe me, Mother Rose."

The next night Rosie felt awkward as she glanced around the large fellowship hall filled with singles of all shapes and ages. Prissy wanted to sit in the front row, but Rosie insisted on three safe seats near the back door.

While Rosie enjoyed listening to the upbeat songs, out of the corner of her eye, she caught Grace eyeing the cute guitarist. She glanced at her watch as a petite blonde named Barbara announced a March beach trip. But throughout the evening, her eyes had been drawn to a tall, tanned, blue-eyed man with a beard.

"Handsome, huh?" Prissy whispered. "I love the way he gives orders—he must be one of the leaders."

Rosie gave him another once-over. Her eyes stopped at his freshly polished cowboy boots. "It doesn't matter—cowboys aren't my type."

Driving home, Rosie asked Grace, "How did you like the meeting?"

"It was okay. I met a few gals, and I talked to the guitarist, but all I got out of him was his name and that he played college football and he loves fishing."

"What's his name?

"I think he said Tim, or Tom, or Todd. How about you? Did you have a good time?"

"It was okay, but I won't be going back."

The following Thursday evening, Rosie shivered as she opened the door to run a chilling three miles.

"It's only February, and I'm already wishing for spring," she said, shivering. A few weeks earlier she had spent the weekend skiing in Big Bear, the only reason Rosie could think of to be out in the cold.

The phone rang but she ignored it, thinking it might be Prissy trying to insist that she go to another singles' group. But by the fourth ring, she figured it might be Presley calling from his dad's, so she picked up.

"May I speak to Rose?" *Another long-winded salesman*, she assumed since he addressed her as only her family often did. He quickly introduced himself, as all good salesmen do.

"I'm Jesse Atkisson, and I'm calling to thank you for coming to our meeting last Friday night."

"What meeting? Oh, yes, the singles' meeting my friend dragged—I mean, *invited* me to. How did you get my phone number?"

"You filled out a visitor's card, remember?"

"No, I didn't . . . perhaps my friend filled one out for me. Well, thanks for calling."

Rosie was ready to hang up, but as he continued, she felt she was being slowly drawn into his world. Before she knew it, she was talking to the stranger on the other end of the line as if they knew each other. *What did he say his name was? Did I see him at the meeting?* She took a wild guess.

"By any chance, are you the guy who was giving directions and moving chairs?"

He chuckled. "You got it."

I'm talking to the cowboy!

"And how about you?" he asked.

In so many words, Rosie described herself as the brown-eyed brunette with the radiant smile.

He hesitated. "Gee, I'm sorry, but I can't place you. It was a large crowd."

Rosie suddenly experienced an attack of the deflated ego. But then again, her purpose had been to enter and exit without being noticed. Obviously, she had been successful.

"What have you been doing all your life?" he asked.

"Don't you believe in small talk?"

"Sure, later," he answered.

Okay, cowboy, I can bypass small talk. "I was married for sixteen years, and I've been single for three."

"I was married sixteen years too."

"I have a twenty-year-old daughter," she continued.

"So do I. Lynn's married and has a son."

He's a grandfather! Okay, I'll get him this time. "I have a thirteen-year-old son." *Top that, cowboy!*

"Well, what do you know? My son, Jay, is thirteen."

This cowboy has met me step-for-Texas-two-step!

"And I love to dance," she added.

"I don't dance," he admitted.

Then she recalled her three-item wish list. "Oh, that's okay, I don't dance much anymore."

An hour passed as they talked about the good, the bad, and the ugly of their past.

"Rose, may I call you after I finish contacting the rest of my list?"

"Yes, of course . . . and you can call me Rosie." *Grace is the culprit!* "And, uh, what was your name again?"

"Jesse."

Rosie pictured Jesse standing tall in his cowboy boots. "Don't tell me your last name is James."

"My first name is after my father, and my middle name, James, is my grandfather's namesake. My last name is Atkisson."

"Atkisson . . . you're Swedish?"

"Yes. And you?"

"Cook. Rose Adrienne Cook . . . English. Do you remember reading about Captain James Cook in your history books?"

"He discovered the Hawaiian and the Cook Islands in the Pacific. If you're from the Cook family tree, you must love to travel."

"I do, but I haven't, but I would—love to travel the world someday," she stuttered.

"I'm a traveler myself, but we'll talk about that later." Then he hung up.

Rosie's heart began beating rapidly before she stepped out into the cold night air to run her happiest three miles ever. The electricity through the phone line was enough to spur Rosie to finish in record time, and she returned home still dizzy from the phone call. This time when the phone rang, she was sitting, waiting.

"Hi, Rose," her father said cheerfully.

"Oh, it's you."

"Don't sound so disappointed," Talmage said.

"Sorry, Dad, but I'm expecting a call. Can I call you back?

"You sound like you're waiting for a call from someone special."

Rosie blushed. "You'll be the first to know, Dad. Bye!"

Jesse loved to tell stories. "When I was fifteen, my mother dragged me to the Los Angeles Coliseum to hear Billy Graham preach to a record-breaking crowd."

Rosie couldn't contain her enthusiasm. "I was at the Coliseum with my parents that night! Hey, were you the cute blond sitting two rows down who kept flirting with me?"

They laughed, and then Jesse told her about his favorite summer hangout, Surf City. "I nearly drowned in a riptide, but I didn't give up. I jumped right back on my surfboard."

"Huntington Beach was my hangout too." *Were you the blond surfer dude who staggered out of the water on that hot spring day?* She dared not ask; they had already experienced enough strange encounters for one night.

"Where do you live?" she asked.

"On the high desert, but I'm selling my house and my horses so I can move closer to the church."

"So that explains the boots and the beard."

"The boots will go with the horses, but I'm keeping the beard for awhile," he added. "My divorce was hard on my son, so I want to focus on giving Jay some spiritual roots, like my mother did when my dad left when I was a kid."

"Fortunately, my parents had a happy marriage until she died last year. It's the children who suffer from divorce. I wish there was something I could do to take away the pain that Presley went through."

"We can't change the past, Rosie, but we can help make their future better," Jesse said. "Now, speaking of the future, will you be coming to the meeting tomorrow night?"

Don't sound too eager. "I have plans," Rosie lied. *Please, God, don't strike me dead.* "But I can change them."

"I'll meet you at the door. How will I recognize you?"

Rosie hesitated, and then with every ounce of confidence, she answered, "You'll know me because, well, I'm a knockout."

And please, God, let him have a sense of humor to go with those baby-blues.

10

Stuart couldn't forget the World War II ship in the Seattle harbor, so he flew to Washington again. After several months of praying, Shelly and Stuart agreed it was time to buy the ship and begin making plans for their future.

Wearing the little black dress she had purchased on her lunch hour, Rosie strutted through the parking lot in her red patent leathers. She gave her long, permed hair one last fluff as she plotted her grand entrance. "Okay, tummy in, I'll glide through the door, and Jesse James Atkisson will be standing there, impatiently waiting for me. I'll smile, and as we look into each other's eyes, he'll know it's me, the knockout."

As Rosie walked through the door, Jesse was nowhere in sight. She breathed deeply and tried to regain her composure. A knot began building in her stomach when she spotted her cowboy talking, laughing, and standing between two very single-looking ladies. She turned her three-inch heels to make her exit, but as she pushed the door open, something inside told her, *don't leave.* The guitarist started playing so she reluctantly turned and found a seat near the exit. *I guess he can't help it if the women find him irresistible.*

Unknowingly, Jesse sat in the chair in front of her, so she took advantage of the moment to check him out, cowboy boots and all. She finally mustered up enough nerve to tap his shoulder. He turned around to be greeted by one of her knockout smiles.

"Hi there, are you Jesse?"

Jesse's eyes sparkled his approval. "Yes. Are you Rosie?"

She nodded, then looked down, embarrassed.

As he stood, Rosie crossed her legs to show off a bit more skin, but by the time she looked up, he was gone. Disappointed, Rosie uncrossed her legs, only to be surprised by a tap on her shoulder.

"You were right," Jesse said as the band continued to play.

"About what?" she asked, melting under the spell of his baby-blues.

"You *are* a knockout."

Blushing, Rosie decided not to tell him until later that she had been joking. She would not break the spell of this magical moment.

"Would you like to go for coffee after the meeting?"

She didn't hesitate. "Yes."

As he opened the door of his pickup truck, he gently touched her waist to help her up, causing her heart to skip a beat. *Coffee, tea, or—stop that! You must not ruin a perfectly wonderful evening!* she told herself as they sped off into the night.

When Jesse offered to pick her up the following Friday night, she didn't have to think twice.

Jesse arrived at her door carrying a large white box with a red bow.

"Here's a Valentine gift for you."

You're all I need, cowboy, Rosie thought as she opened the box. A white, fluffy teddy bear wearing a big red heart smiled at her.

"Someone for you to sleep with on these cold winter nights."

I can think of someone I'd rather sleep with, she thought, but dared not linger on such nonsense.

Rosie walked outside, looking for Jesse's brown pickup. *Why is he opening the door to that snazzy white Corvette?* she wondered.

"This is Baby. As you can see, I'm a man of many vehicles," he said, smiling.

They took their courtship slow, double dating once a week with their new single friends John and Barbara. They served a God of second chances, and neither wanted to make the same mistakes again. It wasn't easy. Every time Jesse held her hand, Rosie's heart pounded. *Steady, girl,* she told herself. She wondered what words Jesse repeated to calm himself when his heart began to pound.

Their lives were full of challenges, especially when it came to entertaining their two teenagers. "We'll have to do some creative planning and lots of communicating," Jesse forewarned. Rosie could think of better ways to communicate with her cowboy, but he was right. The boys were their priority.

Grace eventually returned to the Friday night singles', and from the moment Tim made his first play for her, she began her own creative planning—she was going for a touchdown. By Christmas, Tim and Grace announced their engagement, and a wedding date was set for April 1988.

Wedding plans were alive and well among the singles' ministry. John and Barbara were busy planning their August wedding and had already signed up for the upcoming February premarital class. In the meantime, Rosie was restless. A year was long enough for any warm-blooded forty-something single woman to wait for a proposal. They talked about marriage, so she couldn't understand what the holdup was.

One night, while having one of their hour-long phone conversations, Rosie sensed a distance in Jesse's voice. "Is something wrong? You don't sound like yourself."

He didn't answer right away, which left Rosie anxious.

"I've been thinking that maybe we're going a little too fast," Jesse said carefully.

Rosie's heart pounded. "And all the time I thought we were crawling," she answered sarcastically. "But you might be right."

"About what?"

"Perhaps we are going too fast, so let's take a breather."

Rosie wanted to catch Jesse off guard and it worked. He wasn't prepared for her extreme response, but wasn't he was the one who had brought up the subject?

Rosie continued to play it cool on the phone, but after they hung up, she broke down. She could hardly see to dial Prissy's number.

"He's having second thoughts about getting married," Rosie cried into the receiver.

"It's the cold feet syndrome," Prissy advised. "Bill got cold feet last month, but he came to his senses."

"Prissy, are you thinking about marrying Bill?" she asked, surprised at her friend's confession. Prissy had met Bill at a large Baptist Singles' happy hour four months earlier after becoming involved in the church's theater group. Rosie had never heard Prissy as happy as when she was chatting about Billy the Baptist.

"We're talking about marriage," Prissy admitted. "But if we do marry, we'll have to elope to Vegas in between his business trips."

"Prissy, we must talk more often; I can't keep up with your life."

"I'll call next week, but I have to run—I'm late for rehearsal," Prissy said.

"I don't want to get married anyway," Rosie told herself as she made her way to the bathroom to take a cold shower. She repeated the mantra each time she was tempted to call Jesse. She thought about him constantly. Her head was saying one thing, but her heart was telling her something else. She held firm until Jesse called her three days later.

"I think we've slowed down enough," Jesse said. Before she could respond, he added, "I miss you."

"I miss you too," she confessed, breathing heavily.

"Can we get together Saturday? We need to talk. Jay's with his mom this weekend."

"Let me look at my calendar. Let me see, Presley will be with his dad, so Saturday will be fine," she said, trying to sound casual.

"It worked! Playing it cool worked!" she sang as she danced herself silly in the privacy of her living room.

They met at In-N-Out, Jesse's favorite hamburger joint. Rosie was munching on a French fry when Jesse began talking of marriage. Then out of nowhere, he hit her with one of his creative suggestions.

"I was thinking, since you've been proposed to, and I proposed to my wife—who later told me she never loved me—I think it would be nice if *you* proposed to me."

She choked on her fry, then took a gulp of Coke, spilling it on her blouse. "What is your reasoning?" she asked as she wiped soda with a napkin.

"Then I would know you're marrying me because you love me."

"That's out of the question," Rosie answered. "I come from the old school where the man proposes to the woman." Disappointed about where the conversation was heading, she took another sip. "Besides, I don't think I'm ready for all this marriage talk."

Rosie loved the blank look Jesse gave whenever he hesitated before saying the wrong thing. Before he could speak, Rosie added, "And by the way, you can call me Rose."

And with that, she gathered her purse and walked out, leaving Jesse alone to finish his cold burger and fries.

By the time she walked in the front door, her phone was ringing. She pushed the off button to the answering machine and let the phone ring, and ring, and ring.

The next morning Rosie overslept, her excuse for not having to see Jesse at church.

Every night she ran farther, and took longer, colder showers. She couldn't sleep, so she read until her eyes fell shut.

Thursday night, as she slabbed on the last bit of Ponds Cold Cream, a voice came out of nowhere. *Rose, do you really love Jesse?*

"Of course, I love him."

Then why don't you make him happy by proposing to him?

"My mind is set in stone about this," she said as she smeared Vaseline on her lips.

She had to almost drag Paul to the altar. Bob proposed in the traditional way—almost on a whim.

What would Mom say? she wondered. She couldn't ask Dad for his opinion—he was vacationing in Morocco. She stared at the phone.

Make *him* happy? She had never thought of a marriage proposal that way—it was supposed to be all about her. But thinking about Jesse caused the cold cream on her face to start melting.

"Well, maybe I could change my way of thinking, just this once. Okay, I will propose to my cowboy!"

Rosie let out a yee-haw and began writing her to-do list. "The proposal will take place this weekend."

She placed the pen on her desk. "Next step, call Jesse and eat humble pie."

Her heart pounded at the sound of his voice. "Are you busy Saturday night?" she asked.

"No, Rose, I'm not busy. Why?"

"Let's get together. I need to talk to you."

"You do? Why?" Jesse asked.

"You'll find out Saturday. Can you pick me up at six?"

"Sure, but won't I see you at Singles tomorrow night?"

"No, I have other plans."

"Other plans?"

He sounded curious. She loved it.

"Yes. Something personal has come up."

Until this week, Jesse knew Rosie's every move . . . how far she ran, what she had for lunch, what book she was reading. But tomorrow night Rosie had a secret—she was going shopping for a ring.

Jesse pulled Baby into the parking lot of the Gondola Getaway in Belmont Shores. Jesse had talked about taking Rosie on a gondola ride for her birthday, but she had refused, making some excuse. The truth was, she didn't want to admit to this adventurous man how fearful she was of water. But tonight she would put her fear aside and step into a boat that would sail them into the sunset, and into their future.

"Rose, what's going on?" Jesse asked as he opened her door.

"You'll see. And, by the way, you can call me Rosie," she said, taking his hand.

"Rosie, you look beautiful." He smiled. "You're a real knockout!"

A good-looking Italian greeted them. "Good evening, I'm Antonio and I will be your gondola driver." He held out his hand for Rosie, but she hesitated.

"Do you have life jackets?" she asked, looking around.

Antonio smiled, still offering his hand. "There is no need for a life jacket. The water is very shallow."

Rosie took his hand and sat down.

Antonio began singing romantic love songs as he rowed the gondola toward the narrow canals and under the low bridges. This was Rosie's cue. As he sang "Love Me Tender," Rosie removed a tiny tape recorder from her purse while Jesse poured two glasses of sparkling apple cider. *I could sure use something stronger,* she thought as she glanced at the murky waters below.

After a few sips, she pulled out a little black box. "Open it," she instructed. He placed his glass down and carefully removed the white satin ribbon.

"Faster," she said impatiently, grabbing the box. "Here, let me help." She ripped off the ribbon and then handed him the box. He smiled as he held a Corvette key ring next to a candle that was flickering on the small table.

He dangled the ring. "This is nice," he said, and then placed it next to the bread and cheese basket.

She picked it up and waved it in his face.

"It's a key *ring*—get it? A *ring!*" She could tell by the look on his face that he was confused, but she would help him along, each step of the way.

Rosie took his hand. "Jesse, I love you and want to spend the rest of my life making l—, I mean, I want to spend the rest of my life making your life happy."

He smiled. "That's *very* nice."

"Jesse, will you marry me?" *Whew, that wasn't so hard.*

"Can I think about it?" he asked, wearing a sheepish grin.

"No, you cannot think about it," she answered.

"Ask me again."

She rolled her eyes. "Jesse James Atkisson, will you *marry* me?"

He hesitated three seconds and then smiled. "Yes, *I will* marry you."

They kissed. And they kissed.

Antonio waited for them to come up for air and then asked, "Are you enjoying the evening?"

Smiling, Jesse turned around to Antonio and pointed to Rosie. "The lady just proposed to me."

"She what?"

"The lady asked me to marry her, and I accepted." Jesse had Antonio's undivided attention. "I had to get my life straightened out before God could bring Rosie to me," he said, smiling at his fiancée.

It was confession time as Antonio shared his backslidden-son-of-a-preacher-man days. "I miss singing in the church choir. I know I need to get back with God," he finally admitted.

"You won't regret it. God has given you a great voice, and who knows, you might end up singing on Broadway," Rosie said.

"Or even better, a beautiful woman might propose to me!" Antonio said, laughing.

"Oh, I wouldn't count on it. You don't know how hard it was to get her to propose," Jesse said teasingly.

"What? Where's that ring?" Rosie asked, grabbing for the box that had slid onto the seat next to Jesse.

"Come here . . . you know I'm kidding!" Jesse said as he pulled Rosie close.

A few moments later Antonio sang "The Lord's Prayer" as the gondola slid through the moonlit waters.

"This is a perfect way to end a night of new beginnings," Rosie said.

When Rosie finally said *yes* to God, Jesse said *yes* to Rosie.

The next morning Rosie called Prissy with the news.

"Rosie, that's wonderful! I feel like an honest-to-goodness cupid!" Prissy chimed.

"If you hadn't called me that cold February night, I wouldn't have met Jesse."

"And don't you forget it!" Prissy laughed. "Have you set a wedding date?"

"We'll marry in *June*, after Grace and Tim's April wedding. In the meantime, I'll start moving our things into Jesse's new condo."

"How is Presley taking all the changes?"

"Like any typical teenager, he wanted to know if he was going to have his own room. I put his mind to rest when I told him he wouldn't be sharing a room with Jay."

"Have you started making wedding plans?" Prissy asked.

"No, but I thought you could help me."

"You can count me in!"

"By the way, how are things between you and Bill? Maybe we could pull off one of those double weddings," Rosie teased.

Prissy waited a few seconds and then blurted, "I have some news too—Bill and I eloped to Vegas a few days ago."

The phone went dead and then Rosie blurted, "Prissy, why didn't you tell me?"

Prissy stumbled over her words. "I was planning to call . . . been busy moving into Bill's house . . . I knew you were going through some hard times with Jesse . . . didn't want my wedding announcement to add to your gloom."

"Don't be silly! Congratulations! And by the way, what's with you and Vegas?"

Prissy giggled. "Yeah, I know! Maybe I should buy some stock in that town—kidding! This is the real thing, Rosie."

"I'm so happy for you—and for me! This is too good to be true! God is so good!"

"He knows how to watch over his girls, doesn't he? Now, we have some serious planning to do—we'll get started next week," Prissy said. "Now, where's my calendar?"

"Is this too much for you, Prissy?"

"Are you kidding? This will be the wedding I never had! In the meantime, I have to get to church!"

Their June wedding took place at Prissy's French Tudor hilltop home. Jay was best man, Grace was matron of honor, and Lynn was a bridesmaid.

Acting like the director of her own play, Prissy ran around orchestrating every detail, with Bill as her new assistant. "I love family affairs!" she said as she straightened Presley's tie. "You are such a handsome usher!"

Grace sang "The Song of Ruth" while all eyes gazed at the bride gracefully gliding down the stairs to take her place next to her groom. Rosie's thoughts were already leaping to their upcoming wedding night. *It's been a long wait, cowboy!* She was visualizing him slowly unzipping her wedding dress when her heel caught in the back of her hemline. Gasps filled the room, and she was about to slide onto the floor when Presley grabbed her arm.

"Take it easy, Mom," Presley said as he held onto her arm.

Keep your mind on the ceremony, girl; it won't be long now, she told herself.

But as hard as she tried, she couldn't stop her imagination from running wild . . . *as her wedding dress fell to the floor . . . oh, my, the ceremony has begun. To be continued*, she smiled, gathering her thoughts back to the moment.

Talmage held out his arm to escort his daughter into the living room that was brimming with close to a hundred guests. Rosie kissed his cheek.

"God has given you a traveling man, Rose," he whispered.

"Yes, it's finally my turn," she said, and then added, "I love you, Daddy."

Pastor Caleb greeted everyone, smiled at Rosie, and then turned to Jesse. He recognized that all-too-familiar look of fear he had seen on grooms who were having second thoughts about taking the big leap.

"Jesse, are you okay?" Caleb asked under his breath.

"I've done a terrible thing," Jesse answered ever so softly.

Rosie turned from her pastor and looked at her soon-to-be-husband.

Jesse had told his pastor of his backslidden divorced years, but this was not the time to bring up his sordid past. Perhaps Caleb should have ignored Jesse's glazed look, but it was too late.

All eyes were on Jesse. Rosie's stomach tightened as she prepared for the worst. She wanted to whisper in Jesse's ear, *This is not a confession booth, my darling cowboy. The past is forgiven, so please, let's proceed with the ceremony*. She was on the verge of passing out when Jesse blurted, "I forgot Rosie's wedding ring."

Sighs of relief echoed throughout the large room, and then rumbles of laughter. Pastor Caleb exhaled, and Rosie began to breathe normally.

"That's okay, hon, I don't need a ring," Rosie said.

Women began passing their wedding rings to Jesse. "Here, you can borrow my ring," Prissy said.

Jesse reached over and handed Tim the Corvette keys. "Here, take Baby, and hurry. The ring is at the condo—on my bed." Tim sped down the hill on a mission from heaven.

Rosie was feeling somewhat normal when she felt a nudge on her arm from her matron of honor. "Mom, where is Jesse's ring?"

Her mind went blank. "Didn't I give it to you?"

"No, Mom. Take a deep breath, and think."

"Umm, I think it's upstairs in Prissy's bedroom . . . in the closet . . . in the pink satin bag."

Prissy ran upstairs to her bedroom.

The case of the missing rings caused an uproar, but the ceremony continued. Grace began singing "The Wedding Song" but her face paled as she stumbled over the words to the second verse; the pianist stopped; everyone stared. Then Grace closed her eyes and began singing, making up words as she went along.

Afterward, Grace found her place beside Rosie, and whispered, "You forgot the ring, and I forgot the words. Like mother, like daughter."

Prissy handed Grace the groom's ring, and as if on cue, the front door creaked open. Cheers went out as Tim walked in carrying the bride's ring.

"Thank God for fast friends and fast cars," Caleb laughed. "Now, let the wedding vows begin."

Through misty eyes, Jesse recited his vows, followed by Rosie reciting her vows from the book of Ruth. "Jesse, wherever you go, I will go. Your people shall be my people, and your God shall be my God."

In the midst of the reception, Jesse pulled Rosie aside and kissed her tenderly. "I have a surprise for you." He glanced at Prissy, who quickly pressed the on button to her stereo. Elvis filled the house and spread outside, across the hillside. Jesse took Rosie in his arms. "May I have this dance?"

"I thought you didn't dance!"

"This is my wedding gift to you. Prissy taught me enough steps to carry me through our song."

Rosie was speechless as "Love Me Tender" filled her emotions with electricity.

After hours of celebration, Jesse and Rosie sped away in Baby, into the night.

Once in the nearby Embassy Suites hotel room, Jesse shed his tuxedo. "Let the wedding night begin," he said as he slowly unzipped Rosie's wedding gown. As the sound of satin fell to the floor, she slipped into the arms of her Boaz. "I've waited a long time for this night," he said, gently kissing her neck.

She began unbuttoning his shirt. "Let's take it nice and slow."

He took a deep breath. "Rosie, I'll try . . . but you're killing me with your touch."

She backed away and then hit him with her knockout smile. "Okay, cowboy, now it's your turn . . . go ahead . . . kill me . . . I dare you."

He grinned, swooped her up in his arms, and carried her to the bed. And slowly, all through the night, they killed each other softly with their words and their touch.

After returning home from their honeymoon in Mazatlan, Mexico, they plunged into their blended family life. Lynn and Grace lived close enough to drop by at least once a week. Jay and Presley had their own rooms. Presley spent hours playing basketball at the church courts, and Jay spent his extra time skateboarding. They were active in the church youth group and enjoyed hanging out with the single guys and gals on Friday nights.

A few months later Jesse accepted the position as singles' pastor, an honor that came with great responsibility. Over a hundred singles gathered on Friday nights. Three years of winter and summer camps, enough volunteer work and activities to keep everyone busy—not to mention the calendar of weddings—Rosie thought life couldn't get any better.

11

Miss Knot had heard of several ship ministries—YWAM, Youth with a Mission; Don Tipton's Friend Ships; and the logos ships, a large book ministry that traveled to ports all over the world donating thousands of books to people of many languages. Perhaps one day she would be included on the prestigious list.

On a cold November night, Jesse and Rosie crawled into bed to read and snuggle. Rosie's latest book was taking her down an English country road, and Jesse's auto magazine had him dreaming of a car twice the price of Baby, when the phone rang. After four rings, it was obvious that neither wanted to answer.

"You get it," Rosie said, not looking up from her book.

"You get it," Jesse mumbled.

After the sixth ring, Jesse reluctantly picked up.

"Hello Luke!" Jesse said with excitement. Jesse and Rosie were introduced to Luke and his wife when they came to minister at the church. Jesse and Rosie were drawn to their love for God and for the nations so Jesse invited them to speak at the singles' meetings whenever they were in town

Luke was calling from Sweden, where he and Lisa were teaching at an international Bible school. Rosie motioned for Jesse to put Luke on the speakerphone.

"We're looking forward to visiting you in the spring," Jesse told their friend.

"I'm calling to invite you to join me on a trip to Estonia and Russia. I'll be teaching in the Bible schools, and I can use your help."

"Will Lisa be going?" Jesse asked.

"She'll already be in Estonia teaching, so we'll meet up with her."

"When?"

"We're scheduled for March."

"We'd love to join you," Jesse said.

Rosie's stomach tightened. Jesse's stories of living in Israel and his travels to Brazil had intrigued her, but go to Russia? Raised in the fifties, Rosie had listened fearfully as her schoolteachers, the news media, and everyone around had declared Russia to be America's dreaded enemy. Prissy's father had built a bomb shelter in their backyard in case of an attack. Rosie had hoped she would be playing at Prissy's house if a bomb ever dropped.

But the nineties were bringing changing times. Communism in Russia was shaky, the world had recently witnessed the fall of the Berlin Wall, the Baltics were preparing to break away from Russia, and the United States was in the midst of the Gulf War.

Jesse looked at Rosie. He recognized that faraway look.

"Luke, let me talk to Rosie, and I'll call you tomorrow." He hung up and gently took the book from Rosie's hands.

"Rosie, don't you want to go to Russia?"

"I was thinking more along the lines of a spring holiday in Sweden."

"I promise that we'll tour Stockholm."

Rosie had spent too many years reading about everyone else's adventures. She had waved good-bye to her father at the airport last year when he boarded a plane for Spain. Was God now giving her an opportunity to make her own journey?

"What am I thinking? Of course, I want to go to Russia."

So in March of '91, the great woman of faith began packing for her first international mission trip.

As they boarded the Boeing 747, Rosie noticed that the plane was barely half full.

"It looks like Gulf War jitters are keeping people from traveling across the Atlantic," Jesse remarked. "That's why we got such good airfare prices."

"So what are *we* doing on a half-empty plane, heading for Russia?"

"It's too late for second thoughts."

A flight attendant interrupted their conversation. "As you can see, we're light on passengers."

"Yes, we've noticed," Rosie answered.

"Would you like to fly business class to Stockholm?"

Settling into the big, comfortable leather seat, Rosie leaned back and smiled. "One man's fear is another man's business class."

Sweden's March weather greeted them with a picture-postcard, snow-covered countryside, sprinkled with quaint red and yellow houses.

"Sweden looks like something out of a travel magazine," Rosie said from the backseat of Luke's car.

Rosie couldn't take enough pictures of Uppsala's picturesque buildings, the canal that flowed through the center of town, the castle on the hill, and the large state Lutheran church that stood regal in the middle of town.

"Enjoy this scenery. Wait until you see Moscow," Luke said somberly.

The next day Luke drove forty minutes south to Stockholm through a mixture of snow and rain. "Winter isn't the best time to tour the capitol," Luke said as he held an umbrella while Rosie took pictures.

"Then we'll have to come back in the summer," Rosie answered.

Jesse's goal for the first few days was to spend time at Living Waters Church. Each evening they stood in the midst of hundreds of mild-mannered Swedes as they prayed and sang with all of their hearts. Bible school students passionate for God attended morning classes. The international class was taught in English, and each afternoon they gathered for the two-hour Prayer School.

Rosie noticed that Jesse was asking Luke way too many questions about the Bible school. Something was going on in his head—and possibly in his heart—but she didn't dare ask.

A gloomy afternoon greeted them when they landed in Estonia. Rosie immediately noticed that the Tallinn Airport was in need of repair and upgrades, not to mention the restrooms needing toilet paper. Rosie came prepared, carrying small sheets of tissues in her purse.

"The Estonians are suspicious of Americans," Luke forewarned. "The airport customs will be strict."

"Oh, great. And here we are carrying over twenty-five Bibles in our luggage," Rosie said, her hands trembling. She prayed silently as they stood in the customs line. "If they find our Bibles, will they arrest us?" she whispered in Jesse's ear. Before he could answer, the customs clerk motioned to Luke. "Come with me."

Jesse and Rosie followed Luke to a small, dimly lit room. *Am I the only one in the room feeling warm?* she wondered. When she saw Jesse perspiring, she knew they were in a tight situation.

"What are they going to do?" Rosie asked Luke anxiously.

"We don't know yet, so smile—and pray," Luke said.

The customs clerk stepped up to the table and began opening their luggage. He was about to toss Rosie's underwear on the table when a man in a black overcoat stuck his head in the door. "Sir, there is a problem that needs your assistance."

"Follow me," the customs clerk ordered. Again, they did as they were told.

An American businessman stood outside the door, sweating and breathing heavily. The customs clerk quickly went through his suitcase and boxes, and as he spread the computer on the table, Rosie thought the man was going to pass out. "Take him in the other room," the customs clerk ordered one of the nearby security guards.

The straight-faced customs clerk checked their passports and visas, and then motioned Luke and his entourage through the gate. The man in the black coat smiled at Rosie and then walked down the hallway, as the customs clerk turned to the travelers next in line. "You must open all your suitcases—now."

Rosie breathed a sigh of relief as they walked outside into the cold air. A young man in a stained, brown trench coat and black wool cap waved, and then held out his hand to Luke.

"I am Volnar. I will be your guide and translator," he announced in broken English as he began packing their suitcases in the van.

Rosie quickly climbed into the old gray van to escape the wintry afternoon, still shivering as everyone piled in.

"The van does not have a heater," Volnar apologized.

That's okay, I'm tough, Rosie told herself as she wrapped her wool scarf around her neck.

"We've just stepped back forty years in time," Rosie whispered to Jesse as Volnar drove down the narrow streets of Tallinn. She had seen movies with similar old buildings, but looking at them firsthand, they didn't look as glamorous as the movies portrayed. Block walls were crumbling and broken windows stood in disrepair in a nearby shop, but the nationals didn't seem to mind as they strolled down the streets, going about their everyday business, untouched by the decay around them.

Volnar turned the van onto a cobblestoned street and then stopped. Large boulders prevented them from going farther.

"This is where we withstood the Russians a short time ago," Volnar proudly proclaimed. There were two army tanks parked behind the boulders as a reminder of their victory.

Rosie shivered. A scene on her TV screen flashed before her. She vaguely remembered watching the news while packing for the trip, seeing boulders and large army tanks in front of a city hall. She hadn't paid much attention to the rioting taking place in the faraway Baltic state. Now she was touching history-in-the-making. *I must pay closer attention to what's going on the world,* she thought as Volnar shoved the van into reverse.

"It will be a two-hour ride to Tartu," Volnar informed them as he headed south.

As hard as she tried, Rosie couldn't get comfortable. The road was bumpy, and she couldn't stop shivering. She stared out the dirty window like a kid. Tired, she leaned her head against the cold jittery window and was dozing off when they hit a pit in the road. *So much for napping on the bumpy road to Tartu,* she thought, yawning.

Two hours later, Volnar dropped Luke off at the house where Lisa was staying and then drove around the block and pulled in front of an old historic home.

"You will be staying here," Volnar said as he pointed to the two-story house. An elderly gentleman greeted Jesse and Rosie at the door and invited them into the living room where a warm fire awaited. Mr. and Mrs. Svalbe spoke only broken English, but they smiled a lot. Mrs. Svalbe led them upstairs to a small guest room and then motioned them to go back downstairs. Rosie glanced around the small room; the twin beds looked inviting. It had been a long day, and all she wanted to do was take a hot bath and snuggle under the warm covers. The aroma of baked bread coming up the stairway beckoned them, so they made their way down to the kitchen.

"The dinner is delicious," Rosie said, although she wasn't sure what she was eating. The Svalbes smiled and nodded. A world traveler once told Rosie it was best not to ask what you're eating in a foreign country until you're finished. Watching the Svalbes smiling and nodding, Rosie decided not to ask.

Later, they sat by the fire with their new friends, drinking strong coffee and smiling at each other. Mr. Svalbe carried on a meaningless conversation, using hand gestures to describe what he was trying to convey. All was going well until Rosie made the comment, "You are so kind. I love the Russian people."

Mr. Svalbe stood up and pointed to his wife and then himself. "Not Russian. We Estonian," he stated proudly. Rosie learned another history lesson on her first international trip.

As Rosie prepared her bath, she looked around the narrow room for a toilet. A sink stood next to the old tub. At the end of the narrow hallway, she spotted a closed door the size of a coat closet, with a WC sign posted above. She figured that going to the toilet must be a very private experience for the Estonians.

The next morning they walked the cobbled streets of Tartu's old town. Rosie drank in the sights of the beautiful buildings. From the town square, small pathways led to shops that catered to the few tourists who browsed through the narrow aisles. Shop owners sold handmade cultural items of wood and other fine textiles. Since the dollar was strong, Rosie was able to buy more than she had anticipated.

Snow began to fall as they stepped into an intriguing hat shop. "Look at this," Jesse said. He placed a beautiful gray fur hat on Rosie's head.

"That would cost over two hundred dollars back home," Luke said.

"I would never shop for a fur hat in California," she said, touching the soft gray fur.

"But you will need this while traveling in the snow-covered terrain," Jesse said as he paid the shop owner for Rosie's first mink hat.

Tartu's Bible school was filled with zealous students who didn't seem to be aware of their lack of worldly possessions. After Luke and Lisa taught the morning sessions, they joined the students in the basement for lunch. Rosie admired the young, energetic student who led the worship, so she took her aside and presented her with a new wool suit she had bought for the trip. Natasha, who spoke fluent English, hugged Rosie. "Thank you so much!"

"You'll get more wear out of it than me," Rosie said with satisfaction.

"I will wear it next year when I go to Sweden for my second year of Bible school," Natasha said proudly.

Rosie hadn't felt this good since the Tijuana week-end many years ago when she sat with Prissy, playing jacks with the little Mexican girls.

"I wish you were here, Prissy," Rosie whispered.

That night Volnar drove the couples to the Tartu train station and gave them specific instructions. "It is very important to stay together at all times. The Russians are suspicious of Americans. Your interpreter will meet you at the train station at the Russian border and will travel with you to Leningrad and Moscow."

As Volnar spoke, a twinge of both fear and excitement grabbed the pit of Rosie's stomach, as if she were playing a role in a Russian spy movie. Would the Russians really consider their group to be American spies? Whatever they thought, she would act cool and responsible.

Rosie held her husband's hand until they boarded the train. Jesse's past world travels had prepared him for this, but the heightened atmosphere of intrigue was new to Rosie.

They found two empty benches in the back of the train. After an hour, Rosie's rear went numb from sitting on the wood seats. Looking out of the smudged window into the darkness, she prayed, "God, I know you're traveling with me, no matter where I end up on planet Earth. And you even gave me my very own James Bond to take care of me . . . well, my own Jesse *James,*" she whispered as she looked over at her husband.

The train was dimly lit, so Lisa and Rosie tried their best to read while Jesse and Luke kept watch on their surroundings as the train moved deeper into darkness.

They arrived at the Russian border soon after midnight, an hour later than scheduled. Their interpreter, Jon, greeted them at the platform, relieved to finally see the four brave Americans.

A few overhead lights cast a dim, gray light throughout the cold concrete train station; the rest of the fixtures were dark from burned-out bulbs waiting to be replaced.

Five solemn Russian soldiers gathered in a corner, while a few cold and tired Russian citizens waited for another delayed train to arrive.

"These people need some joy, so let's pray," Lisa said to Rosie. Lisa had no longer whispered a quiet *amen* when out of nowhere, a little boy came walking by. Lisa smiled and handed him a handful of wrapped candy. He smiled back and then bravely walked over to the soldiers and held out his hands. The soldiers chuckled as they took the candy, and within minutes, the station was filled with laughter.

"Isn't it fun to see how a prayer and some candy can bring such joy?" Lisa said, smiling.

Rosie turned to Jon. "We must find a restroom before we board the train to Leningrad." He pointed to the exit door that led into the darkness. Lisa and Rosie hesitated, then looked at each other.

"When ya gotta go, you gotta go!" Lisa said.

As Rosie and Lisa walked briskly through the falling rain, two soldiers walked toward them, making remarks that only their translator would have been able to interpret. Rosie hoped they were being friendly, not fresh. The young soldiers smirked as they neared. Rosie's heart started beating rapidly. All the stories from the fifties about the Russians not trusting the Americans came rushing back.

Then, out of nowhere, a man in a black coat appeared from behind a concrete building. He walked toward the soldiers, lifted his right hand, saluted, and then began chatting.

Lisa stopped. "Smell that? This is the place," she said, leading the way into the dark building that had no door. "Breathe through your mouth," Lisa said as she patted the damp walls in search of a light switch. Rosie fumbled and searched for toilet paper. No lights, no paper. They pulled out small wads of toilet paper they had tucked in their coat pockets. Carefully, and in unison, they bowed and stooped over the holes in the already wet concrete floor. They took aim, as if trying for an all-important bull's-eye.

"I don't know if I'm cut out for this," Rosie said.

"Of course, you are. If you can aim, then you can go anywhere! Oh, the life of a missionary," Lisa teased as they made their way back to the station.

"You're right, Lisa! I'm an honest to goodness missionary!"

They stopped giggling as they approached the soldiers. The man in the black coat saluted the two soldiers before walking into the darkness.

"Our guardian angel?" Rosie asked.

"They work full-time for us in Russia," Lisa said as they entered the train station.

They boarded the midnight train at one-thirty. The conductors looked at them suspiciously as they took their tickets, and then a big Russian babushka led Luke and Lisa to their compartment. When she returned, she gave Jesse the once-over and then motioned the couple to follow her down the narrow hallway.

Ms. Babushka opened the compartment door to a dimly lit, cigarette smoke-filled room. Two men clad in stained undershirts were lying on the two lower bunks, drinking vodka. As they smiled and raised their glasses to Rosie, she turned to Jesse. Her look told him, *we will not be sharing this compartment with these two overfriendly Russians.*

Jesse beckoned Jon, who was still standing in the hallway. "They need to find us another compartment—now. Luke made reservations for private sleepers."

Jon shook his head. "In Russia, reservations do not always have the same meaning as in America, but I will see what I can do."

Ms. Babushka told Jon the train was full, but she would see what she could do, meaning she expected many rubles for her time and effort.

"I'll stand here in the hallway all night before I go into that compartment," Rosie told Jesse.

The train began moving. They waited for twenty minutes, then thirty, before Ms. Babushka returned. They held the rail and followed her as she wobbled her way to the next car, leading them to a smaller sleeper. Rosie took a deep breath as Jesse opened the door. Darkness . . . silence . . . but no smoke, and no evidence of Russian vodka.

Jesse thanked the tired old woman. "*Spasibo,*" he said as he filled her hands with rubles. She forced a smile, and then she sauntered down the aisle.

Rosie strained her eyes, but all she could see was two motionless bodies sleeping on the two lower bunks.

"We will be arriving in Leningrad at seven-thirty," Jon informed them before he closed the compartment door.

Jesse motioned to climb the narrow ladder. Reaching her point of destination, Rosie plopped down on the upper bunk—coat, boots, and all.

Relieved to be in a somewhat safe environment, Rosie fell asleep to the clikkity-clak-clikkity-clak—until thirty minutes later, when the train screeched to a halt. Another train station. And so it was throughout the night as the night train made its way through Russia—clikkity-clak—screech—stop—clikkity-clak. Rosie had finally reached her REM sleep mode when a loud knock on their door startled her awake.

"You must come immediately," Jon spoke through the door.

"What's going on?" Jesse asked.

"We arrived in Leningrad early."

"What time is it?" Rosie asked, wiping her eyes with a hankie.

"Six o'clock. We have to leave the train before it departs," Jon instructed.

A small light in the lower bunk flickered. A woman and a young boy gathered their belongings and were out the door before Rosie had a chance to say good morning in Russian.

Jon led the Americans from the train into the darkness, and followed the tired crowd toward a large building. Lights glared above as they entered the Leningrad train station. A cup of hot coffee sounded good to Rosie, but they weren't in the good old USA. The station was cold, and no coffee was to be found.

"The driver is scheduled to arrive at eight-thirty, so I have found a corner for everyone to sit," Jon announced.

"And wait," Rosie added as she looked around the historical mint green building.

"Welcome to Russia," Luke said as he removed his gloves.

Rosie was in awe of her surroundings, even if it was in the wee hours of the morning, with no coffee in sight. She never imagined she would be in Leningrad, the background city of her favorite classic novels, *Anna Karenina* and *Doctor Zhivago*. As dawn broke, the solemn Russians began to make their way from one end of the train station to the other.

Their driver arrived around nine o'clock, drove them through the heart of Leningrad, and then dropped them off at one of the many high-rise government co-op buildings that stood tall throughout the city. Rosie gagged at the smell of urine as she walked up five flights of stairs. The hallways were laden with piles of trash, the evidence of a government that didn't care for their people.

"Breathe through your mouth," Jesse reminded her.

Stepping from the hallway into the pastor's flat was like finding a pot of gold at the end of a rainbow. Orange and red sofas, rugs, and tablecloths brought life to a once-drab flat. And the aroma of fresh-brewed coffee gave them hope for the morning.

After they devoured two bowls of porridge and two pots of coffee, the pastor's wife showed the weary travelers to their rooms for a much-needed rest. Jesse was sinking into his REM sleep on the sagging bed when a knock jolted him awake.

"Jesse, you must come with me to the Leningrad Airport," Jon spoke through the door. "Aeroflot Airlines booked your ticket and Rosie's ticket on one flight, and Lisa, Luke, and me on a different flight to Moscow."

Yawning, Jesse slowly dressed as Rosie turned over and wrapped herself in the orange bedspread.

The ticket agent was not about to assist Jesse with the tickets. She was determined to do the minimal amount of work necessary before going home. Jesse learned that words of kindness weren't in their vocabulary. All he received was a clear *nyet*—the Russian's favorite word—No!

An hour later, after translating the situation to several associates, Jon was losing hope. Jesse led him to a nearby corner and whispered, "We must pray for a breakthrough."

Acting as if they were conversing about a football game, they prayed for God to change the situation.

After they waited in line for another thirty minutes, a ticket agent motioned to them. Jon smiled as he turned to Jesse. "They have decided to change the tickets. We will be flying to Moscow together after all."

That afternoon, they took an underground subway to a tourist hotel in downtown Leningrad. They ate hamburgers and drank warm Cokes in the hotel restaurant and were deep in conversation when their server set a clear bowl in the middle of their table. Conversation ceased as all eyes fell on the contents in the bowl.

"Ice!" they shouted in unison.

"Ice for the Americans," the server said in broken English as he placed the cubes in their glasses.

"Little things mean a lot when you're traveling in Russia," Luke said cheerfully.

After two days of successful meetings at the newly established Leningrad church, it was time to board Aeroflot Airlines to Moscow.

While the city slept, they arrived at the airport before daybreak. Except for a few solemn flight attendants and a small group of Russian businessmen, the terminal was empty. They boarded the plane an hour behind schedule and found their seats.

Jesse pointed downward. "The carpet is moving under my feet."

"That is normal," Jon said, smiling as he fastened his seat belt.

Then two pilots stumbled into the cockpit.

"Are they the drunk pilots we saw staggering through the airport?" Jesse asked.

"This is normal also," Jon said apologetically. "And don't bother asking for coffee or refreshments. You'll be lucky to get water."

"Prayer is the only answer for a safe journey when traveling in Russia," Rosie said seriously, bowing her head.

They arrived in Moscow two hours behind schedule. Jon pointed to their host driver, who held a sign that read *Americans*.

Billboards and paintings of Lenin were everywhere. Tall gray statues added to the gloom that hung over Moscow. The driver pulled in front of a large gray tourist hotel. "I will pick you up in one hour."

The rooms were compact, with enough space for twin beds and a desk.

"The water smells like rotten eggs," Rosie said as she wiped her hands with a dingy gray towel.

"But look at the lovely hunter green velvet bedspreads," Jesse commented, hoping to bring something positive to the situation.

After lunch, they walked through the snow until they reached Red Square. Small groups of tourists from Germany were taking pictures. To warm themselves, they walked to the nearby tourist mall, where a group of men stood in line to purchase wool sweaters. Russian women stood in longer lines at the other end.

"They are waiting for their ration of wool socks for their families," Jon explained.

Once outside, Rosie noticed a longer line on a nearby walking street. "Why would anyone stand in thirty-degree weather?" she asked, pulling her fur hat over her already frozen ears. She looked closer, and at the front of the line were men and women waiting in line for ice cream.

"Sometimes they wait for hours, but it's a small delight in their dreary world," Jon said.

As they continued walking, they came across another line of women. "More goodies?" Rosie asked.

"You could say that. They are standing in line to buy makeup. Russian women want to look pretty too. Some save rubles for months to buy one lipstick."

Rosie shook her head. "I'll never complain again when I have to stand in line five minutes in my drugstore back home."

Rosie was looking in the window of an art gallery, admiring a small watercolor painting of Red Square, when Luke came along beside her. "Let's all go inside—now. Don't look, but I think we're being followed."

Rosie's immediate thought was to look over her shoulder, but instead, she darted into the gallery. Looking out the window, she saw two men in topcoats standing about ten yards away.

"They want to make sure the Americans are on the up-and-up, so let's continue shopping. They're probably KGB," Luke said. Jesse removed the painting from the window, purchased it, and handed it to Rosie as the two men stood watching.

Or they could be our guardian angels, Rosie thought as she carried her painting down the walkway toward their hotel.

After dinner, Jon hailed two taxicabs to drive them across the city for a meeting at a pastor's flat.

"Jon will go with Lisa and me," Luke told Jesse as he handed the cab driver a slip of paper with an address. Jon advised Taxi Two to keep an eye on Taxi One.

As he hopped in the taxi with Luke and Lisa, Jon said to Jesse, "Moscow cabbies are a little crazy."

"Thanks for the warning," Jesse said, waving as Taxi One sped through a red light, leaving Taxi Two in his dust.

"Did he do that on purpose?" Rosie asked, but Jesse raised his hand to keep her quiet. The driver waved the piece of paper in the air while driving aimlessly around the city for what seemed like an hour.

"Does he know where he's taking us?" Rosie asked as calmly as possible.

The driver kept shaking his head and looking down at the paper. *We will be lost forever in Moscow central,* Rosie thought, forcing her eyes closed.

The driver pulled over to where a fellow taxi driver was parked and handed him the piece of paper. The driver shook his head and gave the paper back. The taxi skidded off into ongoing traffic. Jesse landed in Rosie's lap. That was enough for Rosie.

"This is great! We have a reckless driver who doesn't know his way around Moscow. Unbelievable."

"In Russia, nothing is unbelievable," Jesse said, climbing off his wife's lap.

If Rosie's stomach wrenched much more, she would have to ask Mr. Cabbie to pull over so she could barf in the gutter. Plus, she needed to find a restroom, fast.

"It's time to pray," Rosie said as she fumbled in her coat pocket for some tissue.

Five minutes later, Jesse tapped the driver's shoulder and pointed to the curb. "Over! Pull over!"

Jesse took the piece of paper from the taxi driver and gave it to the man in a black coat standing next to the curb. The man pointed to the corner street sign, smiled at Rosie, and then walked down the street filled with people.

Five minutes later, they arrived at their destination. Rosie climbed out of the taxi and breathed a sigh of relief. "There are angels in Moscow."

Four days later, they sat in business class on the half empty, sleek SAS airplane, surrounded by smiling flight attendants and sober pilots.

"I'll never forget our days in Sweden," Rosie said.

"And the heart-stopping moments in Russia—drunk pilots and lost cabbies."

"My schoolteachers and the news media may have had their version of America's enemy, but the Russians I came to know are warm, loving people," Rosie said as she fastened her seat belt. "I'm glad I didn't give in to my fears about going to Russia."

She leaned back in her leather seat, but Jesse kept turning the pages of the SAS magazine.

Rosie recalled her prayers of long ago, the ones where she reminded God that she would like to travel the world with him. Rosie smiled. "You remembered."

"I remembered what?" Jesse asked.

Rosie wanted to share her thoughts, but her husband was obviously preoccupied, so she pulled out a book from her overstuffed purse.

Jesse kept opening and closing his magazine. He looked out the window. He twisted in his seat. Jesse was always calm, even when he was flying Aeroflot.

Once in the air, Rosie placed her book in her lap. "Are you okay?" she asked.

"I've been doing a lot of thinking on this trip."

"Yes, I've noticed."

"Well, I'm thinking we should go to Bible school."

She picked up her book. "I'd love to go, someday."

"I'm thinking about the Bible school in Sweden."

Turning a page, she answered, "Uh, yeah, maybe someday."

"I'm thinking about Bible school . . . in Sweden . . . in the fall."

Her book fell to the floor.

12

Miss Knot had become a lady-in-waiting in Seattle's quiet harbor.

Rosie's stomach knotted, similar to the time when she was in Leningrad and ate too many servings of borsch soup. A hundred thoughts ran through her mind. She felt dizzy. She must talk some sense into Jesse before it was too late.

"You're a pastor of a large singles' ministry. You can't pick up and leave all those wonderful people for nine months."

Jesse sat quietly, waiting.

"Let me do the math . . . Grace and Tim are expecting a baby in July . . . we would be coming back to Sweden in August. There . . . see? We can't leave our family—they need us."

She sounded desperate, so he didn't dare interrupt her.

"Besides, we've finished remodeling our living room, so I'm looking forward to spending cozy evenings by the fire with you."

She could have continued, but she was grasping for straws and giving herself a headache. And Jesse knew his wife long enough to know she needed time to think things through.

Rosie stared out the window at the billowy clouds. *He should have waited to talk about this until—until when?* she wondered. Would there ever be a *right* time for Jesse to ask her to leave their family for almost a year? She turned from the window.

"Jesse, you're always so levelheaded. How could you consider going to Bible school now, especially in a foreign country?"

"But I thought you told me that you *wanted* to go to Bible school someday. This can be your someday."

"I do, but *live* in Sweden? This is so sudden. With everything that's going on at home—the new grandbaby, the ministry—"

Jesse stopped her. "You're right. Perhaps it's not the best time."

"We'll talk about this later," she said, picking up her book. After trying to read the first two sentences, she placed it in the seat pocket.

Rosie couldn't think straight, so she faced the window and prayed while the plane's engines drowned her out. "Lord, I have a desire to go to Bible school, but isn't there a school closer to home?"

On and on she prayed as they crossed the Atlantic. She didn't demand, but waited for God to give her some direction.

By the time they landed in Chicago and then boarded the plane for California, Rosie was ready to continue the conversation with Jesse. When they reached thirty-two thousand feet, she took his hand.

"I have to believe you heard from God when we were in Sweden. After spending time at the church, and praying, I also feel he would want us to go to Bible school."

Jesse paused, waiting for her to continue. When she didn't, he asked, "When?"

"In the fall." *There, I said it.*

"Where?" he gently asked.

"Sweden!" she proclaimed loud enough for the person across the aisle to hear.

Jesse squeezed her hand and then reached for his backpack. "Then we need to begin making plans for our sabbatical. Where's my pen and paper?"

Smart man, Rosie thought. *Put it down in writing before I change my mind.*

The guilt attacks began as soon as they landed. The uncertainties about their decision hit Rosie from every angle while she unpacked. She argued with her reflection in the full-length mirror on the closet door. "What grandmother would leave her grandchildren to go to a foreign school? And doesn't Presley still need me around? Jay's living with his mother, so I can't use him for an excuse." She walked away from her silent reflection, wondering if Mother Teresa ever had doubts about her calling.

The following day when Jesse and Rosie met with Pastor Caleb, he approved of their request. However, two days later, when they attended the weekly pastors' meeting, each elder made it clear they didn't want Jesse to leave his singles' ministry for a year.

"I think you're being narrow-minded and selfish," Rosie finally blurted.

"Now, Rosie, don't jump to conclusions," Jesse interrupted, taking her hand.

Pastor Caleb motioned to his elders. "We'll meet later to discuss this. I'd like to talk to Jesse, alone." The elders filed out, and Jesse winked at Rosie as she followed close behind.

Pastor Caleb handed Jesse a piece of paper. "I would like to make you an offer. As you know, Japan is my vision. How would you like to lead two trips to spearhead a future ministry there?"

Jesse sat silently. "I consider this a privilege for you to even consider me. May I go home and pray about it?"

"Of course. Let me know your answer by tomorrow."

That evening Rosie read the piece of paper silently, then out loud. "This is an honor. What are you going to do?"

"I'll spend the night in prayer, and give Caleb my answer tomorrow at the special elders' meeting that he's called."

The next day, Jesse and Rosie met again with the pastor and his elders. Jesse cleared his throat before facing Pastor Caleb. "Thank you for this amazing offer, but if I accept, it would be like the story in the Bible where the young man sold his birthright for a bowl of soup. I cannot exchange what God has called me to do for another man's vision."

Caleb glanced at his elders and then turned to Jesse. "The elders don't think this is the right time for you to leave."

"When is the right time?" Jesse asked.

"They don't know yet."

The room was eerily quiet. Rosie held her breath and found strength in the hand that held hers tightly.

"Is this your final decision?" Pastor Caleb prodded.

Jesse nodded. "Yes, pastor, it is."

Pastor Caleb stood. "Then we must ask you to resign immediately as singles' pastor."

"But we're not leaving for five months," Rosie said. "What's the hurry?"

The elders sat motionless, waiting for the pastor to respond to Rosie's outburst. They could see that she wasn't familiar with church politics.

Pastor Caleb glanced out the window, ignoring Rosie's glare.

Jesse tightened his grip on Rosie's hand, but it was too late.

"Pastor Caleb, the elders are thinking of the inconvenience it might impose on them, not what's best for Jesse," Rosie continued, rubbing her husband's clammy hand. "We'll be gone for nine months, and we'll return with more to give those wonderful people," she added, pointing to the fellowship hall where the single' ministry met each week.

Pastor Caleb looked at the pile of paper on his desk. "This is our final decision."

"I assume you've prayed about this," Jesse said as he rose from his chair. They exited the room, hand in hand, and Rosie knew there was no turning back.

Just like that, Jesse's position as singles' pastor was gone. At the request of the elders, he announced his resignation several nights later at the singles' meeting. Jesse stood brave as he shared their decision to attend Bible school in Sweden. The people showed their love and support by cheering him on. He stammered as he gave the reasons for his sudden resignation . . . too much planning and preparation to continue in a pastoral position. He would never give the true reason for resigning five months before they were to leave. No one needed to know the church politics behind the decision; it would only cause confusion and unrest.

Tough days followed. Pastor Caleb asked Rosie to stay on as his assistant until August. They needed the money, so she agreed. Greeting the elders daily as if nothing had happened was challenging. Rosie knew she had missed her calling. She should have been an actress.

Preparations filled the days. One evening while they were filling out their visa forms at the dining room table, Rosie blurted, "How can we tell the Swedish government that we have enough financial provision for nine months when we don't have enough money to buy our airline tickets? What are we thinking? We must be crazy!"

"Maybe we are, but God called us to go, so he'll provide the finances. We have to trust him."

"I do, but it's scary! Prissy asked me today why we don't go to a local Bible school."

"What was your answer?"

"I told her because God asked us to go to Sweden, and we want to obey him."

"And what did she say?"

"End of conversation."

"Smart girl. Besides, she knows we're levelheaded people," Jesse added.

"There's always a first time," Rosie muttered.

Jesse's eyes narrowed.

"Kidding!" Rosie said.

She studied the checkbook. "Where are we going to get twelve-hundred dollars for our school tuition?"

"Good question," he replied.

She wanted to ask, *and how are we going to eat in Sweden?* but thought it best to call it a night.

The next day, the church accountant knocked on Rosie's office door. "I received a call from the Broadway department store. They're asking for volunteers to help with their semiannual inventory. They'll pay fifteen hundred dollars for a group to pull an all-night shift." Shirley handed the phone number to Rosie. "The singles' ministry has been looking for a way to help you and Jesse; this could be their chance."

Rosie smiled as she dialed the phone number. "Lord, thank you for this miracle."

The singles went into action, passing out flyers that read, "Help send our missionaries to Sweden!"

"Missionaries? I thought we were going to be students," she told Jesse after reading the flyer.

"From pastors to students; now missionaries . . . maybe God is trying to tell us something."

"Maybe I'll end up becoming a missionary after all," Rosie teased.

"Be careful what you speak, young lady. You usually get what you have faith for."

Jesse arrived at the department store early, wondering who would show up on a Thursday to work an all-night shift. An hour passed before the room started filling with volunteers. The store manager walked over to Jesse, rubbing his forehead. "This has never happened before. Too many people showed up, so you can send some of them home."

Everyone had a mind to work, and by ten o'clock, the store manager handed Jesse a check for fifteen hundred dollars. "We've never finished this early. Your group was the best we've ever had. Please consider working for us again," he said as he shook Jesse's hand.

The next morning Jesse called the travel agency to price two round-trip tickets, and somehow he wasn't surprised when the agent quoted a total amount of fifteen hundred dollars.

That afternoon as Jesse was praying, a thought came to him. He hurried to the kitchen, where Rosie was preparing a salad. Since Jesse's forced retirement, coming home for lunch was a welcome break from the hectic church office. She was chopping lettuce when he barged in.

"I'm not on staff, but you're the pastor's assistant, and we're still members of the church, right?"

"Right."

"Why didn't I think of this before? One of the church policies qualifies us to receive partial scholarships for Bible school!"

Rosie's eyes lit up.

"You must write a letter," he said. She put the knife down, and followed Jesse to the computer.

After lunch, Rosie walked into Pastor Caleb's office and handed him the letter of request. By five o'clock, the accountant walked into Rosie's office. "Here's a check."

"Thanks, Shirley," Rosie said, smiling. She tore open the envelope. Inside was a check for half of their tuition. She couldn't wait to show Jesse their miracle.

That evening after they shared the good news with Jesse's mother, her eyes filled with tears. "I told the Lord many years ago that if he provided me with a good job, I would always send you to Christian schools. It wasn't easy being a single mom, but God always provided." She reached for her purse and pulled out her checkbook. "So I might as well finish the job."

Each week, God showed up with another miracle. Barbara and Prissy hosted Tupperware and home decorating parties and gave the proceeds to the Atkisson Missionary Fund. Jesse's friend offered him a part-time position assisting with his air-conditioning business, while Rosie prepared for the upcoming Atkisson garage sale.

Grace stood in the middle of her mother's garage, baffled. "Where do we start?" Clothes were piled in one corner of the garage, and dishes in another. "I've got some junk that I'll donate, and Tim has some old fishing poles that need to go."

"I suggest you check with Tim first. Remember, one man's junk is another man's treasure."

Rosie watched as Grace stuck price tags on all her trashy treasures. The larger her daughter's tummy grew, the more she glowed. Rosie was counting the days until the birth of her grandchild.

Grace sat down and wiped beads of sweat from her forehead.

"Hey, take it easy," Rosie scolded.

Grace had become a beautiful young woman, from the inside out. Through the years, they had built a strong mother-daughter relationship, and now they were friends, which was frosting on Rosie's cake. It never failed—when they walked into a restaurant, the hostess would ask if they were *sisters*. Rosie always smiled, accepting the compliment like any older sister would. Their dark hair, brown eyes, and refined cheekbones reflected their DNA. Grace would follow with a smile, assuming the hostess knew who the younger sister was.

"Mom, I'm sitting here labeling; I can't make it much easier."

Rosie took the labels from Grace's hand. "You've done enough. Now, sit there and look pretty. It won't be long now."

On a warm July morning, the phone rang. "Mom, this is it. Can you meet us at the hospital?"

Five hours later, a healthy baby girl popped into the world. Tim opened the recovery room door and motioned Rosie to join them.

"She's beautiful. What are you going to name her?" Rosie asked.

"I'm sure you have a suggestion," Grace teased.

"As a matter of fact . . . I was thinking . . . how about Priscilla, after Elvis's wife? Or Lisa Marie, after his daughter?"

"What's with you and Elvis anyway?" Tim asked.

"Gotcha!" Rosie said jokingly.

"Actually, Mom, Tim and I have chosen a name," Grace said, cuddling the pink bundle in her arms. "This is Katherine Rose, after her maternal grandmother and great-grandmother."

Tears welled in Rosie's eyes. "Mom would have been honored, and I . . . well . . ." She reached in her purse in search of a hankie.

"We're going to call her Katie," Grace said as she handed her daughter to Rosie.

Rosie beamed as she held her beautiful granddaughter. "Our little Katie Rose, how am I going to part with you?" she said.

"By God's grace," Grace answered.

For the next six weeks, Rosie spent every possible moment with Katie Rose, taking her for walks in the park, giving her baths when she visited Grace, all the things she would miss doing for the next nine months.

Rosie was confronted daily with guilt-versus-follow-your-destiny. And daily, destiny won.

It was still dark when a small group of family and friends escorted the Atkissons to the LAX Airport.

"You better take care of my Mustang," Rosie teased Presley.

"I promise not to go over eighty—kidding!" Presley said, laughing. "I'll have enough money to buy my own car by the time you get back," he added.

Teenagers and Mustangs can be a dangerous mix, but I'll have to trust my son to abide by the rules, she thought as she hugged Presley.

Rosie took Katie to a corner of the departure area. "I'll see you in nine months," she whispered as her tears fell on Katie's cheek. She blotted them with her hankie.

Rosie walked toward Tim and Grace. Tim took his daughter from Rosie, and then Grace wrapped her arms around her mother. "We'll talk on the phone."

"We probably won't have a phone, but we'll write lots of letters." She pulled Grace close. "This will have to do for now."

Forcing a smile, Rosie turned to give Tim a hug.

Afterward, Tim smiled. "Can I tell you a secret?" Rosie nodded. "We're going to try to come to Sweden for Christmas."

Rosie jumped back. "Are you serious?"

He turned to Grace. "I don't think I can keep your daughter away."

"We were going to surprise you, but why wait?" Grace said, grinning.

Once in the air, Jesse took Rosie's hand. He knew she was leaving part of her heart behind. "Hon, the time will fly, and before you know it, Christmas will be here."

Rosie smiled at her husband's thoughtful words. "Ahh, Christmas in Sweden with our family," she sighed. "But now if I want to be in the graduating class of '92, I must focus on Bible school. I haven't been a student in years!"

Rosie looked out the window, and as the engines roared, she whispered, "Saying yes to you, Lord, isn't always easy. I don't know what the coming year will bring, but I trust that you are leading me toward my destiny."

13

Miss Knot continued to sit and wait.

They arrived at Stockholm's Arlanda Airport with passports, visas, a donated computer, and two suitcases full of clothes and personal belongings—with no place to live.

After living in Sweden for a year, Luke and Lisa had moved back home to California, so Luke had called his Swedish friend, Dan, and asked him to pick the Atikisson's up at Arlanda Airport.

They gathered their luggage and then began the search for their Swedish chauffer.

"Look for a tall, thin blond," Jesse told Rosie.

"Oh, that must be him," Rosie said, waving at a tall, handsome man. But he was soon running toward a beautiful young blond woman.

"That's Dan," Jesse said, pointing to a fair, lean gentleman. But the Swede turned and walked toward a woman with two children.

They stood at the terminal entrance for fifteen minutes before a man in his early forties walked toward them, waving. "I am Dan, and you must be the homeless Americans." He smiled as he glanced at their luggage. "I was a student once. You bring back memories of when I moved from northern Sweden to Uppsala with all my belongings," he said as he guided them to the parking lot.

Luke had also asked Dan to drive by Living Waters Church and look on the bulletin board for flat rentals. As Dan drove past the canal that ran through the town of Uppsala he mentioned, "I went by the church to check the bulletin board, and I am sorry to report there are no flats for rent. I read the newspaper this morning, and there is nothing available. This is a university town and most of the students have already arrived, so it is a difficult time."

Rosie sighed as Jesse glanced at her, sitting alone in the backseat of Dan's company van.

Church bells rang as they drove past the majestic Lutheran cathedral. Rosie took it as a sign that there was a flat waiting somewhere in the city. Perhaps not as grand as the seventeenth-century castle that she was staring at through the back window, but who needed a castle? They only wanted a place to sleep.

As Dan pulled into his driveway in the small village of Stroveta. Rosie immediately captured the scent of roses as Dan led them through his garden. He stopped at the door of a tiny room behind the garage.

"My rooms are full in the main house, but my daughters won't mind if you occupy their playroom until you can find a flat."

Rosie glanced through the narrow door. Barbie dolls were sprawled on the floor, along with other girlie items—doll clothes, brushes, and plastic beads.

"I'm new at being a single dad, so telling Lu-Lu to put her toys away is not a high priority."

All Rosie could see was a small, messy dollhouse, but Jesse looked past the clutter. "With some rearranging, this will work fine," he said.

Dan excused himself to go back to work. "I'll be home at six, and I'll fix us something to eat," he said. "Help yourself to my kitchen and bathroom." Then he was gone.

Rosie's eyes were drooping. "I can see that you have a bad case of jet lag," Jesse said, smiling at his wife. "Let's call Grace, and then you can crash on Dan's sofa while I straighten up our dollhouse."

Rosie woke up several hours later, still drowsy from a deep sleep. She sauntered through the garden to the playhouse. Her eyes widened as she looked inside. Once stacked twin beds were now side by side; dolls and all accessories were packed away; their computer was sitting on a small table under the narrow window, waiting to be assembled.

"Our very own playhouse," Rosie said. "After I hang a few clothes in the Ikea closet, we'll be ready for action." But looking into Jesse's bloodshot eyes, she added, "I think it's your turn to take a nap."

"Yeah, I'm tired, but first, how about a little of that *action?*"

Rosie held out her arms as they collapsed on their make-do double bed.

Rosie was straightening the bed when she saw Dan heading for the playhouse.

Jesse looked at his watch. "Aren't you home early?"

Rosie saw the troubled look on Dan's face. "You look like you've seen a ghost."

"The radio has announced communism has fallen in the Soviet Union. Come in the house so we can watch TV, and I will translate for you."

They sat in Dan's living room listening to a Swedish news reporter. Rosie moved next to Jesse on the sofa, while Dan sat in the armchair next to the TV, translating for them.

"We need to learn some basic Swedish, fast. The world could be ending, and we wouldn't have a clue," she told Jesse. He nodded.

The TV station broke for a commercial. "Shall I make coffee?" Rosie asked.

"*Tack sa mycket,*" Dan said.

"Pardon me?" Rosie asked.

"Oh, sorry. I meant to say in English, thank you very much."

Rosie smiled at Dan. "My first Swedish lesson . . . *tack sa mycket.*"

Then Dan spoke in a serious tone. "We are living in a monumental time in history. First, the Berlin Wall came down, and now communism is falling. Thank God Living Waters is positioned for this time in history."

"What do you mean, *positioned?*"

The commercial was still playing as Dan continued. "The church established Russia Inland Missions a few years ago, and now teams will be sent into Russia and Siberia.

Jesse smiled. "Maybe we can be part of a team before we go home."

Rosie glared at Jesse as she walked toward the kitchen. "We've only been here a day, and you're already talking about going to Russia?"

Jesse realized his timing was off; this was not the time to verbalize his thoughts.

Rosie was pouring cups of coffee in the kitchen when the phone rang. In the living room, Dan was glued to the TV, so he motioned for her to pick up.

"Mom, are you okay?" Grace asked. "I heard the news about Russia on *Good Morning, America.*"

"Grace, don't worry; we're fine."

"You're in Russia's backyard, so of course I'm concerned."

"We're in the middle of what's going on, so we get the news firsthand. Actually, it's quite exciting." Rosie couldn't believe the words that came out of her mouth.

School began, and six weeks later, they found a furnished two-bedroom flat, a mere twenty-five-minute bus ride from Living Waters.

Rosie stood in the middle of the spare room with outstretched arms. "This room will make a perfect study."

"And a great guest room for family and friends," Jesse added, remembering those who had committed to travel halfway around the world to visit them. "Free room and board is an invitation that's hard to pass up for Americans who like to travel."

Rosie and Jesse soon became Mom and Dad to the younger students at the largest international Bible school in Europe. The young and the restless enjoyed living independently away from home, but it was comforting to know they could drop by the Atkisson flat for Jesse's famous tacos.

Three morning classes and attending the two-hour prayer school each afternoon found Jesse and Rosie looking forward to their evenings at home. They couldn't afford a telephone, so Rosie wrote a monthly newsletter to family and friends, informing them of what was happening in Eastern Europe, the Baltic States, Russia, and Siberia. When the postman dropped mail into their box, they hurried indoors, poured cups of coffee, and sat at the kitchen table and read letters from home.

"Listen to what Prissy wrote," Rosie said one snowy December afternoon. "Merry Christmas to my personal international journalist. Thanks for the monthly updates. I miss you and I'm praying for you and Jesse. God spoke to me to send you this Christmas gift. Can't write much now; I'm on my way to our church Christmas play. The show must go on!"

Rosie handed the check to Jesse. "We'll put this money aside for our mission trip," Jesse said as he folded the check for three hundred dollars.

"What trip?" Rosie asked.

"The train that's going through Siberia in July."

"Oh, yeah, that one." Her heart jumped every time their mission teacher, Carl Gustav, talked about the train. "But we're from California—we'll freeze in Siberia," she said, sipping her coffee and shivering at the thought. "Remember *Dr. Zhivago?*"

"There's no snow in July, silly," he said, placing the check in his wallet.

"We need to get home as soon as we graduate in May," she argued. "Besides, we don't have the money for the four-week trip."

"We didn't have the money for Bible school, but look around," he said, pointing to the kitchen large enough for a farm table. "We're living in a two-bedroom furnished flat."

"But we need to get back to our family, and to our singles' ministry."

Jesse slammed his cup down on the table, splashing coffee. "Rosie, it isn't *our* ministry anymore. This is a chance in a lifetime, so why are you making excuses for not going?" he asked, trying not to raise his voice.

She wanted to blurt, *because I'm afraid!* How long could she hold out telling him that since she was nine years old, she was afraid of the Russians?

Their trip to Leningrad and Moscow in March was enough to last her a lifetime. Now as Jesse spoke of the Siberia trip, she sat petrified.

Then she remembered the faith class they would be taking next semester. Maybe then she would learn how to overcome her fear. *But what if I fail the class?*

"Rosie? Did you hear me?" he asked as he wiped coffee off the table.

"Yes, I heard you, but I need more time to pray about it," she said as she placed her cup on the kitchen counter. "In the meantime, let's go buy us a Charlie Brown Christmas tree!"

Something always happened in Rosie's heart whenever Carl Gustav taught about Israel. By the end of the mission course, she yearned to join the June graduating class on the Israel trip. She talked on and on about Israel with Tim and Grace over Christmas dinner.

"But we don't have enough money to go to Israel, especially if we're going to Siberia," Jesse said.

"Who's going to Siberia?" Grace asked.

"Who said we're going to Siberia?" Rosie asked Jesse.

Tim handed Katie to Rosie. "Can I come?"

Grace glanced at her husband.

"Kidding!" Tim quickly added.

"Let's make a deal Rosie," Jesse said. "Since we both got A's in our faith class, why don't you believe for Israel, and I'll believe for Siberia?"

"Why don't you both believe for Israel *and* Siberia?" Grace asked.

"I was hoping someone would suggest that," Jesse said, smiling at Grace. "And may all our dreams come true in 1992!"

Jesse and Rosie moved to Dan's home right after June graduation to prepare for their eight-day Israel trip.

"When we return to Sweden from Israel, we'll have just enough time to repack for Siberia," Rosie told Grace on the phone. "It's a miracle that we have the finances for both trips."

"You received a lot of donations over the last nine months," Grace said. "Prissy called and told me that she's traveling through Siberia with you because of her support. Your time in Sweden wasn't only for your benefit, but for everyone who supported you with their prayers and donations."

"I never thought of it in that way."

"We've enjoyed living in your house, but your testimonies have increased our faith to believe that we can buy a house when you return in August."

"You're welcome to stay with us for as long as you want."

"Thanks, Mom, but we'll be ready to find a place of our own. But don't worry, you'll have lots of time to babysit Katie."

Rosie walked outside to enjoy Dan's garden. The roses were in full bloom. She inhaled the sweet fragrance. "Lord, you did remember my prayers as a young girl: I'm traveling with you and the special man you gave me; and even Prissy gets to come along."

14

The ship waited while rust gathered.

Four hundred weary travelers arrived at the Ben Gurin Airport. By mid-morning, the tour buses drove northeast until they arrived at a hotel that overlooked the Haifa harbor.

"You'll be staying at the Haifa Towers Hotel," their bus captain announced.

After eating a breakfast of goat cheese, yogurt, boiled eggs, tomatoes, cucumbers, rolls, and coffee, they met their tour guide outside the hotel to board their bus for Jerusalem.

"I can't believe we're here," Rosie said as she jumped off the bus at the old city. The streets were crowded, and the hot, dry climate reminded her of California, making her feel at home in the small foreign country.

Jesse and Rosie held hands as they walked through the Jaffa Gate and down narrow streets of the Arab section. Handsome dark-skinned men beckoned the tourists to come into their shops. The tour guide appointed thirty minutes for shopping.

Jesse sniffed the air. "Wait! I must go in this store." Rosie smiled; he could never resist the smell of leather. Jesse dropped Rosie's hand and strolled down the narrow aisles of the shop while Rosie stopped at the shoe rack. A pair of brown leather sandals caught her eye.

The shopkeeper smiled as he approached. "May I help you find your size, madam?"

She picked up a size forty. "I'll try these."

"Of course, madam. Are you American?"

"Uh, yes," she said as she buckled the right sandal. *Why does he want to know?* she wondered.

"My brother lives in New York City. I want to go there someday."

Rosie returned his smile. "You'll love America." She finished buckling her left sandal. "And I love your country." Looking down, she asked, "How much?"

The man looked amused. "I give these to you for twenty-five American dollars."

Jesse walked over, carrying a leather wallet.

"That's a good price," Rosie answered.

"She'll take them for twenty," Jesse sparred.

The shopkeeper nodded as Jesse handed him a twenty-dollar bill.

"They love to bargain," Jesse whispered to Rosie. "How much for the wallet?" he asked.

"Fifteen dollars."

"I'll give you eight."

The Arab nodded.

"Keep the change," Jesse said, handing him a ten-dollar bill.

Rosie walked out of the shop wearing her new sandals.

"They'll last for years," Jesse said.

"And they were such a good deal," Rosie said, smiling.

As they walked, Rosie looked puzzled.

"Is something wrong?" Jesse asked, taking hold of her hand.

"He looked at me funny when I told him that I loved his country."

"He's Arab. In 1948 Israel became a Jewish nation."

"But the Arabs and the Jewish people live in peace among themselves, don't they?"

Jesse stopped and pulled her aside from the busy cobblestone path. "When my church sent a small team to Israel in the seventies, we lived on the West Bank. The Arabs welcomed us as family. The people want to live in peace, but as we studied in Bible school, the problems go deeper. We must continue to pray for the peace of Jerusalem, and for these people, both Israelis and Palestinians."

As Rosie walked the streets of the old city, she began to feel connected to the place where Jesus had walked. Later the tour partook of communion in the garden of Gethsemane, and then prayed in the Upper Room. She wanted to take her time in these special places, especially when the tour guide directed the group toward the Western Wall.

Women gathered on the right side of the Wall, swaying back and forth as they lifted prayers to heaven. Rosie waited her turn in line, and then walked forward and gently touched the stones. After placing in the wall a piece of paper that held a personal prayer for her family and friends back home, she closed by praying for the peace of Jerusalem.

Afterward, Rosie watched as men in black robes quoted scriptures and prayed on the left side of the Wall. "Lord, everywhere there is separation. In America, there was separation between the blacks and the whites. Here, there is separation between the Jews and the Arabs, and between the men and the women. Will it ever change?"

From within, she heard, *Yes. One day there will be no more separation.*

She wanted to stay in this holy place, but the tour guide was calling everyone to move on.

After lunch, near the Mount of Olives, Jesse turned to the team captain. "Can Rosie and I take a taxi and meet you back at the hotel?"

"Of course, but be back by dinner," the captain instructed.

Rosie reluctantly followed Jesse down a narrow street. "Where are we going? And why is the bus leaving us behind?"

"I want to find the little church where our group held meetings when I lived here in the seventies."

"Do you think you can find that building after twenty years?" Rosie asked, but Jesse wasn't listening. He was intent on finding a small part of his past.

The blazing sun bore down as they walked the dirt road. Soldiers stood in front of the shops with rifles flung over their shoulders, watching their every move.

"They don't look Jewish to me," Rosie said.

"They're not. We're on the West Bank. Those are Arab soldiers, but they won't bother us. Here, take my hand."

How does he know that? she wondered as she tightened her grip.

Her surroundings brought back the dream she had five years before. She was walking the streets of Jerusalem with a man. Now, here she was, walking in Jerusalem with her husband. But this wasn't the interpretation she had hoped for.

"Let me see, where's that building?" he said, looking around.

The shops were in poor condition, and she stepped in a pothole while two soldiers looked on. Jesse caught her before she landed in the dirt.

Rosie was sweating and her stomach was churning as Jesse led her to an even more rundown section of town. She didn't dare ask her James Bond to find her a toilet—he would only tell her to hold it. After four wrong turns down narrow dirt streets, he stopped. "They must have torn it down." He was clearly disappointed, but Rosie couldn't sympathize. She was scared, and she couldn't understand why her husband wasn't.

A fifth wrong turn led them to a rundown warehouse. "I think that's where we held our meetings," Jesse said, leading her toward the building.

Then just as fast, he looked beyond and saw an army post that overlooked the city below. He took her arm as two Israeli soldiers marched toward them.

"Try to act normal," Jesse whispered.

"We do look suspicious, don't we?" she asked through trembling lips.

The great woman of faith was about to faint as she felt something trickle down her left leg.

Then, from out of nowhere, a tall man in a black coat approached them and pointed to a nearby taxi.

"Yalla! Yalla!" Jesse yelled, motioning for the cab. The dirty sedan pulled up and Rosie dived into the safety of the backseat.

"An afternoon on the West Bank—a day to remember," Rosie said as the taxi sped down the street toward their hotel.

"Tomorrow we'll go to Abu Dis to find the house where I lived for six months," Jesse said.

"Over my dead body!" Rosie answered as she wiped her left leg with a Handi Wipe.

The next afternoon, the tour buses drove the team to the desert near Masada. That night, as Jesse and Rosie lay in sleeping bags furnished by the tour company, Jesse pointed to the sky. "Here is the five-star hotel I promised you."

Rosie stared at the black sky, glittering with too many stars to ever count. "You promised me a five-star, but God has given me a million-star hotel . . . and the man of my dreams."

Jesse slept while the desert dogs howled their moonlight serenade. Rosie turned over and decided to wait until dawn to find the outhouses that were lined up at the edge of the campsite—until she felt something damp between her legs. She dreaded getting out of her bag, but she had been right—the attack of the monthly period had picked an inappropriate time to come calling.

Cramps and all, Rosie joined the group at dawn to trek up to Masada. Hiking in the fresh morning air gave her a sense of well-being, and that afternoon when they arrived at the Dead Sea, she even considered taking a dip, until the bus captain gave them specific instructions.

"The salt in the sea will cause you to float, but do not let the saltwater inside your mouth. People have died from ingesting this water."

"I'm bloated, so I think I'll pass," Rosie told Jesse.

After touring Capernaum, they arrived at the Jordan River to spend a few hours river rafting. Rosie sat in the bus while everyone filed out.

"Aren't you coming?" Jesse asked.

"I'm still bloated," Rosie said as she pulled her T-shirt down once more to cover her stained shorts. The sound of the river's current caused her head to spin.

"Come on, Rosie. The fresh air will be good for your *condition.*"

Rosie and Prissy could never figure out how men always knew what was best for women *that certain time* of the month. Rosie reluctantly followed Jesse to the river's edge, and after taking a few deep breaths, she found herself relaxing as they rafted down the Jordan. She was actually enjoying herself—cramps having all but disappeared—when a current caught the raft broadside.

"Oh no!" Rosie yelled as she lost her balance and fell overboard. Within seconds, she was blowing bubbles beneath the water. She dog paddled to the surface, and then went under again. Her life began to pass before her, when out of nowhere, two hands from underneath grabbed her, pushing her to the surface.

Jesse pulled Rosie up and over the side of the raft as water spouted from her mouth. She clung to him, coughing continuously. After her breathing returned to normal, she looked around at the others in the raft.

"I want to thank the person who dove in the river to save me."

They looked at each other and then at Rosie. Jesse shook his head.

"No one was in the water with you, Rosie. One minute you were under the water, and a few seconds later, you surfaced alone."

Rosie was in no mood to argue—it was the wrong time of the month. But she knew there was someone else with her in that magical river. Driving to the seaside town of Natanya, soaked from her near-death experience, she couldn't figure out what had happened—perhaps an angel? Angel or no angel, she opted to sit in the sand while Jesse swam in the Mediterranean, and vowed to never set foot on a boat again.

The next evening, as their plane flew over the lights of Tel Aviv, Jesse turned to Rosie. "Let's return to Israel someday."

"Someday," she repeated. "But after being away from home for a year, I can't think that far ahead."

"Now we must prepare for our trip to Siberia," Jesse reminded his traveling lady.

She closed her eyes, wondering what Siberia held.

On a hot July afternoon, twenty-five Swedes, twenty-five Russians, and somewhere in the middle two Americans arrived in St. Petersburg.

Jesse glanced around the airport. "Everything looks the same as last year. Only the name of the city has been changed."

Rosie pointed at the Russian men and women laughing as they walked down the street. "But look at the people," she said to Torre, their team captain.

"When communism fell, the people began to feel a sense of freedom they've never experienced," Torre said. Torre traveled to Russia frequently and had witnessed firsthand the changes taking place.

The bus drove to a train station on the outskirts of town. When the bus pulled over, Torre announced, "For security reasons, the train has been moved to a different location."

Rosie gathered her luggage and, trying to be a tough missionary, she began walking in ninety-degree heat in search of the missing train. She stopped to wipe her forehead with a hankie and was getting ready to ask, *Are we there yet?* when she caught sight of a large, isolated hangar-looking building. Then she beheld the big, old, green former youth communist propaganda train.

Rosie didn't know what to expect as she boarded her new home. She stepped up the ladder and walked through the lounge. The dining car was decorated in Russia's favorite colors. Curtains, tablecloths, and accessories were bright yellow, orange, and red. Rosie was impressed by the beautiful hand-carved Russian woodwork.

Torre introduced the team to the train's staff. "These men and women will be serving you." Everyone smiled and nodded. Torre added, "As you can see, our translators are going to be busy in the days ahead."

Jesse and Rosie found their way to the designated sleeping compartment and then dropped their suitcases in the hallway. Once inside, they tried to turn around, but there was only enough room for two bunks and a pullout table. Jesse sat on the lower bunk. Rosie remained standing, wondering how she was going to live in the small, hot, eight-by-four.

"Another small room, even smaller than Lu-Lu's Swedish playhouse," she said.

"It's only for a month," Jesse reminded her.

She unpacked her family picture and placed it on the shelf above the pullout table. Lisa had told her it was important to bring a few personal items wherever you travel to make you feel at home. The rest of their belongings were stored in their suitcases under the lower bunk. When Rosie was finished, she sat next to Jesse on the lower bunk. "I have to remember that less-is-best."

"The people in Russia only know less," Jesse reminded his wife.

The train pulled out of St. Petersburg around midnight. The sounds reminded Rosie of their one-night train excursion from Estonia to Leningrad. Now they were in Russia again, heading for the heart of Siberia.

As Jesse climbed the ladder to the top bunk, Rosie gently pulled at his leg.

"Hey, Jessinski, I've never done it on a train."

Jesse stopped mid-ladder, climbed down, then slid into her bunk and began gently rubbing her back. "There's always time for first-times," he said as he kissed her moist neck.

Afterward, they were lulled to sleep by the clickity-clack of the big-green-train-that-could.

As dawn broke, Rosie peered out of their small window. Green fields were sprinkled with bright pink, yellow, and orange flowers, vegetable gardens, and tiny summerhouses. The Ural Mountains stood regal as the train passed through the mountainous ridges.

Rosie had just finished dressing when Jesse called, "Climb up here and look." His head was inches from the ceiling. "We're going to change bunks," he said. "There's not enough room for me up here." He didn't ask; he informed.

The mayor and the city officials greeted them as the train pulled into the station. The first morning Rosie stepped off the train onto the dusty Russian soil, an eerie feeling came over her. She looked around at her unfamiliar surroundings. *Here I am, somewhere in Siberia. If someone snatched me up, no one would even know,* she thought.

Before her stomach had a chance to knot up, a reassuring voice from inside whispered, *I would know.*

Once again, that still, small voice came at just the right time.

The teams left by nine-thirty and were driven to city prisons, hospitals, orphanages, and senior homes. Clothing, hospital medicine, and other useful items donated by local Swedish churches and hospitals were distributed.

A beat-up van transported Rosie's team to a women's convalescent home in a village in the Siberian countryside. A large woman greeted them at the door. "I am Yovita," she said loudly.

Agnetha, their translator, stood next to Semret, the Swedish team leader, ready to assist. They entered the large unkempt building and walked through a dark, musty hallway. Rosie started to gag, so she began breathing through her mouth.

Yovita led the team into the darker living room, where old women shouted for no apparent reason. Cots lined the living room walls—some empty, some with women trying to sleep. The screaming concerned Rosie—it didn't seem normal. Johan and Anna, two young Swedes, were stunned into silence. The whole scene was like walking into a Stephen King horror movie, except Rosie didn't see a director's chair.

Yovita escorted them to a small office and then excused herself to find the house doctor. Semret had been traveling through Russia for several months with the Operation Jabotinsky teams, so she knew what needed to be done. She bowed her head.

"We take authority over every foul spirit that would try to keep us from giving the gift of love to these people. We dedicate this time to you, Lord."

Semret had only just pronounced her *amen* when a handsome Russian in a white jacket walked in. As Semret rose from her chair, he held out his hand. "I am Dr. Petronevich, the house psychiatrist."

Rosie nicknamed him Dr. Zhivago because of his dark, caring eyes, and because she couldn't pronounce his name.

As Semret spoke, the doctor's eyes focused on Semret's neck, giving Rosie a chilling feeling. "What is that?" he interrupted.

Semret looked down, assuming he was inquiring about her T-shirt. She pointed to the Russian letters. "Our train is traveling to these fourteen cities in Siberia."

"I am not speaking of your shirt. I am looking at your necklace," Dr. Zhivago said.

As Semret clutched her Star of David necklace, she shared how their church in Sweden began Project Operation Jabotinsky to help Russian Jews migrate to Israel.

"I am a Russian Jew," the doctor said.

The team was all ears.

"The Jews are persecuted in different ways in Russia, and the situation is getting worse. My wife and daughter are doctors, but we fear for our lives." He scribbled something on a piece of paper and then handed the paper to Semret. "Perhaps you can help us."

Rosie's heart went out to this handsome Russian. *If only he and his family could hop on our train,* she thought.

By the time the meeting began, the pandemonium had turned to calm. Over a hundred women sat, waiting in the large living room. Rosie opened by singing a simple upbeat song in Russian she had learned the night before. Old women clapped as Rosie sang, and when Semret shared her testimony in English, the women stared at her as Agnetha translated her message to Russian.

"God loves you. He will give you strength to face each day, and he will give you eternal life. Who would like to receive the Lord Jesus today?" Semret asked. As the women raised their hands, Rosie remembered a day many years ago when a missionary came to her church and asked the same question. And now, here she was, thousands of miles from home, living her dream—traveling with him. She whispered, "Lord, have I thanked you lately for all you've done for me?"

As the team headed for the front door, Rosie noticed an old woman lying on a narrow bed in a small, dark room, alone. Rosie motioned to the translator, and together they sat and listened to the old babushka. "I have been waiting for seventy years to talk to someone about my Lord," the woman slurred in her native tongue.

"My sister, God brought me all the way from America so you could talk about him."

As the lady smiled, gold teeth shining, sharing how God had kept her safe through many hard years, Rosie knew it was a mission-from-God that brought her to this Siberian village. She felt as if she had been transformed into Mother Teresa as she took a glass of water from the small table and lifted it to the lady's wrinkled lips. She was having an epiphany moment. *Lord, again you are reminding me that my life is not all about me. It is about being a comfort to another sister, even in a faraway country. Thank you that I can be the answer to this babushka's prayers.*

Rosie bent over and gave the woman a hug—her body odor didn't bother her one bit—and bade her farewell. The Russian babushka smiled through gold-filled teeth at the happy American grandmother, and asked, "Will I see you again?"

"Yes, we shall meet again," Rosie answered, as beads of sweat dripped down her back.

There were no crowds to cheer, no VIP—very important person—to pat her on the back. None was necessary for Rosie to feel like the Mother Teresa of Siberia.

The next day Semret delegated Rosie to take her place as a team leader. "But I don't feel prepared to lead," Rosie argued. "What if I find myself in a similar situation as yesterday?"

"You will do exactly what we did—pray," Semret answered. "I must lead another team today."

Rosie took a deep breath, and away they drove in the back of an old Russian army van, headed for a small rural village. After driving through the countryside for an hour, the team arrived at an old, broken-down building near the center of town. Trash was piled at the entry door. Rosie could smell someone's leftovers from weeks gone by. "Where do we get these connections?" Rosie asked her interpreter.

"From the city officials," Agnetha replied, glancing at the rat scurrying from one trash pile to another. "This is the best they can offer."

After climbing four flights of stairs, they were greeted at the door of 4C by a young woman. "I am Yovi, Korrina's neighbor," Agnetha translated. Yovi led them into the living room.

"This is Korrina. She lives alone, and I care for her daily needs."

Korrina didn't stand to greet the team, as most of the hospitable Russians did. Instead, she sat on her sofa and smiled. Rosie looked further. In the corner was a wheelchair.

Korrina couldn't stand because she had no legs.

Rosie sat with Korrina drinking chai and chatting. "God loves you so much that he sent me from America to tell you how he wants to give you comfort."

As Rosie spoke, her mind raced. *Who do you think you are, you spoiled American girl with legs, to tell Korrina how much God loves her? How can Korrina think God loves her when she has no legs?*

Rosie was about to back off when Korrina interrupted her thoughts. "I want your God."

Oh, ye American of little faith, she thought as she prayed for Korrina.

The team held large meetings every night for a month in former Communist party theaters where propaganda meetings were once held. The Swedish dance team performed musical mime that presented the gospel of Jesus Christ. After the performance, hundreds of Russians made their way to the front of the theater to receive Christ. The team was nearly crushed by eager converts as they pushed forward to grab free Bibles, tracts, and books.

Each night the weary team arrived back at the train after midnight, but as they met in the lounge car to share the day's activities, they were energized by the testimonies. Rosie's little compartment became her haven as she collapsed in her bunk each night. By the time they pulled out of the station to begin the trek toward the next city, Rosie was lulled to sleep by the train's clickity-clack.

Throughout the month, the team met Christian organizations from America who were helping reach the vast country for God. There was no talk about who had the largest or the best church—no competition here—only stories about how God was changing lives throughout Siberia.

As their plane crossed the Atlantic heading for home, Jesse leaned close to Rosie to reminisce about their year. "The time in Bible school and Israel has taught us a lot about her history and God's eternal plan for Israel."

Rosie smiled as she leaned back. "I loved our trip to Siberia—I even met some Russian Jews. The Russians are warm, loving people."

Jesse touched her arm. "Maybe this year was preparation for our future. Perhaps we'll return to Russia someday."

Rosie began to squirm in her seat. "Israel *and* Russia? I don't see how that's possible." Then she looked in her husband's eyes. Did she see disappointment? . . ."Uh, you might be right. But for now, all I can think about is going home to our family."

15

When Stuart and Shelly discovered the vision for their ship while attending Bible school in Sweden in 1993, Miss Knot was delighted to be getting attention from local churches and organizations.

Rosie was grateful to live only ten miles from work. The southern California traffic was getting heavier by the day. Their friend Luke was now pastor of a growing church and Bible school, so when he offered her the position of Bible school administrator when they returned home from Sweden, Rosie jumped at the chance. She was in her element teaching classes, writing articles for the monthly newsletter, and spending time with the students. Since graduating from Living Waters Bible School two years earlier, she understood the value of studying the Bible.

But even driving her Mustang the short distance sometimes got to her. It took all her willpower not to honk at the rude, fast-driving, lane-changing drivers, especially after living in slow-moving Sweden.

Rosie never read while driving nor did she apply lipstick while behind the wheel, but one vice she would never give up was sipping coffee from one of her many travel mugs. However, while driving home over the Fullerton Pass this particular February afternoon, she felt an urge to pick up the two-sided green flier that Pastor Luke had handed her as she walked past his office.

"I returned from Seattle yesterday, and I thought you might want to write a column in the school newsletter about what's going on with this World War II ship. I'm sure Jesse will be interested."

"Thanks, I'll read it tonight," Rosie said, taking the flier from his hand. She continued walking, travel mug in one hand, purse, briefcase, and flier in the other. She was on her way home to spend a quiet evening with Jesse.

The flier lying on the passenger seat began blowing toward Rosie, as if it were beckoning her to read it. She took a sip of coffee, placed the mug in the cupholder, and then picked up the green piece of paper. Rosie slowed down as she read aloud, "God is bringing Russian Jews home to Israel, and you can help."

"Hey, lady! Watch where you're going!" a teenage boy yelled out of his car window while passing.

There. She had become another wild California driver.

Her love for Israel was evident to her family and friends, but she hadn't heard about the ship MS *Restoration* until this moment. Tears filled her eyes as the words jumped off the page. She placed the flier on the seat.

Crying and driving isn't a good combination either, especially with hair blowing in your face. But Rosie couldn't hold back her hair nor her tears, so she rolled up the window and drove home through moist eyes and tossed hair.

She pulled in the garage, gathered the mail, and dropped it on the kitchen table. She was tempted to stuff the flier in her briefcase, but instead, she placed it beneath Jesse's much-awaited car magazine, along with a few bills and occupant letters.

She headed for the bedroom to change for her evening run. As she passed the hallway mirror, she caught a glimpse of her reflection—permed hair tumbled from the wind and bloodshot eyes. Pulling a hankie from her purse, she shook her head. "You look like a woman who's experienced a bad day at the office—or the latest version of Cher," she told the forty-eight-year-old woman staring back at her. She dabbed her eyes and then leaned closer to the mirror. "Come on, get your running shoes on; it's time to hit the road."

"Hon, I'm home!" Jesse yelled as he walked through the back door an hour later. Working fifteen minutes away at the Home Depot for the past two years fulfilled Jesse's passion to help people with oftentimes impossible projects. After somewhat challenging conversations, the customer's satisfaction made it worthwhile. He came home tired, but somewhat content.

Jesse stopped to glance at the mail, purposefully looking for his March issue of *Motor Trend*. After thumbing through a gas bill and a few occupant letters, he found his treasure. "It's here!" As he picked up the magazine, a green piece of paper fell to the floor. Curious, he picked it up and read it. "Hmmm, interesting." He placed the flier next to the occupant letters, grabbed his *Motor Trend*, and exited the kitchen.

Later, while reading in bed, Rosie asked, "Did you happen to see the green flier Luke gave me today?"

"Yeah, I read it."

Rosie was curious to hear his comments before he went back to oohing and aahing over his car magazine. Before she could ask, he had already gone to the kitchen and came back holding the flier.

"A World War II ship in Seattle—soon to be christened the MS *Restoration*—that was given to a church in Sweden by an Alaskan sea captain is now being restored to transport Russian Jews from Sochi, Russia, to Israel. Needed: short-term and long-term volunteers."

Jesse paused. Rosie noticed his eyes lighting up, which meant the words had penetrated his heart. He loved adventure, but he was levelheaded and right now the most sensible thing for them to do was to stay put. But the combination was lethal. She knew he was thinking this matter through before going into his move-into-action mode. *Perhaps he's deciding how much we should donate to the project,* she thought, feeling a sense of relief.

"Should we give a donation?" she asked.

"I wasn't thinking along the lines of money." He hesitated. "Why don't we take a week in March to volunteer on the ship?" He handed Rosie the flier, which she quickly placed on her bedside table.

"Are you suggesting we donate a week of our two-week vacation?"

"Sure! Let's go to Seattle for a good cause, and then we'll plan a seven-day Caribbean cruise for the summer."

Rosie's eyes widened. "A cruise? I don't think so," she answered. "Do I have to remind you that I can't swim? We can fly to an island, but I will not spend seven days on a ship surrounded by water."

"So much for surprises," Jesse said, picking up his car magazine.

"What surprise?"

"Never mind," he said as he slid under the covers.

By the sound of Jesse's voice, Rosie knew he was up to something, but she decided not to pursue the matter. Instead, she turned to her travel magazine. Since living in Sweden for a year, two weeks maximum was as long as Rosie could take being away from her family.

Then she glanced over at Jesse. "Well, maybe I can handle a week on a ship that's safely moored in Seattle."

"And with Jay and Presley sharing an apartment, we have nothing holding us down," he added.

"Perhaps a week in Seattle would be nice for the empty nesters."

The next day Rosie was working in her office at the Bible school when Pastor Luke walked in with clenched lips. She recognized that look when he was in deep thought. He had worn it when they were being followed by the KGB in Moscow. And now with the Bible school in full swing, he was busier than ever teaching, counseling, planning mission trips, and all the while clenching his lips.

Pastor Luke sat down as Rosie poured two cups of coffee. She was taking her first sip when he got straight to the point.

"I've been praying about the upcoming mission trip to Cuba, and I don't feel it's the right time to take a team back."

Rosie nodded in agreement as she took her second sip. Then he handed her a familiar-looking green flier.

"Did you talk to Jesse about the ship that's laid up in Seattle?

Rosie choked on her third sip. "Funny you should mention the ship," she said, wiping spilled coffee off her fresh white shirt. "Jesse read the flier last night, and he's—*we're*—thinking about taking a week next month to volunteer on the ship." *There, I said it.*

"Maybe this would be a good opportunity for you and Jesse to take the Bible school team with you."

"Uh, that's a great idea," Rosie answered. Pastor Luke always knew how to throw her a curve when she least expected.

After Rosie finished wiping coffee off her desk, she called Jesse with the news. That night she rang Prissy.

"We always wanted to go on a mission trip together. Besides, you *owe* me," Rosie reminded her friend. Of course, Rosie knew she could never repay Prissy for dragging her to the singles' meeting where she had met her lonesome cowboy.

"Sure, I'd love to go. Bill will be out of town on business, and I'm in between acting classes."

"Grace and Tim will be on the team, so it'll be like a reunion."

"I forgot Grace was in Bible school," Prissy said.

"And Tim is dying to check out the old World War II ship."

"Are they bringing Katie?" Prissy asked.

"The ship isn't childproof, so Tim's mother offered to babysit."

"Then it's settled. You're heading for Seattle with your groupies in tow," Prissy teased.

Torre, the Living Waters' representative from Sweden, greeted the team at Sea-Tac Airport. "It is good to see you both again. The ship can really use your team's help," Torre said to Jesse.

Jesse patted Torre's back. "As I recall, whenever there's a difficult or challenging project, you're the man delegated for the job. You can make the impossible happen."

"And I can use your assistance in many areas on the ship," Torre said.

"I couldn't pass up the chance to work on a World War II ship," Jesse said, smiling. Torre glanced at Rosie.

"Oh, me too!" Rosie added, trying to sound as excited as her husband.

Seattle's March rain couldn't dampen the eagerness of the fifteen Bible school students. As they drove through Seattle, they gazed through water-stained windows at green rolling hills, the evidence of the benefits of Washington's rainfall. As they headed toward the outskirts of town toward the Ballard Bridge, the World's Fair Needle reflected the sun shining through the clouds. Twenty minutes later, Torre turned off the paved highway onto a dirt road. At a chain-link gate, the guard motioned them through, and the two vans parked close to the dock to prevent the team from having to walk through too many potholes.

"There she is, the MS *Restoration*," Torre said, pointing to an old ship tied up to the dock.

The team stood, gazing at an old, rusty ship.

"Yep, there she is, in all her glory," Jesse said.

"You mean, lack of glory," Rosie said sarcastically. "Pictures sure can be deceiving."

The smaller-than-life photo on the flier had shown a beautiful ship, ready and waiting to begin her journey across the Atlantic. The picture didn't fit the ship Rosie was staring at.

"This ship looks like it couldn't cross a lake, much less an ocean," Grace whispered to Rosie, her mouth hanging open.

"Did you have to say that?" Rosie asked her daughter. But Grace was right. If ever Rosie had judged a book by its cover, it was now. Her head was spinning with questions before they started walking up the gangway. "Torre, how much work has to be done before the ship is seaworthy? From her looks, she needs a total overhaul."

Everyone nodded.

"Is there an extreme makeover available for ships?" Prissy asked.

"Can this big heap of steel be transformed into a seaworthy vessel by a handful of volunteers—in a matter of weeks?" Grace asked.

"You are full of good questions," Torre said. "Yes, there is much work to be done, and from her outer appearance, she does need a makeover. But there is good news." He turned toward the men.

"Her engine and basic equipment are seaworthy. With patience, prayer, and much work, she will be ready to sail in a few weeks."

Before Torre could answer any more questions, a bellowing voice brought their attention to the top of the gangway, where a tall, handsome gentleman in his mid-sixties, wearing beige work clothes, was standing.

"Halo, everyone! I am Captain Alain Beck. Welcome aboard."

Torre had told the team about the Finnish captain and his wife as they drove to the port. "Captain Alain has years of experience on large oil tankers traveling through the Suez Canal and other parts of Europe and the Middle East. The captain and his wife, Tina, are volunteering their time to fulfill a dream that God gave Tina several years ago. Until now, it was a seemingly impossible dream, but now it is a reality."

"What dream?" Rosie asked.

"Tina had a dream they would one day transport Russian Jews to Israel."

"Impossible dreams can come true," Rosie said, thinking of her dream to travel the world.

A tall, slender woman in her fifties joined the captain at the gangway, her shoulder-length brown hair blowing in the breeze. She held out a strong hand to Rosie. "I am Tina. Welcome to the *Restoration*." Tina's bifocal glasses could not hide the gleam in her eyes.

Captain Alain pointed toward two large doors at the top of five-step staircases on deck. "You may get settled before I give you a tour. The men will bunk in hold two, and the girls will sleep in hold three. The lighting is not so good, so keep your flashlights ready."

"Will the married couples be together?" Rosie asked shyly.

"Absolutely!" Captain Alain bellowed. "Henrik will lead the way to your cabins located in the superstructure."

"Can I come with you? Henrik is a hottie!" Prissy whispered to Rosie. "And that scar on his face is fascinating—like a swashbuckling pirate."

"Hey, don't forget—you're married," Rosie teased.

"I'm kidding, but a girl can look, can't she?" Prissy said, jabbing Rosie's side.

The couples followed Henrik through a large, steel door.

"This part of the ship is called the superstructure—we call it the Iron House. Be careful stepping over the bulkheads," Henrik warned as he opened the large hatch. "Both entrances to the superstructure—starboard and port—are quite high."

Everyone lifted their right leg up and over, holding onto the steel wall to keep their balance, and then, like clockwork, they brought their left leg up and over. Rosie followed, lifted her right leg, but somehow her left leg caught on the bulkhead.

"Oh!" she gasped. Jesse turned and caught her as she was about to land on the steel floor.

"Quick response, Jesse," Henrik said, smiling.

Rosie's face turned red.

"You will get the hang of it soon," Henrik said.

"Hopefully before I break a leg," Rosie said, still blushing.

As Henrik led them down a dimly lit hall, Rosie noticed an office to her left.

"This is the ship's office," Henrik said. "And Bjorne, the first engineer, has the cabin on the right."

Henrik led them up a flight of stairs. Rosie noticed that everything seemed to be unusually narrow.

Henrik pointed down the hall. "When we head to sea, the second and third captains will live in these cabins. The second and third engineers will live around this narrow hall. But now we use them for volunteers who stay for a long period of time."

Henrik motioned Tim and Grace to the right, Mike and Alex left, and Jesse and Rosie straight ahead. Within seconds, they were standing next to their cabin doors.

"It looks like we're going to be a close-knit neighborhood," Rosie said, and then turned to Henrik before closing their cabin door. "Henrik, what is your job on board?"

"In Sweden, I am an electrician by trade, so on board, my job is to have all electrical functions in working order by the time we sail," he answered in proper British English.

"Did you get your scar on the job?" Rosie asked.

Henrik frowned. "No. I was a little reckless on my motorcycle in my younger years."

"You're not that old."

Henrik gently rubbed his scar. "I'm twenty-four. I was eighteen when this happened."

Embarrassed, Rosie changed the subject. "Are you going to sail with the ship?"

"Oh yes. I took a year off from my job in Sweden to work on her."

"She must be quite challenging."

"Yes, she is, but I am loving every minute. I feel I was created for this challenge," Henrik answered proudly. "Now I must return to my work. I'll see you at dinner."

As Rosie inhaled fresh paint, she caught a glimpse of a few challenges, and as she closed the cabin door, the first one stared her in the face. The small, compact room barely gave her room to turn around.

She sat down on the nearest bunk. "Did you see the dusty halls?" Rosie asked.

Jesse sat next to her. "Look on the bright side. Our cabin will be easy to clean." He stood and pointed. "And look at these lockers. Don't they remind you of your high school gym lockers?" Jesse opened a metal door, and then banged it shut.

The clanking sound brought back flashbacks of Rosie's high school P.E. days. She had dreaded changing into her gym clothes in the large, humid locker room for her physical education swimming class. The hotter the days, the stuffier and smellier the locker rooms. Rosie always prayed she wouldn't have phys-ed first period—her freshly teased hairdo would be ruined for the rest of the day. But to her dismay, her fall sophomore schedule read: first period, swimming.

The beginning of California's school year was always hot, so the girls had to postpone wearing their new wool dyed-to-match skirts and sweaters until later in the fall. One hot September morning, Rosie decided she would wear her white spaghetti-strap dress, the one she saved for church. After splashing around in the shallow end of the outdoor swimming pool for thirty minutes pretending to swim—and almost drowning—she showered and then swung open her locker door. Before she could react, the crisp white dress tumbled onto the wet, concrete floor. She picked it up and discovered a big, wet patch on the lower backside. The spot quickly dried, but a beige stain followed her for the rest of the day. Rosie couldn't understand why the boys chuckled as she walked by in the hallway, until after school when Prissy walked up from behind and said, "What is that awful stain on the back of your dress? Did you start your period?"

"Darn that wet gym floor!" Rosie muttered as she forced Prissy to walk behind her to the school bus. "I almost drowned, and now this!"

"That is one memory I'd like to forget," Rosie mumbled to Jesse. "And do you remember two years ago when we traveled on the Trans Siberian Railway and our sleeping compartment had been no larger than a linen closet, with enough room for only us and a hundred Russian mosquitoes? At least this freshly painted cabin is the size of a walk-in closet. And the white walls do give the room a World War II shabby-chic look."

"That's my girl." Jesse glanced at his watch. "Come on, we need to hit the deck for the captain's tour."

Piles of what looked like junk sat on the main deck. Fifty-five gallon drums of who-knows-what were stacked next to hold one.

"The ship was once converted into a museum, but the owner ran out of money so he had to sell her," Captain Alain explained.

"Thus, the piles of junk . . . uh, treasures," Rosie assessed.

Captain Alain led the team through the superstructure and then down a flight of stairs. Rosie held tight to the slick handrail as they carefully made their way to a gigantic room. She began perspiring, so she pulled a hankie from her pocket. "This must be what hot flashes feel like," she said, wiping her forehead.

Captain Alain spoke loudly to be heard over the booming noise. "This is the engine room. The engineers are constantly testing the engine. Please do not touch anything, or you will be devoured by grease!"

Rosie quickly moved her arm away from the wall she was leaning against as if the grease were poison. "Yuk—too late! I've been initiated," she murmured as she discovered a brown spot adorning her white T-shirt sleeve.

"And I've got a grease smudge on my new jeans," Prissy scowled.

"Do you want to borrow my hankie?" Rosie asked, but Prissy wasn't listening.

Silence filled the room when the engine shut down. A tall, lanky man in his thirties, dressed in gray coveralls, smeared in grease, appeared from the other end of the room.

"I am Bjorne, the chief engineer," he told the group. "I arrived from Sweden last month, and I will sail with the ship." He smiled shyly and then proceeded with his work.

"This engine will take the ship to places she has never been before," Captain Alain said. "Engineers and electricians work daily to prepare for departure. This is where precision is of the utmost importance. She can look like a million dollars on the outside, but if anything goes wrong in the engine room, we could be in for some challenging times at sea."

The thought of the large engine dying in the middle of the Atlantic made Rosie's stomach churn.

"Are you okay, Mom?" Grace asked, remembering her mother's fear of water.

"Oh, I'm fine. Thank God I'm only here for a week."

"And we're safely roped to the dock," Grace added.

Captain Alain led the group up a flight of stairs on the opposite side of the engine room. Centered in the middle of the superstructure was the galley. There were no windows, only overhead lighting and a few portable fans blowing for ventilation. Wiping her forehead, Rosie whispered, "Do not volunteer for galley duty."

"What did you say, Mom?" Grace asked.

"Uh, I think I'm having another power surge—hot flash."

"You can't be . . . you're too young," Grace said with conviction.

The aroma of something Italian reminded Rosie's stomach that she was hungry. The captain introduced everyone to the local galley girls, Valentine and Deena.

"I hope you like what we're preparing for dinner," Deena said as she tossed lettuce in a large tin bowl.

Valentine and Deena began chopping onions and slicing tomatoes as the team looked on from the other side of the cafeteria-style window. They were both Lane Bryant model material—beautiful and buxom, and proud of it. They looked at home standing next to the fans as they prepared dinner. The hungry volunteers' sense of smell awakened, so Captain Alain announced, "Let us continue the tour. Please follow me to the bridge."

The stairway took them past the couples' cabins on the second floor, past the third floor, to the top floor of the superstructure. The bridge, with its large windows on all sides, overlooked the bow of the ship and provided a panoramic view of Seattle's skyline. But Rosie looked further into the future.

"What beautiful sights at sea will be seen from this room." She pictured the captain giving orders in his confident manner. "Is this your favorite place on the ship, Captain?"

"Absolutely!"

Everywhere volunteers diligently worked, scraping rust and chipped paint off the ship. Others slapped on fresh paint. Metal gray and white were the decorator's choice for the decks and the superstructure. A pretty young woman, covered with paint, kneeling on her hands and knees, caught Rosie's attention.

"Hi, I'm Rose, but everyone calls me Rosie."

"Hello, I'm Jeanine, but everyone calls me Jeans. Welcome aboard," she said as she tied back her long, blond hair. She smiled and then went back to her painting project.

Rosie caught up with the team as they entered the first level of hold one. "I feel like an actor on the set of a World War II movie," Prissy said as she made her way down into the dark cavity of the ship. The captain flipped on a light switch. Rosie breathed unsteadily as they proceeded downward, to places she never knew existed on a ship.

"Are you okay?" Prissy asked.

"Of course," Rosie panted.

"Are you claustaphobic?"

"No," Rosie answered, still breathing heavily.

"Well, I am!" Prissy replied. "I'll meet you on deck."

Rosie was tempted to follow, but she was determined that a little darkness, dust, and close quarters would not push her to miss the rest of the tour.

Piles of World War II paraphernalia filled the corners of the large hold.

"Some of these objects will be kept as mementos from a war fought over forty years ago, but most will be tossed overboard into the dumpsters by the end of the week," Captain Alain said.

"Listen to this, Captain." Tim began reading from one of the torn boxes he found lying in a corner. "Life boat and life raft rations, packed by the Chemical Service Company, Baltimore, Maryland, approved by US Coast Guard: seven ounces of pemmican; seven ounces of malted milk; seven ounces of ration 'C' biscuit; seven ounces of chocolate."

"I know you are hungry, but please do not open. Those will be kept as mementos," the captain said, laughing.

Overhead lights in hold two lit the large room filled with stacked furniture. Donated carpet was rolled up. Rosie found an old army green flashlight in a corner. "Dad has a flashlight like this."

"I bet he doesn't have any of these," Tim said, holding up a crumpled pack of Camel cigarettes. "I found these under a rusted bunk."

Another flight of stairs led downward to a dimly lit cavern. Bunk beds that once held US troops were stacked at the end of the room. Rosie noticed small fans attached to the standing bunks.

"Not many conveniences," Grace observed. "No wonder the government stored her in mothballs after the war—she's too old to be of much use."

"Ouch! I'm the same age as this old gal, and I hope to have some good years left," Rosie reminded her daughter.

As the team walked toward the exit, Rosie caught a glimpse of a shadow lurking in a far corner. "Do you see that?" Rosie asked Grace.

"See what?"

"There's a shadow over there."

"You've been reading too many mysteries, Mom," Grace said. "Come on, let's catch up with the team."

Rosie stood motionless. "Many soldiers survived the war, while others went on to meet their fate in the hereafter. Grace is right, too many mystery stories trying to invade my imagination," she said as she fumbled to turn on her flashlight.

She hurried to catch up with the others, but as she glanced over her shoulder, the shadow turned a corner and then disappeared.

"I'm outta here! Hey, Grace, wait for me!"

Rosie almost toppled down the four stairs as she exited the hold onto the deck. She caught herself as Captain Alain announced, "What you see is the ship of old. She is going to war again, but this time she will fight a different kind of war."

The captain had Rosie's attention.

"For those of you who don't know, Operation Jabotinsky was organized several years ago to help prevent persecution of Russian Jews. Unlike the times during World War II, we will not stand by and watch this tragedy happen again," the captain added with conviction.

"I can't wait to hear more about O. J.," Grace said.

"Not to be confused with the notorious O. J. Simpson," Rosie added.

In the lower bow of the ship, there were small rooms where electrical equipment, plumbing parts, paint supplies, and cleaning products were haphazardly stored. Rosie bumped into a half-empty paint can as she walked through the passageway, smearing gray on her jeans. She was slowly being initiated into the ship's restoration.

"Now, let us go to the troop mess for dinner," Captain Alain announced in his oh-so-proper British English.

In the midst of the grease, dirt, and clutter, Rosie discovered something wonderful. The gallant galley girls would be cooking and serving all the meals. All the team had to do was walk through a line, fill their plates, and continue around the corner to the troop mess.

Tina led the group through the line, assisting them when necessary. "Valentine and Deena show their dedication to the project in the food they prepare three times a day, plus two fika breaks—Swedish for coffee, food, and conversation," Tina explained.

Rosie filled half her plate with potato salad. "This is definitely my kind of dining experience."

"Where does all this food come from?" Prissy asked Tina as she piled her plate with pasta.

"The food is donated from local churches and organizations that support the ship's mission," Tina explained.

Throughout dinner, Rosie noticed Jeans sitting in a corner, writing on a notepad in between bites of salad. Rosie's curiosity got the better of her.

"Are you a writer?" Rosie asked as she stood next to Jeans's table.

Jeans looked up. "I journal every day, and I write my family, friends, and church members to keep them updated on the ship's progress. Many of them are supporting me as their mission project."

"What a great idea."

Jeans was already back to her writing before Rosie finished her sentence.

"I'll let you get back to your writing."

Jeans nodded, and Rosie took that as a clue to end the conversation.

Some friendships start small, Rosie thought as she walked to her table.

16

Miss Knot loved the attention she was receiving, especially from the energetic California team.

The after-dinner coffee and dessert time had everyone feeling like they were on a minivacation, until Captain Alain kindly interrupted the mood.

"Attention, everyone. Every morning at seven, we gather for prayer in hold two. Breakfast is at seven-thirty, and work begins at eight. Torre will give work assignments after breakfast. I suggest you go to bed early. Have a good night's rest." And with that, the captain disappeared.

"The captain rises before dawn and works late into the night," Torre told Jesse and Rosie. "He's in his sixties, but he's as fit as any man onboard, and he doesn't plan on retiring from the ship's mission anytime soon."

By nine o'clock, Jesse and Rosie climbed the stairs to their cabin. After bedding down in their bunks—they could literally reach out and touch each other—Jesse tossed to and fro.

Finally, Rosie asked, "Can't you get comfortable?"

"I'm okay . . . I was thinking . . . there's so much plumbing to do before the ship sails. Shower stalls, toilets, sinks—old and new—must be installed and repaired." Jesse sighed. "And the steward department could use some help."

Rosie had years of experience cleaning her own homes, even taking housecleaning jobs to earn money while the kids were in school.

"What are you getting at?"

"They could use our help again," Jesse said. "We could come back for another week before they sail."

"So much for a relaxing summer vacation," Rosie murmured.

"We won't make any decisions now. Let's pray about it for the rest of the week," Jesse said as he leaned over to kiss Rosie goodnight. She grabbed his T-shirt and pulled him closer. "Hey, cowboy, we've never done it on a ship before," she whispered.

"Hey, now, what are you getting at?" he teased as he climbed out of his bunk and slid next to her warm body.

The travel alarm sounded at 6:15 a.m., waking Rosie from a deep sleep. She opened one eye and caught a glimpse of Jesse dressing in his work clothes. *Such a hunk*, she thought. He was halfway out the door by the time her feet touched the cold floor. "What's your hurry?"

"Gotta go—I'll be back," Jesse said, and then hurried down the hall to the nearest head.

Shivering, Rosie dressed in a long-sleeve T-shirt and a pair of faded jeans. She was brushing her teeth over the sink when Jesse returned carrying a cup of freshly brewed coffee. *What a sweet way of saying, "good morning hon, and thanks for a great roll in the bunk,"* Rosie thought as she took the cup from his hand. Taking a sip, she winked before making a mad dash down the hall to wait her turn in line for the head.

Captain Alain arrived in hold two a few minutes before seven and greeted everyone with a hearty good morning. Tina began praying at exactly seven, ending at seven-thirty sharp.

Rosie was making her way to the galley when—oops! Prissy reached out and caught her by the arm. "Remember to step up and over. Got it?"

Embarrassed, Rosie snickered, "Duck and step. Got it."

"Don't feel bad; I fell on my butt in the middle of the night when I got up to go to the bathroom—I mean, the head," Prissy said, chuckling.

"We hope you enjoy your breakfast, Priscilla," Valentine chimed from the other side of the galley window.

"Enjoy? Valentine, I'm delighted that you and Deena love to cook," Prissy said as she piled scrambled eggs on her plate.

"Please, everyone calls me Val."

"And everyone calls me Prissy. All the fifth grade boys thought I was stuck-up. And then my best friend here—"

Rosie nudged her forward. "Miss Priss, you're holding up the line."

"It's a long story. I'll tell you later," Prissy said, carrying her tray to the troop mess.

Rosie enjoyed getting to know the local volunteers. In the midst of all the talking and laughter, she again noticed Jeans writing on a notepad.

"Are you writing a newsletter?"

"No, I'm writing Bible verses that I read this morning."

"I missed you at prayer."

Jeans put her pen down. "I was there, in the corner."

"Oh, well, sorry to bother you. Catch you later."

"Sure," Jeans answered as she continued writing.

"She's stuck-up, isn't she?" Prissy asked when Rosie returned to their table.

"Takes one to know one," Rosie teased. Prissy made a face, and Rosie kicked her under the table. Prissy was laughing when the captain walked into the troop mess.

Rosie was organized and Jesse was punctual, but they had met their match with Captain Alain. By eight o'clock, he was motioning Torre to give out the daily assignments.

The women were to clean and paint, so Henrik wasted no time in leading Grace, Prissy, and Rosie to the bow of the ship.

"Love that scar," Prissy said, rubbing her finger on her cheek.

"Hey, remember?" Rosie answered, pinching her behind as they entered the dark narrow passageway.

"Not for me, silly. I'm thinking for Jeans."

"Stop playing cupid; that's my job," Rosie teased.

Henrik pointed to the messiest room in the bow. "This is the plumbing room, where you will be working." He smiled as he turned on the overhead light. He then left them standing in the middle of the room, wondering where to begin.

Rosie pointed to the middle shelves. "Those are female parts, and these are male parts."

"What's this?" Grace asked as she picked up a strange-looking object.

"That's a half-inch coupling."

"Where did you get all your knowledge, Mom?" Grace asked.

"I worked in a hardware store when I was sixteen," Rosie declared.

"And you're also married to a former pipe fitter," Prissy added.

"That's true, before he was a pastor. But we never have time to discuss work—we have more important things to do."

The girls giggled as they donned their coveralls and gloves to begin their assignment. They separated parts and then threw them into designated piles on the floor. They worked through the early morning hours, and Prissy was belting out the sixties song "Rescue Me" when a loud bell declared the ten-o'clock fika break.

Hours later, the plumbing room was finally organized. "Now, let the painting begin," Prissy announced as she opened a five-gallon paint can and handed out brushes.

Rosie began painting away with the ship's color of choice, steel gray. Her artistic side began to flow as she stroked the cabinets with her brush.

Grace pointed to her mother's dark tresses. "Look, Prissy!"

"What's wrong?" Rosie asked.

"I didn't know you had gray hair," Grace said.

"I don't!"

Rosie had been a Nice 'n Easy girl since she turned thirty, when gray strands started popping up in the midst of her black tresses. No one knew her little secret except Prissy, her hairdresser.

"Remember the song from *South Pacific*?" Prissy asked as she stood in the middle of the room. She grabbed a piece of pipe for a microphone and belted out, "You'd better wash that gray right outta your hair! You'd better wash that gray right outta your hair—"

Rosie and Grace cheered.

"Your own Nice 'n Easy version," Prissy said.

Rosie grabbed a bandana and wrapped it around her dark locks. "That's right. No gray for this forty-something gal."

The girls exited the plumbing room as soon as the dinner bell chimed, wearing their grease and paint like badges of honor. Rosie noticed that others were wearing badges of their day's work—paint-splattered faces, dirty hands, and greasy clothes. Looking around, she noticed something else they were wearing—smiles on their tired faces.

The March temperatures dropped with each passing day. By lunchtime on Thursday, Torre decided to bring all the work indoors.

"It's snowing!" Prissy yelled as she ate her last bite of pizza.

"Snow in Seattle? It's a known fact that in Seattle, you don't tan—you rust. Prissy, maybe you're hallucinating from too much work," Rosie teased as she jumped up and ran to a porthole.

Fluffy white cotton covered the deck. "I'm experiencing my first snowfall—on a World War II ship!" Prissy cheered.

"This is a day to mark in my journal—snow in March," Jeans said as she walked back to the table where her journal lay.

The week of labor had worked its miracles. Piles of trash were thrown overboard into the dock dumpsters. Scraping and cleaning made way for a newfound shine on the decks and beyond. There was still much to do to make her seaworthy, but for now, the California team had done their part.

That night Rosie was reading in her bunk, happy to be horizontal, when Jesse came over and snuggled next to her.

"After working on the ship for a week, what do you think about coming back?" Jesse asked.

"Won't the ship be sailing soon?" she asked, her eyes staring at the shabby-chic ceiling.

"They're scheduled to sail next month. But I've been thinking, and praying . . . why don't we make a commitment?"

Commitment? "What kind of commitment?"

Jesse took in a deep breath. As he exhaled, he blurted, "A commitment for a year."

Rosie's book fell to the floor. She sat up. It was her turn to breathe deeply. She tried to compose herself. Deep breaths always worked, but not this time.

"What are you talking about?" She didn't give him a chance to answer. "Are you talking about sailing on this ship?"

Jesse nodded.

"How could we? We left our family two years ago to live in Sweden for a year, so why would you consider packing up again? We have responsibilities." Rosie took another breath. Still, no composure. "Why would you want to sail across the Atlantic? You almost drowned in a riptide, remember?" Another breath, deeper this time. "Besides, you know I can't swim! There, I said it. The thought of leaving this port makes my head dizzy."

Jesse picked up her book and tried handing it to her. She refused, so he held onto it.

"I don't want to read. I'm not finished speaking my mind. Another thing—whenever we counsel people, we explain to them that in life's journey there will always be immediate needs they'll want to help with, but first they need to pray, then pray some more, and ask God specifically what he wants them to do," Rosie stated matter-of-factly.

Jesse stared at the floor. "You're right."

Please, God, help my husband come to his senses, Rosie prayed as she sat, frozen at the thought of being surrounded by the vast Atlantic. She could have continued on with her excuse list, but as her husband stared at the floor, she was reminded of another place in time—their wedding day, and her wedding vows. It was the Ruth Factor—*wherever you go, I will go,* Rosie had vowed to her Boaz.

Rosie cleared her throat. "On the other hand, as we agreed, I've been doing some serious praying this week too."

Jesse looked in her eyes.

"You mentioned on the plane home that our year in Sweden and our trips to Israel and Siberia had been a preparation for our future. My insides froze when you spoke those words, but now I admit since coming onboard, I've been feeling a sense of wanderlust. And I confess that I need to overcome my fear of water, but I was hoping I might overcome it in a swimming pool."

Rosie took Jesse's hand. "But most important, if God is calling us to sail on this ship, then we must obey, whether I *feel* like it or not."

There, I said it. And furthermore, "I think I can handle a year on this ship. But if I can't . . ."

"Yes?"

"If I can't, will you promise to fly me home?"

Jesse opened his arms. "I promise!"

The book dropped to the floor again, where it remained for the rest of the night.

The team spent their last evening at one of Seattle's waterfront restaurants devouring all-the-shrimp-you-can-eat. They reminisced about their week from heaven—and hell. Prissy's back ached, Tim's shoulder was ready to give out, and Rosie's knee pounded from her fall on the freshly painted deck. But all the pain couldn't compare to the camaraderie they experienced—working, eating, laughing, and praying side by side.

After dinner, Torre invited Jesse and Rosie to join him at his table.

"Jesse, as you know, we need your expertise as a pipe fitter and plumber. And Rosie, you are greatly needed in the ship's office and the steward department,"

Torre explained. "Your high energy and your words of encouragement are also what we are looking for." He stopped to give them a moment for his words to sink in. "Have you thought about volunteering on the *Restoration?*"

They had not spoken to anyone, but a similar incident had occurred the night before when Rosie had joined Tina in her cabin for an evening chat. Rosie noticed Tina staring at her, but she often stared at the Americans, as if she were trying to understand their rapidly spoken American English. Most of the time, Tina looked at them pensively, as if she knew their secrets.

"Am I talking too fast?" Rosie slowly asked Tina.

"No, but I have been wondering . . . have you and Jesse thought about sailing with the ship?"

Rosie stared back into Tina's eyes. "Why do you ask?"

"From the day you arrived, Alain and I thought you and Jesse would be perfect for the ship."

Embarrassed, Rosie had looked away, as if Tina had read her personal mail. The two women had spent time together every day over the past week, sharing their testimonies over coffee, talking about their families, their hopes, and their dreams. Tina was someone Rosie could confide in. If Jesse and Rosie decided to sail, she would need a friend like Tina.

"We're praying about it, but let this be our secret," Rosie said. Tina had a twinkle in her eyes, as if she already knew their decision.

"I can install the toilets, and Rosie can clean 'em," Rosie heard Jesse say, bringing her back to the moment.

Torre laughed. "What a team!"

Jesse reached for Rosie's hand under the table. "We'd like to volunteer on the *Restoration* for a year."

A chill went up Rosie's spine when Jesse spoke the word *year.* She knew that feeling of doubting God's voice. It was the same apprehension that attacked her two years earlier when they made the decision to move to Sweden. And as before, she chose not to let those feelings get the best of her.

Torre reached for his briefcase. "These applications are a formality. Fill them out when you get home and then fax them to the ship's office as soon as possible."

Jesse flung his arm around Rosie as they walked back to their table. "I can't believe by next month we'll be sailing across the Atlantic!"

She shivered. "Golly, I can't either." *This better be God,* she thought.

17

Miss Knot missed the California team. But there was talk that the lady and her man might be returning.

Rosie's busy schedule never allowed her much time in the kitchen, but two days after they returned home, she prepared a special dinner for her family. She would feed them well before announcing their plans to be gone for a year. She cooked a large batch of southern fried chicken with all the trimmings. Over dessert, Jesse shared about Operation Jabotinsky's network in Sweden and Russia and its mission to help transport Russian Jews to Israel.

"That must take a lot of people working together," Lynn said as she wiped mashed potatoes off Liam's little face.

"That's why they're asking for volunteers to sail with the ship," Jesse said.

Grace spilled her water on the tablecloth. "Volunteers?" she asked as she walked to the kitchen for a rag.

"I thought the kids were supposed to be the ones taking off on wild adventures, not the parents," Presley teased.

"I'd love to volunteer. I bet the fishing will be great," Tim said. He glanced at Grace, who was peering at him from the kitchen. "But I have a family to feed," he quickly added as he sliced a piece of cherry pie.

"Are you thinking about volunteering?" Jay asked his dad.

"Only for a year," Jesse answered.

Grace stood in the kitchen doorway. "Did you say a year?"

There's that word again, Rosie thought.

"I'll be happy to car-sit for you again," Presley said, taking a bite of pie. Grace had mentioned to Rosie that he had washed and waxed her Mustang faithfully while they were in Sweden, so she was going to ask him anyway. Rosie never had time to wax her eyebrows, much less her car. "We'll talk about that later, Presley," Rosie said.

"Be sure to send us a postcard from all the exotic ports," Lynn said. Rosie knew Jesse's daughter would be too busy raising two sons and holding down a productive accounting job to pine their absence.

"I'll be the manager of my mortgage company by the time you get back," Jay said.

Jesse smiled. "Son, with all the hours you put in, you'll be the president!"

Grace was quiet all evening, which bothered Rosie because her daughter was usually the one asking questions and giving her support. *I'll talk to her tomorrow, when we're alone*, Rosie decided as she fed Katie a spoonful of vanilla ice cream.

Rosie was loading the dishwasher when Talmage came in with his coffee cup.

"Rose, don't worry about Grace; she'll be okay. Now with Katie, I'm sure she wants you to stick around."

Rose glanced at her father's shaky hands and then looked him in the eyes. "Where do you get such insight, Dad?"

"From living with your mom for forty years. If she were here, she would gather you and Grace in a room and make you talk it out until you both came eye-to-eye on the matter."

"I wish Mom were here."

"The important thing to remember, Rose, is that you have to follow your dreams. If God is calling you on this mission, then you must obey him." He took her steady hand. "I'd volunteer with you, but Doris would miss me too much." He smiled. "Besides, I did my duty on a knot ship many years ago."

"Now it's my turn to carry out the family tradition," Rosie said, giving her dad a hug.

Later that night, Rosie cried in the shower. When she crawled under the covers, Jesse noticed her red, swollen eyes. Jesse fluffed her pillow. "The year will go by fast."

"I remember you telling me that once before," Rosie said, sniffing. "Is it really all that important to obey God? I'm sure he won't strike me dead."

"Of course he won't, but don't you remember the peace that came when we obeyed him when we went to Bible school?"

"And to Israel . . . and on the train . . . it was a dream come true," she said as she wiped more tears on Jesse's T-shirt. "Thanks for reminding me. Now, first thing tomorrow, we must tackle our to-do list."

"I've already started. I'm putting the house-for-rent sign up tomorrow, and I gave notice to my boss today."

"What did he say?"

"He wished me well and told me to come back to the Home Depot when I return. Tomorrow we'll make a doctor's appointment for our physical exams and a note stating the good health of *Restoration's* future sailors."

Rosie smiled and then snuggled closer. "You're the most organized person I've ever met. Now, come here so I can reward my sailor."

Within two hours of the for-rent sign going up, a Korean couple called to make an appointment to see the Atkisson home. "Our daughters can walk to school," Mrs. Chen said. "This is exactly what we are looking for." They agreed to the monthly payment, so they gathered around the dining room table. Pen in hand, Mr. Chen began to sign the contract. Suddenly he pulled away.

"Is there something wrong?" Jesse asked.

"I read here that the lease time is twelve months. We have to stay fourteen months, until our daughters finish school."

"But we're going to be gone for only twelve months—from May to May," Rosie replied.

"Excuse us for a minute," Jesse interrupted, and then led Rosie to the kitchen.

"Rosie, only God knows exactly how long we should be gone."

"Yeah, I guess you're right. I'm sure we can stay with Tim and Grace for two months if we have to," Rosie said.

"I think Katie would love having you around," Jesse added. Rosie smiled at the thought.

They returned to the dining room. "Fourteen months will be fine," Jesse said as he held out the pen to Mr. Chen.

"I hate garage sales," Rosie said a week later, while tagging a third pair of black three-inch heels.

Grace placed a sticker on a green vintage vase. "*Hate* is a strong word for a garage sale, Mom."

"Okay . . . I dislike garage sales."

"Why's that?"

"They take up too much of my time and energy."

"But they do have their purpose." Grace held up a green and turquoise, tie-dyed, loose-fitting sack dress. "First, you're getting rid of all unnecessary objects you've accumulated over the years." Rosie giggled as Grace tagged the dress for one dollar. "Someone will buy this to wear for a Halloween costume," Grace said, winking. "And second, the money will come in handy."

"You're definitely right about that!" Looking at Grace grimace at another vintage outfit that she couldn't part with at the Sweden-or-Bust garage sale two years earlier, Rosie was thankful her daughter was there to help out.

Rosie slowly carried the last box of unnecessary items and dropped it on the garage floor next to Grace. "Ugh! The old back isn't what it used to be."

"I'm fading fast too," Grace said, pushing the box away.

Rosie dropped a pile of faux purses on a nearby table. "I'm ready for a fika break. I'll boil some more water for tea, and pour myself a cup of coffee."

Grace glanced at her watch. "I need to get home."

Mother and daughter had always made time in their busy schedules to sit over a cup of coffee and share their thoughts, from husbands to children, from decorating to traveling, from spiritual matters to world politics. Rosie wanted to hear about Katie's preschool open house, but Grace seemed to be in a hurry to leave.

"Is everything okay at home?" Rosie asked.

"Everything is fine, Mom."

"You seem so quiet lately."

"I'm just tired."

"Grace, I know you too well—you have enough energy for three people."

"Well, since you asked, I can't understand why you're leaving again. I thought it was a wonderful opportunity when you went off to Sweden—you've always wanted to go to Bible school. And volunteering on the ship for a week was great—we had a fantastic time. But now you're leaving again—for another year!"

I shouldn't have asked, Rosie thought.

"I hope this Operation Jabo—whatever it's called—is worth missing another year of your granddaughter's life." Grace picked up her cup and headed for the kitchen door. "I have to pick up Katie. I'll see you later."

"I was hoping you would—," was all Rosie could get out before the kitchen door slammed, "—understand."

But how could she expect Grace to understand, when she didn't? "Okay, Lord, I'm open for any advice you can give me," she prayed as she finished tagging the last of her trashy treasures.

Rosie went inside to tackle some cleaning chores. She tried singing as she scrubbed the bathtub. She whistled while she swished the toilets. "And just think, once you're on the ship, you'll be doing even more tedious cleaning."

She stood up. "Stop it, Rose Adrienne Atkisson! You will love cleaning all those toilets, yes, you will," she said as she shook the toilet brush at her reflection on the freshly Windexed mirror.

Rosie exited the bathroom and sat down on her bedroom floor beside a cardboard box. "What to take, what to leave behind," she said, staring at the overstuffed box. Jesse was running errands, but she could hear him saying, pack light. "I won't need the floral dresses with the flashy heels and matching purse, and the jewelry will be of no use." She sighed. "Life will be simple onboard. I prefer jeans and a T-shirt to nylons and bling anyway."

April showers pounded against the bedroom window while Rosie packed her fourth box for storage. Perhaps it was the rain—or the fact that her daughter didn't understand why she was leaving again—but she broke down.

"Go ahead, get it out of your system; you'll feel better," she told herself. She was right. After a few more sobs, she took a deep breath, wiped her eyes, and then taped the boxes closed.

She walked across the hall to Jesse's office. Her tummy flip-flopped as she caught sight of the world map hanging on the wall above his desk. "Oh, my, look at that big ocean." Then it hit her. "What if that old ship stalls in the middle of the Atlantic? Will there be a ship, or anyone, out there to rescue us? No one came to the *Titanic's* rescue in time, and down went the *Poseidon*." She sank to the floor. "Who am I trying to fool? I'm not sailor material. I can't even swim."

Memories of her experiences with boats came flooding back . . . canoeing down the Colorado River and losing her paddle to a raging current, forcing Prissy to paddle upstream for an hour . . . and the time she rafted down the Jordan River and fell overboard.

Then she remembered Jesse's riptide story—he was seconds from drowning . . .

It was spring break of '65, and Jesse had gone to Huntington Beach for a few days to do some beach witnessing with the Nomads, the Christian high school version of Campus Crusade for Christ. But before hitting the beach, Jesse and his friend Patrick wanted to catch a few waves, so Jesse grabbed his surfboard and they headed for the pier.

Jesse was shooting the curls when, suddenly, out of nowhere, an undertow grabbed him and took him under. The next thing he knew, his surfboard disappeared, and the current pulled him farther from the shore. Fear grabbed him as the deadly current dragged him deeper.

He finally surfaced, gasping for air. He looked around for his surfboard and for Patrick, but neither was in sight and the shoreline was drifting farther away. But he was determined to fight for his life. Jesse was tired—he couldn't do it alone.

"God—glub—I need—glub—help!"—glub.

As Jesse resurfaced, he caught a glimpse of Patrick, paddling near the shore on his surfboard. Jesse tried swimming toward him, but couldn't. As the waves continued to pull him under, he remembered the words of a fellow swimmer—"if you're ever caught in a riptide, never swim straight to shore . . . swim with the current . . . swim with the current."

With every ounce of energy, Jesse began swimming parallel with the shoreline, until he was at last a few hundred feet from Patrick. With his last burst of energy, he swam toward his friend.

Tired and limp, Jesse tried to act like a cool teenager. He grabbed his board from Patrick and carried it to shore. Walking on shaky legs, he even smiled at a pretty dark-haired beauty as he limped away. He was thankful to be alive, so that evening, Jesse was the first to testify to the Nomads.

"God must have something special for me, because today he saved my life."

God gave Jesse eternal life when he was eight, but that day, at the cool age of seventeen, God saved him from one mean riptide. The almost-deadly incident could have kept him on the shore forever, but Jesse chose to put that day behind him and obey God . . . .

Rosie glanced at a poster hanging on the opposite wall. The words spoke to her so deeply that she had bought the poster at a garage sale. "You cannot discover new oceans until you are willing to lose sight of the shore," she read aloud. "I don't know who made that quote famous, but he must have been one brave soul . . . hmm, maybe it was a woman who spoke those words."

She breathed deeply. "This must be my time to discover what awaits me over the horizon. There must be oceans of dreams waiting for me! Yes, it's a big ocean, but no matter where I go, Lord, you'll be traveling with me."

Rosie removed the poster and the map, rolled them up, and then placed them in a tube, along with all of her oceanic fears. "There's only going to be enough room in our small cabin for the necessities of life—and a whole lot of faith."

Later that afternoon, she read over her list of necessities to pack. "If you can't carry it yourself, don't take it," she said to herself, quoting Jesse.

"I'll need a year's supply of Nice 'n Easy, makeup, a few pair of jeans, shorts, T-shirts, pajamas, and some winter clothes."

As she wrapped her Russian wooden boxes and Scandinavian candelabras in bubble wrap, she thought about this season of her life. She had been going about her everyday tasks—working at the Bible school and spending her evenings and weekends with family and friends—with ease. When she had questioned God about her simple life a few months ago, he answered, *You are in the right place, for now.*

When she finished taping her Euro-treasure box closed, she picked it up to carry it to the garage.

"Ow!" A slight pain in her left knee jarred her to a halt. She slowly set the box on the floor. "I hope these legs that carried me on all those 10K runs—and on my prized half marathon—will be able to take me up and down all those stairs for a year." She smiled as she remembered a verse Prissy had recited before every race. She quoted from her Message Bible, as if she were making small talk. "He wraps us in his goodness; we have eternal beauty, and he renews our youth—we're always young in his presence."

Rosie smiled as she thought of Prissy. "I wish you were here, girlfriend, to help me pack."

Rosie stuffed the next box—no to red heels, yes to comfortable tennis shoes. When she came across her favorite pair of running shoes, she decided to take them along, but before packing them, she dashed out the door for a slow run-and-gab session with her eternal running partner.

May's flowers blossomed, but with all the packing, Rosie was too busy to notice until Prissy gave them a bon voyage party in her garden the evening before they departed. Everyone promised to write, and Rosie pledged to return home in a year.

Jesse unloaded the luggage at the curb while Rosie hugged and kissed Katie good-bye. Rosie moved toward her daughter as she stood silently next to the curb. Every time Rosie had planned to have a mother-daughter talk, either Grace was busy or Rosie had some last-minute item to attend to.

"Grace, you know how much I love you. This trip has nothing to do with . . ."

Grace stopped her. "Mom, I know. Just promise me you'll return home safe."

"Of course. And I promise this will be my last trip."

Horns honked while the traffic cop motioned Grace to move her car. Rosie gave her one last hug.

Katie waved, "I love you, Gama! See you soon!"

Rosie took one last memory picture of her granddaughter through the window of the black SUV.

Grace remained the stoic daughter, keeping her emotions hidden. Like her mother, she had a way of covering her feelings. Rosie would wait until she was flying above the clouds, in the solitude of the Alaska Airlines Boeing 747, to have her meltdown.

As the plane gathered speed, Jesse grabbed his wife's hand. "Here we go on another journey."

Rosie stared at her husband. His voice had the same excitement she had heard the night she proposed to him. He was smiling, and his eyes were sparkling.

She squeezed his hand. "You are so ready for this adventure. You can pick up and go anywhere, anytime." Rosie leaned over and kissed his cheek. "I think I'm ready, too. On your mark, get set, let's go!"

So, in the spring of her forty-eighth year, holding Jesse's hand, Rosie lost sight of her safe shore. Not knowing what horizons lay ahead, she assured herself that God knew where they were going. And that would have to do.

18

Miss Knot was happy to see the California lady and her man return. He looked excited; she looked apprehensive.

Torre greeted Jesse and Rosie at SeaTac Airport, and after loading two large suitcases and two fifty-pound boxes in the van, he drove toward the outskirts of Seattle. The sun peeked from behind the clouds as they neared the dock where the *Restoration* was moored.

"We might get some rain tonight," Torre said.

"When do we set sail?" Rosie asked.

Torre hesitated, but Rosie didn't find that unusual. After living in Sweden, she knew it often took a few seconds to process from English to Swedish and then answer in their polite British English. But Torre was taking more than a few seconds.

"We are going to set sail in May, aren't we?"

"There is much work to do before we can sail."

That was a polite answer she didn't want to hear.

"What seems to be the holdup?" Jesse asked.

"When we brought the ship to dry dock yesterday, we were told that the bottom of the ship must be sandblasted, and then she must be painted."

"Dry dock? Sandblasted? Painted?"

"Dry dock is where the work underneath a ship is done," Jesse said, trying to take the pressure off Torre.

"We will also have to check the hull's thickness for safety. For maintenance reasons, we have to change the anodes," Torre continued.

Sandblasting, hull thickness, anode maintenance . . . words the men were using to gently warn Rosie of the days to come. How could she have been so naïve to think they would sail in a week after their arrival?

Rosie removed her sunglasses. Reality stared her in the face as they walked through the dry-dock parking lot toward the ship. The vessel looked much larger out of the water. And much older.

"Unfortunately, dry dock affects the crew as much as the ship," Torre said. Torre glanced at Rosie.

"And as of now, we are considered part of the *Restoration*'s crew," Jesse stated proudly.

"Dry dock is necessary to update the ship to meet her requirements to sail. Now the water is drained from the dock, so the work has begun. We do have electricity, but there will be no water on the ship while we are in dry dock," Torre said apologetically.

"No water?" Rosie asked. Suddenly a flashback of another waterless time passed before her. The summer of '92, when she had stood on a grimy dock in a train yard in St. Petersburg, Russia . . .

Ninety-degree heat greeted the mission team. They walked a mile across railroad tracks, dragging their suitcases toward a big green train where they would live for the next month. Before boarding, a stout-looking conductor gave instructions. The interpreter translated from Russian to English for twenty-five Swedes and two Americans.

"We have no water on the train until we leave the station," he stated matter-of-factly in his thick Russian accent.

After snooping around the old abandoned hangar-like building where they once cleaned and maintained trains, Jesse found an old hose.

"Hey, look—running water!"

A handful of Swedes helped Jesse wire up a large hose, creating a shower in the back of the building. The brave ones ran through the beige, warm, rushing water, clad in their Euro-swimsuits and rubber sandals.

"Come on, Rosie!" Jesse yelled, holding the hose.

"I'll take a shower in a banya in the next town," she answered, and then walked back to the train before Jesse had time to persuade her. She spent the next half hour in her cabin, lavishing herself in a private Handi-Wipes spit-bath.

She soon discovered that bathing in Russia's stuffy, smelly bathhouses in the middle of Siberia would be one earthy experience she could live without. "Thank God for Handi-Wipes," she prayed each night . . . .

"I survived a month in Siberia without the comforts of home, so I can surely survive a few days in dry dock," Rosie told Jesse as they walked toward the gangway.

Jesse shook his head as he looked at the ship.

"It's evident we're going to have a slight delay in our departure," Torre said, as if he had read Jesse's mind. "How long the delay, I cannot say."

He either doesn't know, or he's afraid to tell us, Rosie thought.

"Usually when a ship is dry-docked, no one is allowed to live onboard," Torre continued.

Rosie was ready to volunteer to fly back home when Torre added, "But this particular dry dock is closed for business, so the crew has been granted permission by the bank to live onboard. This is a miracle, because most of the crew is from out of state, or from Sweden, and they don't have anywhere else to stay."

"One woman's dry dock is another man's miracle," Rosie said. Torre's blank look told her that he didn't understand the American saying. "Haven't you heard the saying in Sweden that one man's trash is another man's treasure?"

Torre shook his head. Rosie was about to explain when Jesse intervened. "We're also happy for this miracle."

Torre pointed to the pile of rubber hoses. "There's a few water hoses hooked up from the dock to the ship's deck for special purposes. The galley needs water, and there is one head to wash our hands."

"In other words, we're Waterless in Seattle," Rosie said, hoping her play on words would lighten her mood. Torre and Jesse stared silently at her.

"It's a joke. You know, the movie, *Sleepless in Seattle* . . . Waterless in . . . oh, never mind."

Rosie lagged behind, staring at the World War II vessel as Torre and Jesse climbed the gangway. She wanted to connect with the ship, but didn't know where to begin. She took a few steps closer and patted her side. "Well, old girl, you're going to be my home-away-from-home for a while." After reading *The Little Engine that Could* when she was a little girl, Rosie had no doubt that trains, ships, and planes had feelings. Perhaps not like people, but somehow they could relate to those around them.

"I have an idea, old gal," Rosie said. "I've always connected with my family and friends by giving them nicknames. There's Racy-Gracie, Cutie-Katie, Prissy-Priscilla, Brainy-Barbara."

As she made her way up the gangway, Rosie touched the ship's tarnished features. "I would call you Rusty, but all this rust is temporary. You're in the beginning stages of a makeover that will restore you to your natural beauty."

Rosie patted the rail. "You'll soon help restore Russian Jews to Israel, so I don't want to take away from your soon-to-be-christened name, the MS *Restoration*."

Her eyes lit up. "That's it! Restoration—Resti. I'll call you Resti."

She caught up with Torre and Jesse as they were entering the superstructure. Torre held out his hand. "Don't forget to lift your legs upon entering," he reminded her.

"And step over the thresholds," Rosie added. Tripping too many times on their March trip taught her well. She still had a few bruises to prove it.

"You can use the head across the hall to wash your hands, and the showers are around the corner—for future use," Torre said as he opened their cabin door.

"Oh, if only we could use them," Rosie said, half-joking.

Jesse smiled at his wife. "It won't be so bad. At least we have the dry-dock facilities."

Rosie stayed in their cabin just down the hall from the galley while Jesse went to greet Captain Alain. Looking at her surroundings, she sighed. "Oh, my, these cabins are smaller than I remember." She didn't have the energy to unpack, so she closed the cabin door and walked toward the ship office.

Papers were stacked on three desks, along with a dusty typewriter and an old desktop computer. But it was a worn newspaper that had blown onto the floor that caught Rosie's attention. She picked it up and read the front page. "Well, old girl, it looks like you survived a large gale in the China Sea many years ago. We have something in common; I've survived a few storms myself."

She placed the article on top of a paper pile. "You've had an exciting past, and now, thanks to O. J., you have a bright future. Perhaps we can make some dreams come true together."

Again, she remembered her favorite children's book. "There was *The Little Engine that Could*. Now, Resti, you're going to be The Big Ship that Would."

That moment, a unique friendship was born between a forty-eight-year-old lady and a forty-eight-year-old ship.

19

Resti was delighted with her new nickname and was enjoying her dry-dock makeover. But she could see that the California lady was struggling with her unfamiliar surroundings.

After dinner, the female crew gathered to make the dreaded trip to the dry-dock facilities. Two Swedish women had arrived earlier that day and were ready for a hot shower before retiring to their cabins. Flashlights, towels, and clean clothes in hand, Rosie followed as they trekked across the parking lot. They turned two corners, being oh so careful not to step in the oil spills. They formed a single line and walked up the stairs, and then shined their flashlights on a sign that read *Dry-Dock Restrooms and Shower Facilities*. They hesitated.

"We must enter at our own risk," Ana-Karin said as she held the dirty wooden door open while Deena flipped on a light switch. Rosie gasped and began breathing through her mouth as she walked past the toilets and urinals. She pointed to a scratched door with a tin sign that read *Shower Room*.

Ana-Karin, a tall, energetic Swedish nurse, led the girls through the doorway, turned on another light switch, and then wiped her hand on her jeans. Rosie's eyes fell upon grimy cement floors, cobwebbed corners, and shower stalls with torn curtains, brown stains, and green mildew she swore was moving.

It was all Rosie could do to keep from letting out a *yuk,* but it was her first day on board and she wanted to make a good impression.

The group was about to turn and walk out, completely discouraged with the mess, when Ana-Karin spoke out in Swenglish—a mesh of English and Swedish.

"This might be acceptable for the men, but this is no place for rejectional ladies."

"Don't you mean respectable?" Rosie asked.

Ana-Karin blushed. "Of course, that is what I meant."

"We agree, Ana-Karin, but what shall we do?" Rosie asked.

"I have a suggestion," Deena chimed. "Let's all pitch in and rent a cheap motel room across the street, and then take turns using the clean bathroom."

Rosie checked her armpits. "I brought a year's supply of Handi-Wipes so I can wait another day for a shower." She held out her box. "Handi-Wipes anyone?"

"Aren't those American nurses?" Ana-Karin asked.

Deena chuckled. "You're thinking of Candy Stripes!"

Ana-Karin cut her off. "Cleaning this place will be my job while we are here. I'll begin first thing in the morning."

Rosie was so grateful for Ana-Karin's enthusiasm that she dashed back to the ship and filled three large pails with cleaning equipment, bright yellow plastic gloves, and gallons of bleach. That was the least she could do for the energetic nurse.

The next morning after breakfast, the girls watched in admiration as Ana-Karin marched over to the dry-dock facilities. Rosie and Britt, the new Swedish steward, followed close behind, carrying the cleaning supplies.

Later, when the girls returned to see if Ana-Karin needed more cleaning products, they were amazed to see the difference the shapely Swedish nurse had made in such a short time. Her massive labor of love was heaven-sent. Rosie whispered to Deena, "I think the *Restoration* has found her own personal Martha Stewart."

Rosie was typing a thank-you letter to Starbucks for their recent donation when Grace called. It had been a few days since their arrival, so she was anxious to hear the latest news.

A few minutes into the conversation, Grace announced, "Tim's taking me on a Caribbean cruise in June for my graduation gift."

"How wonderful! After nine months in Bible school, you deserve a vacation. Maybe next year Jesse and I will fly to the Caribbean," she said, picturing white sandy beaches and palm trees blowing in the wind.

After they hung up, Rosie cried. She was homesick, and the dry-dock facilities didn't help matters one bit. Then she glanced down at the half-written thank-you letter. "Wait a minute," she told herself, "there is no time for tears!"

She dried her eyes and then delved into the office work. After one letter, she gave up and dialed Prissy's number.

"You're where?" Prissy asked when Rosie told her they were stuck in dry dock.

"Obviously, you aren't familiar with the term *dry dock* either, so let me explain. You won't find dry dock advertised on the travel channel, and dry dock is not a weekend getaway on a romantic waterfront. Dry dock is a dirty, isolated place where you would only consider sending your worst enemy."

Prissy chuckled. "In that case, I'm glad we're best friends."

After a few more minutes of Rosie's whining, Prissy interrupted, "Thanks for crying on my shoulder, but I'm late for the theater. Love ya . . . bye!"

"Good-bye, my friend, and thanks for the sympathy."

Rosie sat alone in the dusty office, fighting back the tears. "Pull yourself together, lady. There's no time to feel sorry for yourself. It's time to move forward . . . everyone else is."

She walked out of the office, grabbed a cup of coffee from the galley, and then closed the door to their cabin. She sat down on the hard floor and began unpacking, first the two large suitcases and then two large boxes. Soon the floor was covered with clothing for every season.

"Summer clothes will be stuffed in the lockers, fall clothes shall be shoved in the suitcases under the bunks, and winter clothes will be stored in the boxes in hold two."

Several hours later, neck and shoulders stiff from sitting on the floor, still knee-deep in clothing and a year's supply of Nice 'n Easy, Rosie stared at her surroundings.

"How am I going to live in this shabby-chic cracker box for a year? Is it too late to change my mind?"

She closed her eyes and remembered another tiny room she had lived in not so long ago. "Six weeks in a Swedish playhouse. As tiny as it was, I have to admit, those were some of the best days of my life."

Rosie opened her eyes. She was still lying on a pile of T-shirts. "Daydreaming isn't getting me anywhere. I'll stretch my legs, grab a cup of coffee, and go to the head."

As she walked down the gangway toward the dock facilities, the sun's warmth took her back to sunnier days in California, but the piercing noise of sandblasting equipment brought her back to her rainier days in Seattle.

Within an hour Rosie was back to sorting shirts with heightened caffeine energy when she came across a long forgotten white T-shirt with fourteen Siberian cities listed on the front in bright red.

"I don't remember packing this." She held the shirt close to her heart as sweet memories came rushing back of traveling across Siberia on the Trans Siberian Railway. "I once lived in a tiny sleeping compartment on the big green train that could. Now I live in a small cabin on the big blue ship that would." She smiled. "My rhyme of life . . . I like it," she said as she sprawled out on the cool, hard floor.

Rosie was still sorting, sipping, and remembering, when Jesse appeared at the door.

"We have a visitor from California."

"A visitor? Now?"

John stuck his head in the doorway.

"John! What a surprise! What are you doing here?"

"Just another quick business trip. I thought I'd drop by to see how my former singles' pastors are doing."

John took a long, hard look at the cluttered cabin and gasped. He must have seen Rosie's look of helplessness, because his look of shock soon turned into one of pity.

"I'd invite you in, but—"

Jesse came to her rescue. "Join us in the troop mess."

Spending time with an old friend over a cup of coffee was the energy boost Rosie needed.

When Jesse and Rosie met John and Barbara at the Friday Night Singles, they discovered they had something in common—they were also single parents. They were married two months after Jesse and Rosie, and after flying to Hawaii for their honeymoon, they had been vacationing in exotic places ever since.

As they sat in the troop mess sipping donated Starbucks, John looked around. "I don't know how you do this."

Handsome as ever, John had arrived in one of his spotless business suits, but by the time Jesse finished taking him on a condensed tour, dust covered his once-shiny shoes, he had a greasy smudge on his Perry Ellis white shirt, and his expensive aftershave could not hide the aroma of diesel oil.

118

As they strolled on deck, John kept repeating, "You guys must be crazy!"

"Crazy?" Rosie asked. "Maybe a little different, but not crazy." Rosie wanted to change the subject. "When are you and Barbara leaving for Hawaii?"

"Next week. I'm so stressed from work that I'm counting the days. Barbara's already planning a cruise for September." John looked at the pile of trash in the corner of the deck.

"You must be stressed living on this ship."

"Maybe a little challenging, but not stressed," Rosie said.

"We have our moments, but we're on a mission for God," Jesse reminded his friend.

"And we're following our dreams," Rosie added.

John shrugged. "I can't understand how you can leave the comforts of home to live in rust, but I won't argue your point." John did his best to take the surroundings in stride, until he asked to use a restroom.

"Sorry, there's no water onboard, but you can use the dry-dock bathroom," Rosie said, pointing to the dock's facilities.

That did it. Within minutes, John was looking at his watch, ready to make his exit.

"Can you stay for dinner?" Rosie asked.

"Uh, no, sorry, I've made other plans, but maybe some other time."

"Yeah, when we're back in our big, clean house," Rosie teased.

A week later when Pastor Luke came to Seattle for a conference, he was surprised to find the ship still in dry dock. His face told Rosie that he was thinking along the same lines as John.

"We have donated Starbucks coffee," Rosie chimed. "Would you like a cup?"

His smirk turned to a smile. "I'd love a cup."

After chatting awhile in the troop mess, Rosie asked, "Can you stay for dinner?"

Pastor Luke glanced at his watch. That said it all.

"Sorry, not this time; I've already made plans."

As they walked Pastor Luke to the parking lot, he stopped. "Is there anything I can do for you?" he asked, as if they were trapped in a prison camp.

"We need to get the ship out of dry dock as soon as possible, so pray for the funds to come in."

Pastor Luke agreed to pray for the ship, for his friends, and for their sanity.

Rosie tackled her daily assignments like any other of her past jobs. Daily, she cleaned the office, the bridge, the troop mess, the soon-to-be crew's lounge, showers and toilets, and the first engineer's cabin. Then there were the long, endless hallways. When grease was tracked in from the engine room or dust from sandblasting, Rosie was there with broom and mop in hand.

When it wasn't raining, the World's Fair Needle reflected the afternoon sun as Rosie made her way up the stairs to one of her favorite places onboard. She rubbed on the old ship's bridge, giving her the tender loving care she deserved. "Resti, this view makes dry dock bearable," she said to her friend. As she glanced out of the large windows, she pictured the *Restoration* gliding over the mighty waters, guided by her captains and their maps.

Adjacent to the bridge was the map room. Although Rosie didn't understand the nautical language, the maps captivated her.

"Resti, these maps are going to guide you toward your destiny," she said, dusting the long table. "And perhaps toward my destiny too."

While Rosie busied herself in the steward department, Jesse assisted Mike in sandblasting the bottom of the ship by day and into the night. After spending a week with the mission team in March, Mike returned to donate another week to sandblast and spray paint the ship. He was the best in his field, giving him the title of Mike-the-Dry-Dock-King.

Among the projects needing attention, old lifeboats were in need of repair, and new lifeboats and safety equipment were required. These were the projects Stuart Lang thrived on.

20

Resti *grinned from starboard to portside when the Alaskan sea captain and his wife came to live on board.*

The atmosphere changed the moment Stuart Lang stepped on the gangway. His bold laughter could be heard from bow to stern. An experienced mariner, Stuart's love for the sea and his zest for life was as contagious as his warm smile and hearty laugh.

Rosie liked his wife the moment she shook her hand. In contrast to Stuart's fair Norwegian heritage, Shelly had the olive complexion of a Mediterranean beauty. Rosie admired this woman who had given up everything to follow her man across the seas and continents of the world. Shelly was the perfect mate for Stuart.

After dinner, Stuart and Shelly invited Jesse and Rosie to join them for coffee in the captain's mess.

"Have you met my son, Clive?" Shelly asked.

"He's my number one plumbing assistant," Jesse said proudly. "With all that blond hair and blue eyes, I guessed he was Stuart's son."

Shelly smiled. "Clive is my son from my first marriage. He stayed in Seattle with my sister to finish his high school junior year while we were in Bible school in Sweden. Now he'll homeschool on the ship for his senior year."

"You must be happy to have Clive with you," Rosie said, thinking of Presley and Jay.

"I'm delighted he wants to sail on the ship with us."

"What young man wouldn't want to sail the seven seas?" Stuart said, laughing.

Rosie took a sip of coffee. "Stuart, can you tell us the story of how you donated this ship to the church in Sweden?"

"Rosie, they're tired from their flight from Sweden. Give them a day or two before you ask them for an interview," Jesse said.

Shelly smiled. "Stuart doesn't mind; he loves telling the story."

"Shelly and I were in a meeting listening to Pastor Hans share about Operation Jabotinsky. According to Bible prophesy, the Jews will return to Israel in the last days, and the Gentiles will help. Operation Jabotinsky's mission is to provide a way to locate Russian Jews who have the desire to move to Israel. Pastor Hans told of the many church members who are working in Russia."

Stuart put his cup down. "The Jews want to take their possessions to Israel. They're using air transportation, but they need a better way. When Pastor Hans announced they needed a ship to carry the passengers and their possessions, Shelly and I were touched."

"We went home to talk and pray," Shelly said. "Afterward, we agreed to loan our ship to the church for the Operation Jabotinsky project. The next day we met with Pastor Hans."

"He must have been surprised," Rosie said.

Stuart chuckled. "It's not every day someone has such a large ship."

Shelly's eyes twinkled. "After we returned home that night, God told us we couldn't loan our ship; we must *give* them our ship. Now we were the ones who were surprised!" After the shock wore off, we said, *Okay, Lord, we'll obey.* The next day we couldn't wait to give Pastor Hans our latest update. He accepted the offer, sight unseen."

"I'm honored to be second captain," Stuart said in his gruff voice.

"We sold our house in Alaska, and we're content to live onboard to help with the restoration," Shelly said.

Rosie felt guilty as she sat longing for the comforts of her home.

The next day Rosie was shaking her dust mop over the side of the ship when she noticed a young woman walking up the gangway carrying a backpack and a worn suitcase. She looked familiar, but Rosie couldn't place her. Piercing blue eyes, blond hair, and solid build. Definitely Scandinavian. *I wonder if she just arrived from Sweden*, Rosie thought.

"Hello, I'm Rosie. Can I help you?"

"No. I'm looking for someone," she said, dropping her backpack and suitcase on the deck.

"Ellen!" Stuart yelled from the upper deck. "I'll be right down."

"Do you know Stuart? He's one of the captains. He and his wife gave the ship to—"

"Yeah, I know the story," she said, looking at the captain as he walked toward her. "Hello, Stuart."

He attempted to give the young woman a hug, but she stepped back. "It's been a long time, Ellen. I'm glad you could make it." He stood and admired her from afar. "You look great!"

She glanced around. "I wish I could say the same for your ship. It looks like I arrived too early. I can see that the old tank won't be going anywhere for a while."

Ellen stared at Rosie, making her feel like an intruder, so she started to walk away, until Stuart called after her.

"Rosie, I want you to meet my daughter, Ellen."

"Oh! Hello, Ellen. I'm glad to meet you," Rosie said, holding out her hand.

"Ellen, this is Rosie; she works in the office and the steward department."

Ellen nodded at Rosie and then turned to Stuart. "Where do I put my stuff?"

Rosie quickly withdrew her hand and then glanced from Ellen to Stuart. "That's why you look so familiar. You're the female image of your father."

Silence.

"Can I help you find your way?" Rosie quickly asked.

"No," Ellen answered, picking up her backpack.

Stuart grabbed Ellen's suitcase. "Thanks, Rosie, but I'll show Ellen to her cabin."

Rosie watched as father and daughter walked into the superstructure.

Rosie made a habit of reading her Bible every evening before delving into one of her historic novels. Tired from the day's work, Rosie often had to force herself to recite a few Bible verses.

This night she opened to II Corinthians. "That's why we live with such good cheer. You won't see us dropping our heads or dragging our feet. Cramped conditions here don't get us down. They only remind us of the spacious living conditions ahead. It's what we trust in, but don't yet see, that keeps us going."

Rosie sighed. "Yes, that's what I'm dreaming about—spacious conditions that lie ahead." She closed her Bible and picked up Bodie Thoene's *Vienna Prelude*.

As Jesse sandblasted into the night, Rosie was lost on a dark cobblestone path in Vienna when she heard a soft knock on the door.

"I saw your light under the door. May I come in for a minute?" Tina asked in her proper British English.

Rosie opened the door wide for her new friend. "Of course."

"Captain Alain and I have been talking. Since you and Jesse will be on the ship for a year, there is a large cabin in the back of the ship, starboard side. It needs some work, but there is a surprise waiting for you there."

Rosie had just settled into their cabin so she wasn't about to move, but she didn't want to sound ungrateful. "Thank you, Tina. We'll look at the cabin in the morning. By the way, what do you know about Ellen?"

"Why do you ask?"

"I don't want to sound snoopy, but she seems so aloof, as if she doesn't want to be here."

"From what Shelly told me, Ellen's mother and stepfather . . . how do you say in America . . . kicked her out of their house in Montana."

"You mean, they *asked her to leave?*"

"Yes, that sounds better," Tina said softly.

"Oh, that's terrible."

"Shelly invited her to sail with Stuart so they can spend time together. It would be good for us to make her feel at home."

Rosie nodded. "I've already tried, but I'll do my best to make her feel welcome."

The next morning after prayer, Jesse and Rosie walked to the end of the hallway that led to the stern of the ship.

"This is it, across the hall from my cleaning supplies closet," Rosie said.

Jesse opened the door and walked in, but Rosie stood in the hall. "Oh, my," she gasped.

Jesse said, "This was originally the cook's cabin. Let's see, I can remove four of the bunks, leaving us with two. Then we'll have lots of space. There's major work to be done, but I think I can handle it."

Rosie stepped in. "I don't know. It looks like a lot of work for a few extra feet of space." As she rattled on, Jesse walked several steps further and then shoved open a stubborn door.

"Look, Rosie."

Rosie stopped babbling and looked through the door.

"A toilet and a sink—and a shower! A big, roomy bathroom!" she shouted. "So this is Tina's surprise!"

"The shower needs parts, the sink is missing, and the toilet is broken."

"Like you said, it needs lots of work, but that shouldn't be a problem for my personal plumber," Rosie teased.

"I can have it up and running by the time we leave dry dock," Jesse promised.

Tina and Captain Alain were in the troop mess finishing breakfast when Rosie danced in.

"We'll take it!" Rosie chimed.

Every night after dinner, Jesse and Rosie headed for their new B&B—Bigger-and-Better—bungalow. Rosie scraped, cleaned, and painted the main cabin, while Jesse worked in the head.

"Once we leave dry dock, we'll be able to flush the toilet with a large pail of water."

"Such a small sacrifice compared to walking down the gangway in the middle of the night—in the rain," Rosie said, smiling.

"Remember, I install, and you clean," Jesse said as he presented Rosie with her new scepter, an old plastic toilet brush. "I promise to buy you a new one at Fred Meyers."

One night after dinner Rosie was cleaning her paintbrushes when Jesse walked in carrying an old sink.

"Look what I found in the storage hold! It'll shine up like new. Next, I'll need to find extra shower fixtures when we go ashore."

"Since the ship is so old, won't it be hard to find parts?" Rosie asked.

"The shower will be the most challenging, but I'll ask Stuart; he knows every plumbing shop in Seattle."

A few nights later, while Rosie was moving their clothes to their B&B, Jesse came in carrying a small piece of furniture. "Captain Alain thought you could use this desk he found in one of the holds."

"A writing desk! What a perfect place to write postcards, letters, and journals."

Jesse dusted off the rusted metal table. "I'm thinking more along the lines of your first great American novel," Jesse said, smiling.

21

High and lifted up, Resti was sandblasted down to the bare bones. No more faded red and rusty beige. She would soon show off her new colors of blue and white, along with her new name, the MS Restoration.

Torre walked into the troop mess and requested the steward department to report for duty underneath the ship.

"Why?" Rosie asked.

"The sandblasting is finished, and now the sand and paint must be loaded into the large dumpsters to prevent polluting the water," he explained. "Since we are pressed for time, everyone must help shovel."

"After spending hours cleaning the superstructure, you're asking us to go outside and shovel?" Ellen demanded.

As soon as Torre walked out, Ellen made her intentions very clear.

"I'm out of here. I'm going shopping." She looked at Rosie. "Do you want to come?"

Rosie was tempted to follow Ellen to the nearest shopping center, but looking at Tina quietly gathering cleaning supplies, she said, "I guess I'll go below—but just for an hour."

Tina and Rosie watched Ellen march off the ship, purse in hand. "I guess there's some advantages of being the captain's daughter," Rosie stated.

Covered with sand and grime, Rosie mumbled as she shoveled, swept, and coughed her way across the asphalt. Then there was Jeans, covered with sand from head to toe, and not one complaint to be heard from her pretty little hankie-covered mouth. Beautiful as ever, she shoveled right alongside the men.

"This is a far cry from cleaning the superstructure," Rosie murmured. "Ellen's right; we didn't sign up for this."

Rosie slid a blue bandana from around her hair and wiped the sweat from her face, spit particles into it, and then wrapped it back around her head.

Jeans pulled her hankie down. "This too shall pass. Besides, hard work is good for us," Jeans said, all the while showing a gritty smile.

"You're such a happy camper," Rosie said, forcing an even grittier smile back at Jeans.

After hours of working alongside Jeans, Rosie hoped to learn how to get down and dirty—spit-spit—without complaining.

"Now look who's bringing in the dirt," Ellen said to Rosie that afternoon as they stood in the shower room line. Before Rosie could reply, Ellen flung the shower curtain closed.

Rosie faked a grin. *This, too, shall pass.*

Ana-Karin snubbed Rosie as she pointed to her greasy flip-flops. "Rosie, you must learn how to clean up behind you."

"Behind me?"

"And in front of you. Look at the grease on your rubbers."

Remembering all the hard work Ana-Karin donated to the shower room, Rosie faked yet another grin. "You're right. I'll try to be more careful—and by the way, these are called flip-flops, not rubbers."

At dinner, Torre informed the crew, "Now the hull must be checked for thickness, the saltwater inlets need to be inspected for saltwater systems, and the large brass propeller has to be polished."

"We must continue to pray for the money to paint the ship," Stuart added.

"The list seems endless, but we can consider these overwhelming tasks as challenges," Tina said.

"If I wanted challenges in my life, I would have stayed in Montana," Ellen complained.

"Challenges make us stronger," Tina said. "Whenever obstacles cross our path on this ship, we send out a prayer alert, headed up by our steward department leader and chief cook." Tina turned to Urma.

Urma's blue eyes shimmered, causing the tiny wrinkles around them to fade. She had arrived from Sweden a few days earlier, with a reputation of being the best chef in Olstrum and praying with the tenacity of a madwoman until the answer came. As she worked in the galley, she could be heard down the hallways, praying in Swedish at the top of her lungs.

"Urma is our mighty Swedish prayer warrior," Tina informed the stewards.

"The key word is patience, dear one," Urma said, smiling at Ellen.

Ellen's eyes widened as she gathered her tray. "Okay, I get the message—challenges are good for us, and patience is the key. Gotcha! But I don't know how I'm going to listen to all that praying for a year! See ya later," she said and then walked out of the troop mess.

The next morning, Torre squirmed in his chair until it was time for the morning announcements. "A Seattle businessman read about our ship in a local newspaper. When he heard the exterior would be painted the colors of the Israeli flag, he gave a large donation for the paint."

Mike and his power team cheered at the news, and so Project Spray Painting began and was completed within a week. Afterward, the crew stood admiring their ship, her bottom half a deep nautical blue, and her top half the color of snow.

"I don't think it's by chance she was painted the colors of the Israeli flag," Rosie told Mike.

"It's no accident," Mike agreed. "She's a ship with a special mission."

A week later, Torre announced, "The *Restoration* passed all inspections, so she can leave dry dock. We will have a celebration on the Fiesta Deck."

The big question everyone wanted answered was *when*?

The galley girls tried to keep the crew's spirits up by using every step forward to celebrate, so that evening the steward girls prepared the Fiesta Deck for the evening festivities, while the galley girls prepared a feast to commemorate Dry Dock Graduation.

There were two worlds on the *Restoration*. There would always be the work-to-be-done areas throughout the ship, but then there was the solitude of the freshly painted Fiesta Deck. The stern overlooked Seattle's skyline, so twinkle lights were hung to reflect on the water to give a festive atmosphere. The aromas coming from Stuart's grill often filled the evening air.

The evening before Mike returned to California, the galley girls prepared a farewell party fit for the sandblasting king. The Four Preppy Plumbers sang "Leavin' on a Jet Plane," and afterward Torre presented Mike with a gift of appreciation for all his hard work.

Through tear-filled eyes, Mike shared, "This has been a labor of love. I'm going to miss all of you, but I'll especially miss the *Restoration*. I will never forget her."

Torre solemnly announced at breakfast, "As helpful as the bank has been, our outstanding invoices must be paid in full before they will allow us to leave dry dock."

"How much do we need?" Ellen asked.

"Thirty-nine thousand dollars."

Rosie's mouth dropped.

"We're being held hostage!" Ellen said.

"The amount is more than Living Waters had anticipated, and our local bank account doesn't have the funds, so we'll have to wait," Torre concluded. Then he glanced at Urma. "And pray."

And so they waited, they worked, they prayed, and they did their best to be patient. Well, to a point. As the crew sat in the troop mess, it was evident everyone wanted to escape dry dock. Some were just more verbal than others.

"I didn't come all the way from Montana to be held captive," Ellen said as she sat with the young and restless crew.

"And I didn't come all the way from California to be—" Rosie started, but Urma stepped in to interrupt Rosie before she could finish a sentence she might regret.

"It is vital that we continue to pray *together* for the money, and as we lift our voices to God, he will answer our prayers."

Rosie sighed. *She's right, so stop complaining. You'll only make matters worse.*

Rosie glanced over at Jeans. She came to morning prayer, but she always sat in a corner to pray while everyone joined together to pray for specific needs.

And then there was Ellen. She rarely showed up at all, and when she did, she would saunter in twenty minutes late and then stand in another corner slurping coffee, with her eyes wide open. When Rosie complained to Jesse about this, he asked, "How do you know Ellen has her eyes open?"

Oops. Caught.

On the other hand, Rosie noticed other happenings among the crew, like the morning when Bjorne, the first engineer, had electrical difficulties, and Henrik stopped what he was doing on the bridge to give him a hand in the engine room. And the day Jesse needed some assistance with a fire line, and Jeans jumped in to help. And the afternoon Deena was too tired to peel one more potato, so Val took the knife and began peeling away.

Days passed. It was a day like any other day—prayer, meals, and work. Rosie and Ellen were cleaning the troop mess, and all the while Ellen was complaining about her cold shower the night before. Rosie was getting ready to quote the Jeans *this too shall pass* line, when out of nowhere, a loud, rushing noise came from outside. Rosie and Ellen strained to look through the nearest porthole.

"Move over so I can see," Ellen said, nudging Rosie, forcing her to move to the next porthole. "The dry dock's filling with water!"

They heard the deck crew cheering, so they jumped over the doorway to join them outside.

"How can this be?" Rosie asked.

"Maybe the money fell from heaven," Ellen said sarcastically as she pushed past Rosie.

"You're starting to sound like Urma," Rosie answered as she jumped over the hatch door.

"Oh, puleeze!" Ellen said, rolling her eyes.

Stuart yelled to the deckhands, "We're starting to float! Get moving!"

Captain Alain called the port to request a tugboat to guide them to Ballard, while the crew moved fast and furious, grabbing belongings off the dock and disengaging electrical wires and water hoses.

When the tug arrived, Stuart and the more experienced boatswains worked with the journeymen, showing them how to move around the deck. Rosie noticed how quickly Jeans caught on, obeying every command with precision.

The engineers were positioned in the engine room, heeding every order the first officer gave from the bridge. The women kept out of the way, watching from the monkey bridge. Everyone except Ellen. Rosie chuckled as Ellen tripped over ropes and hoses, cursing with every mistake she made.

The water continued to rise until the ship's bottom was submerged.

The roar of the engine, the creaking of the steering mechanism in the stern of the ship, and the hum of the large propeller sent a fresh sense of excitement through Rosie's weary body.

"All this noise is like music to my ears," Rosie told Tina.

"These sounds will become familiar to you in the days ahead," Tina said, smiling.

"Tina, how did we manage to escape dry dock?"

"The dock owners agreed to accept payments until we are paid in full, but our debt must be paid before we leave Seattle."

"God will bring us the money," Urma said with confidence.

It was at moments like this that Rosie's faith grew.

Rosie had anticipated the ride from Lake Union to the Ballard Bridge for weeks. The breeze against her face and the sound of the waves splashing against the ship gave her a sense of freedom she hadn't felt in a long time. She joined with the rhythm of the ship, swaying back and forth as they glided across the bay toward the Ballard Bridge.

"This is our breakthrough trip! We're finally leaving the wilderness of dry dock!" Rosie declared as she lifted her arms in victory.

"This is a small taste of what sailing on the high seas will be like," Tina said, smiling.

After safely docking, everyone was enjoying an afternoon break on the Fiesta Deck when a large truck pulled up, breaking the silence. Torre motioned the driver to drop the delivery at the end of the dock.

"Now what?" Ellen asked as she walked to the rail.

"The dock owner is providing these nice, portable toilets. They'll be convenient until the waste tanks are in working order," Torre explained.

"But I thought we had water onboard now."

"We are piping in water for minimum use. We will have one shower and one head in working order. And, of course, enough water for the Galley."

Three blue porta-johns stood tall in Seattle's afternoon sun, beckoning to be occupied.

"They're much more inviting than the dry-dock facilities," Rosie said as she walked down the gangway.

As she turned the corner, one of the blue doors opened, and she stood face-to-face with Alain, their distinguished captain. She shyly nodded, thinking it probably wouldn't be the last time they would meet at The Blue Rooms.

Once up the gangway, she rounded the corner in time to hear the last of a father-and-daughter conversation.

"You did a good job on deck today. How would you like to work with the deck crew in the afternoons?" Stuart asked Ellen.

"Yeah, I guess so. I'm bored to tears in the steward department. I'd rather work outside," Ellen answered. She glanced at Rosie as she walked by. "You'd like that, wouldn't you?"

Acting as if she hadn't heard a word, Rosie ignored the remark and headed for the cleaning closet to begin her afternoon chores.

Rosie couldn't hold her frustration any longer. That night in bed, she blurted, "Can you believe Ellen wants to be part of the deck crew? She can't even clean a toilet, so how can Stuart think she can work on deck?"

"Did you stop to think that maybe Stuart would like to have his daughter working with him?"

"She just wants to work with the guys. Now I'll be the only one cleaning the superstructure!"

"Rosie, calm down. Can't you and Shelly handle the superstructure until the rest of the Swedish volunteers arrive?"

"Of course, but it's the principle of the matter. Anyway, Ellen doesn't like me."

Jesse shook his head. "Does this remind you of another incident you told me about that happened many years ago?"

Rosie thought, but she couldn't remember any incident as annoying as Ellen.

"Remember when you first met your neighbor Priscilla?"

She grimaced. "Yeah. Prissy and I did not get along."

"And *why* was that?"

"We rubbed each other the wrong way."

"No, Rosie. If you recall, Prissy wasn't the one with a problem. *She* rubbed *you* the wrong way because she was always late, she was boy-crazy, she loved the dramatic . . . shall I go on? Then once you got to know her, you became best friends."

Rosie raised her hands in resignation. "Oh, no, not again," Rosie sighed, getting Jesse's point.

She picked up her novel, turned a few pages, and then placed it back on the writing table. She picked up her Bible instead.

22

As the volunteers worked endlessly on Resti, *she was looking better every day.*

There was a sign-up sheet for Auswich—a nickname Ellen gave the gas-eating, exhaust-burning van that had been donated to the ship by a local church. The rule was: first come, first serve.

Each evening a group would hop in—Ellen said the fumes alone made her feel as if she was on an LSD trip—and take a trip to one of Seattle's many points of destination. Some nights Val would take a run to a nearby video store to rent a girl's-night-in movie. They enjoyed gathering in the newly painted crew's lounge to watch movies appropriate for the ship's theme—*Exodus, Miss Rose White,* and *Fiddler on the Roof.* After swooning over the newly released chic-flick *Sleepless in Seattle*, they piled in the van and drove to nearby sights where the box office smash had been filmed.

Jesse and Rosie enjoyed spending evenings relaxing at nearby coffeehouses, where college students, seniors, and odd couples went to hang out.

"Starbucks is definitely onto a great moneymaking coffee idea. They should spread their wings and consider going statewide," Jesse remarked as he sipped his vanilla latte. "And if they're successful, they might even consider going nationwide, and who knows, even worldwide."

"I wouldn't go that far," Ellen said sarcastically. "That's dreaming way too big."

Rosie wondered if Ellen had any dreams.

"Our cabin is finished, so while I'm finishing the head, you can enhance our home-on-steel," Jesse said in hopes of cheering his wife after her latest bout with homesickness.

When Tina invited them for an evening at the Fred Meyers Discount Store, Jesse accepted immediately. Jesse's task was to find items that would turn the cabin into a comfortable home at sea, so he made his way to the appliance department. He found a refrigerator small enough to fit in the corner of their bathroom, next to the toilet. The four-cup coffeemaker Prissy had given them would fit snuggly on top.

Rosie busied herself in the home improvement section. She chose an area rug to cover their freshly painted floor, sheets and bedspreads for the bunk beds, and a plastic lawn chair for the corner of the cabin—all in Jesse's favorite color, hunter green. With her shopping tasks completed, Rosie steered her basket toward the small appliance department.

"I found the solution to our no air-conditioning dilemma," Jesse said as he held up two small fans. "I'll attach them to the bunks. They'll be lifesavers in the Caribbean."

"I have my own personal MacGyver," Rosie said proudly. Jesse always came up with great ideas, thus his nickname.

They arrived back at the ship with arms filled with treasures and hearts full of anticipation for the voyage.

When Jesse finished making the beds with their new linens, he grabbed Rosie's hand. "Hey, let's try out our new sheets. Which bed, mine or yours?"

"How about *both*?"

The following Saturday, a local volunteer asked Jesse, "What do you need for the voyage?" Rosie walked up behind her husband as he answered, "We've bought everything we need at Fred Meyers, but there is one item we can't afford. You see, we're going to be on the ship for a year, so Rosie would really like us to sleep together. A double mattress is on top of her wish list."

"Me! What about you, my affectionate, hands-on husband!" Rosie said teasingly after the volunteer walked toward the superstructure.

Jesse winked. "A double bed would be nice."

A few days later, while Jesse finished repairing the showers in hold two, he noticed a double mattress wrapped in plastic, leaning against a wall in the hallway.

"Do you know where this mattress came from?" Jesse asked Torre.

"A man who assisted you with the showers brought it aboard. He said it was a gift for the California plumber."

Jesse read the note that was attached to the mattress: Happy sailing. Enjoy!

Jesse spent days working to get the mandatory fire lines up and running. He was exhausted at the end of each day, but the bed project put a zing in his step.

After tearing down the two single bunks, he used several boards that were stored in hold two to frame their bed, building it high enough to store luggage and boxes underneath. After splashing a coat of white paint on the bed frame, he announced, "Voila! Our new love bed!"

"I can't wait to test it out," Rosie said, smiling.

On their next trip to Fred Meyers, Rosie purchased bed linens for double-size bedding, and Jesse bought a large fan to hang at the foot of the bed.

"Now we're ready for action, er, ready to set sail," Jesse said.

Rosie didn't know if it was the new mattress or the fact they were able to snuggle every night, but her MacGyver woke up every morning with a smile on his face.

Volunteers drove straight from their jobs to spend a few hours working before they headed home; others worked on their days off. Some were skilled; others worked wherever they were needed, just to be part of the ship's destiny. War vets loved to work on the ship. The *Restoration* brought back memories of their World War II days, giving a new sense of value to the salty seniors.

Then there were the younger volunteers.

Rosie noticed that the pretty outgoing blond wasn't afraid to get down and dirty. And someone else was noticing the tall, blue-eyed flight attendant.

Bjorne and Nicole began spending their coffee breaks and lunches together. She definitely brought out the best in the shy Swede. He smiled more, laughed more, and talked more when she was around.

Rosie was a cupid at heart. She loved watching their friendship turn to love. Bjorne had no idea when he came to America to volunteer as first engineer that he would find love. *Telephones and ships*, Rosie thought, smiling. She was still learning firsthand how life was full of wonderful surprises.

The next morning, Torre announced to the crew, "To hold more water on the ship, we will clean out the water tanks, since they have been sitting empty for many years. Unfortunately, the men are too large to fit in the cramped areas."

He turned to the women. "Do we have a volunteer?"

"Count me out," Val said, chuckling. No one would argue with buxom Val. Torre was looking for someone more petite to fit into the small quarters.

"Don't look at me!" Ellen said, shaking her head. Torre hadn't even glanced her way. "I'll clean, scrape, and paint, but I'm not crawling into some small, black pit!"

Everyone heard her message, loud and clear.

Rosie avoided eye contact, focusing on the tile floor that she would soon be sweeping. She didn't know exactly what size woman Torre was looking for, but when she looked up, he was glancing her way. "I'm too tall," Rosie said before he could speak.

Jeans raised her hand. "I can do it."

Rosie sighed in relief.

"It figures that Miss-I-can-do-anything would volunteer," Ellen said in between slurps of coffee.

"Do you need help?" Henrik asked Jeans.

"Thanks, Henrik, but we've got it covered," Torre answered.

Jeans wasted no time in climbing into the dark abyss. She took her breaks and then climbed back down into the first water tank, resurfacing for the next meal. This went on for days. The men cheered the brave young woman on. Rosie had to admit that Jeans looked as pretty in her grease-stained coveralls as she did in her freshly laundered T-shirts and jeans. And Rosie wasn't the only one who noticed. Several of the young men had their eyes on Jeans, but she didn't seem to care. Her focus was on God, the ship, and her journal.

A week later, Stuart proudly announced, "Thanks to Jeans, the two water tanks are ready to store water. When the water begins flowing through the ship's pipes, we can use all of the sinks, showers, and toilets."

Cheers filled the troop mess. "A good reason to celebrate," Urma said. There was no doubt that Jeans was the ship's grease angel.

"You're just a modern-day Joan of Arc, aren't you?" Ellen said to Jeans as she tugged at Henrik's shirt. "Come on, let's get our coffee."

Henrik winked at Jeans as he brushed her shoulder. "Nice job, Joan . . . I mean Jeans," he said.

"Thanks," Jeans answered, blushing.

"Come on, Henrik!" Ellen called.

"Uh, later," Henrik said to Jeans, and then turned to follow Ellen to the galley.

"Ellen doesn't mind interrupting, especially when it comes to Henrik," Rosie said to Jeans as they ate breakfast.

"So I've noticed," Jeans said, stirring her oatmeal. "But that's okay. I'm not interested."

As Jeans daintily filled her spoon with oatmeal, Rosie got the impression that Jeans hadn't had much experience with boys. Since the ship was full of young men, perhaps the time had come for her to spread her angelic wings a little.

That evening while Rosie was reading her Bible in bed, Isaiah forty-three caught her attention. "The God who builds a road through the ocean, who carves a path through the pounding waves . . ." Then another verse jumped off the page. "Forget about what has happened. Don't keep going over old history. Be alert, be in the present. I am about to do something brand-new. It's bursting out, don't you see it? There it is!"

Rosie looked around the cabin. "Lord, I left my home and family. That's history. Now, in the midst of getting ready to travel the seven seas, I could say that you're going to do a brand-new thing."

She closed her eyes. "I can't see it yet, but I'm going to be more alert and live more in the present."

She placed her Bible on the table and then patted the hull. "Resti, you're beginning to feel like a love boat in more ways than one."

Movies, popcorn, and scenic drives made the waiting bearable. But time was running out for some of the Swedes, who would soon need to return home to families and jobs.

They all still believed the money would come for the *Restoration* to sail. But when?

23

On Resti's *christening day, a star was born. Her next chapter was about to begin.*

On a rainy June morning, Torre stood in the troop mess with the hopes of shedding some sunshine on the dismal day. When he announced that Pastor Hans was coming for the *Restoration*'s dedication ceremony, the crew cheered. Their thoughts turned to dedication day.

That afternoon, a professional company painted the ship's name on the starboard, portside, and stern. Amid empty paint cans, the crew stood on the dock admiring the bold blue letters that read *MS Restoration*.

Resti, your blue letters look like a shawl wrapped around your white evening gown," Rosie said.

"You have quite an imagination," Ellen said. "And I *imagine* this old ship talks back to you?"

"Didn't your mother read *The Little Engine that Could* when you were a little girl?" Rosie asked.

Ellen grimaced. "My mother didn't have time to read to me. She was too busy with her singing career."

"I didn't know your mother was a singer."

"She's not, but at least her connections landed me a job at the local radio station," Ellen said as she walked away. Rosie wanted to ask about Ellen's career, but she was already halfway up the gangway.

Alone, Rosie walked up to her freshly painted friend. "Don't mind Ellen. Perhaps one day she'll catch your dream."

Pastor Hans led the Swedish group up the gangway.

"He doesn't look Swedish," Ellen commented.

"Not all Swedes are blond," Rosie said, watching the pastor's dark hair blowing in the breeze.

In perfect English, Pastor Hans introduced the new crew—Lizzie, a blonde Swedish galley girl; Olga, an even blonder steward; Daniel, a young boatswain; Arne and Sven, engineers; and Else, a nurse.

Pastor Hans followed Captain Alain and Stuart to the superstructure, and Henrik led the Swedes to their cabins.

"I'll never remember those weird names," Ellen said, shaking her head. "But I certainly won't forget him."

By the time Daniel, the good-looking Swede, shook hands with everyone, he had already discovered Jeans. But Ellen interrupted the moment.

"Tell us about yourself, Daniel."

He smiled at Ellen as he pushed a few blond curls from his eyes.

"I'm from Stockholm, and I have come on this ship to see the world." He proceeded to smile at Jeans. She blushed and then walked away.

"Now that's a face to remember," Ellen said with a devilish look in her eyes.

Rosie would keep a close watch on the new boy. The gleam in his eyes told her he had a way with the women. Rosie walked over to Tina. "Do you know anything about Daniel?"

"His father is Torre's friend. Daniel needs to get away from his druggy friends, so he asked Torre if Daniel could volunteer for a year." She paused and then added, "I hope the decision was not a mistake."

"I was thinking the same thing. Did you see the glimmer in the girls' eyes when he came onboard?"

Tina nodded. "I'll make sure he reads the ship's policies and procedures manual regarding male and female relationships."

"We'll keep a close watch on him," Rosie said. "But sometimes you can't stand in the way of true love."

"Are you referring to Bjorne and Nicole?" Tina asked with a twinkle in her eyes.

At that moment, Rosie realized Tina was also a hopeless romantic.

The sky opened as the tour began, so with umbrella in hand, Captain Alain carefully guided Pastor Hans around the puddles. Hans peeked into every nook and cranny.

An hour later, the crew gathered in hold two, where the large vacant area had been converted into a comfortable living room. Brown sofas and orange chairs were positioned to divide the large room into three conversation areas. Today they were arranged to face the chair where the pastor would sit.

Rosie arrived early to get a seat close to Pastor Hans. Ellen and Jeans arrived late and stood next to the door until Daniel motioned for them to sit next to him. Ellen smiled at the invitation and sat between Daniel and Jeans.

"I am delighted to finally see and touch this dream come true," Pastor Hans began. "First, I want to thank you for the hard work you are doing. You are part of God's prophetic plan, so I want to tell you how this dream began."

"How long is this going to take?" Ellen asked, rolling her eyes.

"Shh," Urma said, but Ellen ignored her.

"In 1993, while I was hosting one hundred Russian pastors in Israel, God spoke to me." Pastor Hans looked around the room. "I shared with them about the historical mission that lay ahead of them to help those Soviet Jews who want to make *aliyah* to Israel. They caught this vision and returned home to begin networking throughout Russia."

"I don't believe in visions or dreams," Ellen said to Daniel. She stood. "Want to join me?"

Daniel smiled and then stood to follow her.

Rosie whispered, "You should stay."

Daniel and Ellen looked at each other.

"You need to stay if you're serious about the ship," Rosie said.

Ellen sat down with a thud; Daniel followed. Rosie caught Stuart shaking his head as Shelly whispered her famous *yikes*.

Pastor Hans stood, solemnly looking around the room.

"Let me say one more thing. This journey is God's plan for this ship. As the crew, you need to be prepared physically and spiritually for the days ahead."

The crew was silent. And for once, so was Ellen.

Seattle's weather showed mercy by bestowing a day of sunshine for Dedication Day. Rosie and Ellen decorated the Fiesta Deck with blue tablecloths and then placed white daisies they had purchased at the local outdoor market in the center of each table. Potted plants welcomed the guests at the bottom of the gangway. Volunteers brought extra food, flowers, and chairs.

The television media and local city officials were greeted by the ship's uniformed officers. Over seventy people gathered on the dock as Pastor Hans spoke about the *Restoration*'s mission to transport Russian Jews from Russia to Israel. After the dedication prayer, the captains stood on the dock and flung a bottle of sparkling cider into the side of the freshly painted ship.

"We christen you the MS *Restoration!*" Pastor Hans proclaimed.

Glass smashing against metal brought a roar of triumph throughout the crowd.

"Now, let the celebration begin!" Captain Alain bellowed.

A buffet of turkey, ham, and herring was served on the Fiesta Deck, along with Swedish and American side dishes. A large blue and white cake represented the *Restoration*'s colors.

Laughter rang throughout the ship as Israeli folk songs filled the air. Everyone was commemorating all the days of hard labor and celebrating the days that would soon follow.

Later that evening, after the last visitors disembarked, the crew gathered in the lounge to watch the taped ceremony on the local TV networks.

"Isn't she beautiful?" Val sighed.

"Yes, she is quite photogenic," Tina added as she flipped from channel to channel.

Within minutes after the news broadcasts, the phone number that had been posted on the bottom of the TV screen kept Rosie busy in the office for several hours.

24

Everything seemed to be moving full speed ahead for Resti *and her crew.*

Long after the Swedish pastor's departure the next morning, the crew's fresh sense of joy and renewed faith in the *Restoration*'s destiny could be felt throughout the ship. The media coverage brought donations and eager volunteers.

It was late afternoon and Rosie was busy typing thank-you letters in the office when Jesse appeared at the door. "Rosie, you left your coffee cup on the deck; you need to get it now."

Jesse seldom spoke to her in that tone, especially in public. *Can't he see that I'm busy?* "I'll get it later," she answered curtly.

"You need to go get your cup, *now*."

Shelly and Stuart looked up from their desks. *He must have had a bad morning, or maybe he needs some time off the ship,* Rosie thought. Embarrassed, she decided to handle the situation with grace. She walked to the door, giving him her *we'll-talk-about-this-later* look. She brushed past him and then stopped in her tracks. Looking up at her with big brown eyes was a little girl who looked all too familiar.

"Katie!" Rosie screamed. Katie jumped at her grandmother's outburst and then smiled.

"Hi, Gama!"

Rosie swept Katie up into her arms and smothered her with kisses. When she looked at Jesse, he smiled and pointed down the hall at a tall, dark-haired beauty.

"Surprise!" Grace yelled as she walked toward her mother. "This is my graduation gift from Tim. The Caribbean trip was to detour you." Glancing at Jesse, she added, "We've been planning this trip for weeks."

Holding Katie, Rosie kissed her daughter's cheek. "Of all the surprises I've had, this one takes the prize!"

She turned to Stuart and Shelly. "Did you know about this?"

"We sure did," Stuart bellowed. "Now, go and have fun."

After dinner, Grace stood admiring Jesse and Rosie's head. "I can't wait to use your shower."

"I hate to disappoint you, but we're having temporary pipe problems." Rosie picked up a plastic bucket. "But our toilet works just fine."

Rosie walked Katie down the hall for their evening shower. Suddenly, darkness surrounded them, and Katie let out a scream and reached out for Rosie's hand.

"Gama, I'm scared."

"Oops! The generator went out," Rosie said, trying to make a game of the darkness. As Katie began to cry, two flashlights made their way toward the girls, lighting up the hallway.

"Here, carry this to the shower room," Jesse told Katie as he handed her a flashlight.

Rosie and Katie giggled as they showered by flashlight and then made their way back to the cabin. The generator eventually kicked on, but Katie insisted on sleeping with her flashlight.

Jesse volunteered to sleep in hold two so the girls could have a slumber party, but after Grace fell out of bed onto the hard floor for the second time, she gathered a pillow and a blanket.

"I'm glad you have a rug to soften the blows, but my body can't take another fall. I'm going next door to sleep on the lounge sofa," Grace said, closing the cabin door behind her.

Although Rosie could stretch out, she cuddled Katie in her arms until her granddaughter fell asleep.

The girls spent their days making faces at the seals at the Seattle Aquarium; Grace read Katie *The Little Engine that Could* at the Children's Library; and they strolled through the Market Place to buy fresh fruit and souvenirs. Too soon, their time together was over.

As Grace packed her suitcase, Rosie handed her an envelope. "Here, give this to Dad. When I called him, he asked for a picture of the ship."

Grace placed the letter and photo in her purse. "I'll give it to him next week when he comes over for Katie's birthday."

Grace bent over the bed and gave Katie a good-night kiss and then stepped over the threshold. "My last night to sleep on the lumpy crew sofa."

As soon as Katie drifted off to sleep, Rosie tiptoed next door. She knelt down and gently touched her daughter's hair, awakening Grace from her slumber.

"Sorry to wake you. I just needed to be near *my* little girl."

The dock lights gave off a dim glow through the portholes of the newly decorated room.

"I'm actually going to miss this lumpy sofa." Grace sat up and looked around. "Mom, after being here these past three days, I realize you were right about volunteering."

Rosie sat close to her daughter. "Grace, at first I blamed Jesse for this trip—you know how he loves adventure. But after working on this ship these past weeks, something inside is compelling me to help the Russian Jews. I don't understand it, but I have to follow my heart."

"Mom, you don't have to explain. I know you have to go on this journey. I was just being selfish."

Then Grace embraced her mother. *There are times when a daughter's hug can say more than words*, Rosie thought as she crawled back into her bed, next to Katie.

The next morning, Rosie drove back from the airport in silence. Jesse tried small talk, but he knew it was better to leave his wife to her memories of the past few days. Once back at the ship, she excused herself and went to their cabin to hide out for the rest of the day. She was lying across the bed when Jesse walked in. He sat next to her and began rubbing her back.

"Rosie, I know it's hard with the girls gone, but you should be grateful you had a few wonderful days with them."

She sat up and forced a smile. "I am grateful, and I thank you for giving me the best surprise ever."

As they embraced, Jesse glimpsed at the calendar sitting on the writing desk. There was a red circle around the date. June twenty-fifth. His heart sank.

"Rosie, do you know what day it is?"

"Of course . . . it's Sunday."

"Today is our anniversary."

"You remembered," Rosie sighed.

A knock on the door broke the uneasy silence. Jesse opened the door to find Stuart standing in the doorway wearing one of his famous grins.

"What's going on?" Jesse asked Stuart, curious.

"Some local friends gave us a . . . what do you call it . . . oh, a love gift. So we have a surprise for you and Rosie."

"A surprise . . . for us?" Jesse asked.

"We're inviting you to go on a road trip with us to Port Townsend."

"When?" Jesse asked.

"As soon as you get your pants on," Stuart teased.

Looking at her weary husband, Rosie smiled from the bed. "We'll be ready in five minutes."

She would have preferred to stay in their cabin and feel sorry for herself, but she could see that Jesse needed a break from the ship. She took hold of her emotions, and as they walked down the gangway toward Stuart's used Mercedes, Rosie took Jesse's hand. *Today is not about me. Today is about my cowboy.* "Happy anniversary," she whispered.

Stuart drove to the town where Shelly was raised. They slowly cruised through the base where *An Officer and a Gentleman* was filmed. They feasted on shrimp and salmon at the Sea Galley, a quaint little seaside restaurant. They nibbled on dessert as they watched the sun set over the water.

They caught the midnight ferry back to Seattle. Tired from the day's journey, they were happy to return home.

Rosie lay in bed and took a moment to thank God for his special surprises and then turned over and thanked Jesse.

"It's the Fourth of July, and we're still stuck in Seattle," Ellen complained as she threw red, white, and blue tablecloths across the Fiesta Deck tables. Rosie took one and began spreading the plastic cloth while she hummed "The Star Spangled Banner."

"Why are you so happy?" Ellen asked.

"I'm thankful to live in the United States of America. Aren't you?"

"I never think about it," she said as she walked into the superstructure.

At precisely nine o'clock, the crew stood on the deck of the World War II ship to watch the fireworks going off across the bay. Rosie's heart swelled with pride as a local radio station played "God Bless America" to the timing of each firework.

"Does your radio station do anything like this for the Fourth?" Rosie asked Ellen.

"Are you kidding? We're lucky to get sparklers in our small town."

Rosie wondered how Ellen's voice sounded coming from a radio.

"Do you miss your job?" Rosie asked.

"No, I don't miss anything about home," she said, turning toward the bow of the ship.

Stuart blew the *Restoration*'s deep horn and Rosie held one hand over her heart and the other on Resti's rail as she declared, "I'm proud to be an American!"

25

May, June, July. Resti *sat in port, waiting for a departure date.*

Rosie had settled into her new life, dust and all, and had no time for regrets, until the morning Captain Alain announced, "The crew must have two mandatory typhoid shots before we sail."

"We don't need those shots. Besides, they'll only make us sick," Ellen said.

Oh, how Rosie wanted to believe Ellen. Noticing the color slowly leaving Rosie's face, Tina leaned toward her. "You might have a few side effects," Tina said in her reassuring way.

Captain Alain gave Ellen a larger-than-life frown and then continued, "A local medical clinic has donated their vaccines. Ana-Karin will give the first shot tomorrow, and next week she will perform the second one."

Rosie's fear of needles ran a close second to her fear of water. As soon as a needle touched her skin, she would begin to feel lightheaded, as if she were on the verge of a fainting spell. Now, after hearing Ellen's remarks, Rosie began experiencing premature side effects, so she excused herself to hide out in her cabin.

She sat in her plastic green chair. "Inhale . . . now exhale . . . yes, that's it . . . inhale, now exhale." She prayed, "Okay, Lord, if I have to have these heavy-duty shots, then give me the courage and stamina to take it like a man—a seaman."

Rosie went to bed dreaming of needles and fainting spells, with not one faith dream to be found.

The next morning Rosie showed up at the temporary infirmary in the captain's mess, smiling and acting like a tough sailor.

"Pull down your shorts and remain standing," Ana-Karin instructed.

"That's easy for you to say. When was the last time you had a typhoid shot?"

Ana-Karin ignored her as she prepared the six-inch needle. Rosie quickly looked away and continued babbling, "I could never be a nurse—the thought of sticking a needle in another human's flesh brings little spots to my eyes and tingly noises in my head."

"You think too much about the needle. Try focusing on something pleasant," Ana-Karin suggested. "How do you Americans say it? Find your happy place."

Rosie held onto the table, trying to find the happy place that the Swedish nurse seemed to know so much about. Her eyes faced the porthole, careful not to spy the shiny needle that Ana-Karin was aiming at her bottom. She flinched as the sharp object pinched the flesh of her right cheek. "Ouch!"

"That wasn't so bad," Ana-Karin said, all the while smiling as if she actually enjoyed watching Rosie flinch. "You can go now."

Rosie quickly pulled up her shorts and walked out. Nurse A.K.—Rosie's nickname for Ana-Karin—was smirking, so Rosie didn't bother to thank her. All she wanted to do was clear the premises.

Later, Rosie heard that some of the crew had to retire to their bunks with nausea, headaches, and weakness. To her surprise, she felt sure-footed.

"You're becoming quite the trooper," Rosie proudly told herself as she carried on with her chores.

Ellen resigned herself to taking the shot, and she teased her roommates for their weak behavior.

"There's nothing to those needles," Ellen said as she blared Elvis' "All Shook Up" on her cassette player. Her roommates ignored her by pulling their pillows over their heads.

The following week, Rosie arrived early for shot number two, smiled at Nurse A.K., and lowered her shorts without being instructed to do so. She held her breath and clinched her teeth—not even an ouch this time.

Afterward, head held high, Rosie staggered down the stairs, determined to make every attempt to carry on as usual. She changed her mind when her head started to spin.

"If I can make it to my cabin, I'll be fine," she told herself. She had learned from her past fainting experiences that when dots start appearing in front of the eyes, it was time to sit down and put head between legs—fast . . . a humbling position for anyone.

She spotted a five-gallon paint can sitting next to the first engineer's cabin, so she sat down and placed her head between her legs and began breathing deeply.

"What are you doing?" Bjorne asked as he stepped out of his cabin.

"Oh, I'm reading the label on the can."

"Upside down?"

Bjorne held out his grease-stained hands. "Here, let me help you."

Reluctantly, Rosie allowed him to slowly guide her to her cabin. She plopped onto the bed.

"Thank you, Bjorne. You can go now . . . I'll be okay."

"May I tell you a secret?" he asked softly as he stood in the hallway.

"Of course. I love secrets," she whispered, trying to be polite.

Bjorne stepped closer. "I don't like needles either."

"You don't?"

"I've been a seaman for years. I have no fear, except for the fear of *the needle*."

Rosie leaned back on her pillow. "Thanks for sharing; it will remain our secret."

"I have another secret," Bjorne said in his almost perfect Swenglish.

Rosie sat upright. "I'm listening."

"Nicole and I are going to pronounce our engagement before we sail."

"Pronounce? Oh, do you mean *announce?*"

Blushing, he answered, "Yes, yes, that is what I meant."

"Congratulations! You make a darling couple." Suddenly, all of Bjorne's secrets were making Rosie feel much better. "Will Nicole move to Sweden? Where will you get married?"

Bjorne held up one hand. "Hold on! You'll have to ask Nicole; she is planning the wedding. For now, she will continue working as a flight attendant, and after the ship arrives in Stockholm, she will fly over to meet my parents."

Rosie was ecstatic by all the firsthand news.

Bjorne stepped toward the door. "By the way," he added, "did you know that Ellen is in her cabin? And she is sicker than a—how do you say in American?"

"Sicker than a dog?"

"Yes, she is sicker than a dog," he said, winking.

Rosie smiled at the news, and after Bjorne closed the door, she burst out laughing. "Ellen is sicker than a dog!"

Bjorne and Rosie bonded that day.

After lunch, Torre told the crew about an American Jewish businessman who had heard about the ship. "He wants to pay for three hundred thousand liters of marine diesel fuel, enough to take the *Restoration* to Stockholm."

"Our prayers are answered daily," Urma said with arms lifted.

"He asked us to keep the transaction quiet."

"Why?" Rosie asked.

"Most of his business colleagues are of Middle Eastern descent. When they heard he was investing in an international transport project, he avoided giving them details."

The crew was hanging on his words. "Go on, Torre," Jesse said.

"Mr. H—as I must call him—told me that if they find out about the ship transporting Soviet Jews to Israel, they might take their multimillion-dollar investments elsewhere."

"What is done in secret will be rewarded in the open," Urma said, lifting her flabby arms again.

Torre turned to Captain Alain. "He mentioned that if they find out about his contributions, there could be consequences."

Rosie gulped and wanted to pursue the conversation, but Jesse started gathering their dishes. "Well, it's time to get to work," Jesse said, rising from the table. "Come on, Rosie."

She followed her husband, but she was curious to know what consequences Torre was referring to.

Miracles arrived on the gangway daily. Within two weeks, Mr. H also donated money for Stuart to purchase a GMDS—Global Maritime Distress System. "Whew! Now we'll be safe at sea," Rosie said when Stuart handed her the receipt for the radio equipment.

"Rosie, with God at the helm, we're always safe at sea."

"Stuart, I love your way of thinking." Rosie turned to her computer and began writing a thank-you letter.

"Don't bother writing him, Rosie. Remember what he told us?"

Rosie stopped typing. "What Mr. H does in secret will be rewarded openly. God bless Mr. H."

The office kept Rosie busy writing thank-you letters to the many donors. She kept a list: two radar units valued at twenty thousand dollars, donated by a Finnish businessman; Archie, a retired volunteer who worked six days a week on the ship, donated a thousand dollars; the Church Emmaus donated four thousand dollars; Urma's Swedish friends who lived in Ballard donated five thousand dollars; two businessmen who survived the Holocaust bought two computers and a printer for the office.

Dry and canned goods were stored in hold three, and frozen foods were stored in the large stand-up freezer downstairs next to the engine room. After Jesse gave a German couple a tour of the ship, they drove to a local market and brought back twenty frozen turkeys. Several local Russian churches donated five hundred pounds of frozen chicken. Rosie talked to a representative from Seattle's largest coffee company, who told her they were going to donate three hundred more pounds of coffee.

"And may God prosper Starbucks!"

Two local hospitals stocked the infirmary with medical supplies; three local libraries donated four boxes of books, giving the ship a library-at-sea. Rosie enjoyed filling the bookshelves. Bodie Thoene's *Warsaw Requiem* and *London Refrain* jumped out at her as she removed them from the box. "I'll read these for starters," she said, placing them aside.

The books helped Rosie to ease her homesickness, but after turning off the reading light, Rosie's thoughts and prayers turned to her family. She drifted off to sleep remembering Presley's laugh . . . Jay's sense of humor . . . Lynn's smile . . . lunches with Grace . . . playing with Katie Rose in the park . . . .

The next day, Stuart motioned Jesse and Rosie to join him and Shelly at their table for lunch.

"I have some good news."

"We love good news," Rosie said.

"We've received the final paperwork for flagging the *Restoration* under the Panamanian flag."

"I'm curious—why Panama?" Rosie asked.

"Thousands of ships from different countries sail under the Panamanian flag because it comes with less pressure." He hesitated and then added, "But oftentimes it proves hazardous because of the piracies on the high seas."

Rosie gulped. "I thought pirates went out with the *Pirates of the Caribbean.*"

"Pirates are alive and well at sea, especially in the waters where we're heading, and they seem to be attracted to Panamanian flags."

"Yikes," Shelly whispered before she prayed, "Dear Lord, bless this food."

"And please, Lord, protect us from the pirates of the Caribbean. Amen," Rosie added, trying to keep her sense of humor.

"Amen! Now let's eat, mates," Stuart said as he dipped his spoon in Urma's famous Swedish stew.

The pace was picking up. Rosie spent hours in the upstairs captain's mess with Stuart and Captain Alain preparing port documents, making sure everyone had their updated seaman's papers. Rosie beamed with pride the day Stuart presented her with a red Panamanian seaman's book. Later in her cabin, she repeated, "This isn't a dream, Rose Adrienne Atkisson. You are an official seaman."

Since the ship had no stabilizers, the ballasts were vital for correct balance. After the dock cranes lifted the heavy weights into the holds, two vans that had been donated from a local church to be transported to Russia were tied down on deck and covered with heavy blue tarp for the voyage.

Stuart continued working on the challenging project of finding, purchasing, and preparing lifeboats and first-aid equipment. He told the crew, "We have the mandatory equipment to sail to Sweden. We'll purchase canister lifeboats when we arrive in Stockholm."

In the midst of the last-minute preparations, Grace called Rosie. "I have a surprise for you. Lisa has asked me to meet her in Russia in October, so I can spend a few days with you in Stockholm."

"Daughter, you have made my day!"

"I'll give you more details once you arrive in Stockholm."

"I'll try calling you at sea our new ham radio—it's like a shortwave radio system," Rosie said.

"By the way, Grandpa loved the picture. He said the *Restoration* looks strangely familiar . . . reminds him of the knot troop carrier he was on in the China Sea."

Rosie smiled. "I plan to spend more time with him when I return home. I want to hear more of his war stories."

"If you can catch him! As we speak, Grampa's touring Morocco with the Savvy Senior Tours," Grace said, laughing.

"I'm happy for Dad. Jesse told me he wants to be traveling when we're in our seventies."

"How did you respond?"

"I told him, *Let's get this voyage over first.*"

"Good for you, Mom," Grace said. "I'll talk to you soon. Love you."

Holding back tears, Rosie whispered, "Love you more. Bye."

Rosie gathered her cleaning supplies. "Lord, you are always full of surprises." Picking up broom and dustpan, she declared, "Now I'm ready to leave this safe harbor!"

PART TWO
The Voyage Across the Pond

A ship in the harbor is safe, but that is not what a ship is built for

26

Over the years, many ships had passed through the Chittenden Locks, but this day, all eyes were on the World War II ship MS Restoration.

Back and forth, side to side, the movement began. The *Restoration* slowly made her way from Ballard toward the locks before making her escape to the blue Pacific. Seagulls flew above Rosie's head as she stood on the monkey bridge. Not knowing what to expect, she planted her feet firmly on the deck and grabbed the rail to keep from falling.

"You won't fall on this leg of the trip," Tina said, smiling at Rosie's antics.

Rosie released the rail. "Tina, this is something right out of the pages of one of my adventure novels. I'm actually leaving my safe harbor and heading out to worlds unknown."

As the ship made her way through the Chittenden Locks, friends waved and cheered, and a Messianic congregation danced and sang on the dock as Israeli songs floated through the air.

Rosie stood next to Tina, waving their last farewells to their Seattle friends. Rosie's eyes filled with tears. "Tina, life's journey has few poignant moments, and for me, this is one."

Tina patted her arm. "My dear, before the end of this journey, there will be many more." Tina walked away, leaving Rosie alone to savor her special moment.

The music soon faded as the *Restoration* headed toward Puget Sound.

After they cleared the locks, Stuart gathered the crew for a meeting. "I'll give you a short briefing of the days ahead."

"Haven't we heard this before?" Ellen asked.

Stuart refused to respond to his daughter's sarcasm. "After sailing south along the coast of Washington, Oregon, California, Mexico, and Central America, we'll make our passage through the Panama Canal."

Stuart glanced at Ellen whispering in Daniel's ear. He cleared his throat to get her attention. She rolled her eyes.

"By next week, we'll be in Caribbean waters; we'll cross the Atlantic, and we should arrive in Stockholm by mid-August," Stuart said. "We'll be at sea for approximately thirty days."

"I could be riding my horse back home in Montana. Instead, I'm stuck on this tank," Ellen said as she smacked away on her bubble gum.

"And I could be home playing with my grand—." Rosie caught herself mid-sentence. Instead of joining in with Ellen, she decided to take a walk and enjoy her new surroundings.

Rosie had spent a lot of time thinking about this maiden voyage. After all the *Restoration*'s years in storage, Rosie seriously wondered if the big hunk of steel would make it through the Panama Canal, much less across the Atlantic. The captains vowed that she would, but Rosie was sure that they wondered too.

"Lord, we're not supposed to judge a book by its cover, but in this case, I'm wondering how far this ship will be able to take us."

The answer would come as they moved forward, step by step—in Resti's case, nautical mile by nautical mile.

When she returned from her walk, Captain Alain was still answering questions about the voyage.

"We will slow down at two in the morning to allow the Seattle pilot to disembark. When you wake up, we will be sailing on the Pacific."

Ana-Karin stepped forward. "The Pacific may be a little rough, so I suggest you wear these bracelets to prevent sea sickness. We also have seasickness pills in the infirmary."

"How do you know you won't get seasick if you're wearing one?" Ellen asked.

"It's wise to wear one if you have never been to sea," Ana-Karin said matter-of-factly.

"I'll be fine," Ellen said.

"The decision is yours," Ana-Karin said curtly as Ellen walked away.

Rosie took Ana-Karina's suggestion and placed the bracelet around her left wrist, and as an added precaution, she took a few seasickness pills.

Exhausted from the day's excitement, Jesse and Rosie were in their cabin at nine. They climbed into bed, and within minutes they fell asleep in each other's arms.

Daybreak. Stillness. Silence. They were stopped dead in the water. Rosie sat up, then stood on the bed and looked out the porthole. "It's too soon for something to go wrong!"

"I'll find out what's going on," Jesse said as he buttoned his shirt.

He returned fifteen minutes later, carrying Rosie's morning coffee.

"What happened?"

"The ship's compass broke," Jesse said as Rosie reached for her cup. "Without a compass we could end up anywhere, so it's better we break down now rather than somewhere in the Pacific. Who knows, we could end up in Hawaii."

Rosie smiled. "Hawaii? Hmmm."

"I can't believe we're stranded before we got started! Now it'll take forty days to get to Stockholm," Ellen muttered at breakfast while slurping her coffee.

"Better now than later," Rosie said, repeating Jesse's words.

Ellen glared at Rosie and then grabbed her cup and walked out.

"Did I say something wrong?" Rosie asked Jeans.

"No, but what little I know about Ellen, she probably considered your remark a rebuke. She doesn't like anyone challenging her."

"Especially her father. So, why is she here? It's obvious she's miserable."

"Shelly told me Ellen has been somewhat rebellious since her parents' divorce."

"*Somewhat* is an understatement," Rosie said, sipping her coffee.

"Her mother married a few months after the divorce, and it didn't help when Stuart moved to Alaska and married Shelly a year later."

Rosie shivered at the word *divorce*. "My son was ten when I went through my divorce and he had some rough years."

Jeans looked over to the table where Jesse was joking around with Clive and Henrik. "I didn't know you were married before. You and Jesse act like you've been together forever."

"You could call us kindred spirits," Rosie said. She remembered how the young women in their singles' ministry always related to that remark.

"That sounds nice."

"Yes, we're true soul mates," Rosie added. Then she frowned as she thought of the rebellious daughter. "Tell me more about Ellen."

"Ellen lives on a ranch in Montana with her mother and rich stepfather. Her mom can't do anything with her, so Shelly thought this would be a good bonding time for Ellen and Stuart."

"I hope Shelly's right," Rosie said, shaking her head. "Looking at the situation now, they could either bond or bomb."

"Let's hope for bond," Jeans said, glancing at her watch. "Well, time for work."

Torre announced at lunch that the dock owner was flying a compass to the ship, so they would be up and running in a few hours.

"We won't be stuck in Puget Sound after all," Ellen said, munching on a mouthful of salad.

Rosie didn't dare comment, in fear of setting Ellen off.

Three hours later, the compass was delivered; and within two hours, Henrik had it installed. The roar of the engine and the creaking of the steering mechanism was music to everyone's ears. As the shoreline disappeared, the blue Pacific welcomed the *Restoration* with balmy waters.

Standing on deck, Rosie quoted her favorite saying, "Resti, old gal, you cannot discover new oceans unless you are willing to lose sight of the shore." She took a deep breath. "I'm as willing as I'll ever be, so what are we waiting for?" She patted the ship's sturdy rail. "Let's get going!"

The next morning was clear and warm, so after cleaning the troop mess, Rosie looked for an excuse to go on deck. She volunteered to help Jesse roll up fire hoses, and then afterward, she took a walk on what was now her front yard. She could see why Ellen preferred working outdoors. The fresh air, sunshine, and gentle breezes were invigorating after working in the superstructure all morning. She could soak in the beauty that surrounded her for as far as her eyes could see.

"Lord, I'm enjoying my first cruise. Well, it's not exactly a cruise—I work my tail off for my meals, and there's no fancy lounges to lounge in," Rosie said as she basked in the serenity of her first day at sea.

Too soon, she was jarred out of her sense of well-being.

"Rosie! I need you to help me in the laundry room," Ellen yelled from the superstructure.

"Cinderella's stepsister is beckoning," Rosie said, patting Resti.

"Coming, Ellen."

"There will be a special dinner to celebrate our first day on the Pacific," Urma announced after lunch. By the time the five o'clock bell rang, there was a feeling of fiesta in the air.

The Swedes feasted on grilled salmon, while the Americans opted for grilled chicken. They ate, laughed, and shared their moments of doubts, fears, and faith that had brought them to this place.

"We have much to celebrate. We have been tested many times, but our faith and patience have brought us this far. Our reward is the beautiful, peaceful Pacific," Captain Alain boasted.

"There is truly a God in heaven who has heard our prayers," Torre said, as he took another bite of salmon.

"He better hear us while we're on this boat," Ellen added, munching on her chicken.

As the sun made its way to the edge of the water, Jesse and Rosie strolled in their steel front yard.

"I'm sorry we didn't fly to the Caribbean this summer," Jesse said.

She had forgotten. As the waves gently lapped against the ship, Rosie took Jesse's hand. "This will do just fine. I feel like we're on a special sea cruise—with a mission."

It was inevitable.

"We're in smooth waters, so we'll have our first lifeboat drill in thirty minutes," Stuart announced after breakfast.

"If everything is going so smoothly, why do we need to have a drill?" Ellen asked her father.

Rosie was getting ready to say, *I totally agree!* when Stuart added, "Listen and obey orders—your life may depend on it."

The thought of an emergency at sea that would force the crew to evacuate to lifeboats made Rosie's head spin. It was the same reaction she experienced with typhoid shot number two.

"Step one, go to your cabins and retrieve your life jackets; then wait for the alarm to sound," Stuart instructed.

By the time Rosie stepped in their cabin, Jesse had already fastened his extra-large orange jacket and was holding her size medium in his hand. To keep her mind occupied, she began singing her favorite Bobby Darin song, "*Somewhere beyond the sea, somewhere waiting for me . . .*"

"Rosie, I know you're nervous, but there's nothing to fear. This is only a drill."

"I don't see why we have to do this."

"You sound like Ellen," Jesse said as he handed her the life jacket.

She grabbed it, annoyed that he would compare her with smart-mouthed Ellen.

"What do you suggest we do, Rosie? Wait until the ship starts to sink?"

His comment made her face turn chalk white. She was still fidgeting with her first hook when the alarm blasted for everyone to hit the deck. Jesse helped fasten the rest of her hooks and then stated matter-of-factly, "You need to practice fastening your vest."

"We won't need to use them," she said confidently, trying to snap herself out of such a fearful state.

"Just in case, you need to have this procedure down."

"I know—my life may depend on it," she said as she stepped over the doorway.

They walked briskly down the hall toward the deck, passing Ellen and Daniel standing in the hallway, chatting as if nothing was happening.

Not my business, Rosie thought as she brushed past the two rebels. *Let them dog paddle around in the deep blue sea for a few hours, and then maybe they'll listen up.*

Team One filed into the portside lifeboat while Team Two filled the starboard boat.

Jesse gently pushed Rosie toward the portside lifeboat, but she stopped dead in her tracks.

"I can't get in," she said.

"Yes, you can. I'm right here with you. Now, step in," Jesse said.

She didn't budge.

"What's the holdup?" Ellen shouted from the back of the line.

"Nothing! Just wait your turn!" Rosie yelled. Anger overtook fear as she stepped into the shaky lifeboat.

The boatswains lowered the swaying boats over the sides.

"We won't lower them into the water, but you can get a sense of how it feels," Stuart said.

Sitting in the boat high above the Pacific, Rosie immediately got the idea of what it would feel like to wait in the cold, unsure waters for hours, possibly days, to be saved by a ship passing in the night.

"I've had enough," she told Jesse. "Let me out."

Ellen and Daniel laughed as the boat swayed back and forth. The boatswains carefully guided them back to the deck.

Stuart took Rosie's hand to help her out. "We'll be having several more drills in the course of the journey, until everyone feels comfortable with the procedure."

"I will never feel comfortable with this procedure," Rosie said, stepping onto the secure deck.

"Sure you will," he said, smiling.

"Oh great, more drills—something exciting to look forward to," Ellen said as she climbed out, refusing her father's hand. "Make sure that Rosie is in our boat again. She's a hoot to watch!" Then she walked over and stood next to Daniel.

"Now, Clive will demonstrate how to put out a fire in the engine room," Stuart said, pointing to his stepson, proud of his enthusiasm.

"A *fire*? My, this is getting serious," Ellen said, mocking Stuart.

Jesse and Stuart helped Clive dress in a heavy, fireproof suit and a yellow helmet. He ignored Ellen's remarks as he performed the demonstration.

"My stepbrother looks like a mini-astronaut," Ellen laughed.

"Those two are as different as night and day," Tina whispered in Rosie's ear.

"As different as black and white."

Stuart handed Rosie a fire extinguisher. "Your turn, Rosie."

Ellen giggled as Rosie's trembling hands held the heavy red container.

Rosie aimed at the small fire burning directly in front of her, but missed by a foot. She pulled the plug and repeated the procedure, but missed again. "We'll have no need for lifeboats and fire extinguishers on this journey anyway," Rosie said.

"Amen, sister," Ellen laughed.

"Well, we finally agree on something, *sister*," Rosie said as she dropped the extinguisher in Ellen's arms.

As soon as the wind picked up off the California coast, Rosie devoured two seasickness pills, which still left her feeling drowsy. To keep her mind alert amid the tilting and swaying, she began quoting Psalm twenty-three as she cleaned toilets.

"He leads me beside still waters—"

Tilt—splat. The forward motion knocked Rosie, face-first, into the toilet.

"Enough!" Rosie screamed as she threw the toilet brush across the room and then slammed the door behind her. "I must gather my emotions," she told herself as she ducked and lifted her way toward the deck.

"Rosie, dear, what's wrong? Have you been crying?" Urma asked as she wiped Rosie's face with a dishrag.

"Are you missing your family?" Tina asked.

"Oh, don't worry about me, girls, I'm not crying. I was just attacked by a toilet. I've worn toilet water before, but this is definitely not my scent." She handed Urma her dishrag and pulled out a hankie. By the blank look on their faces, she knew they were clueless.

"You know, toilet . . . toilet water . . . perfume . . . oh, never mind . . . it's no big deal." She changed the subject. "So, what are you up to?"

"We're praying for San Francisco," Tina said. "Will you join us?"

Anything to keep from cleaning toilets. "I'd love to."

After praying for an hour, Rosie began to feel lightheaded, so she made her way to her cabin to rest. She had been sleeping for about twenty minutes when, suddenly, a heavy pressure seized her, tighter and tighter. She was having a hard time breathing. Still in a dreamlike state, she called out, "God, help me . . ."

With every ounce of energy, she sat up. The pressure left. Shaking, she staggered to the head and looked in the mirror. *Was I dreaming, or was it real?* she asked her reflection as she wiped beads of perspiration from her forehead. She bowed her head. "Whatever that was, I thank you, Lord, for watching over me as I sleep."

Twelve-foot swells greeted day six. The ship rocked and rolled all day and into the night, to the rhythm of Ellen's loud music. Too many complaints pushed Stuart to the brink.

"Ellen, your late-night music is keeping your neighbors—and your roommates—awake," he yelled, banging on her cabin door. "Jailhouse Rock" raged as she opened her door.

"What's wrong?" she asked nonchalantly.

"Please, turn Elvis down. There's a ten o'clock curfew, remember?"

Ellen shook her head as she closed the door. "All Shook Up" followed Stuart up the stairs to the bridge.

Rosie had settled into an evening ritual. Her legs often ached from standing and walking on the hard floors all day, so she was content to be horizontal with her books. She had finished Bodie Thoene's *Vienna Prelude* in Seattle, so she was eager to begin *Prague Counterpoint*.

After listening to the news on his shortwave radio, Jesse inserted his earplugs. He could never get used to hearing the Monster Mash, Rosie's nickname for the steering mechanism directly below their cabin. Within minutes, he was out for the night until his next 4 a.m. watch.

Rosie had turned off her reading light and was sleeping soundly when—bang! Something startled her awake. To keep from stumbling around in the dark, she grabbed her flashlight. She followed the noise to the vacant cabin next door. She turned on the overhead light and spied the culprit—a locker banging open-shut-open-shut.

An hour passed when—crash!

"Later!" She pulled the sheet over her head, too tired to pursue the noise. When she made her nightly jaunt to the head, she almost tripped over something lying on the bathroom floor. She closed the head door to keep from waking Jesse and then squinted as she turned on the overhead light. The wind scooper had blown out of the porthole onto the floor.

"Jesse can install it in the morning," she said as she washed her hands, then returned to bed.

She was dozing when—crash! Bang!

"That's it! I've had enough!"

As she slid off the bed, she glanced at Jesse lying in the moonlight shining through their porthole.

"Maybe I'll get some earplugs," she muttered as she dragged herself across the hall. She flinched as another crash greeted her in the hall—the utility closet door was opening and closing to the rhythm of the sea.

"Ellen, you must close the door *tight*," she said as if Ellen was standing in front of her.

Rosie secured the door, and from that night on, she made sure that all items within earshot were securely fastened before turning out the lights.

The swells continued throughout the night into the next day. Deena did her best to prepare a Mexican fiesta, much to Jesse's delight. But after savoring a larger-than-life burrito, Jesse's stomach began to feel queasy. The next day, he passed on dinner when he heard the menu.

"Liver at sea with twelve-foot swells? Someone needs to talk to the galley girls," he said to Rosie as they lay in bed listening to their stomachs growl. She knew her husband too well; he had probably overextended his food intake.

The swells were so bad that Rosie was awakened with what sounded like the storeroom's refrigerator door flying open. The next morning, when Deena found everything from milk to mayonnaise toppled onto the floor, she made a big sign—*Lock fridge door! Tack sa mycket! (Thank you!)*

Day ten brought smoother waters, so Stuart increased the ship's speed from ten to twelve knots. Two knots made a big difference that night—anything that could rattle and vibrate, did. Rosie couldn't take it any longer. She inserted her earplugs. She clung to her bed, wishing the ship had those stabilizers she had heard about. "The sleeping giant has awakened," Rosie moaned.

Around three-thirty in the morning, off the coastal waters of Mexico, the *Restoration* was greeted with a fierce anger.

An unfamiliar dampness filled the air as Jesse dressed for his 4 a.m. shift. A strong wind blew massive sheets of rain into their portholes, forcing Jesse to close them for the first time.

"We won't need these for a while," he said as he tossed the wind scoopers in the corner. "Hi-ho-hi-ho, it's off to work I go," he sang as he kissed Rosie good-bye. "Hold on tight, and I'll see you in the troop mess at eight."

The steering mechanism below their cabin sounded like dragons fighting to keep the ship on course. Rosie feared the roof might cave in at any moment as torrential rain whipped down on the deck above. "So, this is what it's like to be trapped inside the belly of a whale."

Little did she know that in the wee hours of the morning, the MS *Restoration* had received a warning that they were sailing directly toward Hurricane Hector.

27

Something felt strangley familiar to Resti. *The strong winds reminded her of her rough days on the China Sea.*

The purring fans attempted to cool the cabin, but with the portholes closed, the air was too thick to bear. Rosie hooked the cabin door open, allowing air to flow in from the hallway. "Now I won't feel isolated," she told herself. "And I'll be able to hear movement in the hallway in case we're instructed to abandon ship."

Until now, everything on the ship seemed to be battened down, but Rosie jerked as a crash came from the galley storeroom. She glanced at the alarm clock. Six a.m.

An hour later, Rosie heard Deena let out a discouraging, "Oh no! Someone forgot to fasten the hook on the refrigerator door! Pickles everywhere—and my potato salad I made last night is slathered all over!"

"I can't take this," Deena howled. She sounded, and most likely, *looked*, as green as the pickles she attempted to clean off the floor. She had been swollen and nauseated for days. Bracelets, pills—nothing worked.

Rosie decided to brave the turbulence. "If Deena can make her way to the galley, then I can get to the troop mess for—yuk—breakfast," she told herself as she brushed her teeth.

A large wave crashed against the ship as Rosie staggered down the deserted hallway, knocking her against the wall. Her stomach churned with each toss. She had taken her seasickness bracelet off days ago, thinking she had the stomach needed to travel over rough seas. Big mistake.

Rosie held onto the doorknob as she looked around the empty room. "I think I'll skip breakfast too." She felt resilient enough to stumble to the cleaning closet across from her cabin to gather a cleaning bucket and mop.

"Oh!"

Previously neatly-stacked products were scattered on the floor, so she bent over to pick them up.

"Ouch!" A bottle of Windex found Rosie's forehead. She threw the blue plastic bottle in the bucket. "Ellen, you are going to hear about this."

She slowly walked down the hall to the nearest head and bent over the toilet, swishing the brush around, when another big wave hit, tilting her forward—splat!—all over her face.

"Not again!" She grabbed a hankie from her pocket. "That does it! I'll never clean another toilet while sailing on rough seas, and when in doubt, I'll scrub the shower stalls," she vowed.

Rosie left the supplies in the corner of the head and swayed to and fro back to her cabin to recuperate from her unexpected event. She pulled herself up on the bed and prayed, "Lord, I'm scared. Please keep us safe in the midst of this storm."

Rosie grabbed her Bible, embraced it, and then thumbed through the pages, hoping to find some comforting words. Her trembling hands stopped at Isaiah forty-three. She tried to drown out the sound of waves beating against steel by reading out loud. "When you pass through the waters I will be with you, and through the rivers, they shall not overflow you." She sighed. "Okay, this is good." She raised her voice. "Thus says the Lord, who makes a way in the sea, and a path in the mighty waters." She had read these verses before, but today, as the *Restoration* listed back and forth in the mighty Pacific, they gave her the comfort that she desperately needed.

As the ocean's surge tossed the ship with a vengeance, she felt as if she were on a roller-coaster ride. When she was a teenager, she had loved going to the Long Beach Pike with Prissy. They paid twenty-five cents to ride the large wood roller coaster over and over. They lost their stomachs on that crazy ride. But unlike a roller coaster, Rosie had no way of knowing how this unpredictable ride was going to end. Wondering how Jesse was holding out in the engine room, she began praying for him.

Below, in the engine room, Jesse was going through his own roller-coaster experience. His 4 a.m. shift in the engine room began in one-hundred-degree heat. The Finnish second engineer, who spoke very little English, nodded a good morning as Jesse took his place of duty next to the engine lever. Each time the propeller rose out of the water, Jesse made sure the lever didn't drop down and shut off. The worst thing that could happen would be to stop dead in the water. When the large propeller fell back into the water, sweating and nauseated, Jesse staggered to the sink and barfed.

After Jesse spent the first two hours making his way back and forth, Bjorne, the Swedish first engineer, came in for his shift.

"Are you okay, Jesse? You are looking pale," Bjorne yelled over the engine.

"I have to sit here and make sure the engine doesn't cut off."

Bjorne stood over Jesse for a moment. Then he pulled a large rag from his pocket and tied it around the lever. "There! Now you are free!" Bjorne shouted.

Jesse saluted Bjorne, wiped his forehead with a damp cloth, and then walked over and sat by the sink. He placed his head between his legs and wondered why he hadn't figured out that solution on his own.

By 8:15, Jesse was headed for the vacant cabin next door, anxious to fall onto the empty bunk.

Rosie lay in the depths of the *Restoration* praying for Jesse and doing her best to think comforting thoughts. "Remember, sailor, you're on a mission . . . you're on a mission . . ."

As the hours wore on, she hummed, *The sun will come up tomorrow,* until she finally drifted off into slumber.

28

Resti's crew depended on her to weather the storm, so she was determined to prove herself seaworthy, as she had done forty-some years ago.

"We are moving away from the hurricane, and Hector has now turned into a tropical storm," Captain Alain announced the next morning to those who showed up at breakfast.

"What's the difference?" Rosie asked, thankful to have survived the night.

"A hurricane is very serious; a tropical storm is dangerous, but not as critical," the captain explained.

"Does it matter?" Ellen asked. "We're feeling the sea's wrath, no matter what Hector's title is." Rosie could tell Ellen was seasick, but she made it a point to never miss a meal.

Ellen grabbed her tray. "I must report to the bridge for duty. I get to watch Hector from the best seat in the house."

Around nine o'clock Rosie climbed to the bridge and stood in the passageway next to the map room. The windows facing the front of the ship revealed more than she had anticipated. She felt helpless, trapped, and stranded in time.

"Oh, my God!" Rosie gasped. She watched wave after wave pound over the deck, rising to the third story of the superstructure. Riding the turbulence inside her cabin with the portholes closed was one thing. Now, looking through the water-soaked windows of the bridge made the whole experience a raging reality.

"This is it—I'm going to die at sea," she whispered. One look at Stuart confirmed it. No Norwegian laugh. No small talk. He communicated to the engine room by the EOT—Engine Order Telegraph—making one request after another.

"We need more RPMs. We don't have enough to hold into the wind."

Stuart glanced at his daughter, who was standing at the wheel. Ellen's blue eyes stared soberly toward the gray turbulence. For once, she quietly waited for her father's words.

"Midship right away . . . keep straight . . . thirty degrees . . ."

The training Stuart had given Ellen paid off; she obeyed every command, swiftly and correctly.

Rosie took hold of the hallway rail and whispered, "Resti, you're a fighter, so don't give up now."

As the old ship continued to press forward into the gale, Rosie exited down the stairs, leaving father and daughter to bond.

Later that morning, curious to see how things were going, Rosie made her way back to the bridge. The crew with 12-to-4 p.m. shifts were in their positions. Captain Alain stood stoic, speaking sternly to Jeans, who stood at the wheel. He communicated to the engine room via EOT. The captain's steadfast eyes peering out over the ship's flooding deck told her they were in trouble.

Hector's anger roared, covering the *Restoration*'s main deck with the ocean's fury. The two vans secured on deck, covered with large blue tarps, tilted as if they were about to be thrust overboard by the Pacific's rage.

Rosie carefully made her way down the stairs. Once in her cabin, she raised her voice to pray, in hopes of preventing her premature entry into the hereafter.

By mid-day she became restless, so she staggered down the hall, mop and pail in hand, to see if her services were needed in the superstructure. The lights were off in the galley, signaling that the galley girls were off-duty-get-your-own-coffee-and-grub.

Rosie swayed toward the troop mess to check for spills. She glanced in the door and caught a glimpse of Stuart sitting alone, attempting to eat a self-made brunch of burned toast, two hard-boiled eggs, orange juice, and coffee. His somber countenance spoke volumes—he was tired, and stressed. He looked up as Rosie shuffled toward him and forced a smile to give her a sense of security she desperately needed.

"Hi, Rosie. How are you?" he asked as he sipped his juice. A wave hit, causing the liquid to paint his beige shirt a subdued orange.

Rosie was tossed aft. "I've been better. I should have kept my magic bracelet on," she answered, trying to keep the conversation light.

"Aw, this is nothing. Just relax and go with the waves. It'll be over in no time."

"I tried relaxing, but it didn't work. Did the weather report say the storm would be over soon?"

"No, but I can tell by looking at the sky."

Rosie nervously looked through the porthole, but all she could see was massive gray clouds as the rain continued to hit the glass.

Okay, Stuart, whatever.

"Would you like a boiled egg?" he asked.

"No, thanks. I'm having a hard time holding down Ritz crackers."

Just as Stuart picked up an egg to peel, another wave hit, pitching the oval object out of his hand and onto the floor. Rosie held onto the table as they watched the egg roll from one side of the mess to the other. Back and forth. Portside to starboard.

Stuart broke into laughter, and Rosie knew, deep inside, that all would be well.

Rosie took refuge in her cabin. She lay between the fans, stomach churning, as if she were in the depths of her Whirlpool clothes dryer. Sick and tired of the continuous roller-coaster motion, she prayed for Hector to hurry and fade away. "I've had my twenty-five cents worth, thank you. Now I'm ready to hop off."

But unlike the Pike's roller coaster, there was no way for Rosie to exit.

Jesse's daily experience in the engine room was hot, humid, and tiring. Once off duty, he went directly to the next-door cabin to crash and moan.

"Can I get you anything?" Rosie asked, peering in at her husband's ghostlike state.

"No, I'll be okay. By the way, Shelly popped her head in the door a few minutes ago. You're needed at the head next to the office, and take your mop and bucket." Before his head hit the pillow, he did a double take of his wife. "What are you wearing?"

"Just in case," Rosie said, patting her orange life jacket. She knew when Jesse let out a soft chuckle that she had gone too far, so she swayed next door and dropped the jacket in the green chair, and then staggered down the hall to the head.

Rosie gagged as she opened the door. Flowing over the toilet, onto the floor, was evidence of Deena's homemade chili, combined with chunks of onions.

"No way! Who would be stupid enough to eat chili in this storm?" As she turned to make her getaway, *Do unto others* ran through her mind. Rosie stopped, then reluctantly grabbed a mop and dipped it in the suds-filled bucket. Thus began her forced labor of love.

Rosie had no sooner finished wiping the now-gleaming porcelain when her stomach began to churn. She bent over in time to watch her Ritz crackers disappear into the sparkling toilet basin and then run over onto the floor.

"Why isn't this toilet flushing?" she screeched.

The door opened, and Jeans took the mop from Rosie's hand. "Here, let me help you."

"I'm going to complain to the head plumber," Rosie said after she finished barfing up her last cracker.

"I think you better wait until your plumber is feeling better," Jeans said, smiling. "Go to your cabin; I'll take care of this."

Once in bed, Rosie took several deep breaths and did her best to lie still. "Maybe I am trying too hard. I'll do what Stuart advised; I'll go with the waves, and like Esther said in the Bible, if I die, I die."

As Rosie spoke Esther's name, another thought came to her—a fearless thought. She sat up in bed.

"I'm not going down without a fight," Rosie proclaimed. "I know how to pray boldly, and this is as good a time as any to do battle for this ship." She grabbed her Bible.

"Lord, according to your word, I can speak to this mountain to be removed. Right now, Hector is our mountain. So I say, Hector, you be still!" Rosie fell back on her pillow and waited for an answer.

Rosie faded in and out of sleep, dreaming that Hector was inviting his partner, the *Restoration*, to perform an intricate dance. This particular dance would not be a gentle waltz . . . this day the dance would be a tumultuous flamenco, full of fire and passion—a love-hate relationship. And like all flamenco dances, it would soon end.

Rosie slept into the night, and by the next day, the *Restoration* had danced her way out of Hector's arms. The Pacific was once again Resti's waltzing partner.

"May I say a few words to the crew before dinner?" Rosie asked as she glanced over at Ellen sitting next to Daniel, taking a French fry from his plate.

"Of course," Captain Alain answered.

Rosie stood and tapped her fork on a glass to get everyone's attention. "When Ezekiel prayed for the dry bones to rise up, they came back to life. In Seattle, we prayed for the *Restoration*'s bones to rise up, and now she's not only looking good, but she's running beautifully." The crew cheered as Rosie bragged on their ship.

"We would have escaped Hector if she had been faster," Ellen said, chomping on a French fry.

"But she kept trudging ahead, rather than giving up," Rosie reminded Ellen, who responded by her famous rolling of the eyes.

After dinner Ellen invited everyone to the crew's lounge to watch her H. H.—Hurricane Hector—video. The minute she pressed the play button, her roommates gasped. There they were, lying in their bunks, pickle-green, trying their best to ride the waves of Hector. Ellen aimed the video at the porthole as the ship bobbed up and down, and then took aim at the girls, looking as if they were trapped inside of a front-loading washing machine.

"You're cruel to show that video," Henrik said as they watched Deena barfing in a trashcan.

"Good audio too!" Daniel said, laughing. Ellen had finally won Daniel's attention.

Although Hurricane Hector brought many of the crew to their knees, he indeed had brought out the worst in some of those he had tormented.

Everyone was finally feeling normal. Everyone except Deena. She spent most of her time in her bunk, never quite recovering from Hector. And her complexion had a cabbage-green tint, which wasn't a good sign. Rosie couldn't imagine Deena having to suffer through another storm in the Caribbean or while crossing the vast Atlantic.

When Rosie heard Captain Alain and Stuart suggest that Deena take a water taxi to shore in Panama and then fly to Sweden, the galley girl immediately agreed. Rosie figured that she had already mentally begun packing the moment Hector came to torment.

29

Resti *knew this was how life at sea was supposed to be—playing with dolphins, birds, turtles, and whales, not worrying about wars, pirates, and seasickness.*

The water off the coast of Central America was as calm as a sheet of glass. But something was missing. "Where are all the ships?" Rosie asked Stuart while cleaning the bridge.

"The Pacific is a large mass of water with a variety of ship lanes; there's room enough for hundreds of vessels to travel out of sight from each other."

All Rosie could see was water and sky melding together, blending into one large abstract painting. Suddenly Rosie felt alone. She prayed as she walked down the stairs, "Lord, please let me know that we're not alone out here."

During the morning fika break while Rosie walked on deck, she heard strange screeching sounds coming from the front of the ship. She climbed the steps to the bow. "Urma! What are you doing?"

Urma turned and waved. With Urma's feet thrown over the front rail, the screeching, straggly-legged birds landed on either side of her. There she sat in the midst of her feathered friends.

Jeans pointed. "Look, everyone! Urma is sitting with her new groupies!"

"Keep a close watch overhead, Queen Urma!" Ellen warned. "Yuk! Too late!"

Urma screamed and then smiled as she wiped the splotchy white crown off her head with a rag she pulled from her apron. "It's a sign," she said, laughing.

"Aren't you afraid of falling overboard?" Rosie asked, ready to toss her a life buoy.

"Not at all. We Swedes know how to swim!"

Hours later, Rosie was scrubbing the troop mess floor when she heard Henrik shout, "All hands on deck!"

Rosie shuddered. The fire bell wasn't ringing, although they were due for another lifeboat drill. She wouldn't take a chance; she scurried to her cabin and fetched her life jacket, and then walked briskly to the main deck, life jacket securely buckled.

"Why is everyone heading for the bow?" Rosie asked Henrik.

"Look in the water."

Afraid to look, she asked, "Is it a dead body?"

"Rosie, you have been watching too many pirate movies," Henrik said, glancing at her attire. "And why are you wearing your life jacket?"

Ignoring his remark, she peered into the water. "Dolphins!" she shrieked.

"There must be twenty or thirty leaping and swimming in the wake of the bow," Henrik said.

Ellen aimed her video camera at the water. "Look! There's a mother, and her baby is mimicking her every move!"

"Look around, mates!" Stuart shouted from the bridge. "We're traveling at eleven knots, and the dolphins are gliding right along with us."

As far as they could see, dolphins were leaping in and out of the surrounding waters. "They're giving us a special performance," Rosie said as Ellen continued filming.

At sunset Rosie strolled to the bow. "I want to be like Urma, bold and brave." But as she threw her right leg over the rail, her eyes caught a glimpse of a wave crashing against the ship. "Oh! I'm not ready for this!"

Rosie was walking toward the superstructure, feeling weak and defeated, when she heard Jeans laughing on the port side of the ship.

"What's going on?" Rosie asked.

Jeans was peering through her binoculars, Daniel standing at her side, Ellen close by Daniel's. "There's a mysterious-looking bird walking on the water."

"I've never seen anything like this on the Discovery Channel," Ellen said.

"Perhaps this should be on the Miracle Channel," Urma said.

Ellen strained her eyes. "Look closer, Urma. The bird isn't walking on the water." Suddenly, a large turtle emerged from beneath the surface.

"That bird is standing on top of a huge turtle!" Rosie said.

Then, as if the turtle knew he had a captivated audience, he submerged, leaving his rider to once again glide along the top of the Pacific.

"I've heard of the tortoise and the hare; now there's the tortoise and the bird," Ellen said, trying to be funny for Daniel, but he had already walked away with Jeans.

Rosie gave a polite giggle for Ellen's sake, but she was already trailing close behind Daniel.

The tortoise and the bird made Rosie temporarily forget her moment of defeat. She would try again later, but for now, she prayed, "Thank you, Lord, for showing me that we're not alone at sea."

The next afternoon, as they neared the coast of Panama, Stuart announced from the bridge, "It's whale-watching time!"

Binoculars in hand, the crew spied several pilot whales romping in the surrounding waters.

"We're having our own SeaWorld," Rosie said gleefully.

"When we get to Sweden, I'm going to use the birthday money Mom gave me to buy a pair of binoculars," Jesse said as he peered through Stuart's expensive ones.

Rosie kissed Jesse's cheek. "If anyone deserves a nice pair of binoculars, it's you, my handsome sailor."

Jesse grabbed her waist. "If you keep that up, I might let you borrow them."

Rosie looked up at the sun. "Isn't it time for a little afternoon delight . . . I mean . . . fika?"

Jesse glanced at his watch. "It's exactly three o'clock. Now you're telling time by the sun . . . you are becoming quite the sailor."

At sunset, Stuart shouted over the bridge speaker, "Land ahoy!"

Out of nowhere, ships of all shapes and sizes began appearing.

"It looks like our California freeways," Rosie told Tina.

"Do you miss California?" Tina asked.

"I don't miss the crazy traffic," Rosie answered. "But I admit that I'm relieved to see land."

Tina pointed to the ships. "They are waiting their turn to go through the Panama Canal. The *Restoration* will soon find her place in line. Because of her age, she will have specific inspections to pass before she is allowed to travel through the three large locks."

Rosie patted the rail. "Poor Resti, her age is always being thrown in her face."

"We can relate to that," Tina chuckled. "The engineers are preparing for the passage. The canal is on a tight schedule, so one ship's breakdown could tie up the canal for hours."

"Breakdown?" Rosie asked.

"Any engine problems in the canal could cost us an enormous amount of money."

And so, the *Restoration* waited in the harbor for her passage.

Three sticky days later, two Panamanian inspectors, Jose and Fernando, arrived on the pilot boat to begin the inspection.

"When we heard that a World War II ship was scheduled to pass through the locks, we were curious. May we have a tour of the vessel before we begin the tests?" Jose asked.

"Absolutely," Captain Alain said, eager to show off the *Restoration*, especially to the doubting port inspectors. He had been a captain long enough to know that Jose and Fernando would be surprised at her condition.

After the tour, Fernando remarked with little expression, "Now, let us see what her engine can do."

The captains and the inspectors disappeared into the superstructure while the crew remained on deck. Henrik volunteered to be the crew's spy.

After each test, Henrik scurried down from the bridge to give the results, and then he dashed back up to the bridge until the following test was completed. The results were always the same—the *Restoration* passed with flying colors.

"There is one final test. Due to her age, the engine has to successfully stop and restart three times in succession," Tina explained.

Rosie rubbed the rail. "Okay, Resti, no matter what your age, you will not fold under pressure. You will take these tests in stride, like everything else you've done so far."

The crew held their breath each time the chief engineer was instructed to turn the engine on, then off.

Inhale—engine on—exhale. Thank you, God.

Engine off.

Inhale—engine on—exhale. Thank you, God.

Engine off.

Inhale—engine on—exhale. Thank you, God!

"The MS *Restoration* has passed all of her inspections!" Captain Alain announced over the loudspeaker. Cheers resonated throughout the ship.

Jose shook his head as he confessed to the captain, "All the inspectors in the office waged bets on whether this old vessel would pass her inspections. We're pleased to see how well she has done."

"This vessel is in very good condition; she can go anywhere," Fernando added.

The words were welcome assurance to the captain's ears, and they were like *music* to the crew's ears.

"Resti, today you have really strutted your stuff!" Rosie proclaimed.

Captain Alain prepared to call for a water taxi to pick up Deena, but Fernando insisted on taking her ashore. "We will save the senorita time and money."

It was a bittersweet moment as Deena bid the crew good-bye, but it became more on the bitter side as she looked down the side of the ship. She froze in her tracks.

"I'm petrified to climb over the rail!"

"Senorita, this is the only way you can get off the ship," Fernando said. He smiled and then climbed over the rail. "Here, let me help you."

On cue, Deena hoisted herself over the ship's side and then slowly made her way down the wobbly ladder. She lost her balance and screamed.

That was Rosie's cue. "Hold on, Deena! You can do it!" Then she whispered, "Your freedom depends on it, girlfriend."

Everyone sighed in relief as Deena jumped onto the inspection boat without putting a mark on her Lane Bryant pantsuit.

"See you in Sweden!" Deena yelled, waving as the boat sped off, causing her to lose her balance and fall into Fernando's arms.

"I think Deena will enjoy her ride," Tina teased.

"Especially if she keeps losing her balance," Rosie said, chuckling.

Once in the office, Rosie could tell by the solemn look on Captain Alain's face that something was wrong. Frowning, he gave Stuart the news. "Before disembarking, Jose advised me of the amount of money we will need to pay the Panama office before we can pass through the canal."

"How much?" Stuart asked.

"The amount is much greater than we expected," he said. "I'll use the ship's mobile phone to contact Sweden immediately so they can wire us the money."

After leaving several messages, the mission department secretary returned Captain Alain's calls.

"Hallo," he answered cheerfully.

"As you know, we have finished the summer conference, and now the offices are closed," the secretary reported.

"No, I did not know," he answered.

"Every year after the conference, the staff goes on holiday for a week."

"Please have someone call me as soon as they return," Captain Alain answered, obviously disappointed.

After dinner, Stuart made the announcement that they would be laid up in the harbor for a week.

"We're stranded for a week? That's just great!" Ellen said as she rose from her table. "Here we sit while they're on a holiday. Why wasn't anyone organized enough to have the money available to us?"

Stuart frowned as he watched his daughter walk out. "Don't be upset with her. Ellen only stated what the crew is thinking," Shelly said, glancing at Rosie. She nodded her agreement.

"But why does she have to be the one who always does the verbalizing? Why can't she keep her mouth shut?" Stuart picked up his empty cup and headed for the galley.

The days dragged. To pass the time, the girls sat on deck with their fans, drinking iced tea and shooing mosquitoes while they counted the ships passing by on their way to their destinations. Rosie wrote in her journal in between swatting:

A large container vessel is transporting Volvos from Sweden; a larger container ship is bringing BMWs from Germany. Empty oil tankers are heading back to the Middle East, beautiful yachts are sailing to the Caribbean, and cruise liners are heading for exotic ports of call. And look—a huge yellow Dole Pineapple ship is carrying thousands of pineapples to the east coast, and there's a small destroyer escorting a submarine to some unknown destination.

Daily, Rosie sat writing, sweating profusely and drinking enough tea to float her to Sweden. Having read *Danzig Passage* made her wonder when the *Restoration* would make her passage.

For safety reasons, Captain Alain requested that no one go ashore, and although they were surrounded by water, he asked the crew to refrain from swimming due to notorious varmints lurking beneath the surface.

But Daniel couldn't take the mosquitoes or the isolation any longer. Or maybe he couldn't handle all the rules. He shed his T-shirt and then dove into the water, only to climb up the porta-ladder covered with large red bites on his muscular arms and legs, tanned back, and other unmentionable places. Ana-Karin couldn't figure out what had bitten him, but Daniel's wounds convinced the crew they were better off sitting on deck swatting annoying mosquitoes.

"I'll be glad to put some lotion on your bites, Daniel," Ellen volunteered.

"No, that's okay," he answered.

"Would you like a glass of iced tea?" Jeans offered.

"I'd love some," Daniel said. He then followed Jeans to the galley, leaving Ellen standing with a full bottle of mosquito repellent.

After dinner, Rosie overheard Daniel talking with several of the young crew in the troop mess. Clive and Henrik walked out. Twenty minutes later while Rosie stood shaking a dust mop over the side of the railing, she heard a motor start up. Her eyes widened as she observed the ship's skiff cruising out toward the shoreline filled with four rebels.

"Captain Daniel, come back for me!" Ellen yelled.

"I feel a mutiny coming on," Rosie said to Jeans as they watched the small boat turn around.

Captain Alain was standing at the porta-ladder when Daniel returned for Ellen.

"You cannot take the skiff," he scolded Daniel. "We must do everything possible to prevent any unexpected accidents."

"You worry too much, Captain Alain," Daniel said sarcastically as he watched the captain walk away.

Stuart walked up to lend a hand with the skiff. "Sorry, guys, but no matter how harmless it seems, you have to obey the captain's orders."

"Well, it's obvious the captain isn't worried about winning any popularity contests," Ellen said over her shoulder as she followed on the heels of Daniel.

"Daniel doesn't take orders too well," Jeans told Rosie. "He's used to doing things his way; that's how he got into trouble back home."

"How do you know so much about him?" Rosie asked nonchalantly.

"Sometimes we talk at night on the monkey bridge," Jeans admitted.

"What kind—" Rosie caught herself. She wanted to know what kind of trouble Daniel had been in, but thought it best not to pry.

The superstructure and the holds held hot, stuffy air. Rosie spent most of her nonworking hours in the shade of the steamy deck. She kept track of the days they were held hostage by writing in her journal.

Four days, five days. No breeze, only mosquitoes.

By day six, Rosie was pacing the deck. Tina sensed what Rosie was feeling, so she took the opportunity to recite one of her favorite *vitamin* scriptures at morning prayer. "This will get you through the day: Don't try to get out of anything prematurely. Let patience do its work so you'll become mature and well-developed, not deficient in any way." Tina smiled at Rosie. "If there's one lesson to be learned here, it is the P word."

"The P word?" Ellen asked from the far corner.

"Patience," Rosie answered. "Thanks, Tina. Some of us needed to hear that." She glanced at Ellen before climbing the stairs.

After lunch, Captain Alain announced, "We have received a wire transfer from Sweden, so we must prepare to sail."

Rosie wrote in her journal: *Patience works! Our prayers were answered today, and I believe our cheers could be heard all the way to the other end of the Panama Canal.*

The *Restoration* neared the canal entrance at sunset. The sun was the size of a tangerine, but slowly disappeared by the time the vessel began her passage through the first set of locks. Rosie donned her mosquito-netted hat and joined the stewards and galley girls on the monkey bridge to view the event.

"Two Panamanian pilots and their crew boarded and took their places at the helm," Shelly informed the women. Rosie was always impressed by Shelly's knowledge of the sea. "This is the only time a captain must give place at the helm to the expertise of a local pilot. The locks have areas where there are only two-foot spaces on each side of the ship."

Once darkness fell, the dock's bright lights allowed the crew to view each procedure. The first three locks were similar to Seattle, but on a much larger scale. The large locomotives, called "mules," were hooked to the ship to pull her through to keep her from touching either side of the dock. She moved slowly at two knots.

Rosie forced herself to go to bed around midnight, but she woke up every hour and leaned against the hull and gazed out of the porthole. Green and red lights lit the shoreline to guide the ship. Trees draped in moss gave off a Disneyland feel. Rosie was ten years old again, riding the jungle ride. Jesse slept, too tired to get the Disneyland feeling.

Rosie finally dozed off, wondering what the morning would bring.

30

Resti had plowed through Hurricane Hector, passed the Panama Canal's inspections, and now she was cruising on Caribbean waters. Someone was definitely watching over the old gal.

"Here is your morning coffee, madam. If you go on deck, you can experience the lovely Cara-bee-un sunshine," Jesse said in a West Indies accent.

Rosie chuckled at her husband's antics. "Thank you, mahn," she answered, and then hurried on deck to capture the Caribbean feeling. A hot and sticky morning greeted her, minus the Panamanian mosquitoes. After morning prayer, she found a place next to Ellen at breakfast.

"This isn't the season to be sailing in the Caribbean," Ellen said, taking the last bite of her pancake.

Rosie looked up from her plate. "Why do you say that?"

Since working on the bridge as a helmsperson, Ellen kept Rosie updated on the weather conditions. "Haven't you heard? This is hurricane season."

Rosie dropped her fork. "What?"

"That's right," Ellen said, wiping syrup from her lips. "The delays in Seattle and Panama forced us to sail at the height of the season. Why do you think we met up with Hector?"

The desire for breakfast suddenly disappeared, but Rosie tried to act unaffected by Ellen's remarks. She pulled out her lip gloss from her pocket. "I'm finished. Ellen, would you like the rest of my pancakes?"

Ellen grabbed Rosie's plate and delved into the warm pancakes covered with butter and maple syrup. Nothing seemed to interrupt Ellen's appetite. Rosie excused herself to go to the galley for a glass of water. With an upset stomach, the last thing she needed was to watch Ellen scarf down her food.

At twilight, Rosie sat on the Fiesta Deck, keeping a close watch for any sign of hovering clouds. She was relieved when only a velvet breeze swayed the ship to and fro. She watched luxury cruise ships passing in the night, their music traveling across the sea and their bright lights flickering on the water. Rosie imagined the fun and games going on, mingled with food galore.

Later in her cabin, she wrote: *The muggy nights in my cabin are insufferable. As our surround-sound fans hum nonstop, their currents of moving air try to make the room bearable. Earlier tonight while relaxing in a plastic deck chair, I watched a Carnival ship sail toward another fun-filled destination. Then as I gazed up at the star-filled sky, I was content to be on my own private cruise, sipping donated Starbucks. I am right where I'm supposed to be, and no amount of loud music, bright lights, and gourmet food can bring me this kind of satisfaction.*

Tina and Rosie had something in common—they loved to sunbathe. They spent most of their afternoon breaks at the Restoration Day Spa—the monkey bridge—soaking up the sun, the therapeutic warmth penetrating their tired bodies. After an hour, Rosie would head to her cabin to take a cool shower—part of the day-spa experience—leaving Tina alone to read and doze for a few extra minutes.

How many people can gaze at the ocean while showering? Rosie thought, looking out of the porthole from her shower stall while the water cooled her sun-kissed shoulders. *Not many,* she mused.

Around three in the morning, the *Restoration* stopped dead in the water. Just as the ship's constant noise lulled Rosie to sleep each night, so the absence of the roaring engine woke her. She sat up in bed, feeling helpless and scared. After she shook Jesse awake, he dressed and went to see what was going on.

Captain Alain had been prewarned in Seattle of Haiti's volatile and unpredictable political climate. The Haitian patrol gave strict orders, via radio, forbidding all ships to sail near their island. They knew the consequences of not heeding the warnings—arrest, and most likely, jail.

Twenty minutes later Jesse returned wearing a solemn look. "We've accidentally entered Haiti's troubled waters. The old third captain's lack of the English language has proven to be detrimental—he failed to heed the patrol's warnings."

Rosie stared at her husband, speechless.

"The patrol boat is alongside of the ship. They're coming aboard to search."

Rosie's heart felt as if it would pound through her chest. "We don't have anything to hide! Will they arrest us? Will they put us in jail?" Before Jesse could answer, she blurted, "I guess they can do whatever they want; we're in *their* waters."

Jesse kissed Rosie's cheek. "Stay here and remain calm. I'll be back when I have more news."

Rosie knew she was going to throw up, so she took her praying position next to the toilet. As she knelt, her mind ran wild. This was nothing like the Caribbean cruises that John and Barbara had always bragged about.

Rosie was still kneeling when the door opened. She was thinking *handcuffs* when she looked up to see Jesse standing in the doorway.

"Are you okay?" Jesse asked as he helped her up.

"That depends." Her eyes begged for a positive report, but his eyes said negative. "The captain talked to the police and apologized for our mistake. They're communicating to the mainland on what to do with us."

Rosie fell backward into the green chair. Jesse bent down and took her chin. "This isn't the time to draw back, Rosie. We need to pray that we have favor with the mainland police."

Rosie nodded in agreement as she looked into his cool, calm eyes.

"Where's Tina? I want to be with her," Rosie said, rising from her chair.

"She's in her cabin. It's better you stay here," he said, sitting her back down. "And you might want to lock the door behind me."

Click.

"Oh, God, I'm too nervous to pray. I ask for your angels to protect us . . . and please, Lord, I don't want to go to prison!"

An hour later there was a knock on the latched door. "Who is it?"

"It's me," Jesse shouted through the door.

She fumbled with the lock. "Well?"

"After the captain explained that we would leave the vicinity immediately . . ."

"What?"

"Let me finish, Rosie." Then he smiled. "They reluctantly agreed, but they're going to keep a close watch on us until we're out of their waters."

Rosie fell into the chair. "No handcuffs after all. Thank you, Lord!"

"They've never seen a ship like the *Restoration* in their waters, so they were quite concerned."

Rosie laughed nervously. "Come to think of it, we haven't seen a ship like Resti sailing in *any* waters. Let's pray she doesn't draw any more unwelcome attention."

Once again the engine roared.

"Come on, Resti, let's get as far away as possible from this danger zone."

"There's a great swell pushing us away from the Bermuda Triangle, which is unusual for this time of year," the captain announced at morning prayer.

"I didn't think anything was unusual with God," Ellen said, pointing to heaven.

"Ellen, you are absolutely right," the captain said, trying his best to be polite.

"I didn't know we were near the Bermuda Triangle! Hopefully we'll get away from here and make up for lost time," Ellen commented as she made her way toward the galley.

"It's good to see you at prayer, Ellen," Rosie said as Ellen brushed past.

Ellen stopped, her eyes narrowing. "I'm not a morning person."

Recalling Elvis blaring from Ellen's cabin into the wee hours, Rosie couldn't help herself. "Well, maybe you should try going to bed a little earlier."

Instead of retaliating, as Ellen usually did, she silently walked out.

"See if I ever share my pancakes with you again," Rosie muttered as she exited the superstructure. She needed to be alone—to cool off—but instead she ran into Ellen, staring out to sea. Rosie's first thought was to turn the other way, but she gritted her teeth and kept walking.

When Ellen caught sight of Rosie, she started to walk into the superstructure, but before she could escape, Rosie asked, "When did you become an Elvis fan?"

Ellen's face softened. "When my brother was little, he tried to say Ellen, but all that came out was something that sounded like Elvis."

Rosie smiled. "That's cute. I've been an Elvis fan for years; I even named my son after him."

Ellen's eyes widened. "You named your son Elvis?"

Rosie smiled. "Oh, no, nothing that extreme. I named him Presley."

"Presley's a cool name. When my brother and I were teenagers, we started collecting Elvis records. Every time I hear an Elvis song, I think of Josh . . . he's a real character."

"Where's Josh now?"

Ellen frowned. "He took Mom and Dad's divorce real hard, so he dropped out of high school and left home." Ellen cleared her throat. "I felt even more abandoned after he left."

"Do you ever talk to him?" Rosie asked.

"No, but I wish he were here," she said, blinking back tears.

"I know how it is to be rejected."

"You? Miss Perfect with your perfect life?" Ellen asked, looking into Rosie's eyes.

"It's almost perfect, but it wasn't always. My first husband chose his friends over me, so we divorced when Grace was only one. But Paul admitted later that he wasn't ready to settle down."

"Did Grace ever see him again?"

"Oh, yes. Their story has a happy ending. They reunited when she was eighteen."

Rosie took a deep breath. "Then, after sixteen years of marriage, my second husband had an affair with a younger woman."

"And what about your kids?"

"Bob dumped me, but he never stopped loving Presley and Grace. And for that, I am grateful." Chuckling, Rosie added, "As the saying goes, I was no *spring chicken*, but I never considered thirty-eight as being *over-the-hill*."

Ellen stared at Rosie. "How can you laugh about such a horrible thing as divorce?"

"I know it sounds cliché, but time can heal all wounds—it's our choice."

Ellen shook her head. "I'll never forgive my mother for leaving me and my brother. Sure, she said she'd come back, but not before she kicked Dad off the ranch and moved her boyfriend in."

Rosie could see the pain on Ellen's face as if it had happened yesterday. "It took more than time to heal me, Ellen. I had to ask God for help. He began to change my heart, and eventually my circumstances started taking a new direction."

"I don't believe in God anymore," Ellen said harshly. She glanced at her watch. "Well, it's time to get to work. See you in the laundry room."

Rosie watched as Ellen walked into the superstructure. "Yes, Ellen, you're a character too, but God loves characters."

As Rosie walked toward the superstructure, she whispered, "Lord, help me love Ellen the way you do."

Ellen and Rosie stood back-to-back sorting dirty clothes as the midday sun bore down on the steel roof.

"As soon as we arrive in Sweden, I'm flying back to the conveniences of the good old USA," Ellen said, wiping her forehead with a hankie.

Rosie searched her pocket for her handkerchief. "Ah yes, those luxuries I've taken for granted. Too hot—turn the switch, and voila!—cool air!"

"Oh, here—I forgot to give this back," Ellen said, handing her a familiar-looking stained cloth.

"Keep it," Rosie said, wiping the sweat on her T-shirt. "I've got more in my cabin."

Ellen turned to walk out of the furnace big enough for only two washing machines and two dryers. "I've got to get some air."

A north wind tossed a pile of just-sorted towels onto the floor, and then a wave knocked Rosie from one wall to the other. She kicked the dryer and stubbed her big toe, which didn't help her already-sinking morale.

"What am I doing here?" she murmured, looking upward. "What does sorting greasy work clothes and washing dirty overalls have to do with my so-called destiny?"

She stopped complaining long enough to hear, *I have called you to sort dirty laundry because I am refining you for the days ahead.*

"*Refine?* I studied that word in Bible school. It means to remove impurities in order to become more elegant." She recalled how the Israelites had to be refined before they were allowed to enter the Promised Land. It took them forty years.

"Lord, are you saying I have impurities to deal with?"

There was an uncomfortable silence. She hesitated before asking the big question.

"Like, what?"

Like, pride.

She knew she shouldn't have asked.

"Pride? Me?"

She remembered, and then quoted a verse from Isaiah. "Do you see what I have done? I have refined you, but not without fire. I've tested you, like silver in the furnace of affliction."

She leaned against the dryer. "I get it. I'm in this laundry room to be refined, so I can do what you've called me to do—with a joyful heart."

She picked up a towel and began folding. "It looks like I might be baking in this humid little laundry room for a long time, but hopefully not forty years!"

Resti helped turn Rosie's mundane tasks into fun little games. Each morning Rosie stood on one side of the room and waited for the next wave to roll any loose objects to the middle of the floor; then she'd sweep the nuts, bolts, and hardened green peas into her dustpan. Afterward, she'd take her dancing partner—the mop—and glide from one end of the room to the other, swaying to the rhythm of the sea until the black and white tiles glistened.

One morning Ellen caught Rosie dancing in the troop mess.

"What are you doing?" Ellen asked.

Rosie quickly picked up the bucket. "Oh, I was just cleaning . . . and thinking about my friends . . . and wondering how they would adjust to living on this ship without the luxuries of home."

"My friends would hate it. This indoor cleaning is driving me crazy, but at least I get to spend my afternoons working on deck," Ellen said as she swept a bolt into her dustpan and then exited the troop mess.

"I'm glad you're on deck too, so I don't have to listen to your complaining," Rosie murmured.

Ellen turned around. "What did you say?"

"Oh, uh, I said that I'm glad you're on deck too so you can help with the painting."

After lunch Rosie made her way to the monkey bridge for her afternoon day spa. She looked forward to spending an hour reading, writing, and chatting with Tina.

Tina positioned herself to face the sun and then spread her yellow towel on a rusted lounge chair. She fidgeted in her orange tote bag for her Bible and tanning lotion.

"To be honest, Tina, I'm surrounded by all this water, and yet I feel as if I'm alone in a drought."

Tina turned a few pages in her Bible. "Listen to this from Isaiah. 'Jehovah shall always guide you and satisfy your soul in drought and make fat your bones. And you shall be like a watered garden, and like a spring of water, whose waters fail not.'" Tina closed her Bible and then reached for her lotion.

Rosie patted her expanding waistline. "I can do without the fat bones, thank you."

Tina pulled her hair into a ponytail, looking as Swedish as she sounded. "Did you ever think that God might be turning your adventure-at-sea into your restoration-at-sea? You do not have to be in the middle of the ocean to feel alone."

Rosie nodded. "Yeah, I've been in a room surrounded by people and felt so alone that I wanted to walk out. Like the night I showed up at the singles' meeting and stood waiting by the door for my cowboy."

Tina smiled as she remembered Rosie's story of the night she met Jesse. "But you see, you were in the room full of strange singles, but God was guiding you, just as he is now," she said, rubbing Coppertone on her shoulders.

"I think you mean *strangers*," Rosie corrected.

"Oh, yes, that's what I meant! Sometimes my English is not so good!" Tina laughed. "But I imagine there were a few strange singles there, but you only had eyes for one handsome cowboy."

Rosie dozed for a few minutes and then glanced over at Tina. She needed to talk to her friend about something that had been on her mind since she boarded the ship.

"Tina, do you believe there are angels traveling with us?" If anyone could set Rosie straight, it would be her Swedish friend.

Tina casually placed her sunglasses on with her left hand and then waved her right arm, as if she were pointing toward an invisible object. "Absolutely! We are surrounded by angels."

"Have you seen any angels lately?" Rosie asked, looking toward Tina's right arm.

Tina paused. "No, but that does not mean they are not here." She looked straight at Rosie. "Why? Have *you* seen any?"

Rosie pointed in the direction of hold two. "When we were in Seattle, I saw a large shadow down below. At first it felt strange, but then a peaceful feeling came over me."

"On special occasions, God allows us to see angels."

Rosie sighed as she lay back in her chair. "Well, I'm still not sure it was an angel."

Tina gathered her belongings. "I have something for you. I will bring it to your cabin before dinner."

"Do you have a book on angels?"

"No," Tina chuckled. "Just a little something that might cheer you up."

Tina stopped by Rosie's cabin on her way to dinner, carrying a Fred Meyer bag.

"Oh, Tina, you shouldn't have," she said as she pulled out a wild-looking blouse.

Tina patted her waistline. "I had fun wearing it, but now it's too small."

In her wildest imagination, Rosie couldn't picture prim and proper Tina wearing the brown and black spotted blouse. *Hmmm, perhaps I need to take a closer look at this conservative Swedish woman,* Rosie thought, smiling.

The problem was, Rosie didn't *do* leopard. Leopard was not her style. But she would not offend Tina. "Thank you so much. Now it's my turn to have fun wearing it," Rosie said as she gave her friend a hug.

"Are you feeling better?" Tina asked softly.

"Much better. After talking with you, I don't feel alone. If I may quote a familiar saying, *You can fool some of the people all the time, and you can fool all the people some of the time, but you can never fool God.*"

"We have a quote something like that in Swedish," Tina said, chuckling.

"With God's help, I'm going to face each situation head-on."

"Remember, Rosie, you are not alone."

"Yes, I know."

Rosie closed the door and then forced the leopard into her already-jam-packed locker, wondering when she would ever have the nerve to wear it.

31

As the Restoration *glided over the vast Atlantic, she noticed that the California lady was keeping her own personal hurricane watch.*

Most of the crew came to dinner showered, but this particular evening as Rosie walked past the table where Arne, Bjorne, and Lennart sat, the combined odors of fuel oil and grease—mixed with garlic—began to eat away at her appetite. She mashed her boiled potatoes with her fork, glaring at their table, all the time trying to keep her emotions intact.

Ellen reached for her second roll. "Those men should have the consideration to shower before they come to dinner. It's enough to make me lose my appetite."

"I don't see that happening anytime soon," Rosie teased as she watched Ellen slather butter on the roll. "But I sure have to agree with you on this one."

Tina spoke up before Rosie had a chance to continue. "It's hard for the men to be away from their loved ones for so long. They work into the night to fill the empty hours, so you can understand why they don't shower before dinner."

"I guess you have a point," Rosie said.

"Humph," Ellen muttered through a mouthful of potatoes.

Tina glanced at Rosie. "Our men are fortunate to have us here."

Tina took the wind out of Rosie's sail, but lit a fire under Ellen.

Ellen gathered her plate and utensils. "Well then, I guess I better go find me a man! Hey, Daniel!" Ellen yelled across the room. "Have you showered?"

Before he nodded, she was halfway to his table. "Great! Then I'll join you for dessert."

"I don't think Ellen understood my point," Tina said.

"Does she ever?" Rosie asked, smirking.

Rosie watched Arne and Bjorne laughing at one of Lennart's jokes. Lennart's wife and two children were waiting for him in Stockholm, Arne's girlfriend was missing him in Uppsala, and Bjorne spent most of his time pining for his bride-to-be that he left behind in Seattle. Working and eating together day after day gave the men comfort while they were separated from their loved ones. The smell of grease and oil faded by the time Rosie finished her dessert.

Rosie walked briskly to the weekly Thursday night Operation Jabotinsky meeting in hold two. The large room was full. The only unoccupied seat was a folding chair next to Ellen, so she sat down and opened the notebook that Tina had handed out to the crew in Seattle.

Ellen thumbed through her pages. "Where are we?"

"Oh, that's right, you weren't here last week," Rosie replied matter-of-factly. "We talked about our Jewish heritage and what they have given us."

"And what's that?" Ellen asked, placing her smudged glasses on her sunburned nose.

"The Bible," Rosie whispered.

Ellen turned toward Tina. "Okay, I'm ready."

Tina slowly turned the pages of her notebook, not feeling one bit intimidated by Ellen. "Tonight we will discuss the peresecution of Jews throughout history. Anti-Semitism, secular or religious, should not be accepted. The Christian church needs to be aware of what they have done to the Jews in the past."

"Like the Crusaders?"

Tina looked at Ellen. "Very good, Ellen."

Ellen grinned. "I studied world religions in college."

Tina continued. "Israel is foremost on God's prophetic agenda. If you want to know where we stand in his timetable, read the Bible and look to Israel. The news media will be covering the Middle East and Israel more in the days ahead."

"Is the news media biased?" Ellen asked. "And does God love the Palestinians?" When Ellen did show up, she came full of questions.

"Yes, and yes. Of course, God loves the Palestinians," Tina answered. "God has blessed the Arab nations with much land, oil, and riches. However, God has chosen the Jews and the Jewish nation of Israel to show his timetable to mankind throughout the ages. In Genesis seventeen, God promised Ishmael a huge family and a great nation. Then God made an everlasting covenant with Isaac."

Tina thumbed through her Bible. "This is where we come in. Who would like to read?" Tina looked around the room, happy to see that she had everyone's undivided attention. Jeans raised her hand to volunteer, and began, "Surely the isles shall wait for me, and the ships of Tarshish first, to bring thy sons from afar, their silver and their gold with them, unto the name of the Lord thy God, and to the Holy One of Israel, because he hath glorified thee."

"I've never heard this before," Ellen said, adjusting her glasses. She read the scriptures again to herself.

"The ships of Tarshish are the Gentile nations. Today that includes you and me," Jeans explained. Her love for Israel showed in the hours she spent studying the Bible. "By working on the *Restoration*, we've become a living part of these Old Testament prophecies coming to pass."

A sense of fulfillment flooded Rosie as she closed her Bible. "So that makes my steward tasks a privilege," Rosie said proudly.

"I guess you could say that, if you call cleaning hairy shower stalls and scrubbing soiled toilets some kind of privilege," Ellen chuckled.

Before Rosie could comment, Tina closed in prayer. Ellen quickly looked at her watch. "Well, enough of this serious talk. In fifteen minutes, there's going to be a few hot games of Tile Rummy in the captain's mess." She glanced at Rosie. "Are you going to join us?"

"I'm not sure," Rosie answered.

"Well, don't say I didn't ask."

While everyone filed out, Jesse motioned for her from across the room. He read her lips, *Later.* After he nodded, Rosie moved to a more comfortable chair. Tina tapped her on the shoulder. "Why don't you come to the captain's mess with us?"

"I need some time alone."

Tina smiled. "Of course. Turn off the lights on your way out."

Rosie was satisfied to sit alone in the quiet, freshly painted living area of hold two. "I'm sitting in this room, on this World War II ship, participating in prophecy. And in a few weeks, these rooms will be filled with Russian Jews."

Suddenly, she didn't feel alone. She looked over her shoulder just as a tall dark shadow passed through a distant hallway.

"Hello," she called out.

No reply.

That was enough. Rosie gathered her notebook and Bible, and then climbed the stairs in record time, flipping the light switch to the off position. She took a deep breath as her feet hit the deck, glad to be topside.

Rosie paused for a moment to look at the star-filled sky. She had stopped many times to admire God's creation, but this evening, as the waves repeated their pattern and the sea's mist moistened her face, she heard a voice whisper, *Notice the waves. They never stop. They continue rolling. That's how my love is for you—never-ending.*

"God, I cannot fathom your love," Rosie whispered into the wind. "But as long as I stay in the center of your will, I can feel your love—even on this old ship, in the middle of the Atlantic."

She caught sight of Tina entering the superstructure. "Hey, Tina, wait up! I think I'll play some Tile Rummy after all."

There were those who sought various forms of evening entertainment, so besides scheduling the weekly International Ping Pong Tournament, Henrik established the almost nightly IGN—International Game Night—in the captain's mess. Jeans was in charge of the popcorn, and Shelly brewed the coffee while Henrik set up the tables. Americans, Swedes, and Norwegians joined the festivities, drinking coffee and eating popcorn while they waited for the losers to move out so they could move in to play.

Game night always began with everyone speaking their own version of the English language. The Norwegians chatted away in proper British English, while the Swedes talked in Swenglish—an amusing combination of Swedish and English. In return, they loved teasing the Americans about their openmouthed English.

Rosie didn't take Tile Rummy as seriously as some of the others, but tonight she pursed her lips, determined to give it her best shot. She undoubtedly succeeded because she finally landed at the winner's table with Ellen, Arne, and Ana-Karin, three of the most competitive players on board. She smiled confidently as she sat down.

"What are you doing here?" Ellen asked, as if Rosie had sat down at the wrong table.

"I've won all my games," Rosie said, still grinning.

Ellen and Ana-Karin shook their heads. As the game progressed, Ana-Karin turned from speaking her lovely British English to conversing with Arne in their native Swedish. Ellen joined in with her rough version of the language, which brought an intimate outburst of laughter among the trio throughout the game. Rosie would have laughed, but how could she when she didn't have a clue as to what they were saying? So she sat, on a slow burn, trying to concentrate on the game.

The weeks of Nurse A. K.'s inconsiderate behavior had already worn on Rosie, but there was no place to run when she became frustrated with her sharp, cutting tones. She certainly couldn't jump overboard, so she resigned herself to face the situation head-on.

Thirty minutes and three Swedish jokes later, Rosie looked up and glared into Ana-Karin's eyes. She took a deep breath. "Excuse me, but am I invisible?"

Arne's mouth dropped, and Ellen's eyes widened in disbelief.

"Could you please turn the conversation back around to English?" Rosie asked. It was more of a request than a question.

Ellen stuffed her mouth with popcorn, and Arne sat silently, waiting for Ana-Karin's response.

Ana-Karin's eyes glimmered. "Turn back around? Of course, I can turn back around," she answered in her sweet-as-honey tone. Smiling, she slowly rose from her chair, turned completely around, and then, ever so slowly, sat down.

"There. I have turned back around."

Ellen spewed popcorn across the table and then broke out laughing at Ana-Karin's quick wit, with Arne soon joining in. Rosie's silence spoke multitudes. Ana-Karin began moving her numbered chips around on her board as if nothing had happened.

Rosie's face turned red, and her hands began to shake. She tried to keep cool, but the harder she tried, the hotter she got. "Excuse me for a minute," she said, rising from her chair. She walked over to the corner bookshelf, grabbed a binder, thumbed through the pages, and then walked back to the table.

"Here, read this . . . out loud." Rosie shoved the *Restoration*'s Policy and Procedure Manual in Ana-Karin's face.

Ana-Karin read ever so slowly, "English is the first language to be spoken at all times while on the *Restoration*."

Rosie looked at the numbers on Ana-Karin's board. "You would have lost anyway!"

Before Ana-Karin could respond, Rosie left the premises and retreated to the solitude of her cabin. She slammed the door, sat in her green chair, and proceeded to have a serious American English meltdown. "I can't believe her! She thinks she's so great! So funny! So—"

The cabin door opened. "What happened up there? Are you okay?" Jesse asked.

"I can't take Ana-Karin's weird humor anymore. She knows I can't carry on a conversation in Swedish, but she spits it out anyway!"

Jesse knelt down and put his arms around her. That's when the dam broke. Her tears covered his T-shirt.

"When we get to Stockholm, I'm going to fly home. You can stay."

"Now wait a minute. Will you listen to me?"

She only shrugged her shoulders.

"It takes a lot of effort and energy for the Swedes and the Norwegians to speak English day after day. It's only natural for them to want to speak in their native language."

She pulled away. "But Ana-Karin does it to bug me! And tonight Ellen joined right in, with Arne following right behind her. And now you're siding with her too!"

"I'm not siding with anyone. If you know she's doing it on purpose, then don't let her bug you. It's your choice. Of course, she should speak English, but try to put yourself in her shoes."

"But I feel so isolated when everyone is speaking their own language. They might as well be saying blah-blah-blah."

After listening to herself mumble for what seemed like hours, she came to the conclusion that she must be sounding a little blah-blah-blah herself, so she decided to give Jesse a break.

"Go back upstairs. I'll join you later."

She went in their head, closed the door, sat on the toilet lid, and tried to gather her thoughts. Jesse hadn't fully convinced her, but he did shed light on a somewhat dark situation.

"Okay, Lord, next time this happens, I promise to put my American feet in Ana-Karin's Swedish shoes."

Feeling better, Rosie went to the galley. She couldn't take another hour of board games, so she poured a cup of coffee and then joined Clive, Dottie, Val, and Filippa in the troop mess for some late-night conversation. The younger crew always had something interesting to talk about.

"I love working on the ship, but sometimes the nights can be so boring," Dottie said, thumbing through an old *Glamour* magazine she had purchased in Seattle. "And I miss my boyfriend."

"I've noticed you've started to let your natural beauty show more, Dottie," Clive teased.

"Is that supposed to be some kind of American compliment?" Dottie asked in her thick Greek accent. "I work on deck all day; I don't need make-up."

It's true, Rosie thought as she looked around the room. *There is no makeup to be found on any of these young women.*

"Why bother?" Filippa, the shy Swedish cook scowled. "There is no one on board who would appreciate it."

"Perhaps that would change if you'd put a little lipstick on those pale lips and brush your hair first thing in the morning."

Just as Dottie threw the magazine at Clive and Filippaa tossed him a dirty look, a *leopard* darted across Rosie's mind.

"Don't go anywhere! I'll be right back," Rosie said. She scurried to her cabin, opened the locker, yanked the leopard blouse from a hanger, and then pulled it over her head. She stuffed the front with two pillows and then stuffed her form-fitting sweats—front and behind—with towels. She teased her permed hair until it stood straight out. She covered every inch of her face with thick Cover Girl makeup, smeared on Maybelline's Red Hot lipstick, laced her high-top lavender tennis shoes, grabbed her purple plastic makeup case, and headed for the troop mess. She barged in the door, making her grand entrance.

"Hello, everyone! I'm Stella Starlight, the famous Hollywood makeup artist! Who would like a makeover?" She looked around the room. "Or should I say, who *needs* a makeover?"

Giggling, the girls raised their hands.

Ms. Starlight placed her hands on her hips. "I can see that I have my work cut out for me!"

Clive rushed to his cabin to retrieve his camera to take before and after shots. Dottie, the dark, sultry Greek; Filippa, the tall, blond Swede; and Val, the buxom American redhead, were ready for Ms. Starlight's Extreme Makeover.

Afterward, Dottie stared in the mirror at her newfound outer beauty. "When I return to Greece, maybe my boyfriend will propose!"

"Dottie, dahling, I guarantee that he won't be able to resist you," Ms. Starlight said.

Rosie beamed as she thought of Tina. Because of one Swedish woman's generous heart, what began as just another boring evening at sea ended with laughter ringing through the hallways and newfound dreams in a simmering relationship.

32

. . . south on the Pacific, east on the Caribbean, and across the pond. After forty days and nights, the Restoration *was nearing her destination.*

"Land ho!" Captain Alain shouted over the intercom mid-morning. "Steady as she goes, mates. We are entering the English Channel."

Rosie dropped her mop and dashed to the deck. Beyond the gray mist lay the first sight of land since Panama.

As they sailed through the English Channel, Val pointed to the tall, majestic cliffs. "They're beautiful—and so white," Val said, peering through her binoculars.

"Those are the famous white cliffs of Dover that so many English songs are written about," Tina said.

"Why can't we stop in England?" Ellen asked her father. "We're behind schedule anyway, so a few more days won't hurt."

"We need to push toward Sweden, but we'll stop when we return en route to Israel," Stuart answered.

"Well, I probably won't be on the ship."

Stuart looked at his daughter. "Why not?"

"I'm going to tour Europe and then I'm going to fly home." Ellen looked at her watch. "Oh, it's time for coffee, I mean, fika." And with that, she headed toward the superstructure.

Rosie patted Stuart's shoulder, trying to comfort a father who was trying to reach out to his daughter. "Don't worry, Stuart. Ellen still has time to change her mind."

They neared the shores of Denmark and sailed by Hamlet's castle. By late afternoon, another body of land appeared. Captain Alain announced, "Ladies and gentlemen, please look to portside. You are now beholding Sweden!"

"Is it true? Can we really see Sweden?" Val asked as she directed her binoculars portside.

"Absolutely!" Tina answered on her husband's behalf, proudly pointing to her homeland. "There are over twenty-four hundred small islands called archipelagos along the Swedish coastline."

Red summerhouses peeked from wooded areas on the islands, reminding Rosie of the postcards she had collected when she lived in Sweden. Boats of all sizes were moored on the docks, some used for fishing, others for recreational rowing.

Cameras clicked as the crew took pictures of the sights. Val sounded like a schoolgirl who had arrived at Disneyland for the first time. "We're in Sweden! We're in Sweden!"

"Val really knows how to express herself," Ellen said sarcastically.

"We can all take lessons from her free spirit," Rosie answered, smiling at the enthusiastic galley gal.

Later that night, the *Restoration* silently tossed back and forth on the North Sea. The absence of the engine's roar woke Rosie.

She nudged Jesse. "We're stopped dead in the water."

He dashed to the bridge and returned with good news.

"All is well. The captain requested a bunker from Amsterdam to fuel the ship," he announced as he climbed into bed. He was asleep within minutes, and when the engine started, Rosie whispered, "Resti, you've given us a safe trip. I'm proud of you."

Rosie slept as the old ship sailed toward Stockholm.

A cool September breeze welcomed the *Restoration* as she neared Stockholm's harbor, but by the time they reached the secluded dock where they would tie up, the breeze had become a strong north wind.

In the distance, at the bottom of a steep hill, a group of a hundred people stood bundled in warm coats, hats, and gloves. Peering through the ship's binoculars, Rosie spied familiar faces. "There's our friend Dan and his family."

"Look! There's Deena!" Val said. "She looks happy to be on land."

The wind continued to carry the ship farther from the dock. The boatswains and deck crew threw ropes directly to the men on shore, but the wind tossed the ship, taking her farther out. Again, the crew threw ropes, but to no avail. They fought against the wind and were wearing down, but they had worked too hard to consider waiting for the wind to subside.

After struggling with nature for over an hour, the last ropes were tied. The gangway was lowered and secured, and Pastor Hans and Helene led the upward procession. As the captains and the crew greeted each visitor,

Rosie wondered what might have been without the prayers of these faithful Swedes.

Pastor Hans announced to the crew, "After many days at sea, you have arrived safely on Yom Kippor, and after tomorrow's morning church service, there will be a celebration in your honor."

Rosie could already smell the aroma of salmon and ma-ma's meatballs. "Tomorrow we'll be in Swedish heaven."

"A meal that I won't have to cook—what a delight!" Val said.

Rosie noticed a stirring on the gangway. "It looks like the Swedish crew is already jumping ship."

"They're eager to return to their loved ones and a much-needed rest," Stuart said. "Some will return, but the weekend leave will become their ritual, leaving us Americans to hold down the ship."

Rosie and Tina watched as Ellen walked over to interrupt Daniel as he was saying good-bye to Jeans. Daniel and Jeans had spent many hours getting to know each other while crossing the pond, and although Jeans swore to Rosie that there was nothing between them other than friendship, Daniel's eyes were a giveaway.

"I'll be here when the ship sails to Israel," he told Jeans. Then he politely turned to Ellen, who was listening to Daniel's every word. "Will you be here?"

"Uh, I don't know." Looking at Daniel and Jeans standing together, Ellen decided she wasn't going to give up so easily. "But I'll see you while I'm in Stockholm, won't I?"

"Maybe," he answered, walking down the gangway toward his brother's car, waving at Jeans.

Henrik yelled at Daniel, "Wait for me! You're supposed to give me a ride to the bus station, remember?" He turned to Ellen. "Will I see you in Stockholm?"

"I doubt it," she said as she walked toward the superstructure.

Ellen escaped to her cabin, and soon Elvis was blaring down the halls toward the deck. "Elvis helps her when she's feeling rejected," Rosie told Tina as they stood at the gangway.

"I'll miss you," Rosie said, hugging her friend.

"We'll invite you and Jesse for dinner, and you can soak in my bathtub," Tina said, remembering how Rosie missed her long bubble baths back home.

Later, after the Swedes had departed, the ship was especially quiet. Jesse took Rosie's hand and led her down the gangway. "Come on, it's our turn to touch land." They stood on solid ground, swaying back and forth, as if they were still at sea. "Stuart said it might take awhile before we stand motionless on land," Jesse said as they strolled down the dirt road.

"Hello, friends!" their friend Dan yelled from the dock. "Don't go too far! We want to take you to dinner in Stockholm."

Rosie smiled at the sight of Dan and his bride.

"Our first Swedish meal in old-town Stockholm," Jesse said, waving.

"Let's go," she said as they swayed toward their Swedish family.

Jesse and Rosie returned to the ship that evening to a quiet troop mess. Stuart, Shelly, Ellen, Clive, and Jeans were sharing a solemn fika.

"Here's a going-away present before I fly home to Washington," Val said as she placed a platter of her special peanut butter cookies on the table.

"With Urma gone to her village and Deena off to Bible school, we'll have to improvise in the galley until we set sail," Shelly told Rosie as she munched on a cookie.

"We're going to miss your delicious cooking, Val, but if you're as good a teacher as you are a chef, then your students are going to love you," Stuart said as he reached for a second helping.

Shelly looked at her stepdaughter. "Ellen's a great cook. She'll make us some mouthwatering pizza."

"Sorry, but I can't help out," Ellen interrupted as she grabbed a handful of cookies. "I'm going to be touring Sweden for a few weeks."

Stuart changed the subject. "Let's play a game of Tile Rummy—in American English," he said, glancing at Rosie. He was doing his best to cheer the group while trying to keep his composure upon hearing Ellen's unexpected plans.

"Yes, this is a day of celebration—we arrived safely in Sweden!" Val said.

Shelly began stacking cups. "We have another big day tomorrow, so I think we need to get a good night's sleep."

"Yikes, you're right," Ellen said and then made her exit.

Once in bed, Rosie tossed while Jesse fiddled with his shortwave radio, trying to find the BBC news channel.

"I miss the roaring engine and the steering mechanism fighting under our cabin. Tonight there'll be no swaying to the beat of the sea's rhythm to lull me to sleep."

"Huh?"

"Oh, nothing." She pulled the covers back. "I'm going to the galley for tea. Can I bring you a cup?"

"Uh, no, I'll be dozing off after the news, but a kiss will do."

"A cup of Jeans's chamomile tea will relax me," Rosie said as she filled the large pot with water. Down the hallway, Elvis was singing, "Are You Lonesome Tonight?"

"Yes, I'm lonesome tonight. I miss the crew, especially Tina. I even miss Ana-Karin," she admitted as she poured hot water over a tea bag. Walking toward her cabin, she heard laughter coming from the troop mess. She peeked through the half-closed door. She smiled as she watched Clive, Jeans, and Ellen improvising some sort of talk show. She giggled as the girls, decked in large-brimmed straw hats, faced Clive's video camera, talking with thick southern drawls.

"This is Ethel and Gertrude telling you how to plan for your future!" Ellen said in a southern accent.

"Join us for *The Plan for Your Future Show!*" Jeans announced in a deep, syrupy tone.

Clive stopped filming when he heard Rosie laughing. When he motioned her to join them, Ellen rolled her eyes, but Jeans waved. "Come on in."

Rosie was about to decline when Ellen added, "Yeah, we could use some older ideas."

"That does it—I'll *show you old*," Rosie muttered under her breath. "I'll be right back," she told Clive, ignoring Ellen's remark. She hurried to her cabin in search of her long-lost friend.

"What's going on?" Jesse asked as he watched Rosie fumble through her lockers.

"I'm looking for Aunt Eunice. She's been with me for twenty years—she can't hide from me now."

As Rosie pulled out a box from under the bed, Jesse smiled as he remembered all of Rosie's comedy skits portraying her infamous Aunt Eunice.

"Here she is," she said gleefully, stuffing one of Jesse's sweatshirts and sweatpants with towels. Then she slathered makeup on her face to make her look like an over-ambitious senior citizen—from deep red lipstick and rouge to dark penciled eyebrows. She pulled her hair in a tight bun, plopped a large straw sun hat on her head, grabbed an apron from the cleaning closet, and then placed a pair of reading glasses on her nose. Voila!

"Hello, Eunice!" Rosie announced as she looked in the bathroom mirror.

Jesse burst into laughter as Eunice made her grand entrance from the head. "That old lady never fails to scare the daylights out of me! Those comedy skits that you and Prissy wrote have certainly paid off!"

Eunice waved as she stepped over the door. "Bye, shugga! Don't wait up—I have a show to do."

Ellen's mouth dropped as Aunt Eunice entered the troop mess. Jeans and Clive roared as the senile lady walked toward the table, slightly bent over, waving a toilet brush as if it were a magic wand. She sat her padded behind down between Ethel and Gertrude and announced, "Okay, young man, start shooting *The Plan for Your Future Show*, starring Ethel, Gertrude, and their ever-lovin' Aunt Eunice."

Two hours later, exhausted from laughing and improvising, Rosie climbed into bed, thanking the Lord for her new friends, Ethel and Gertrude. She hoped that their paths would cross again before the journey was over.

The next morning a church bus slowly drove down the steep hill to pick up the crew.

"I'm excited to be visiting the church before I fly home," Val said as she gazed out the bus window at the sights of Stockholm.

"Who knows, maybe I'll go to the Bible school someday," Jeans said.

"I'm planning to go next year," Clive said proudly. Shelly smiled at her son and Stuart listened for a response from Ellen, but she sat silently, staring out the window. She wasn't about to commit to anything.

Torre escorted the Americans into the large auditorium, where they joined the rest of the crew. They were given headsets for English translation. Song lyrics were posted on two large screens on either side of the podium, one in Swedish and the other in English.

After the worship service, Pastor Hans called for the crew to stand on the platform. Rosie had never stood in front of two thousand people, so her knees began to shake as Pastor Hans began. "We have given you updates of the *Restoration*'s journey from Seattle to Stockholm, and during the summer conference we tapped into the ship's radio so Captain Alain could report on how God was giving them such good weather while crossing the pond. Now we will pray for God's blessings to be upon the crew for all the work they have done."

After the luncheon, Pastor Hans presented each crew member with an individual framed certificate that included commemorative Israeli stamps. Silently, Rosie read:

Thank you for your valuable achievement on the maiden voyage of MS Restoration *across the Atlantic Ocean to Sweden. We believe that God will bless you abundantly according to his promises.*

Signed by, Hans & Helene Södereng, Founders of Operation Jabotinsky, September 18, 1994, Uppsala.

"We'll frame these when we get home," Jesse said.

Rosie thought a moment and then smiled. "But for now, this is our home."

33

The World War II ship happily sat in Stockholm's port while ships of all shapes and sizes passed. No wars, no unfriendly waters. All was peaceful, until one cold September night . . .

As autumn settled in, the sun took its time rising over the nearby hill. Energized by the crisp mornings, Rosie spent her breaks strolling down the dirt road that ran parallel to the dock. She sipped her coffee and admired the trees that flaunted their colors of reds, yellows, and oranges. California's fall season couldn't compare with Sweden's colors.

Part of her morning ritual was waving to passengers on the ferries sailing to Finland and Estonia. She even waved to the small seaplane that circled the ship several times a week, but they weren't as friendly—they never waved back.

The days grew shorter and colder, so Rosie made her way to the depths of hold two to unpack their box of sweaters, gloves, coats, and flannel pajamas. She repacked the box with their summer attire, keeping a few light sweaters in case those strange little flashes came back. The worn, stained T-shirts weren't worth keeping, but rather than toss them, she used them for cleaning rags. Living on the ship was teaching Rosie the value of recycling.

On the mornings she cleaned the bridge, Rosie often stopped and gazed at the shoreline across the waterway. A charming two-story, old world home intrigued her. She wondered who lived behind the green door. As far as she could see, there was no activity in or around the house.

"Perhaps a large family once lived there," she told Jesse at dinner.

He smiled and shook his head as he sliced a piece of ham. "I'm always amused at your curiosity about people you don't know. You should write a book, Rosie."

Before taking her dishes to the galley, she looked out the porthole and glanced at the old house. A light was on downstairs, and then a few minutes later, a lamp brightened an upstairs room.

"Jesse, look! There is life inside that house."

Jesse joined her at the porthole.

"I wonder if an elderly couple lives there, or perhaps a woman longing to find love . . ."

"Rosie, if you don't know someone's story, you're determined to make one up, aren't you?" Jesse teased.

It was little things that helped the days go by faster—like wondering who lived in that old house across the waterway.

September 28, 1994. Rosie hadn't slept well. She woke up with a headache, so she took two aspirins and headed to the galley for a second cup of coffee. Elvis was belting out "Jailhouse Rock" under the crack of Ellen's door, so Rosie knocked, then peeked in and saw Ellen brushing her teeth over her sink.

"Are you coming to prayer?"

"Nope, but I'll be on time for breakfast," Ellen answered, spraying toothpaste all over the mirror.

Some things never change, Rosie thought as she walked to the galley.

Rosie spilled her coffee all over the floor the minute the hall phone rang—she still wasn't used to being hooked up to the dock's landlines.

"Oh, great! Now I have to mop up this mess! And why isn't Stuart answering the office phone?"

The phone continued ringing, so Rosie picked up.

"Tina! Good morning. It's so good to hear from you, but why are you calling so early?"

"Haven't you heard?" Tina sounded desperate.

"Heard what?"

"I need to speak with Stuart to tell him the ferry ship *Estonia* sank last night."

"No!" Rosie screamed.

Rosie dropped the phone and ran to the office.

"Stuart, something terrible has happened."

He looked up from his paperwork.

Rosie sat in the office chair, half-listening to Stuart as he made several phone calls. The *Estonia* was like a beautiful city, with shops, restaurants, and lounges to keep passengers entertained as they crossed the Baltic Sea.

"Stuart, I waved to *Estonia*'s passengers every day," Rosie said through tears. "My dad sailed on the *Estonia* when he visited us two years ago."

Stuart was too disturbed to give any comfort. "I must make more phone calls."

Rosie flashed back two years to when her father had flown from California to stay with them in their three-room flat for three weeks. He had sailed to Tallinn on the *Estonia*. Rosie shivered at the thought of what might have been.

Captain Alain and Tina arrived bringing newspapers for the Swedish volunteers. They gathered in the crew's lounge around the TV to watch as the news media gave regular updates on one of the worst tragedies in Scandinavian history. Rosie sat with a blank look on her face, wishing she had learned more Swedish.

Tina sat down next to Rosie and Jesse. "I'll translate for you," Tina said. "The sea was rough, and the lower deck's large door was not closed tight. The water filled the lower deck, causing the vehicles to move toward one side of the 510-foot-long ferry. In a matter of minutes, the ship began filling with water and listing."

Tina stopped to catch her breath, obviously overwhelmed by the tragedy. "Those who moved quickly jumped overboard to safety, but most of the people were frozen from fear." Tears filled Rosie's eyes.

The days ahead were filled with sorrow. *Estonia's* tragedy resonated throughout the world. One hundred thirty-seven people survived, but 852 loved ones lost their lives that night when the ocean seized control. Rosie knew, deep inside, that her peace must come from knowing that she was in God's care, whether at home, in a foreign country, or at sea. Her prayer was simple. "Lord, I'm weak compared to the sea's mighty anger. This tragedy shows how much more I need to trust you."

Strangely, Rosie never saw another light in the old home across the waterway.

The days grew even shorter as the crew prepared to set sail into those same rough waters. By the time October's harsh winds blew, Grace's visit was a breath of spring air for Rosie.

"Tim's mom is an angel to help with Katie while you're gone," Rosie said as they drove through Stockholm toward the harbor.

"She knows how important this trip is to me. I'm looking forward to Russia, but I'm happy to be here with you for a few days," Grace said as Rosie drove down the hill toward the dock.

Grace's mouth dropped. "Oh, isn't she beautiful! She looks quite regal, Mom." Grace hesitated, then continued. "When we heard about the *Estonia*, I have to admit—"

"The *Restoration* is going to be fine," Rosie interrupted. "She's old, but she's determined to reach her destination." She did not want to talk about the *Estonia*. "You'll be sleeping with me. Jesse is going to sleep in hold two, like in Seattle."

"Our own little slumber party," Grace said, smiling as they walked up the gangway.

Rosie and Grace talked for hours while they walked through Stockholm's old city. They watched the changing of the guards at the castle, and then ate lunch in a quaint Swedish café.

"The weather is much nicer than it was when you came to visit us two Christmases ago," Rosie said as they exited the café.

Grace pulled her hat over her ears. "The Swedish autumn is beautiful, but I'm still freezing."

Rosie removed her jacket. "I can't understand—one minute I'm cold, and then the next minute I'm burning up . . . must be the changing of seasons."

Grace spent a week in Russia helping teach in several Bible schools, but when she returned to Stockholm, she admitted to Rosie, "Russia has given me a bad case of homesickness. I miss Katie so much." Rosie knew the feeling all too well, and that night, as Grace drifted off to sleep thinking of her daughter, Rosie lay awake, already missing hers.

The next morning, Rosie and Grace donned their stoic manner as they hugged and kissed at the airport—it was their protection against falling apart in public. Rosie would have her meltdown behind closed doors.

That afternoon, Shelly found Rosie alone in the troop mess, crying in her coffee. She went to the galley and returned with a fresh cup and set it down in front of Rosie.

"Thanks," Rosie said, wiping her eyes with a napkin.

"It's hard being away from your family, isn't it?" Shelly asked as she sat down across from Rosie.

"I often wonder if I did the right thing to leave my family again. You and Stuart are fortunate to have Clive and Ellen traveling with you. Clive's hard work and lighthearted ways make Jesse's daily tasks a lot easier."

"I wish I could say the same for Ellen," Shelly said.

"Maybe Ellen isn't as lighthearted as Clive, but she's a very unique young woman. Since our eventful *Plan for Your Future* nights, I've come to understand and enjoy Ellen's sense of humor."

"I'm sure you've heard that we've had some rough times with Ellen, but she's finally beginning to warm up to Stuart," Shelly said. But something in Shelly's voice sounded unsure.

"How are you and Ellen doing?"

"She avoids me, but that's okay. The life of a stepmom is rough, but my main concern is Stuart. I want them to be close again. As for Ellen and me, I'm believing for a miracle."

"I'll believe with you," Rosie added. "Speaking of miracles, when are we sailing for the Black Sea?"

Shelly shook her head. "No one seems to know. We're waiting for the lifeboats to arrive. Many of the Swedes have returned to their jobs until a sailing date is announced."

"We've come so far. I'll be very disappointed if I'm not on several trips before we have to fly home."

"We have to keep praying, and have patience."

"You're always so positive about everything. What's your secret?" Rosie asked.

"Yikes, I've never thought about it. I guess I've learned over the years that there are some circumstances that I can't change. I get up every morning at four-thirty to pray and read. Maybe that's my secret."

"Duh, ya think?" Rosie said, chuckling.

As they laughed and talked, Rosie knew how blessed she was to have Shelly onboard.

Several days later, while Rosie was sorting laundry, a loud noise overhead distracted her. As she stepped onto the deck, a familiar-looking seaplane was circling the ship. Rosie's stomach knotted, but she was determined not to give in to her fear. Stuart darted out of the superstructure, obviously disturbed by the overhead intrusion.

"We've been warned about groups who dislike organizations who help Russian Jews," Stuart said. "That's why Pastor Hans delegated security guards to be on duty twenty-four-seven."

The pilot killed the engine about fifty feet from the stern, allowing the plane to slowly float toward the ship.

Stuart yelled, "Please identify yourself!"

Three men silently stared at the ship through the plane's small windows, as if they were taking mental notes. The front-seat passenger snapped pictures.

"I'm calling the coast guard," Stuart told Jesse as he dashed to the office.

"Is this the ship that will take Russian Jews to Israel?" the pilot shouted.

"What type of accent is that?" Rosie asked.

"Shhh," Jesse whispered.

The passenger took several more pictures, and then the pilot started the engine. The plane was gliding out of sight by the time Stuart returned.

"This incident proves that we aren't physically equipped to protect ourselves," Stuart said.

Rosie cleared her throat and then stated boldly, "Ultimately, God is our defense."

Stuart shook his head. "Well, he certainly has his hands full!"

34

November's harsh north winds blew, and still there was still no word when the ship would sail. When several churches in Sweden and Norway invited the Operation Jabotinsky team to share their story, Resti swayed with glee at the thought of sailing again.

Bundled in hats, gloves, and wool scarves, the deck crew continued the never-ending task of scraping and painting. When the work on the bow was finished, they proceeded toward the stern. The sea's elements continued the never-ending process of creating rust, no matter where the ship was laid up.

The crew was warming themselves in the troop mess when Stuart returned from the office. "I talked to Torre on the phone, and I have some good news. We have been invited by several coastal Swedish churches to speak. Then we will sail to Bergen and Oslo, Norway."

The crew applauded the news.

"We'll give tours during the day and hold meetings each evening to share about Operation Jabotinsky. The dance team will demonstrate a variety of Israeli songs and folk dances."

Shelly sat quietly as the crew talked.

"What's wrong?" Rosie asked.

"I wish Ellen was sailing with us."

"So do I, but it was her choice to trek around Sweden."

Shelly stood up. "But who knows? Maybe she'll come back. Meanwhile, my assignment is to find uniforms for the crew. Would you like to be my assistant?"

The ship's walls had been slowly closing in on Rosie, so she took every opportunity to jump ship. "I would love to; when can we leave?"

After walking the streets of Stockholm for hours, Rosie and Shelly stumbled upon a small tailor shop on the east end. The sign in the window read *Rea—Sale: bus uniforms. "Our kind of place,"* Shelly said as she opened the shop's squeaky door.

Shelly stood in front of a mirror. "Look! These white shirts with the buttoned flaps on the shoulders give a nice nautical touch."

Rosie held out a smart-looking navy blue jacket to go with a pair of navy slacks. "This will be perfect for the ports-of-call tours." She smiled as she

197

stood at the mirror, picturing herself decked out in uniform in some faraway port.

"The shop owner can have them ready for us in a week. Let's celebrate by having a fika in town before we head back to the ship," Shelly suggested.

"That sounds wonderful. I'm starting to catch a little ship fever myself."

"Are you sure you're not having a slight case of hot flashes?" Shelly teased.

"Who, me? Heavens no—I'm too young for those," Rosie said as she removed her scarf and gloves.

A week later, while Rosie and Tina were having their afternoon fika on deck, they spotted Ellen hiking down the hill with her backpack tossed over her shoulder. As Ellen walked slowly up the gangway, Rosie asked, "What brings you back so soon?"

"I ran out of money," she answered as she marched toward the superstructure.

Tina shook her head. "Shelly told me that Ellen receives a monthly check from her mother."

"So why can't she just be honest enough to admit that she misses us?" Rosie asked.

"I believe that some day she will," Tina said as she sipped her last drop of coffee.

It was a happy reunion for the crew as the *Restoration* set sail on a windy November morning. Ana-Karin handed out bracelets and seasickness pills for those who feared the North Sea. She handed a bracelet and two pills to Rosie. "These are for you. I remember that you were ill on the voyage over," she said.

"Oh, yes, thank you," Rosie said, taking Ana-Karin's thoughtful care package.

The ship pulled into the port of Oskarshamn late in the afternoon. Team One wasted no time going ashore. Rosie and Shelly sought shelter from the harsh wind in a quaint shop at the village square. A bell that hung on the front door announced their entry. They were greeted with a cheerful, "Velkomen! Sit here by the fire and have some coffee to warm you."

"I think we're the only people in the streets," Shelly said as she took the coffee from the shop owner.

"Is it a blustery afternoon for the Americans, yes?" the shopkeeper asked, handing Rosie a wool lap blanket.

"How can you tell we're Americans?"

"As soon as you open your mouth, it is a dying giveaway."

"Oh, you mean a dead giveaway," Shelly corrected, chuckling.

"Oh yes, that is what I meant. I am still learning English," she said, laughing.

The next afternoon, Pastor Hans and Helene came aboard in Helsingborg. After spending the night in the Atkisson cabin, the pastor jokingly reported to Jesse, "There were dragons fighting below your cabin all night!"

As the ship pulled into Gothenborg's harbor, Jesse told Pastor Hans, "Those same dragons lull Rosie to sleep every night."

A thick morning fog settled against the hills as the *Restoration* sailed into the port of Bergen, Norway. Team One was down the gangway before breakfast.

"Let's eat on shore," Jesse told Rosie. The cobblestone road led the team toward the center of town. Daniel pointed to a nearby hillside. "I'll lead a group to the top, and then we'll ride the gondola that overlooks the bay."

"I want to shoot some videos up there," Ellen said, smiling at Daniel as she stood next to him.

Daniel turned to Jeans. "Are you coming?"

"Sure," she answered timidly.

Ellen's face turned to stone.

"Let's find a place to eat," Jesse said to the rest of the team, trying to break the embarrassing silence.

Henrik followed Jesse. "Now you're talking my language!"

Jesse spotted a *best pancakes in town* sign that beckoned the hungry crew to come inside. They stuffed themselves with butter and sugarcoated pancakes.

After breakfast, Clive and Henrik shopped while Jesse and Rosie walked along the docks. Boats and yachts were moored in the bay, a sign of people who loved to sail when the weather permitted. This was not one of those days. There were old vessels with evidence of fishermen who had kept their dates with the sea. Robust men in colorful Windbreakers and galoshes stacked their catch of the day along the aisles of the outdoor markets.

By lunchtime, they couldn't ignore the aroma of fresh seafood drifting from the cafés. After the team ate, Rosie looked admiringly at the young men's purchases. "I love your Norwegian sweaters," she told Clive and Henrik. For now, they were on a strict budget, so she would be content to sip Norwegian coffee with her hot Swedish husband.

After the evening meeting, a familiar-looking Norwegian lady with rosy cheeks took Rosie aside and placed a package in her arms. "I have something for you. Please open."

Rosie remembered giving the volunteer a cheerful good morning as they left the ship that day. Rosie tore the paper and then held out a beautiful, hand-knit red sweater. "You shouldn't have!" Rosie hugged the woman with one arm while holding her new sweater with the other.

"How did you know I wanted one?" Rosie asked as she held the sweater to her chest.

She smiled. "An angel told me."

The next afternoon the *Restoration* sailed south through the fjords, arriving in Oslo the following day. As they docked next to an ancient brick castle, Torre announced, "We will stay in port for two days, so you will have time to see the capitol's sights."

Jesse found a pay phone on the dock and returned to their cabin out of breath. "Bobby and Rebekka will pick us up in thirty minutes. Rebekka wants to show us her hometown."

As Bobby drove through the city, Rosie compared Oslo's streamlined architecture to Stockholm's old-world charm. The air was brisk as they walked through the famous Vigelansparken Park. As darkness fell, Rosie pointed to the lights below. "This view is breathtaking. The city lights are like jewels sparkling in the night."

"It is a beautiful sight, but it looks like our boys have found their own breathtaking objects," Rebekka said, pointing at their husbands.

Bobby and Jesse chuckled at the nude bronze statues standing throughout the park. "The trees aren't the only objects that are bare," Bobby joked.

"She must be freezing," Jesse said, standing under a nude statue.

Rebekka frowned. "American men need to toss their *Playboy* mentality aside and learn to appreciate God's creation as beautiful art forms."

"But, honey, I'm a red-blooded American. Isn't that why you married me?" Bobby teased as he held her close.

Rosie pulled her wool cap over her ears and walked over and stood beneath the female bronze to duplicate her bawdy pose.

"Now, Jesse, take a picture—for art's sake."

They window-shopped along the narrow cobblestoned streets in Oslo's Old Town. Rosie was admiring the colorful Norwegian scarves when Rebekka handed her a handful of Norwegian kroner. "Here, this is for all the hard work you have done on the ship. Buy something especially for you."

Rosie chose a beautiful burgundy scarf to match her coat. "Thank you, Rebekka. I'll remember you every time I wear it," she said, hugging her.

They dined at McDonald's in Old Town, and reminisced late into the evening of their Bible school year together. Bobby glanced at Rebekka. "We're moving back to California in a few months, so call us when you get home."

"We'll be home in May, so call us when *you* return," Rosie said with conviction as she glanced at her watch. "But for now, we better get back to our *home at sea*."

The *Restoration* left Oslo's port at dawn on the fourth Thursday of November. The galley girls prepared two large Seattle turkeys they had saved for the special occasion.

"We will celebrate a traditional American Thanksgiving at sea," Urma announced as she began peeling two large bags of potatoes.

Two hours later, as the aroma of turkey filled the halls, the sea began her roar. The captain had hoped to miss the rough gales that had been predicted, but it was too late. Four hours later, the brown and beautiful birds sat alone in the galley.

By eight o'clock that evening Rosie's tummy felt like a washing machine. Her stomach rolled with each wave. Jesse gulped down two seasickness pills before dressing for his evening watch. "Can you fix me a Thanksgiving plate for later?" he asked.

"I'll try, but the thought of going near turkey and dressing makes my stomach churn."

Jesse kissed her on the cheek as she glanced toward the head. "Can you hand me two of those pills? I have a feeling we're in for a long, rolling night."

The *Restoration* made it through the gale by the third day. Feeling better, Rosie sang Barry Manilow's "We Made It Through the Rain" as she stuffed her plate with leftover dressing and sweet potatoes.

"It's good to hear you singing again," Stuart said as he filled his plate with turkey and gravy. "Is there a special reason for the serenade?"

"I have my appetite back; that's something to sing about. And once we arrive in Stockholm, we'll be that much closer to sailing to the Black Sea."

Stuart walked silently back to the galley. Rosie never liked it when Stuart was quiet. That meant he had news that he didn't want to share . . . or that he *couldn't* share.

35

The Restoration *had something else in common with the lady: neither liked cold weather. So together they waited for orders to sail to warmer waters.*

On a snowy December morning, Torre announced, "As most of you know, the winter months are not good for sailing on the North Sea."

"No, I didn't know. What are you saying?" Ellen asked loud enough for everyone to hear.

"Keep quiet and listen," Henrik said, shaking his head.

Rosie smiled at Henrik's gesture. Although he complained about Ellen's antics, the twinkle in his eyes told Rosie that he was growing fond of her.

"Humph!" Ellen said, twisting in her chair.

"Ice is forming on top of the waterways," Torre continued.

"I've noticed the icebreaker ships heading out every morning, but I never thought the ice would hinder us from leaving," Rosie said.

Torre cleared his throat. "Due to the many other delays, especially the fact that we haven't received our mandatory safety equipment, we have missed our window of opportunity to depart."

"What are you saying?" Rosie repeated Ellen's words, half-afraid to hear Torre's answer.

"The *Restoration* will have to wait until spring to sail."

"Yikes," Shelly whispered.

Ellen slammed her coffee mug on the table. "Damn!" She glanced at her dad. "I mean, darn."

"There is much work to do, so the time will go by fast," Torre said, trying to console the disappointed crew.

Ellen's eyes glared. "That's easy for you to say. You're only forty minutes from home. I'm stranded six thousand miles from my home—and it's almost Christmas!"

Ellen said what every homesick American was thinking but was too polite to say. Rosie was about to voice her opinion when Jesse grabbed her hand under the table and squeezed it. Rosie shook it off. "Don't do that—you know how much you hate it when I grab your hand under the table."

Jesse gently took Rosie's hand. "You need to calm down before you speak."

The last thing Rosie wanted was to be categorized with Ellen—self-centered and foolish—so she refrained from saying something she would most likely regret.

That evening, after losing two games of Tile Rummy, Jesse joined Rosie in their cabin. He sat on the bed beside her.

"Are you still sulking?" He tried making eye contact, but she pretended to read. "Rosie, things aren't going as planned, but moping isn't going to make things better."

She turned a page. "I don't think anyone has planned *anything* for this ship."

"You're right. The *Restoration* is a new experience for the Swedish church and for all of us. That's what this journey is all about."

Rosie turned another page. "Do you have to be so philosophical?"

Jesse took the book and then looked her in the eyes. "You don't want to sail into angry waters, do you?" he asked, then placed the book back in her hand.

The terrible memories of the ferry *Estonia* passed before her. She tossed the book onto the desk. "Good point."

"And we need to make a decision."

"About what?"

"Our year on the ship will be up in May," Jesse said.

"Oh, my. I haven't thought that far ahead. By the time the ship sails to Russia and then to Israel, it will be at least fourteen months."

"We can stay and work on the ship until then, or we can pack up and be home by Christmas," Jesse said. "It's up to you."

That magic word *home* pulled at Rosie's heartstrings. But the magic ship, *Restoraton*, had already begun to make a home in her heart as well.

"Let's not make any decisions tonight," Rosie said.

After breakfast Jesse peered through the troop mess door. "Come on, let's go on the monkey bridge. I want to take some pictures of you and the *Restoration* covered with snow."

"But it's too cold outside!"

"Rosie, come on outside and play!" Jesse demanded, all the while giving her his warmhearted smile.

She bundled up in her coat, gloves, and cap, and holding a cup of coffee, she crunched her way onto the upper deck.

"You look like an ice princess," Jesse said as he snapped away.

"A *freezing* ice princess," she said, sipping her already cold coffee.

By the time Jesse took the last picture, Sweden's winter beauty had cleared the cloud that had been hanging over Rosie since last night. She brushed the snow off the railing. "Resti, you look like a bride, all draped in white. If you can stand this weather, then so can I."

Rosie was about to step inside when she heard laughter echoing from the main deck. "Oh, those crazy Swedes," she said, shivering, as she watched Clive and Henrik playing football in the snow. She walked inside and poured another cup of coffee, dreaming of warmer days.

The continual snowfall made it impossible to drive down the steep, icy road, but that didn't keep the volunteers away. They parked at the top of the hill and then slowly made their way down, sometimes sliding on their behinds.

Rosie was decorating the troop mess and listening to Elvis sing "Blue Christmas" when the hall phone rang.

After a formal greeting, she replied, "Hello, Dan! I'm happy to hear your voice."

"Our neighbors who recently toured the Restoration are going to spend their Christmas in Norway, so they invited you and Jesse to stay in their home."

They had made so many wonderful Swedish friends over the last two years—they were like family. She longed to see her own family, and yet, she didn't want to pass up the opportunity to serve God on this special mission. Family—or mission? California—or Resti?

"Oh, Dan, we would love to!" Rosie answered gleefully.

She turned Elvis off and began singing "Deck the Halls" as she finished hanging the holly. She couldn't wait for Jesse to get off his afternoon shift to tell him of her decision. They would sail on the MS *Restoration* in the spring.

"Christmas Eve in a real house," Rosie said as she climbed the stairs. "And a bathtub!" she shrieked.

"I'll know where to find you," Jesse teased as she filled the tub with bubbles.

Rosie soaked by candlelight for an hour while soft violin music played on the radio. She would have lingered, but Jesse reminded her that they had a Christmas Eve engagement at Dan and Bigge's home a few blocks away.

They walked hand in hand in the falling snow. The traditional Christmas candlelight glowed in the windows, inviting family and friends to come in out of the cold. Dan greeted them at the door.

"Velkomen!" Bigge yelled from the kitchen. The aroma of Christmas dinner filled the air. Rosie unzipped her boots, unbuttoned her coat, and then made her way to the Christmas table. A red tablecloth was covered with Swedish delicacies of fresh salmon, various cheeses, hard bread, boiled potatoes, Swedish caviar, and Rosie's favorite holiday drink, Julmust. After dinner they shared in a traditional gift exchange. They ate green-frosted Queen Anne's cake and drank Swedish coffee late into the night.

"I love Swedish Christmas," Rosie said. "Being here with you makes it easier when we're away from family.'

"And we love sharing holidays with our American family," Dan said.

"God always provides for his children when they are away from home," Bigge said.

Torre opened his home to the American crew for Christmas Day dinner. Shaking out of her snow-covered coat, Rosie joined the Family Lang by the fire. Ellen was in a lighthearted mood as she sat by Stuart, giggling at the funny-looking elves that hung on the Christmas tree. "The Swedes have such silly traditions," she said teasingly.

"As do the crazy Americans," Torre joked.

"Oops, sorry!" Ellen replied.

Rosie and Jesse glanced at each other. It was the first time they had heard Ellen apologize for anything. Rosie could sense that Ellen was trying her best to be part of the family atmosphere.

"Especially the crazy American Norwegians," Torre added, smiling at Stuart and Ellen.

"Okay! Okay!" Ellen smiled at her father. "I thought we were all in the same family of God. And here's a toast: may we all survive in 1995!" she proclaimed.

"Here, here!" Stuart agreed.

The Scandinavians continued playing their snow games on deck as the harsh winds of January cut the warm-blooded Americans to the bone. Rosie stared out the porthole. "When I get to the Mediterranean, I'm going to sunbathe on the monkey bridge, like I did so many weeks—no, months—ago."

Jeans looked up from her journal. "When we arrive in Greece, I'm going to stuff myself with Greek salad at the local cafés."

"Yikes, you girls talk about sunbathing and eating. All I want to do is read in the shade of a big, tall olive tree," Shelly added.

Somehow, talking about the days ahead helped take the chill off their freezing Swedish days.

Rosie's birthday came in with a blizzard. Shelly and Rosie were decorating the troop mess with red ribbon left over from Christmas when Jesse walked in from his trip to the local market. He tossed a bag in front of Rosie. "Here are our Christmas pictures."

Rosie stared at the woman in the photos. "Yikes—who is that lady?"

Shelly chuckled. "Yikes, it sounds like you've been around me too long."

"What?"

"You're stealing my line," Shelly teased.

"Oh, sorry . . . I can't help myself," Rosie mumbled, her eyes glued to the Christmas photos. She couldn't take her eyes off the plump lady smiling back at her. "Did someone turn the heat up?" she asked as she removed her sweatshirt.

Shelly and Tina smiled at each other. "No, Rosie, but if you ask me, I think your internal thermometer must be a little off," Shelly said.

But Rosie wasn't listening; she was having a real Kodak moment. "I weighed myself at the Norwegian house after Christmas, but I couldn't figure out the scale's kilometers, so I went downstairs for another piece of fudge. I can see that was a big mistake." She pinched her waist, grabbing the evidence of the months of potatoes, bread, and pancakes that had settled into her middle, and beyond. But the pictures couldn't keep her from biting into a freshly baked Swedish bun.

"I don't understand. You would think climbing all these stairs every day would keep me trim," she said, taking another bite.

"Perhaps your body is going through some changes," Tina suggested.

"Hey, save room for your birthday cake—it's the first cake I've baked in over a year," Shelly said.

"Oh, don't worry, there's plenty of room for cake. I'll think of something to do about my dilemma *after* my party."

Rosie's answer came two days later when Ana-Karin came aboard with her arms full of bags.

"It's good to see you," Shelly said as she poured Ana-Karin a cup of coffee.

She placed a large brown bag on the troop mess table. "I'm visiting friends in Stockholm, so I decided to stop by to say hello." She smiled at Rosie. "A local bookstore donated some books and videos for the ship's library."

Rosie's eyes lit up as she reached for the book bag, but Ana-Karin intervened and handed her a smaller package.

"Here, Rosie, this one is especially for you."

Rosie opened the package, curious to see what it contained. *Could it be that Ana-Karin has bought me a birthday gift?* Rosie wondered.

"A workout video," Rosie said, holding it up for Shelly and Tina.

"Don't wave that video at me!" Shelly said. "I'm happy with my love handles."

"Here! Here!" Tina chimed.

Rosie stared at the video cover of a beautiful, thin blond holding a pair of what looked to be fifty-pound weights. Then she turned to Ana-Karin.

"How thoughtful. Is this for me?"

Ana-Karin nodded. "Yes. I thought you could use it."

Rosie glared at the nurse. "And you are welcome to join me anytime. Have you looked in the mirror lately?"

Shelly stared across the table at Rosie as if she had said a swear word. Didn't Rosie remember how Ana-Karin could retaliate against anyone, at any time, with her honey-coated words? Shelly poured the nurse another cup of coffee. "Here, let's drink up."

Ana-Karin took a sip and then smiled. "I'm going to start my workout program when I return to home."

"Now that I have this video, I'm going to start the Restoration Workout Hour, and when you return to the ship, you can join us."

"I look forward to it," Ana-Karin said as she took a bite of Rosie's leftover birthday cake.

"In the meantime, no more potatoes, no more Swedish buns, and no more . . . well, less . . . of this," Rosie said as she bit into another slice of cake.

As February's ice age bore down, the ship's generator acquired the annoying habit of breaking down. When this occurred, the engineer on duty would diligently work on the temperamental machine until it was once more up and running.

Jeans lit candles in the troop mess, and the crew huddled together at the smaller tables. They passed time telling stories, and even though the candles gave off a cozy atmosphere, by the generator's fourth breakdown, Rosie couldn't take it any longer.

"Come with me," she ordered Jesse. Shivering, they made their way to their cabin. They bundled up together under layered blankets and held each other close. They steamed up the portholes and talked of winters past in their warm California homeland.

36

Resti was looking prettier every day with her new interior colors of green, orange, and blue.

By early March, the holds had been painted, giving them the makeover they desperately needed. Anders, a retired painter, arrived at eight o'clock five days a week to oversee the project. "The Russians will love these bright colors," he said, admiring the vivid fresh colors.

Rosie touched the fresh paint. "Resti, you're glowing from head to toe—I should say, from bow to stern."

Jesse turned to Clive. "Speaking of heads, it's time to get back to work." The plumbing duo had finished their work in the kitchen on level one of holds two and three, and now they were installing new heads and showers.

Deep on the second level of hold two, the center of the main area was converted into a sitting area, with furniture donated by the Swedish furniture store Ikea. Brown sofas were arranged on each side of the black coffee table, with chairs of orange and green scattered around.

Small cubicles were built around the sitting area to accommodate four people each. Bunk beds were installed on either side of a narrow aisle, leaving enough space for the passenger's personal belongings.

At the end of the hallway was the rec room, where a Ping-Pong table was set up at one end. "This is where the Restoration Workout will be held," Rosie informed Ellen as they passed by the doorway. "Are you going to join us?"

"When does it start?"

"As soon as possible."

Ellen caught Rosie glancing at her behind. "Yeah, sure. I could use a workout or two before I fly home."

"When are you leaving?" Rosie asked.

"I'm not sure; it depends."

"Depends on what? Daniel?"

Ellen blushed. "I guess it shows, huh?"

"It's quite obvious."

"I've never been one to hide my feelings. But he doesn't give me the time of day."

"Are you playing hard to get?"

Ellen's eyes widened. "Me? Play hard to get? Never! Why? Do you think that would work?"

Ellen seemed truly interested in Rosie's input, but the truth was, Rosie didn't know what would work with Daniel. He was boisterous, self-assured, and too cute for his own good. And he only had eyes for Jeans.

"Let me think about it," Rosie said. "In the meantime, we'll begin our workouts."

Spring's sunshine began to touch the March air and melt the snow. Rosie busily typed thank-you letters in the office while morning sunbeams danced on her computer.

Stuart scratched his head as he looked through the stack of contributions.

"It's amazing how this project has stirred so many people. I couldn't handle this correspondence without you. Shelly's not a computer girl."

Rosie chuckled. "And she's not a cook, and I can relate to that. But I don't know another woman who would give up everything to live on a ship. Shelly is very special."

"Special she is. I couldn't do this without her," he said as he looked around the small room.

"From what she's told me, this is her dream too. And I'd say that God is providing for your dreams to come true."

He picked up another piece of paper. "He certainly is, but we're still waiting for the lifeboat canisters to arrive. We must have them before we sail." He winked. "We have to keep praying."

Rosie resumed typing. "The equipment will come at just the right time."

"What donations have we received so far?"

Rosie picked up the two-page list. "Dan's company donated and installed a beautiful industrial kitchen; McDonald's donated five hundred serving trays; a Christian relief organization donated five hundred cups and mugs; and a hardware store in Smaaland donated all the cutlery."

Rosie looked up. Stuart was grinning over his coffee. She took a sip of her lukewarm liquid and then continued. "A Swedish textile company gave a hundred sets of bedclothes in colors blue, green, and orange to match each room in hold two."

She turned the page. "Ana-Karin is returning to help Doc with the donations for the infirmary. And the food list is endless: seven tons of chicken and hundreds of pounds of potatoes, carrots, and peas, and hundreds of pounds of Swedish coffee. Shall I continue?"

"I get the picture—we are on our way!" Stuart bellowed. "Let the typing continue!"

The crew held their breath every time Torre stood to make his morning announcements.

"Let's see . . . it's mid-March, so what will he say today—that we'll have to wait until summer to sail?" Ellen asked as she chomped on her last piece of bacon.

"He's smiling, so maybe we'll be sailing soon," Shelly said.

Ellen ignored her stepmother's comment as she took a bite of her last pancake.

"You have braved the cold winter, and now spring is here," Torre began.

Ellen prodded Torre. "Yes, yes, go on."

"If the safety supplies arrive, the *Restoration* will depart sometime this summer."

"Summer?" was the first thing out of Rosie's mouth.

"Yikes," Shelly whispered yet again.

Ellen scraped the last of her scrambled eggs into her spoon with her fork. "You can say that again, Shelly. It looks like I'll be taking another trek somewhere."

"We're not leaving until summer? Jesse and I have to be home by July! This means that we might not be helping the Russian Jews at all."

"Rosie, calm down," Jesse said; then he asked Torre, "How long is the trip from Stockholm to the Black Sea?"

"Approximately two weeks, but we'll stop in England and Athens to give tours to the local churches."

"We'll get to tour Greece!" Ellen cheered.

Rosie rolled her eyes. "Don't you ever think about anything besides touring?"

"Rosie, lighten up. You were young once, remember?" Jesse said half-teasing.

"Yeah, but right now I'm feeling my age—forty-nine and menopausal!"

Ellen smiled. "Are you joking? You're old enough to have menopause?"

"Don't go there, Ellen," Rosie scowled as if Ellen had used a swear word.

Torre came to their table and sat down next to Jesse. "I couldn't help overhearing, Rosie. Is there anything wrong? I don't know that term in Swedish."

Rosie blushed. She was in no mood to touch the menopausal subject with a male Swede. "I haven't been feeling myself lately. I should go to the doctor, but we don't have insurance."

"I'll call my wife, and she'll find you a doctor in Uppsala," Torre said sympathetically.

"Thank you, Torre," Jesse said with a sigh. "I can use some help."

Rosie glared at Jesse. "And what does that mean?"

Jesse knew he had lit a fire in his wife, so he took her hand. "I meant, *we* can use some help."

On their way to the doctor, Jesse and Rosie dropped Ellen off at the train station in downtown Uppsala.

"Have fun," Rosie said as Ellen gathered her backpack from the backseat of the church van. "When will you return?"

"I don't know. I'll call Dad, and he'll keep me posted." Ellen slammed the back door and then opened it. "I hope everything turns out okay at the doctor," she added.

Surprised, Rosie rolled down her window. "Why, thank you, Ellen."

As Ellen walked toward the station chewing on a breakfast bar, Rosie smiled. "That girl never fails to surprise me."

After the examination, the doctor's diagnosis was clear.

"With everything you have told me, including the heavy bleeding, hot flashes, and mood swings, the exam shows that you are in the beginning stages of klimakterium."

"Pardon me?" Rosie asked.

"Oh, excuse me . . . the English word is *menopause*, as you call it. I suggest that you take it easy for a few days. I will give you some medication in case you have excess bleeding while at sea."

"Do you have anything for her mood swings?" Jesse asked.

Rosie turned to her husband, but before she could comment, the doctor shook his head and said, "There is nothing a man can do for such a problem except stay clear of the area." Rosie turned to the doctor and caught him winking at Jesse.

"Until you return to America and talk to your physician, try eating healthy foods and try to exercise three times a week."

When the receptionist handed Jesse the statement, he looked puzzled.

"You are volunteers on the *Restoration* so there is no charge."

All Jesse could mutter was, "*Tack.*"

As they pulled out of the parking lot, Jesse patted Rosie's knee. "This is one more miracle to add to our list."

"Don't touch me!"

Jesse quickly withdrew his hand.

"Kidding!"

"Miracles and menopause—quite an emotional combination," Jesse simply stated.

37

Resti *was ready to leave the harbor and begin her journey to the Black Sea, but was her crew?*

The crew cheered when Torre announced they would sail in April.

"I guess you were right after all," Rosie told Shelly.

"About what?"

"You said we'd sail before summer."

"Yikes, I forgot."

"So, why aren't you excited?"

Shelly glanced over at Stuart talking to the engineers. "I'm wondering if Ellen will return in time to sail."

"Stop wondering and start believing, Shelly," Rosie said. "You've seen the miracles on this ship."

"The *Restoration* is our miracle ship, isn't she?"

"In more ways than we can imagine," Rosie said, remembering her *no charge* doctor's exam.

Two weeks later, Rosie was hanging over the rail shaking rugs when she caught sight of a lanky blonde walking down the hill toward the ship.

"Ellen!"

Ellen waved as she made her way up the gangway.

"What brings you back so soon? Did you run out of money again?" Rosie teased.

Ellen slung her backpack onto the deck. "I guess I missed the *Restoration*."

"Is that all?"

"And Stuart . . . I mean, my dad."

Rosie raised her eyebrows. "Anyone else?"

Ellen looked around. "Is Daniel back?"

"He'll return when the *Restoration* is ready to sail."

"Did Torre give us a date yet?"

"We're scheduled to sail in April, but we're praying for a specific date."

She grabbed her backpack and walked toward the superstructure. "Yeah, sure . . . prayer." And then, as if she had forgotten something, she turned around. "Oh, how did your doctor's exam go?"

"Oh, just great! I'm menopausal, so look out!"

Ellen flinched. "Thanks for the warning." She looked up toward the bridge. "Have you seen Stuart?"

"He's working on the monkey bridge. I'm sure he and Shelly will be glad to see you."

"I don't know about Shelly. I think I've become a thorn in her side."

"She wants to be your friend, nothing more."

"That seems to be more than my mother wants."

April showers couldn't dampen the surge of energy that came over the crew as they eagerly worked on last-minute projects. Tired by the end of each day, they sat drinking coffee and laughing at sea yarns that the seasoned seamen told.

Rosie loved listening to the men. "They have some wild stories. I believe half of them, and I pretend to believe the other half."

"Oh, I believe them all," Jeans said, winking.

Ellen rolled her eyes. "I don't believe any of them."

"We'll sail the day before Easter," Torre announced to the crew after breakfast. "Pastor Hans and Helene have invited the crew to their home for a farewell luncheon."

Ellen smiled. "I can't wait to see their mansion."

Torre shook his head and chuckled at her remark. "They don't live in a mansion, Ellen. Where do you get such ideas?"

"And I heard that Pastor Hans had an impressive library," Rosie casually mentioned.

"You shall see for yourselves very soon," Torre said, grinning.

Helene greeted the crew at the door of their modest eighteenth-century home.

"It's not so big," Ellen said, snooping in the library. Rosie stood in awe of the hundreds of books that filled the ceiling to floor shelves . . . some written in English; the majority written in Swedish.

"You look disappointed," Henrik said.

"I just thought all big-time preachers were rich; at least they are in America," Ellen said as she walked toward the dining room. "I'm hungry; where's the food?"

After a Swedish smorgasbord, Pastor Hans led everyone into the great room. He took hold of Henrik's right arm. "I see that working on the ship has given you some muscles."

"Yes, sir," Henrik answered, blushing.

Ellen touched Henrik's left arm. "The ship is definitely not for wimps," she said, smiling.

When the crew settled in, Pastor Hans began. "The *Restoration* is about to embark on a serious journey. It's important that you focus on the ship's mission. You are part of fulfilling the prophetic scriptures to bring Russian Jews from the north to Israel. There are organizations who hate Israel and the Jewish people, and they will do whatever possible to stop us."

Rosie's heart began pounding. *Is it fear or menopause?* she asked herself.

Pastor Hans glanced around the room. "It is crucial that there is unity among the crew, so if you have anything against your brother or sister, you need to go to them and make it right before the ship sails."

The crew listened closely to the pastor's words. Everyone, that is, except Daniel, who sat in a corner, yawning, and Ellen, who was staring out of a large bay window toward the garden.

That night as Rosie and Jesse snuggled under the covers, he noticed her fidgeting under his touch.

"Is this a menopausal thing?" he asked, trying to be sensitive.

"Uh, oh, no. Please, touch me again," she said, taking his hand and placing it around her waist. Jesse smiled as he began his pursuit to the next level. Suddenly she interrupted, "Do you have anything against anyone on board?"

"So that's it," he said, pulling away. "No, I don't. Do you?"

"No, I'm fine. I've dealt with Ana-Karin's nit-picking irritations, and Ellen's I-don't-care-about-anything-but-me attitude." She pulled Jesse close. "So where were we?" She had forgotten all about the pastor's words—until a knock fell on their door.

"Who is it?" Jesse asked, panting.

"It's Jeans. Can I talk to you a minute?"

Rosie gathered her nightgown while Jesse climbed over her, stepped into his shorts, and pulled a T-shirt over his damp body.

"Hello, Jeans."

"May I come in?"

"Of course," Jesse said, opening the door. "Here, sit down."

Jeans looked unsure as she sat in the green chair. Jesse grabbed a stool from the bathroom. Rosie sat up in bed, still holding the sheet as she pulled her nightgown over her head.

Jeans cleared her throat. "Today when Pastor Hans told us to make things right with the crew, I knew I had to talk to you."

Rosie glanced at Jesse, who was looking at Jeans, who was staring directly at her.

Rosie gulped. "Who, me? What did I do?"

"Where do I begin?" Jeans asked nervously.

Rosie bit her tongue.

Jeans stared at the green rug. "First of all, I think the way I pray has offended you."

Before Rosie could answer, Jeans continued, "You see, I'm coming from a different place than you. I've been taught to pray reverently, so that's why I go to a corner during prayer."

Is she saying that I pray irreverently? Rosie wondered.

Jeans looked directly at Rosie. "And I can tell that bothers you."

Rosie had to hand it to Jeans—she was the most honest gal she had met in a long time. Now she was obliged to be just as honest.

"You're right. Jesse is always reminding me that the crew comes from different walks of life and not everyone is going to do things the way I think they should. And sometimes that bothers me."

"And most of the time it shows," Jesse added, winking at Jeans.

Rosie enjoyed the pure honesty of the moment, so she continued, "Like you, I was raised in a denomination where we prayed quietly. But when I went to Bible school, I learned there were different types of prayer. There are times to pray quietly, and there are times when we must pray stronger, and sometimes pray in the spirit. When we're baptized in the Holy Spirit, we're given a heavenly language that we can use at any given time."

"I've heard Tina and Urma talking about the Holy Spirit. I'd like to hear more," Jeans said.

"Let me try to explain. When we have corporate prayer in the mornings and on Thursday nights, it's our responsibility to come together in unity—it's written in the ship's manual."

"You seem to know the ship's manual by heart," Jeans said.

"Rosie can be quite black and white when it comes to rules," Jesse said.

"But since I've been on the ship, I have become more flexible."

"Except when that old mini-pause kicks in," he said jokingly. By the look on Rosie's face, he knew he'd better back off. "But she's much better."

Rosie turned to Jeans. "I admire your honesty for coming."

"I had to clear the air."

Rosie slid off the bed. "You did the right thing." She took the young woman's rough hands. "But more important, you must be free to be who God wants you to be. I can tell you now that I won't be putting any more of my expectations on you."

Jeans looked relieved when Rosie gave her a hug at the door.

Back in bed, Jesse leaned over and wrapped his arms around Rosie, ready to take up where they had left off.

"Can I read something?" she asked as she opened her Bible.

"Uh, sure," he said, adjusting himself.

"Let nothing be done through strife or vain glory, but in lowliness of mind let each esteem one another better than themselves. Do all things without murmuring and disputes."

Rosie placed her Bible on the nightstand and sat upright. "So what if someone prays differently? So what if their prayers are soft when I think they should be loud? It's their heart that matters, not the outward appearance. If someone wants to pray sitting down instead of standing, God doesn't care. What matters is that I show the love of Christ. I should know this by now!"

Jesse sat up and kissed Rosie's cheek. "Hey, calm down. This is a lesson we already know, but sometimes a reminder is needed when we start to slide back to our old religious ways of thinking." She nodded, and then he took her in his arms. "Now, where were we before we were interrupted?"

Rosie smiled as he moved closer. He kissed her, and she responded eagerly.

There were probably knocks on other cabin doors that evening, but Jeans's knock on Rosie's door brought the two women to a new level of friendship.

Pastor Hans presented the crew members with individual certificates at the church service a week prior to the *Restoration*'s departure, and then he prayed for their journey. As his hand touched Rosie's forehead, the power of God knocked her backward so fast that the usher didn't have time to catch her. *Bam!*—onto the carpet-covered concrete floor. A *Bong!* went off in her head, and for an instant she felt a headache about to attack, but surprisingly, it never transpired.

"You don't even have a knot on your head from the fall," Jesse said as he felt her head. "It's like something padded your fall."

"Could it be my angel at work?" she asked, rubbing her head.

"It could be, and may he continue working."

Family and friends gathered at the dock on Passover to bid farewell. The crew bustled to load last-minute food and supplies in the holds and large reefer. Rosie was in the office helping Stuart tie down the computers and office equipment when Torre walked in. "Where are the lifeboat canisters?" he asked.

Stuart stood straight and then cleared his throat. "They haven't arrived, but we'll be staying in Greece for a week, so we'll tie up loose ends there. The canisters will be shipped directly to Athens in time to sail to Sochi."

Torre looked concerned. "This journey depends on those lifeboats arriving in Greece on time."

"Torre, everything we've prayed for has come to pass, so we must believe the lifeboat canisters will arrive in Athens on time."

Torre's face softened. "You are right, Stuart. It is all about faith. Now, let us head for the high seas!"

The Swedes had treated the American crew like royalty through the long, cold winter. The *Restoration* was their queen, and now she was ready to take her royal court to the Promised Land.

PART THREE
The Voyage to Israel

He protected us on our entire journey and among all nations through which we traveled. Joshua 24:17

38

The MS Restoration *was heading for uncharted territory with her royal court. Only God knew what this journey held for the World War II ship and her crew.*

Tired from their first day at sea, the off-duty crew retired early to their cabins. The only noise that could be heard floating down the halls was Elvis singing "Heartbreak Hotel" in competition with the engine's roar.

Silence, and then the gentle swaying back and forth. Rosie sat up in bed and switched on her reading light. She shook Jesse's arm, waking him. He rubbed his eyes. "What's wrong? What time is it?"

Rosie glanced at the clock. "It's after midnight, and the ship has stopped dead in the water."

Jesse dressed quickly.

Rosie looked through the porthole. Out of the darkness, a helicopter flew close, shining a light down on the black, rolling sea. Rosie flew out of bed, dressed in her clean yet stained gray sweat suit, and then hurried to the troop mess.

Tina stood, her dark hair tousled, staring out of a porthole.

"What's happening?" Rosie asked as she found her own round window.

"When we entered the Gulf of Finland, the captain received a distress signal from a nearby ferry." Tina turned toward Rosie. "They have a man overboard, so all the ships in the area must heed the call. We're shining our lights on the sea in search of the missing body."

Rosie shuddered, recalling the sinking of the *Estonia*. "Another distress at sea."

"It is Saturday night, and many people drink and party on the ferries as they sail from port to port."

"Will he be saved?"

Tina shook her head. "It is rare for a body to survive these cold waters for any length of time."

Rosie wanted to cry, but she chose to be brave, mimicking the captain's stoic wife.

After tedious hours of searching, the body was not to be found by helicopter or by ship. When Captain Alain gave orders to start the engine, the crew gathered in the troop mess.

Urma bowed her head. "We must pray for the family left behind, who will soon receive the heartbreaking news."

As Tina whispered the last amen, Rosie broke down. She wanted Jesse, but then remembered he had started his four-hour watch in the engine room at four o'clock. Jeans walked over and placed a comforting arm around Rosie's shoulder. Until she could be in the arms of her husband, Jeans would do just fine.

The *Restoration* sailed into the Helsinki port at the dawning of Easter. "It's a new day," Urma announced to the stewards and galley girls as they watched the deck crew maneuver around the main deck. "Now we must prepare for the tours," she said, as the guards took their positions at the bottom of the gangway.

Team One spent the morning touring the capitol. Most shops were closed for Easter, but after strolling through the market square, Jessie and Rosie found a café where they were serving Easter smorgasbord. "The aroma of Finnish coffee is calling," Rosie said.

"Why don't you join us?" Jesse asked Ellen as she watched Daniel and Jeans stroll toward town.

"I guess I don't have anything better to do," Ellen sighed as she reluctantly followed them into the café.

Rosie tried making small talk as they ate, but Ellen was too focused on gnawing on her crab legs to answer.

"Do you have any plans after we arrive in Israel?" Jesse asked.

Ellen wiped her mouth with a napkin. "Yeah, I'm going to tour Italy."

"What about your mother back home in Montana?" Rosie asked.

Ellen's eyes narrowed. "What about her? She's too busy making my stepfather happy to care how long I'm gone," she said, slurping her coffee.

"I thought you might decide to stay on with the ship," Rosie said.

"You must be kidding! Stuart . . . my dad . . . tries too hard, and Shelly drives me crazy with her *yikes* and kindness."

"Maybe you should give Stuart a chance. And Shelly only wants what's best for you."

Ellen interrupted, "Stop right there. You don't know what you're talking about."

Jesse charged to Rosie's rescue by changing the subject. "Well, tell me, Ellen, how do you like traveling by ship?"

"I'm starting to climb the walls," she said, grabbing her napkin again. "If I were back home, I'd be working on my internship at the radio station, and my favorite pastime is riding my horse. I love the ranch . . . well, until lately."

"What's changed?" Rosie asked. *Here I go again, treading on sensitive ground.*

"Everything. Nothing's the same. Dad's gone and Mom's with that selfish old bastard—excuse me—old coot." Ellen looked down and wiped her eyes with her soiled napkin. Rosie grabbed a hankie from her purse and placed it next to Ellen's plate.

When Ellen picked up the clean handkerchief, she noticed the *E* embroidered in the corner.

"What does the *E* stand for, your maiden name?"

"No . . . the *E* stands for Elvis. My best friend gave it to me as a joke." Thinking of Prissy made her smile. She hadn't realized how much she missed her friend until she thought about the surprise going-away party Prissy had planned for them. Elvis music blared through Prissy's house, and a large cake with a guitar sat in the middle of her dining room table. When Rosie had opened the small box with a white hankie, she was touched when she saw the magical *E* embroidered on the corner.

"Take this wherever you go," Prissy said. "In remembrance of Elvis, and me."

Ellen looked at the gray letter. "So the *E* is for Elvis."

"I was eleven when our family drove to South Carolina for Christmas. When I saw Elvis in his first movie, "Love Me Tender" I was a goner." Ellen laughed along with Rosie.

"When did your love affair with Elvis begin?" Rosie asked.

"I already told you about my brother. When I was a little girl, Dad would tuck us in bed and sing "Love Me Tender" in Norwegian."

Rosie was caught off guard as Ellen opened up her broken heart. While Ellen talked, Rosie discovered that she wanted to help Ellen mend it.

The Gulf of Riga welcomed the *Restoration* with smooth waters. Riga's port resonated Latvia's rich culture. The old town was close by, so after the morning tours, Jesse and Rosie walked to town and shopped for small souvenir boxes. Afterward, they found a courtyard, where they sat in a local café to sip espresso.

By midday, Jesse's feet began to swell, so they walked back to the ship, where he rested in the solitude of their cabin. He lay horizontal into the evening and was asleep by the time the crew boarded a bus for the evening church meeting. Rosie was reading her latest Bodie Thoene novel, *Munich Signature,* and was somewhere deep in the Black Forest when a knock on the cabin door brought her back to Riga.

"Hallo, family Atkisson!" a young Latvian man yelled, waking Jesse from his sleep. "My pastor sent me with a car to pick you up for tonight's meeting," he stated boldly.

"You were sent to personally pick us up?" Jesse asked, yawning.

"You went to Bible school with my pastor, and he longs to see you at the meeting," the man answered.

"He *longs*?" Rosie repeated, recalling how their European friends used the term to express their desire for something.

Jesse looked at Rosie. "If he *longs* to see us, then surely my feet can bear up for a few hours."

By the time they arrived, the Israeli songs and dances had ignited joy throughout the large auditorium; and by the end of the meeting, Jesse's strength had been restored, and the pain in his feet had disappeared. He grabbed Rosie and joined the circle of dancers. "Come on! It's been a long time since we've danced."

39

After the tragic event in the Gulf of Finland, Resti *enjoyed the uneventful days on the North Sea. The Shoreham port official guided the old ship through the narrow lock as if she were the* Queen Mary. *If only her World War II knot-cronies could see her now!*

As the *Restoration* glided through the Strait of Dover toward the coastal town of Shoreham, England, Rosie managed the laundry without a splash from the washing machine, and she vacuumed the crew's lounge without losing her balance. She had earned her sea legs and she was proud of them, but she still took extra caution when cleaning the toilets.

The *Restoration* slowly entered Shoreham's lock, and to prevent bumping against the narrow lock, the boatswains lowered large inner tubes on the port and starboard sides of the ship. Once settled, the guards reported to their respective positions, and the rest of the crew divided up for their shore leaves.

With limited time and budget, Rosie had only two wishes. "First, I want to have lunch in an authentic tea room. Second, I want to eat fish and chips on the Brighton Pier."

"How do you know so much about Brighton?" Jesse asked.

Rosie reached in her purse for a magazine she had purchased in Seattle. "I read about Brighton in my *Victoria* magazine."

"Well, let's see what I can do for you, Queen Rose," Jesse teased as the team began their walk to Shoreham Village.

"We're catching a bus for Brighton in the town square for those who want to join us for tea," Henrik said, glancing at Ellen.

But Ellen was busy trying to make conversation with Daniel, who still only had eyes for Jeans.

"I would love a spot of tea," Jeans replied in her playful British accent. She moved away from Daniel and walked toward Henrik.

Ellen smiled, then led the rest of the team toward the shopping square, with Daniel following close behind.

Why isn't Daniel staying with Jeans? Rosie wondered.

"Are you sure you don't want to join Ellen's group?" Rosie asked Henrik.

"I am very sure," he said, rubbing his scar. "Good riddance to them both."

This love triangle is getting more complicated by the minute, Rosie thought. Trying to help lighten the moment she asked, "Before we catch the bus, would anyone like to join me for a cup of java to go?"

Jeans smiled at Henrik. "No, I'll wait for English tea."

As Rosie stood in line in the café, two young ladies were chatting away at a nearby table. She paid for her coffee, and then walked over and stood next to their table. The older lady stopped talking and looked up.

"Can I help you?" she asked coldly.

"Oh, I'm sorry. I'm just so happy to be in a country where I can understand what you're saying without an interpreter," Rosie said gleefully. Now both women stared at her.

"I'm not eavesdropping. I'm listening to your lovely British accents. May I join you?"

Before the ladies had a chance to answer, Rosie pulled up a chair and proceeded to tell the women the condensed version of where she had been living for the past year.

"Oh, tell us more," begged the younger Brit. They stared openmouthed, as if Rosie were conducting a book reading at a local bookstore.

"You should write a book," said the younger woman.

"I'll buy one," promised the older lady.

"Even if it's written in American English?" Rosie teased.

"Of course. My mother taught me to speak American English after she visited her aunt in New Jersey," chimed the young woman.

Rosie laughed. "My, the Brits do have a sense of humor."

The girls were still giggling when Jesse poked his head in the café and motioned to Rosie. The bus had arrived, so Rosie gave a hearty cheerio and ta-ta to her new British fans, and then ran to catch the red double-decker.

Rosie felt like a real tourist as she dashed up the narrow flight of stairs and grabbed a seat in the first row.

They laughed when the bus turned a corner. "Riding on the wrong side of the road is a real leaning . . . uh, I mean *learning* experience," Jeans said, leaning against Henrik on every curve.

"I don't think I'll venture to drive in jolly old England," Henrik said. Jeans chuckled at all of Henrik's silly remarks.

They walked the cobblestone paths of Brighton until Rosie found a quaint English teahouse. "This one is beckoning me to come inside."

"May we sit by the fireplace?" Jesse asked the hostess.

"Of course," she said, and then led them to a cozy corner by the roaring fire. "Are you from America?" she asked Rosie.

"Yes, but please don't hold that against them," Henrik replied, winking.

Jesse and Henrik downed the finger sandwiches, ordered another plate, and drank a pot of tea.

"What's for dessert?" Henrik asked, wiping his mouth on a cloth napkin.

When the server brought scones, cream, jam, and another pot of tea to the table, Rosie briefly told the server of their journey.

"You should write a book," she suggested.

"That's a jolly good idea," Rosie giggled.

When Rosie looked around the room and noticed a mother and daughter laughing and chatting at a nearby table, Jesse took her hand. "I know what you're thinking."

"I miss them so much," Rosie said, squeezing her husband's hand. "But, hey, we're on the last leg of the trip. We've come too far to turn back now."

"That's my sailor girl," Jesse said as he kissed her hand.

After lunch they posed for pictures in front of the queen's summer castle, and by sunset Jesse faced the Brighton Pier. "Now, let's find something a little more heartier to eat."

"Here, here!" Henrik said, rubbing his tummy.

As they walked, Rosie observed the Brighton shoreline. "The English beaches are so coarse compared to our smooth California sands."

Jeans observed the rows of blue and white striped lounge chairs. "I can see why they can't lie on the beach."

"And you better wear flip-flops; those pebbles could do a lot of foot damage," Jesse added.

"Oh, look!" Rosie shouted. Above a restaurant on the end of the pier hung a sign advertising fish and chips and the best hamburgers in town.

"We're both getting our wish," Jesse told Rosie as he handed the server his menu. "I'll have your largest hamburger, with extra onions."

"Me too!" Henrik echoed.

Jeans whispered to Rosie, "After today, these men might want to consider joining the Restoration Workout Hour!"

The local newspapers had advertised the World War II ship's arrival. Local churches and organizations flooded the ship for the tours, and listened intently as Jesse told the history of Jewish persecution during World War II.

"Most of the world, including England, closed their eyes to the atrocities that were taking place in Europe during the war era."

Jesse concluded, "I invite you to take a few moments to reflect on your own attitude toward the Jewish people."

Rosie was touched as small groups quietly slipped into the corners of hold one to repent of their apathy toward the Jewish people and to ask God's forgiveness in behalf of their country.

On the last evening in port, the crew boarded two buses. They drove through the beautiful English countryside to an old country church. The sanctuary was filled to capacity. After the dance team sang and danced to Israeli folk songs, Torre eagerly shared the story of the MS *Restoration*.

"Operation Jabotinsky was established to help locate and transport Russian Jews to Israel. This project covers all expenses. The *Restoration* is large enough to transport hundreds, plus all of their belongings. They're happy to have the chance to begin a new life."

Afterward, finger sandwiches, scones, and hot tea were served in the reception room. Still, Rosie continued her search for a cup of hot, black coffee.

A stout Englishwoman standing behind the table noticed Rosie. "May I help you?" she asked.

"Where is the coffee?" Ellen interrupted.

"Madam, this is coffee." Rows of cups were filled with a beige-looking concoction.

Ellen looked closer. "It looks like tea."

"That's because we've already added the cream."

Rosie discovered that the caramel-colored coffee tasted delicious.

That evening, in an English countryside church, Rosie surprised herself by drinking cream in her once black-only coffee world.

"How easy it is for you to pick up foreign habits," Ellen said as Rosie followed her to a table full of finger sandwiches.

"Except for Swedish P and P."

Ellen raised her eyebrows.

"You know, Pancakes and Pea soup—every Thursday."

Ellen delved into the stack of sandwiches. "I actually prefer P and P to these little crustless morsels."

Once on the Atlantic, the *Restoration* stayed within sight of the shorelines of France and Spain.

The warm Morocco coastline enticed the stewards to spend their fika breaks on deck. Ellen clicked her camera, while Clive's video scanned the rugged hillsides.

"Are those old houses?" Ellen asked.

Tina handed Rosie her binoculars. "They are ancient monasteries."

"Who would dare live in such isolation?" Rosie asked as she squinted to see if there was anyone living among the cliffs.

"The monks lived in these solitary monasteries and lifted their prayers to God day and night," Tina said. "I wonder what it's like to be so dedicated to God to choose such an isolated life. If I weren't married, I believe I could go away to pray."

"Not me!" Ellen said, snapping a picture of Tina. "But I can see you in a monastery, Tina."

"But did you ever think that you would be living on a World War II ship?" Tina asked.

Ellen turned to capture a photo of Rosie unaware. "Well, unlike you, I didn't volunteer."

"You're right, Ellen," Rosie replied. "I did volunteer, but it wasn't anything I had planned. This lady never dreamed she'd be living on a World War II ship."

Rosie turned toward the bow of the ship. *I wonder how the monks would have taken to living on this old ship for a year.* She smiled at the thought of them scrubbing, scraping, and painting the old ship in their long, flowing robes.

Rosie walked the deck, taking in the beauty of the rough hillsides. "Lord, I'm glad you didn't ask me to live in a cliff-hanging monastery. You do know what's best for me." She paused to draw in the scent of the sea, and then she embraced the freshly painted rail. "And, thank you, Resti, for giving me a first-class tour of these beautiful shorelines."

Rosie joined Tina and Urma on deck every afternoon to pray for France and Portugal, and now Morocco. One afternoon Jeans put her paintbrush down as Rosie walked by. "May I join you?"

"Absolutely!" Rosie answered, using Captain Alain's signature phrase.

Ellen threw her brush on the plastic tarp. "I need a break too. Where's my camera? I'll take some pictures of you praying."

As they walked portside, Tina quoted aloud from her Bible. "Praise the Lord, all ye nations, praise the Lord all ye—" She tried to continue, but a familiar roar above the ship drowned her words.

Rosie pointed to the sky. "Since we left England, that plane has been flying over. Jesse thinks it's the same one that landed next to the ship in Stockholm."

"We are sailing off the coast of Tripoli, so the captains are keeping a close watch on the plane," Tina said.

Ellen snapped a picture as the small two-engine plane flew out of sight. "That's good to hear, because something is strange about this whole situation."

40

Resti felt at home on the Mediterranean Sea with the Greek sun beating on her deck. Oh, the warmth, the beauty, and the freedom.

The *Restoration* sailed past the barren hills of Greece toward the large Athens seaport of Piraeus. Rosie stood on deck, surrounded by the blue, clear water, overcome with emotion—her dreams of visiting Greece were coming true.

"I'm in Greece!" Rosie cheered. "I can't believe that I'm really in Greece! It's exactly how I imagined some twenty years ago when I picked up my first book on this country."

Every summer Rosie looked forward to taking Grace and Presley to the La Habra Library Summer Story Time. She would drop them off at the Children's Corner, and then head for the travel section to find the latest books on Greece. Once home, she'd lie in her lounge chair and bask in the sun reading exotic tales about the faraway country while her kids splashed in their plastic wading pool. Rosie walked with the old women dressed in their black dresses as they hobbled to the water's edge to watch over their grandchildren, who swam in the cool Aegean Sea, their only relief from the sweltering heat.

"Yikes, you sound like Val when she arrived in Sweden," Shelly teased, bringing Rosie back to the moment.

"I can hear her now, shouting, *we're in Sweden*!" Rosie reminisced. "I wish she were here with us."

Shelly smiled. "Val reminded me of that little girl inside me; I just need to let her out more." And with that, Shelly yelled, "I'm in Greece!"

When they were securely docked, Torre held a meeting on the Fiesta Deck. "You have been working very hard, so Pastor Hans and Helene have a gift for you."

"What are we getting, new paintbrushes and brooms?" Ellen asked.

"Ellen's half-empty outlook on life is shining through once more," Rosie whispered to Tina.

"You will take a ferry to the island of Poros for a day," Torre announced. "For security reasons, Jesse will take Team One tomorrow, and Stuart will lead Team Two the following day."

"This time the glass is half full," Rosie told Ellen.

That night in their cabin, while Jesse showered, Rosie spoke through the plastic shower curtain. "I have two wishes when we get to the island."

Jesse smiled as he stepped out of the shower and grabbed his towel. "And what might they be, dear lady of the sea?"

"First, I want to ride one of those little motorbikes around the island."

"And your second wish?"

Rosie's heart jumped as Jesse's towel dropped to the floor, revealing his tanned, healthy body.

"Well, I've always wanted to sunbathe on a topless beach."

Jesse's eyes widened at the thought of his wife lying in her birthday suit on a secluded Greek beach. He smiled as he walked toward the bed.

"Gotcha!" Rosie laughed, pulling Jesse toward her. "You believed me, didn't you?"

"Yeah, you got me, my little Greek goddess. And now, it's my turn to get *you*," he said as he wrapped his arms around Rosie's hard earned slim body.

The next morning, Team One basked in the sun as the ferry made its way to the island of Poros.

"We need to stay together," Jesse ordered from the dock, but Daniel had already taken off on his own, with Ellen following close behind.

The team caught up with Daniel and Ellen at the motor-scooter rental shop.

"Are you going to join us?" Rosie asked Daniel.

"Yeah, sure," he said, and then pulled his bike next to Jeans.

They drove single file along the narrow road that wound around the island, and then pulled into a small cove to picnic and sunbathe on a white sandy beach.

"This sure beats the freezing winter we had to endure," Ellen said as she took the last bite of her sandwich. "It's hot! Let's go for a swim. Last one in is a loser," she shouted.

Everyone raced to the crystal waters while Rosie sat on her towel.

"Come on in, Rosie!" Ellen yelled from the water.

Rosie shook her head and lay down on her towel. "No swimming for me—ever."

"You really need to consider taking swimming lessons!" Ellen jabbed, then dove in the crystal clear water.

Never! Rosie thought, refraining from answering Ellen.

They spent the afternoon browsing the tourist shops and then sat under large striped umbrellas, sipping their favorite colas. Far removed from the work on the *Restoration*, the crew felt like real tourists. No one wanted the day to end, but as the sun began to turn the sky a brilliant orange, they reluctantly boarded the ferry for Piraeus.

Jesse took a head count. "Where's Ellen?"

"Miss Independence is at it again," Henrik said with a note of sarcasm.

"And where's Daniel?" Jeans asked.

"He's usually not too far from you," Henrik noted.

Jeans blushed. "I think he finally got the hint that I'm not interested in him."

"Well, I think we should leave them here to catch the next ferry," Henrik told Jesse.

Jesse shook his head. "I'll stay behind."

"Someone needs to confront that girl," Henrik said.

"It's none of our business," Jesse said. "Ellen is Stuart's responsibility."

"Hey! Wait for us!" Daniel blurted as he ran toward the ferry.

"I had to find a head—I mean a bathroom," Ellen said, breathing heavily.

"Do you believe that story?" Henrik asked Rosie.

"I choose to believe her, and you shouldn't jump to conclusions."

Henrik shrugged as he glanced at Ellen opening a bag of potato chips.

"Henrik, I do believe you have a little crush on Ellen," Rosie said, smiling.

Henrik's face turned beet red.

"Are you blushing?" she asked teasingly.

His eyes shot arrows at her. "No! I am sunburned."

Henrik turned to watch Ellen munching away on her last potato chip. Then he confessed, "Rosie, I think you are too old to fool."

"I think the word you are looking for is too *wise* to fool—not too *old*," Rosie corrected.

"Now I am blushing. I must practice my English," Henrik admitted.

The Greek sun bore down as the work and the tours continued.

The crew was allowed to go ashore in pairs, but Rosie noticed that Ellen wandered off alone whenever she felt like it. She was Captain Stuart's daughter, which in Ellen's eyes, was like royalty. One morning Rosie watched Ellen from the troop mess porthole as she strutted down the dock. "Why doesn't anyone say something to the captain about her jumping ship?" Rosie asked Tina.

Tina shook her head. "No one dares confront the situation, in fear of hurting Stuart. He gave this ship to this mission, and now he is helping bring her to the Black Sea."

"So Ellen is free to do as she chooses?"

"It looks that way," Tina said.

On their first shore leave, Jesse and Rosie walked to the end of the dock and hailed a cab to drive them to the nearest downtown corner. They strolled along the narrow cobblestoned streets to the shops nestled at the bottom of the Parthenon on the Acropolis.

Rosie discovered that the shops closed for afternoon siestas. "This is a ritual that the fast-paced Americans should adopt."

They enjoyed trekking through the ancient city and walking through the outdoor bazaar, where row after row of colorful linens and exquisite pottery lay on display. Rosie bought small wooden boxes to take home as a remembrance.

When the heat brought about unquenchable thirst, they found a sidewalk café with draping vines, where they sipped tea and dreamed the afternoon away.

At dusk, they walked to a nearby harbor, where outdoor cafés stood side by side. Rosie inhaled the delightful aroma of Greek cuisine.

Jesse took Rosie's hand. "We don't have the money to dine at these exclusive restaurants, but someday we'll return and I'll show you the sights."

Rosie kissed Jesse. "I don't need fancy restaurants; I'm having the time of my life just being with you."

A maitre d' stood next to the curb watching the couple walking toward him, hand in hand. "Come in! Come in! We will serve you delicious Greek salads—for free!"

They continued walking until a good-looking Greek wearing a crisp white jacket standing at the curb beckoned. "Please come in for a Greek salad and tea."

"No, thank you," Jesse said as they brushed by.

"But it is for free."

Rosie turned to Jesse. "How can we resist?" Jesse nodded to the man. "Lead the way."

The maitre d' sat them at a small table next to the busy street. "This will give you a chance to *people watch*—your favorite pastime," Jesse teased Rosie.

A tour bus pulled in the parking space across the street, and within minutes, Jesse and Rosie were surrounded by women dressed in plain cotton blouses and skirts, and men wearing walking shorts, black socks, and brown leather shoes. The host led the tourists to large candlelit tables next to the water.

Later, while Jesse and Rosie strolled along the narrow street, a jolly Greek maitre d' chimed, "Come in, we will give you dessert and coffee—for free!"

Jesse winked at Rosie as the maitre d' seated them at a table close to the sidewalk.

As they were finishing their second cup of coffee, Jesse noticed a tour bus parked across the street. "Look, they're coming our way." The Spanish-speaking tourists walked past them, toward long tables overlooking the harbor. "I get it now. They want their cafés to look crowded."

"And popular! I think we are part of their props," Rosie chuckled.

41

Resti *sensed that there was a mutiny about to take place.*

After sitting in Athens for three weeks, the crew began to talk among themselves.

"The months of waiting in Seattle, Stockholm, and now Athens . . . this is getting to be ridiculous," Ellen said at breakfast.

Torre sensed that Ellen's constant negative remarks could set off a rebellion among her young followers, so he decided he must give them a reason for the delay. "It is mandatory that we finish the lifeboat project before we depart."

"Why didn't you say so earlier?" Ellen asked. "We're adults; we can handle bad news."

Torre looked directly at Ellen. "I was hoping you would say that, because I have more distressing news."

"Now what?" Ellen said.

"A few major decisions must be made this week."

"What decisions?" Rosie asked.

"Just listen, Rosie," Jesse whispered.

"Due to the many delays that we have experienced over the months, many of the Russian Jews are questioning if there is a ship. They are fearful of everything, so this is one more thing to be suspicious of."

"What are you saying?" Ellen asked.

"Most of them have returned to their hometowns, leaving only eight Russian Jews waiting in Sochi. Now Pastor Hans must decide if it is worth using hundreds of gallons of fuel to travel all that distance for only eight people."

Ellen pounded her fist on the table. "We've come this far—we have to go!"

"One thing about you, Ellen, you speak what everyone else is thinking," Rosie said. Ellen just smirked.

"Rosie, hush," Jesse said for Ellen to hear. Rosie gave Jesse a cold glance.

"Pastor Hans is praying, and he will let us know when he makes his decision," Torre said.

The June heat bore down on the deck, making it almost unbearable to stay in the holds and the superstructure. The fans blew twenty-four-seven. By lunchtime, the crew gathered in the shade of the Fiesta Deck to capture a gentle breeze off the water.

Before anyone sat at their table, Rosie whispered to Jesse, "Our time is running out. If Pastor Hans doesn't make a decision soon, we'll have to fly home from Athens. It's evident that we won't be making as many trips as we had originally planned." Rosie looked toward the sea. "We'll be lucky to be on the first trip."

Jesse took Rosie's hand "Don't give up now, Rosie; we have to keep the faith."

"I hate to be the bearer of more bad news, but . . ."

That's all Rosie had to hear from Torre to set her mind buzzing.

" . . . the port authorities called, and they advised us that the *Restoration* has stayed in port longer than scheduled. The space is reserved for a larger, more prestigious vessel that is arriving today."

Rosie let out a sigh. "Oh, is that all? I thought Torre was going to tell us that there wasn't going to be a trip."

Jesse just shook his head. "Thatta girl, Rosie . . . like I said, let's keep the faith," he said half-sarcastically.

She wanted to jab him with a left, but he was too fast. By the time she turned around, he was already out of her reach.

No one knew how good life was in the Piraeus harbor until they approached their new location. Stuart guided the *Restoration* around the bend to the overcrowded dock. Rosie counted twenty ships lined up, side by side, crammed next to each other like sardines. Stuart ordered the first engineer to reverse the engine, and then, stern first, he slowly backed the ship into the narrow space.

Thirty minutes later, Stuart arrived on the main deck in time to hear his daughter complaining. "This place looks like a bunch of ugly apartment buildings on water. How long do we have to stay here?" Ellen asked as she looked down the row of weatherworn ships.

Before Stuart could answer, Torre pointed to the ships on either side. "Excuse me, but there is something more important to discuss than the surrounding scenery. These ships are parked so close that anyone can hop from one ship to the next. There is no privacy—or protection." He glanced at the crew. "Our guards on duty will have to keep a close watch to make sure no one unexpectedly comes aboard from either side. There are warnings of looting and piracy, so our guard duty will have to be taken to the next level."

"Dry dock was bad, but what did we do to deserve such a hellhole?" Ellen muttered.

Henrik turned to Ellen. "Maybe it's because of your complaining that we've ended up in this godforsaken place."

"Henrik, watch your tongue," Rosie said in Ellen's defense.

Jesse looked at Rosie. "I can't believe that you're actually defending Ellen."

Rosie smiled. She was a little surprised too.

"This docking area is where ships stay for weeks, even months, to get extensive work done," Stuart explained.

"But we won't be staying that long, will we?" Rosie gasped.

"It could be worse. At least we have water hookups onboard," Stuart added, hoping to cast a light on the somewhat dark situation.

Rosie scanned the area in disbelief. Across the narrow dirt road, graffiti was scrawled all over the breaker wall that separated them from the sometimes-raging sea. A rotten stench from the large piles of trash on the dock almost knocked Rosie overboard.

Captain Alain contacted the port authorities and requested the removal of the pile of debris at the bottom of their gangway. "Perhaps the Greeks and other foreigners can tolerate the smell, but this is unacceptable," the captain announced.

"I won't be breathing through my nose for a while," Ellen said. "This is a real trap—not to be confused with a tourist trap."

The ladies cheered when an old Greek disposal truck drove up, but their cheers turned to horror when, suddenly, there was a bustle of movement from within the rubbish.

"Eeek!" Rosie shouted.

"Yikes!" Shelly screamed.

A pack of rats scurried from a pile of garbage, searching for a new place of refuge. The men laughed as the girls ran into the superstructure.

"You must promise to keep those varmints off the ship," Rosie yelled to the men as she closed the steel door.

Safe inside, Tina reminded, "Ladies, if you look hard enough, you can always find something good in any situation."

"That's what I plan to do on my first shore leave—look for something good," Ellen said.

After dinner, Rosie caught Ellen leading Daniel off the ship.

"Can we tag along with you?" Rosie asked.

By the look on Ellen's face, it was clear to Rosie that she wanted to spend some alone time with the Viking, but Daniel quickly responded, "Of course, you can."

"I'm coming too," Henrik said. "I want to find out what's at the end of that dirt road on the other side of the hill."

After walking a mile up a winding dirt road, they arrived at the courtyard of a small village. In the cool of the evening, they sat at an outdoor café, eating gyros.

"I can't believe these delicious gyros are only one American dollar," Jesse said, pulling out a few more dollar bills. "Does anyone want another one?"

"I'd love two. And how about an espresso?" Ellen asked.

They drank coffee while sharing stories of childhood memories. Ellen's eyes glowed as she told about the time her first pony bucked her off when she was nine.

Henrik laughed. "You deserved it. I bet you were a brat."

Ellen's eyes shot darts at Henrik, but then she confessed, "I guess I was a troublemaker when I was growing up; it was my way of getting the attention that I deserved."

Henrik bowed his head. "Okay, I've heard enough, Princess Ellen."

Henrik has a strange way of showing his affection for Ellen, Rosie thought. But strangely, Ellen was responding to Henrik with a curtsy and a smile. She was getting the attention from Henrik that she longed for.

As they sat in the square, the village children entertained them by playing soccer in the nearby dirt road. Young and carefree, they were a delight to watch. Daniel joined in their game, and as Rosie watched Daniel play and laugh, she saw a softer side of him. She nudged Jesse. "I see the little boy who grew up in a home with a father who spent his last dollar on booze rather than feeding his children."

"How do you know that?"

She smiled. "Tina; she knows everything."

It was one thing to hear stories from Tina; it was quite another to watch the young man playing with the local children. Daniel related to these dirty-faced kids, and he showed it by buying them an aftergame ice cream.

42

Resti *noticed her California lady wringing her hands and drinking too much coffee.*

Rosie could see they were going to be stuck in Greece indefinitely. She cornered Jesse on the Fiesta Deck at lunch. "We have to be on the first trip to the Black Sea. Otherwise, we'll have to fly home from Athens!"

"Rosie, the timing is in God's hands. All we can do is stay put and pray, and keep the right attitude."

She opened her mouth to respond, but was interrupted by Stuart bellowing over the loudspeaker. "Jesse, report to the ship's office."

"Whew! Saved by the bell," Jesse said, pushing away from the table.

"I'll come with you to see what's going on. We'll talk later," Rosie said, following close behind.

A tall, statuesque Greek greeted them at the office door.

"Jesse! Rosie! It is so good to see you in Greece," Plaka said as he threw his arms around Jesse and then planted a wet kiss on Rosie's right cheek and then the left. His gesture brought a glimmer to Rosie's weary eyes.

"How long has it been since we were in Bible school together? Two years? Three?"

"Three," Jesse replied.

"You look as handsome as ever, Plaka," Rosie said.

Plaka looked at Jesse and then at Rosie. "You both look tired. Perhaps you need a little holiday?"

Jesse looked in his wife's bloodshot eyes. "I'm sure we do."

"That's why I'm here. Jesse, my parents took the ship tour last week, and after hearing your speech, they asked me to invite you to their summerhouse at the seaside village of Forka."

"A summerhouse in Greece—it's like a page right out of one of my books. What a fantastic way to celebrate our anniversary!"

Jesse shook his head. "We'll need to ask Torre's permission to take a leave."

"What if the ship must depart?" Rosie asked.

Plaka smiled. "As you Americans say, the bad news is: there is only a small chance that the ship will leave this week. The good news: I already talked with Torre, and he has given his approval for you to go on a holiday."

Rosie eyes lit up. "When can we leave?"

"How long will it take you to pack?"

Rosie was out the office door before Plaka could write down directions to their holiday getaway.

The Athens train station was bustling by the time Jesse and Rosie arrived by taxi early the next morning. Inside, pigeons sat on the ledges above, waiting to greet visitors. The chipped paint and broken blue tiles couldn't take away from the building's beauty. Rosie was admiring the architecture when Jesse motioned. "It's time to board."

As Jesse moved behind Rosie to step onto the train—splat—splat—all over his right shoulder. Startled, Rosie jumped on the train to avoid a similar happening.

"In Greece, this is a good-luck sign," Rosie said as she pulled out a box of Handi-Wipes from her backpack.

"Then we're going to have a great time," Jesse said as he wiped the sign off his shirt.

They had settled into the most comfortable seats when the conductor came to them asking for tickets.

"We are very extraordinary tourists," Rosie said as she leaned back in her seat.

The conductor pointed to the back of the train. They looked at each other.

"It all sounds Greek to me," Rosie said, joking.

The conductor continued babbling, but they couldn't understand a word. Frustrated, Jesse turned to the woman sitting across the aisle, "Do you speak English?"

"Yes, a little."

"Can you help us?"

"Of course. He tells you that this is a special car. Your tickets are for the tourist car—back there," she pointed. "I am sorry to inform you that he wants you to move."

Embarrassed, they gathered their backpacks. "Now we are considered very ordinary tourists," Rosie chuckled.

As the train moved through the lush, mountainous regions of Lianokladio and Larissa, Rosie noticed the difference between the large tourist train station in Athens and the smaller town stations. Most were unkempt, with graffiti written on the walls and trash everywhere. Rosie swore she saw large brown rats peeking out from under a pile of beer cans.

But when she looked past the buildings and into the eyes of the people, that is where she saw the real Greece. They were always greeted with friendly smiles. She felt at home traveling as an ordinary tourist.

The clean train station told Rosie they were in the northern tourist city of Thessaloniki. Plaka's cousin greeted them at the station and then drove them to the bus depot across town. The bus was stuffy and smelled of old men in perspiration-stained shirts, who had spent their lunch drinking too much wine. Beads of perspiration began forming on Rosie's forehead and in her armpits.

Jesse looked around. "Sorry, Rosie, no air-conditioning."

Rosie stood up and reached for the nearest window. "Then let's open the windows."

Jesse pulled her back into her seat. "We can't. They're stuck."

"So here we are, stuck for two hours in this Greek sardine can."

Rosie began fanning herself with a map of Greece while softly singing, "Happy anniversary to me, happy anniversary to me . . ."

Forka's afternoon heat hit Rosie square in the face as she stepped off the bus.

"Ah, fresh—hot—air," Rosie said, breathing deeply.

They tried cooling off under a nearby shade tree and then walked to a nearby market.

"I'll ask for directions." When Jesse pointed to the address on the wrinkled paper, the store owner shook his head. "No speaka the English."

"That's okay," Rosie told Jesse as she continued fanning herself with the tattered Greek map. "There has to be someone in this town that can speaka the English."

They found a tourist shop in the middle of the town square. Rosie thumbed through postcards for Grace and Prissy while Jesse took directions from the cashier.

A welcome breeze blew in from the sea, so they decided to eat at a local café before walking to the summerhouse. After dinner, Rosie sat back in her chair, sipping iced coffee. The pink sky sent a glow over the seaside village, reflecting a wondrous light on the Aegean Sea.

Rosie kissed Jesse's cheek. "What a perfect place to celebrate our anniversary." Then she kissed him gently on the lips. "And there's more," she smiled. "Later."

Suddenly Jesse was eager to find their Greek love nest.

"My grandmother, she live down that long road, about a kilometer thataway," the waiter said, pointing eastward.

They tossed their backpacks over their shoulders and then walked several blocks until they reached the main street. They crossed onto a dirt road.

"How far is a kilometer? Oh, never mind." Rosie inhaled the aroma of the countryside, while mama goats and their babies grazed in the olive groves.

Jesse pointed to a little white house nestled among an olive grove. "This is it." Colorful rosebushes lined the gravel walkway that led to the front porch. Jesse was digging in his pocket for the house key when a tanned, elderly gentleman appeared on the front porch.

"Hallo, Atkissons! I am Anthony, Plaka's father."

"Did you know we were going to share the house with another man?" Rosie asked.

"I'm as surprised as you, but at least he speaks the English," Jesse said as they walked up the path.

Anthony held the screen door for them to enter. The room was small and dimly lit. "Let me take your packs," Anthony said, and then led them to an even smaller room. "Make yourself at home."

When Jesse turned on a table lamp, two black bugs scurried under the double bed. Rosie bit her tongue to keep from screaming. She looked around the room. "Where's the rest of the house?"

Anthony smiled. "Follow me."

They went back outside and walked around the house to a side door.

"Door number two," Anthony said.

They stepped into a small kitchen. Rosie noticed a narrow door next to a wood table that led to a water closet. Rosie whispered under her breath, "Thank God, there's a toilet."

Anthony's large frame filled the kitchen doorway. "Sorry, no shower." He pointed through the smudged window over the sink. "See the big water tower?"

Rosie caught the moonlight's glow reflecting on metal.

"That is where you take shower." Anthony looked at his watch. "I return home early tomorrow, so now I sleep." Then he disappeared behind door number one.

Remembering her Greek mythology, Rosie turned to Jesse. "There's only one bed inside door number one, so where's Anthony sleeping?"

They tiptoed into the dark living room. Rosie sighed in relief when she heard Anthony snorting from the direction of the sofa. Jesse closed the squeaky door that separated the two rooms.

Later, as Anthony snored only a thin door away, Jesse snuggled close to Rosie. "At dinner, didn't you say there was more?"

"Yes, but *after* Tony the Greek leaves."

"Good morning, Atkissons!" Anthony said as he opened their bedroom door. Rosie jumped, and Jesse answered, "Oh, good morning."

"Come, have espresso with me before I leave for the city."

After Anthony showed Jesse how to manipulate his little Greek espresso machine, he bid them farewell. Rosie quickly washed the cups and plates, and then gathered their beach towels and stood at the bedroom door.

"What's taking you so long?" she asked as Jesse fastened his watch. She took the watch and placed it on the nightstand. "No watches. We're on anniversary time."

The summer season wasn't yet in full swing, so they had the beach to themselves, except for a few tourists playing paddleball.

"Those guys play pretty well," Rosie observed as she pulled out a book from her backpack.

"Yeah, they're good, but those aren't guys."

Rosie removed her sunglasses. From a distance and from behind, she couldn't tell who was who, but as the two slim figures turned around to fight for the ball, her eyes widened.

"Yikes, it's a topless beach."

"Yep."

Without further ado, Rosie grabbed their towels and found a deserted spot where they had eyes only for each other.

"I guess this is as good a time as any."

"Huh?"

"There's only one wish I have in Forka," she said as she unfastened her bathing suit straps. Jesse's mouth dropped.

"Gotcha, cowboy!" Rosie laughed as she fastened her straps. "Don't worry, I'm not going to take it off for the Greeks, or anyone—except you—later," she said, lying down on her towel.

He jumped up. "Come on, let's take a dip in the Med." He walked to the water's edge and then yelled, "Come on, Rosie!"

She sat up. "No, I'm staying right here."

As Rosie watched Jesse dive into the water alone, for the first time ever, she considered taking swimming lessons when they returned home.

While eating lunch and writing postcards at a nearby beach shack, Rosie watched two lanky guys playing Frisbee on the shore. When they turned around, Rosie dropped her pen.

"It's time to move on again," she said as she gathered her postcards. "This is definitely something to write Prissy about," she giggled.

That evening they ate fruit and cheese on the front porch while goats grazed in the olive groves.

"Let's take a walk to find out what's at the end of that road," Rosie said, finishing up the last bite of cheese.

As they neared a small village, Rosie asked, "Have we just stepped back into another place in time?"

Men were gathered at the local pub in the center of town, drinking wine and laughing.

"They're celebrating life," Jesse said.

They continued down the dusty road. Old women dressed in black were sitting on a front porch, sipping tea.

"They're sharing neighborhood gossip. They, too, are celebrating life," Rosie said.

Jesse pointed to a group of young boys playing soccer in a nearby field. "They are celebrating life."

Rosie took Jesse's arm. "Now I think it's time to have our own celebration."

Jesse turned her around and walked her briskly back to their summerhouse.

"Would you like me to fix you an espresso?" Jesse asked as soon as his feet hit the front porch.

He's really hooked on Tony's little Greek espresso machine, Rosie thought as she lit a candle on the porch table. She wasn't in the mood for coffee, but this was her husband's way of celebrating life. "I would love a cup."

She was taking her first sip when Jesse winked. "We've never done it in an olive grove."

Rosie placed her cup on the plastic table. "Now you're talking, cowboy," Rosie said as she led Jesse into the grove.

Afterward, they sat on the porch, sipping cold espresso by candlelight.

Jesse raised his cup. "To life!"

Rosie clinked her cup to his. "Yes, we must celebrate tonight, because who knows what awaits us in Athens?"

43

While an old fishing boat banged Resti *on her right, and an ancient cargo carrier bumped her on the left,* Resti *was becoming as restless as her crew.*

Nothing much changed. Each morning the crew waited for Torre to give them a departure date, and every morning Ellen complained to anyone who was within hearing distance.

"Hurry and wait is the name of the game for this ship. Hurry to Seattle—then wait. Hurry to Panama—then wait. Hurry to Stockholm—then wait. Now we're in Greece, and we're still waiting."

Torre cleared his throat, his way of politely interrupting Ellen.

"Let's discuss the security procedures that will be enforced once we leave Greece. When we near Istanbul, we'll continue the twenty-four-seven guard duty."

"Why?" Ellen asked.

"We've been told that sailing under the two bridges of Istanbul will be a critical place for the ship."

"Why?"

"If anyone wants to attack the ship, the bridges are vulnerable places."

"I shouldn't have asked," Ellen said as she walked out of the troop mess.

That evening, after the younger crew went upstairs to play Tile Rummy, Torre joined the small group who were still drinking coffee.

"What's up?" Stuart asked. "You look like you've just seen a ghost."

"I must make an announcement tomorrow morning. I just received a call from Sweden. Pastor Hans thinks it's best to cancel the first trip because the expense to pick up eight people is too great."

"Yikes," Shelly said.

Rosie was speechless.

Ellen charged into the room, looking around. "What's wrong? Why is everyone so quiet?"

Rosie held back tears. "Oh, nothing."

Ellen sighed. "Good. Now, Rosie, come outside with me."

Surprised that Ellen would invite her anywhere, Rosie followed her to the deck, where the girls were standing by the rail. "Why are you watching the trash bins? Have you finally *lost it?*" Rosie asked.

Ellen chuckled. "The guys are pulling Rat Patrol tonight."

Henrik, Daniel, and three other young men crept down the gangway carrying bags of what looked like rocks, while holding their shovels in a strike position.

"When I count, one, two, three, we'll throw the rocks at the trash bin," Daniel ordered.

"Yes, sir," Henrik said.

"When the rats scurry out from underneath, we'll charge them," Daniel explained.

The men stood alert, waiting quietly for the countdown, trying their hardest not to laugh. The girls held their breath.

"One, two, three!" Daniel shouted.

Rocks clanged against the steel bins. One, two, three rats scurried from under the containers.

"Four, five, six rats!" Rosie yelled.

"I'm losing count!" Jeans screamed.

"The young men scampered, shovels in hand, running toward the enemy!" Ellen bellowed, as if she were giving an on-the-scene news report.

The girls laughed hysterically as rodents scattered in all directions while being chased by their personal G.I. Joe rangers.

"We're having our own reality show," Rosie said, holding her aching side.

Afterward, Henrik promised the girls, "The Rat Patrol will do everything in our power to keep the rats off of the *Restoration*."

Before turning to go inside, Rosie lightly punched Ellen's arm. "Thanks for the invite. It was fun."

Ellen muttered, "Yeah, we can all use a good laugh about now."

The next morning Torre stood in the center of the room. Everyone—except Ellen—stopped eating.

"Pastor Hans called early this morning."

Silence.

"The final decision has been made."

Ellen looked over at her father. He made no eye contact with his daughter.

"What's going on?" Ellen asked Rosie.

Rosie knew the only reason Ellen sat next to her was because she could confiscate her food without having to make another trip to the galley. And Ellen knew that Rosie's eyes were always bigger than her stomach when she filled her plate. Since losing eight pounds, Rosie was determined not to overstuff her plate, but Ellen sat next to her anyway.

"We will sail to Sochi to pick up the eight Russian Jews who are still waiting for the *Restoration*. The people need to see with their own eyes that there is a ship that will take them to Israel. Once the news is out, other Russian Jews will begin filling the port again. We will not back down. This will be our breakthrough trip. We will show our enemy, the devil, that we mean business."

Cheers rang through the troop mess. Rosie yelled, "Thank you, Lord! We'll be on the first trip after all!"

Ellen muttered what sounded to Rosie like an *Amen*.

The crew gathered in hold two every Tuesday evening to pray. This night everyone sensed a special presence of God. Henrik played "Amazing Grace" on his guitar, Tina thanked the Lord for bringing the *Restoration* this far, Urma asked God to prepare the way as they sailed toward the Black Sea, and Rosie prayed for the chosen eight who were waiting in Sochi for the mystery ship.

Afterward, Rosie sat down, feeling lightheaded.

"Are you okay? You look pale," Ellen remarked.

Rosie appreciated Ellen's concern, but she was too weak to answer. Trying to be the brave sailor, she didn't want to make a fuss.

"Maybe you should rest in your cabin," Ellen added.

"I'll go with you," Jesse said.

"This is a night of celebration, so go join the crew," Rosie whispered to Jesse. "I'll join you later."

"Are you sure?" Jesse asked.

She nodded and made her way to their cabin. By the time Rosie's head sank into her pillow, her stomach was churning. In a matter of minutes, her arms and hands went numb. The unfamiliar pain left her motionless, and as she lay in the darkness, she called out, "Please, Lord, make this pain go away."

Fifteen minutes later, the pain was gone. Exhausted, yet relieved, Rosie muttered, "Too many Greek gyros."

She stared out of the porthole, toward the bright light shining on a Greek flag blowing on their neighbor's bridge. The light brought her a sense of hope. "There is a light at the end of this tunnel."

She slowly walked to the head and washed her face, but as she brushed her teeth, her stomach began to feel nauseous.

"Oh no!"

She quickly bent over the toilet. "There, much better. Now I can go outside and play." But by the time she staggered to the green chair, dizziness overcame her. She pulled herself onto the bed. "Well, maybe I'll play later." She soon dozed off into oblivion.

Suddenly, the pain returned with a vengeance. Rosie's arms and hands went numb. A sharp pain crushed her chest; then she suffered shortness of breath. She lay motionless, not able to move. "God, what is going on? I've never experienced this before. Please, help me." Once again, the pain disappeared.

When Jesse returned to the cabin, he found Rosie awake and tangled in their sheet.

"Do you want me to get Doc?"

"No! I'm fine. I just need to rest."

Jesse held Rosie's hand and prayed for her, and by the time he climbed in bed, she was asleep, exhausted from the ordeal.

Two hours later, she awoke in excruciating pain. Jesse was breathing heavily, so she didn't wake him. She could only whisper, "Lord, I feel like I'm dying, but I cannot die now. I must go to Sochi, then to Israel, and then home to my family." She laid her hands on her chest. "I have to live!"

Numbness . . . more pain . . . helpless . . . she lay still . . . she prayed . . . God smiled, and sleep found her.

The porthole reflected daybreak, and as Rosie opened her eyes, she knew the miracle of life had won. All that was left of the night was a piercing headache.

Jesse placed a cool washcloth on her forehead. "I'm going to find Doc."

"No doctor for me," Rosie insisted. "A nurse will be fine."

When Ana-Karin appeared ten minutes later, Rosie explained, "I caught a bad case of the Greek flu." She knew that if she shared all of her symptoms, the wise nurse would most likely send her directly to a Greek doctor, or worse, to a Greek hospital.

Rosie pleaded with Ana-Karin as she held a washcloth on her forehead. "No doctors or hospitals. They might fly me home—I cannot go home yet! I must continue on this mission."

Ana-Karin took Rosie's hand. "I am telling you that Doc should check you."

"Don't tell Doc! I'll take full responsibility for whatever happens—nothing is going to happen!" She removed her hand from Ana-Karin's hold. "But thank you for your help."

Ana-Karin continued in her most beautiful British English. "As it says in the Psalms, the nights of crying give way to days of laughter."

Then Ana-Karin looked in Rosie's eyes. "You must promise me that you will rest today, and I will check on you every half hour. If the pain returns, I will bring Doc to your cabin. I fear that you might have experienced a heart attack."

Rosie took Ana-Karina's hand. "It was nothing. But thank you for caring," she whispered.

Ana-Karin smiled. "Would you like me to *turn back around* to prove it?"

Rosie faintly chuckled as she pictured Ana-Karin turning around in the captain's mess. It wasn't funny at the time, but now as the Swedish nurse sat in the green chair next to her bed, she found humor in her words.

"Things do turn around," Rosie said.

Ana-Karin squeezed Rosie's hand. "But your health must turn around soon if you are to continue on this journey."

"I will make a doctor's appointment as soon as I return home to California," Rosie promised.

After Ana-Karin left, Rosie stared at the ceiling. "Hurricanes and heart attacks . . . miracles and menopause! This is an impossible dream!"

44

Resti figured the strange illness would either break the lady or make her more determined than ever to press on toward their mission.

Hours had passed since Rosie's mysterious illness, but no matter where Jesse was working on the ship, he dropped everything to make sure she was okay. He worked as a team with Ana-Karin, checking her every half hour. "If you have any symptoms, I'm taking you to the nearest hospital," he warned.

Rosie smiled from their bed. "I feel much better. I'm sure it has something to do with the whole menopause thing," Rosie reassured him.

He was concerned, but for now, he had to take her at her word.

Several days later, when Jesse poked his head in the laundry room, Ellen shook her head. "Not again! Aunt Eunice is doing fine. Gertrude is taking good care of her," Ellen said, throwing a dirty pair of overalls in his face. He ducked and then threw them over to Rosie. She caught the overalls and tossed them into the washing machine, chuckling at Ellen's playful gesture. Since Rosie's illness, Ellen kidded around more, bringing Gertrude out of hiding, causing Aunt Eunice to sneak out of the closet.

"Thanks, Gertrude, but I'm not here to check on Eunice. I'm here to tell you that Torre is calling a special meeting in fifteen minutes."

The girls were still giggling when they entered hold two. Rosie noticed Torre's serious expression, so she placed a finger to her mouth, signaling Ellen to quiet down.

Ellen sank in her seat. "Another boring meeting," she said as Torre stepped forward.

"The safety equipment hasn't arrived, so according to maritime standards, we don't have enough lifeboats for our forty-five-member crew and eight passengers."

The crew sat quietly, but Rosie knew what was going through everyone's mind.

Ellen broke the silence. "Does that mean eight crew members will be left behind?"

There. Before Torre could answer, Ellen was in his face.

"So, *who* will be left behind?" Ellen persisted.

Torre waited until Ellen was finished before he began. "The captain and I have decided that each department leader will pray, and then they will choose two from their department to stay behind. This will not be an easy decision, but don't feel too bad for the eight who are chosen."

"How can you say that?" Rosie asked.

"Dottie's parents have invited those who stay behind for a holiday of swimming and relaxing at their villa. Next week they will take a ferry to Israel, where they will join us for the next trip."

"The leaders better be in tune with God when they choose the infamous Electric Eight," Ellen said to her father, knowing that he would be one of the leaders making the decision.

"I believe we'll make the right decisions," Stuart answered softly. "The Electric Eight, as you call them, will be making a sacrifice."

"Sacrifice?" Ellen asked.

"They will be sacrificing their place for the eight Russian Jews," Stuart answered.

"The Chosen Eight," Rosie said, trying to match Ellen's wit.

Later, while Rosie was sorting and Ellen was folding overalls, Ellen was pensive.

"What's on your mind, Gertrude?" Rosie asked, hoping to bring Ellen out of her funk.

"Well, since you asked, who do you think will be left behind?"

Rosie stopped sorting. "Who will be the Electric Eight? That's a tough question."

"Since I work in the steward and the deck department, I have two chances of striking out."

Rosie continued sorting. "Urma might choose me."

"You? I've always looked at you as Miss Perfect," Ellen said.

Rosie thought it was time to be honest with her coworker. "Okay, Ellen, this is hard for me to admit, but I know I've come off as Miss Religious-know-it-all." She waited for Ellen to spew out one of her smart remarks, but instead, she stopped folding. Rosie felt as if she were in a steamy little confession booth, so she began.

"When I'm in the middle of my own challenges, I tend to look at other people's faults so I don't have to face my own faults and fears. Since I've been on the ship, God has shown me some of my character flaws, and since I have no place to run—I certainly can't jump overboard—I've had to face them head-on."

"I'm telling you, Rosie, you should face your fear of water head-on by taking swimming lessons—you know, in case you have to jump overboard," Ellen teased.

Rosie's eyes widened. "Never. I drowned while I was taking swimming lessons in high school, so I faked a note from my mother saying that I was allergic to chlorine."

"You drowned?" Ellen asked, picking up a pair of overalls.

"My mouth filled with water . . . I couldn't breathe . . . I panicked and started kicking anyone who tried to save me."

Ellen's eyes widened. "That was a bad move. You should never kick the swimmer who's trying to save you. But you didn't drown—you *almost* drowned. There's a big difference."

Rosie couldn't tell if Ellen was serious or if she was teasing. *Confession booth closed,* Rosie thought. "Anyway, I'm never taking swimming lessons."

"Miss Religious-know-it-all told a lie to get out of her high school swimming class."

"That's our little secret, okay? God's been dealing with me on my little white lies for a long time, especially since I've been on this ship."

"What's with this ship anyway? Since I've been on board, I've been reading my Bible."

"And I've noticed Elvis hasn't been singing as much in your cabin."

"Yeah, he's had to take a backseat to God lately," Ellen said as she folded the last pair of overalls. "And yes, I do believe in God. I didn't realize how much I wanted to be on the first trip until Torre made the announcement. Oh, well, if anyone deserves to stay behind, it's me," Ellen said as she walked out of the laundry-confession booth.

Rosie continued sorting, and praying.

That night in their cabin, Rosie straightened her lockers and cleaned the bathroom before taking a long, cool shower.

"Are you okay?" Jesse asked. "You seem a little fidgety tonight. Are you having one of those hot flashes again?"

"I wish it were that simple," she said as she climbed into bed. "I've been wrong about Ellen. She's not as stubborn as she appears. I've been doing a lot of thinking, and praying."

Jesse fluffed his pillow. "That's good." Then he pressed the on button to his shortwave radio.

"Don't you want to know what I've been praying about?" she asked curtly.

"Uh, yes. What have you been praying about?" he asked as he tuned in the BBC news station.

"If I have to, I'd be willing to give up my place and give it to Ellen."

Jesse turned down the volume.

"You *what?*"

"I believe this first trip is pivotal for Ellen. If she's chosen to be one of the Electric Eight to stay behind, she'll fly straight home to Montana, to a place where she's not wanted."

"But that's not your problem, Rosie."

"Maybe it is. God knows how much I want to be on this trip, but sometimes he asks us to sacrifice those things that are closest to our hearts."

"You already sacrificed by leaving your family for a year—excuse me, fourteen months."

Jesse didn't have to remind her. She thought about their family every day. But over the months, her desire to be on this ship with a mission had overtaken her longing to be home.

"My family will be waiting for me; Ellen has no one waiting for her."

"Do you realize that if we're not on the first trip, we'll miss our chance altogether?" Jesse asked.

Rosie sat up. "My decision has nothing to do with you. If I stay behind, you'll still be on the first trip, and I'll meet you in Haifa with the other seven."

Jesse sat up and ran his hand through his tousled hair. "I don't understand why you want to do this for Ellen."

Rosie took Jesse's hand. "I believe that if Ellen goes on this first trip and meets the Russian Jews face-to-face, it will change her direction, and who knows, maybe she'll even decide to go to Bible school."

"Wow, this is heavy stuff. You better keep praying before you talk to Torre."

"I know that this is what God wants me to do."

"Are you sure?"

"Yes, but I won't influence the leaders' decisions. I'll wait until Torre makes the announcement."

"You're a wise woman." Jesse opened his arms. "Come here." Rosie leaned into his chest, and he enveloped her with his never-ending love. "I'm proud of you, Rosie. I know how much this trip means to you."

"Stop," she said. "Don't make me cry . . . . I'm certainly no hero . . . I love God, and I want to obey him."

"And I love *you*," Jesse said as he turned off the light and his shortwave radio.

The next morning, the crew was solemn as Torre stood to announce who would stay behind.

"Ladies and gentlemen, let me introduce the Electric Eight," Ellen announced in her Gertrude accent as she grabbed a piece of bacon from Rosie's plate. Giving Ellen her bacon for the last few weeks had helped Rosie fit into her hard-earned size eight jeans.

Torre began by calling Daniel and then six others from the various departments. Rosie closed her eyes and prayed silently as she waited for Torre to announce the last name. *Lord, I'm ready to stay behind, if it's your will.*

Torre stared at the paper, not wanting to make eye contact. "Ellen."

Rosie opened her eyes to find Ellen rolling hers as she gathered her tray. "I'm not surprised; it's just my luck." And then she walked out.

Outwardly, the eight seemed to be taking it like troopers. But Rosie noticed that attitudes changed by lunch.

"I'm not staying in Greece. I'm going to visit my cousin in America," Daniel announced, glancing at Jeans.

"I'll miss you—I mean—*we'll* miss you," Ellen said as she slurped her pea soup.

"Don't bother," Daniel said. Then he turned to Jeans. "Besides, I'm going to look you up when I come to Washington."

Jeans gathered her tray. "Don't bother because I won't be there," she said casually. "I'm staying on the ship until August, and then I'm going to Bible school in the fall—in Sweden."

For a moment, Daniel was speechless. Then he turned to Ellen. "Would you like my pancakes?"

Ellen didn't look up. "Don't bother."

"It doesn't seem fair that I have to stay behind," Ellen said, finishing her last bite. Rosie pushed her plate toward Ellen in hopes of consoling her.

"But you'll have a nice holiday at Dottie's villa."

"That's easy for you to say," Ellen said, and then pushed the plate back. She walked away, leaving her tray on the table for Rosie to clear.

The gesture challenged Rosie's decision.

At dinner, Ellen was especially giddy, almost as if she were acting in one of their *Plan for Your Future* skits. Rosie couldn't help overhear her announce, "I'm not staying with the Electric Eight. I'm done with the ship; I'm going to tour Italy instead."

Rosie couldn't hold back any longer. The clock was ticking. "But that means you'll be missing out on the blessings of the future trips," Rosie said as Ellen licked her chocolate-covered spoon.

"Here, take my cake," Rosie offered.

"Keep your cake. And you talk about blessings? What blessings? Humph!" Ellen walked out of the troop mess, purposefully leaving her tray. "And now I'm going to the office to make my plane reservations."

Rosie found Jesse on deck, staring at the sea wall. "Ellen is in the office making reservations to fly off to Italy! I have to talk to the captain now, before it's too late."

Jesse and Rosie found Stuart and Captain Alain in the captains' mess, working on last-minute details. After Rosie explained that she wanted to stay behind so Ellen could continue with the ship, the captains sat in silence.

Then Stuart leaned forward. "How can you give up your place to someone who isn't interested in helping anyone but herself?"

"When she meets the Russian Jews face-to-face, her heart will change," Rosie answered with conviction.

"How can you be sure?" Stuart asked.

"God brought Ellen on this ship for a reason. He's doing something in her heart that she's not willing to admit yet—but she will."

Captain Alain turned to Rosie. "Then I'll talk to her right away."

Stuart leaned closer. "Why are you willing to give up your place for my daughter?"

Rosie smiled. "When I was praying the other night, God reminded me that two thousand years ago, someone took a chance on me. This is the least I can do for Ellen."

She turned to Captain Alain. "Please, Captain, talk to her soon."

45

Although Resti *had heard of certain dangers lurking on the high seas, she was determined to bring her passengers safely to their destination.*

That night, a knock on the Atkissons' cabin door interrupted a hot make-out session.

"Do you have to answer that?" Rosie asked, panting.

"Yes, but hold that thought," Jesse said as he rolled off the bed and lowered Rosie's handmade curtain. It was Stuart.

"I'm sorry to bother you so late, but tell Rosie that Ellen turned down her offer."

"Did she give a reason?" Rosie asked through the curtain.

"Her only reply was, *Thanks, but no thanks.*"

Rosie tossed most of the night, keeping Jesse awake. "Rosie, you've done all that you can do."

She sat up in the darkness. "You're right. I gave Ellen the chance to stay on. It's not my fault that she's too stubborn to accept my offer." She fell back on her pillow. "And I'm sure she's not losing any sleep over it, so why should I?"

Rosie turned to kiss Jesse good night, but he was already asleep. She snuggled next to him, knowing the situation was now out of her hands.

The next day the crew bid farewell to the Electric Eight, but before exiting down the gangplank, Ellen sauntered over to Rosie. "Last night I did a lot of thinking—and praying. No one has ever given me such an offer. I know how much this trip means to you. If you don't stay on the ship, you'll miss your opportunity." Ellen cleared her throat and stumbled for words. It was Ellen's turn for the confession booth, so Rosie didn't dare interrupt. "I've decided not to go to Italy."

"You're going straight home?"

"Not yet. Actually, I'll be seeing you next week."

Rosie stared at Ellen. "Next week?"

"I'm taking the ferry to Israel to spend a little more time with Dad before I fly home."

Rosie grabbed Ellen and gave her a big hug. "Then I'll see you next week in Israel, Gertrude!"

"You can count on it, Eunice," Ellen said, her blue eyes sparkling.

As the *Restoration* slid away between the two ships on either side of the rat-infested port, Rosie yelled to the Electric Eight, "Next year in Jerusalem!"

Everyone except Daniel shouted back, "Next *week* in Jerusalem!"

The gentle wind on the Aegean Sea gave the *Restoration* a smooth journey as they glided across the waters toward Turkey. The aquamarine glow of the Sea of Marmara shimmered in the sunlight, welcoming the *Restoration* to Istanbul. The engine went dead in the water to wait for the pilot boat.

Rosie stood on deck, captivated by the echoes of chanting and the breathtaking minaret skyline. "Jesse, this is more than my senses can take." She wanted him to share her excitement, but he was looking beyond.

Torre delegated those who would keep guard on the stern and the bow of the ship. "We'll wait our turn to sail through the twenty-mile strait," he informed them. "We shouldn't have any incidents on our entry to the Black Sea, but if the word is out that our ship will be carrying Jews to Israel, this would be the most likely place for an attack."

Below borrowed binoculars, Jesse pointed out to Rosie, "Those are the two bridges that unite Asia and Europe. This is where our ship will be the most vulnerable."

The thought of anyone wanting to harm the *Restoration* sent chills up Rosie's spine. Jesse noticed her shaky hands. "Here, take these binoculars and enjoy the scenery. God's protection is all over this ship."

A few hours later, after a local pilot came aboard, the *Restoration*'s engine roared once more. Rosie absorbed the beauty of Istanbul dating back to the fifteenth century—the Blue Mosque, the Galata Tower, and the Rumeli Fortress. Statuesque buildings of blue, salmon, and red stood regal next to the channel. "I recognize some of the homes from my *Victoria* magazines," she told Tina. "I must return to this exotic city someday."

"My, aren't you a world traveler now," Tina jested.

"Can't a lady change her mind? I love my family more than anything, but now I see that there can be room for both family and missions—and dreams."

As darkness fell, the crew was told to disperse inside. Some met in hold two to pray; others gathered in the troop mess to drink coffee and wait.

As the Bosphorus Bridge stood before them, the guards scanned the bridge through binoculars for any suspicious signs.

Jesse stood poised on the bridge. "Stuart, there's a man bending over the side of the bridge."

"Maybe he's never seen a ship like this before."

Jesse squinted through binoculars. "He's taking pictures of the ship."

Stuart grabbed his camera and handed it to Jesse. "Then take one of him, just in case."

Thirty minutes later, they sailed under the second bridge.

"All is clear," Jesse reported to the captains.

"We did well," Captain Alain said proudly.

"And we shall do well next week when we return with the Chosen Eight," Stuart said.

Above, Rosie noticed a small plane flying over the *Restoration*. "Is that the same plane that we saw near the shores of Tripoli?"

"And in Stockholm? I'm not sure, but I'll take a few pictures anyway. Good job, Rosie," Jesse said. "You have become quite the sailor."

Once on the Black Sea, Tina and Rosie made their afternoon trip to the monkey bridge to bask in the Russian sun.

Rosie looked over the side. "The Black Sea is so green."

"You sound disappointed," Tina said.

"I imagined the Black Sea to be black. Some of these waters are thick and murky, making you wonder what's beneath the surface."

"Over the last two thousand years, hundreds of ships have sunk beneath the surface of the Black Sea, where they still lie," Tina said as she slathered tanning lotion on her legs. "Since the fall of communism, there will be more exploration taking place in these waters."

A cool shower renewed Rosie's energy to finish folding laundry, alone. The steward's number one laundry lady found herself missing Ellen—her prodding and teasing made the time in the small room more bearable. Rosie looked forward to their reunion in Haifa.

Tina called a meeting in the crew's lounge after the three o'clock fika break. "Last-minute plans for the guests are complete." She smiled at Urma. "The chief cook and her assistants have prepared special meals." She glanced at Shelly. "The living room lounges in hold one and hold two look beautiful. The floors are washed and covered with colorful area rugs. The bunk beds are made with green and blue sheets and bedspreads." She turned to Rosie. "The shower stalls, toilets, and sinks now sparkle, and the laundry is finished." Then Tina looked to heaven. "The Lord has truly guided us every step of the way."

The *Restoration* stopped her engine a few miles from their destination. The crew gathered on deck to gaze at Sochi's shoreline.

"Look, I can fit into my jeans," Rosie bragged to Ana-Karin as they stepped out into the late afternoon sun.

"Our exercise program has proved successful," Ana-Karin chimed, patting her tummy. Their daily workouts together and her abrupt illness had brought Rosie an unexpected friendship with the Swedish nurse.

Rosie turned her attention to the shore. "Look at the rolling hills, and the trees growing all the way to the beach."

Tina peered at the pebbled beach from her binoculars. "Sochi is a charming tourist town, where thousands of Russians flock to escape the summer heat."

"It reminds me of some of our California coastal towns," Rosie said, remembering days of summers past. "Who knows, perhaps there will be a special event in Sochi one day."

"When can we go ashore?" Ana-Karin asked.

Tina frowned. "I'm afraid that we cannot go ashore. We must be present when the pilots come aboard."

Disappointed, Rosie turned toward the superstructure. "Well, maybe Jesse and I will have to come back another time."

Tina smiled. "Perhaps Alain and I can meet you and Jesse for a summer holiday."

Rosie chuckled. "Istanbul, now Sochi—sounds like we're planning quite a vacation."

Captain Alain paced nervously, waiting to receive the go-ahead from the Russian port officials to pull next to the dock.

They dined on the Fiesta Deck at sunset, but still no word. They finally went to bed.

It was still dark when Rosie woke to the sound of the engine's roar. Four a.m. Jesse dressed quickly. "Stay here; I'll be back."

Jesse returned within minutes. "Good news—we received the go-ahead to pull into dock."

Rosie dressed and then reported to the superstructure's second balcony. She peered down at the handsome uniformed officers, and the deckhands, looking professional in their freshly laundered coveralls. The boatswains tied the ship and then lowered the gangway.

"There's a lot of work to do before the sun rises," Stuart instructed. "After the cranes unload the supplies, we'll begin loading wood crates with the passengers' belongings."

Jon greeted Jesse at the bottom of the gangway. They stood shivering in the morning chill and reminisced about their previous journey through Estonia and Russia a few years earlier. When Jesse made his way back up the gangway, he motioned to Rosie. "Where's my wool overcoat? I want to give it to Jon."

"It's in hold two—I'll go find it," Rosie answered, smiling. Jesse had purchased the coat in a secondhand shop on a cold winter's night while in Bible school. When they returned to California, it hung in the back of his closet. Now the coat would be put to good use.

The crew held out their hands to greet the Chosen Eight as they walked up the gangway. Tina wrapped her arms around each woman as if she were welcoming an old friend to her home. "Welcome to the *Restoration*," she said. They smiled and answered, "*Spasibo*."

Tina took the stewards aside and gave them specific instructions, as if she had done this many times. "We cannot imagine what our passengers are thinking and feeling as they leave the port. We must allow them personal time and space. They are leaving their homeland and are wondering about this Promised Land they have heard so much about."

The *Restoration* pulled away from the dock as the new day broke. Silently, a mother held her daughter as they watched the shoreline fade from sight. A family of four stood together, holding onto the ship rail and to each other. An older couple, with arms wrapped around each other and tears streaming down their faces, made small conversation in their native tongue.

Rosie and Tina watched from the balcony. "Now I see what the ship is all about," Rosie said as her own tears fell to the deck. "It's about these eight brave souls."

"Yes, the Chosen Eight. But this is only the beginning. Many more will follow. As the Bible predicts, the God of Abraham, Isaac, and Jacob will guide them out of the darkness, into the light, and to a life they have only dreamed about until now."

Rosie put her arm around Tina. "And this is what your dream is all about."

"Yes, this is my dream come true. And what is your dream, Rosie?"

"When I was a little girl, my dream was to travel the world with Jesus, with the man I love. Now, as I am participating in this prophecy on this ship, my dream is coming true."

Together, the two dreamers cried tears of joy.

Once past the breakers, Tina instructed the stewards and their interpreters to escort the passengers to hold two. As Rosie approached the group, she did a double take. The tall, gentle-looking man looked strangely familiar. Then she remembered Siberia, and the house full of crazy old people who lived out in the country.

"Doctor Zhivago!" Rosie chimed as she walked toward him.

He squinted as she approached. "Oh, yes! The frightened little American," he said, laughing. Harriet looked puzzled as she interpreted for the doctor.

"I am so happy to see you," Rosie said. She turned to Harriet. "We met when Jesse and I were on the train in Siberia. I nicknamed him Dr. Zhivago because I couldn't pronounce his name."

He held out his hand toward Harriet. "I am Dr. Petronevich, but you may call me Dr. Zhivago too."

"Very nice to meet you," Harriet said, shaking his hand.

Then the doctor took Rosie's hand. "After your team left, my wife and I decided to contact the Operation Jabotinsky office in Moscow—and here we are!" Dr. Petronevich introduced his wife and two daughters. They followed Harriet down the stairs, dropped their worn suitcases in their living quarters, and then returned to the main deck where Rosie was waiting.

"Oh, the fresh air of freedom!" Dr. Petronevich proclaimed as he hugged his wife and daughters.

Breakfast was served in hold two, but as the sun beat down on the decks, Urma notified the stewards of a change in plans. "It's too hot for them to eat inside, so prepare a place for them on deck."

The passengers spent most of the day topside, sitting in the shade of the upper decks, where gentle breezes cooled them.

The captain invited the passengers to join the crew for dinner on the Fiesta Deck. As the evening progressed, the interpreters barely had time to eat. "Captain, the passengers are eager to talk with the crew. May I interpret for them?" Harriet asked.

"Absolutely," he said.

Harriet motioned to Dr. Petronevich. "Yovita and I are very grateful for this ship, and for your hospitality," Harriet translated. "I was forced to close my practice."

"Why?" Rosie asked.

"Because we are Jewish." He glanced at the crew. "There is much persecution. That is why we decided three years ago to make *aliyah* to Israel."

Dimitri waved his arms. "My wife and I are so happy for this ship. We have waited two years for this journey."

After cake and coffee was served, Harriet walked over to the rail.

"Are you all right?" Rosie asked.

"I wasn't prepared for the impact these people would have on me," she said, wiping her eyes.

"None of us were prepared, Harriet," Rosie said as she wiped tears on her sleeve. "Wait here! I have an idea."

The sea remained calm, so Rosie brought her portable cassette player on deck and requested Jeans to play some of her Israeli folk songs. Music filled the air, and it wasn't long until Dimitri grabbed his wife's hand.

Thanks to the Jeans Dance Studio that was held on board while at sea, Rosie knew enough to form a circle.

"Let the dancing begin!" Dimitri shouted as he clasped Harriet's hand.

The passengers swayed to the music as the *Restoration* made her way over the Black Sea.

Long after bedtime, the two Russian couples sat on deck, late into the night, and shared their life stories.

Rosie helped Harriet serve them extra pots of coffee. "From their conversation, they are very happy to be here," Harriet told Rosie.

Dr. Petronevich smiled at Harriet. "Yovita and I feel like we are on one of those cruises that we have heard so much about."

"I could never afford a cruise for my Natasha," Dimitri said.

Natasha squeezed her husband's hand. "This will do just fine."

Rosie smiled. *Natasha and I think alike.*

46

Darkness fell as the Restoration *neared the bridges of Istanbul.*

"We'll be approaching the bridges of Istanbul during the night. We must handle the situation carefully, as we don't want to bring fear to our passengers," the captain advised.

"Nor to the crew," Rosie added.

At dusk the Turkish pilot boat pulled alongside the *Restoration*. The captain greeted them as they climbed over the rail.

"I'm Kemal, and this is Ahmed," the older pilot said as they exchanged handshakes. "We have heard talk of this ship among certain groups in Istanbul," he said in broken English.

Stuart and Alain glanced at each other.

"I hope the talk is good," Stuart said nonchalantly.

"It's concerning your passengers. Do you have Russians onboard?"

"We have eight Russian passengers."

"We must check their visas," Kemal said matter-of-factly.

"Yes, of course," Stuart answered. "I'll bring their visas along with the crew's papers. Captain Alain will show you around while I get the paperwork from the office, and then we'll meet in the captains' mess."

As Stuart entered the superstructure, he heard Shelly laughing in the troop mess, so he walked briskly down the hall. She was telling Tina and Rosie a sea yarn when she looked up and saw her husband standing in the doorway. One look told Shelly that something wasn't right.

"The pilots want to look at the passengers' visas."

"Yikes," Shelly whispered.

"Oh, my," was all that escaped Rosie's lips.

"This is a normal procedure, but pray that they don't make an issue of the fact that they are Russian Jews."

"Why? What could they do?" Rosie asked.

"If the port officials want to give us a hard time, they can make us turn the ship around and take them back to Sochi."

Shelly frowned. "That could cost us a lot of time and money."

"Not to mention the passengers' disappointment," Tina added.

Stuart motioned to Rosie. "I might need your help with the paperwork."

Rosie gulped, then followed Stuart to the office. Stuart opened the office safe, pulled out eight visas, and held them to his chest. "Lord, we need your help." Rosie continued to pray as they climbed the stairs to the officers' mess, and continued praying as she stood silently in the corner of the small room.

Kemal looked over each visa carefully. "These passengers are Russian Jews. What are you going to do with them?"

"We're transporting them to Haifa, Israel," Captain Alain answered.

"I can see that on the paperwork," Kemal answered curtly. "But why?"

Stuart didn't know how to explain the ship's mission to the Turkish pilots, but he knew he had to give it his best shot. "They want to live in Israel but they don't have the finances, so our nonprofit organization provides their transportation."

Ahmed shook his head. "We must call the port office and discuss this situation."

Then Kemal smiled at the captain. "However, for a small fee, we can allow you to make your passage tonight."

Rosie was ready to blurt out that they were a Christian organization that did not pay bribes when Captain Alain jumped in. "Sir, we would pay the fee, but we have no money. You see, everyone on the ship is a volunteer."

The pilots looked at each other and then broke into laughter, as if the captain had told them a funny joke.

"Volunteers! Then, of course, you have no money! We should have known that no one in their right minds would work on this old ship," Kemal said.

"Plus pay for Jews to travel to Israel," the stout pilot added. The Turkish pilots laughed until their bellies shook. Alain and Stuart didn't think the matter was one bit funny, but they were wise enough to keep silent.

Kemal rose from his chair. "Back to the business at hand. We're not getting anywhere, so let's proceed by going to the bridge."

The pilots followed Alain to the bridge, and Stuart and Rosie dashed downward to the troop mess. "We don't have to turn back," Stuart said, smiling.

Tina raised her hands to heaven. "Thank you, Lord."

"Two bridges to go, and then we're home free," Rosie cheered.

The praying nuns—as Ellen had nicknamed Tina and Urma—prayed as the *Restoration* glided under the first bridge. They sighed in relief and thanked God when they sailed away with no incident.

They neared the Bosphorus Bridge around three o'clock in the morning. The ladies turned off the lights in the troop mess, and then stationed themselves, binoculars in hand, by the portholes. Rosie tensed when she spied movement on the dimly lit bridge.

"Do you see what I see?" Tina asked.

Rosie breathed deeply. "Yes! I see two figures—a short man in the middle of the bridge, and a larger man in a dark coat walking toward him. Why are they out at this hour of the morning?"

"Perhaps he's walking home from a local bar," Tina said.

Shelly gripped her binoculars tighter. "I only see a little guy in the middle of the bridge, and something long is draped over his shoulder—it looks like a rifle."

"And he's carrying a duffle bag," Rosie said.

Tina tried to sound unaffected by the ordeal. "I'm sure the captains can see him from the bridge."

"*Them,*" Rosie corrected.

Urma placed her binoculars on the table and began pacing the floor. "Let's pray! Lord, we are wearing our spiritual armor. We are holding our shield of faith, we are wearing our breastplate of righteousness, and we are carrying the sword of the spirit," she declared. Then she picked up her binoculars and repositioned herself at the porthole.

As the ship sailed closer, the short man in the middle of the bridge placed his rifle down and then reached inside the duffle bag. Rosie's mind raced. "It's a bomb! Oh, God, help us!"

Just then, the ship stopped dead in the water. Jesse shouted from the doorway, "Keep all lights off and stay away from the portholes. The pilots have called the police."

Rosie continued to peer through the darkened porthole. She couldn't take her eyes off the two figures. Suddenly, the larger man walked up to the short man and grabbed the duffle bag from his hand, took the rifle, and then continued to walk toward the other end of the bridge. As he turned around, the slightly built man was running the opposite way, as if he had seen a ghost. The large figure dropped the rifle, fumbled around in the duffle bag, and then disappeared. Two Turkish policemen seized the culprit at the end of the bridge.

"Yikes! Do you see that?" Shelly screamed.

"The police caught the man! Thank you, Lord!" Urma cheered.

"What happened to the other man?" Rosie asked as she turned on the lights.

Shelly stared at Rosie. "What are you talking about, Rosie?"

"What other man?" Tina asked.

Rosie dropped her binoculars on the table, and then plopped into the nearest chair and went limp. "There was an . . . oh, never mind." She looked at Tina. "We'll talk later."

As the ship's engine roared once more, Rosie slowly walked to her cabin. "Thank you, God, for your special forces at work."

47

So far, the World War II vessel had proven that she could conquer any obstacle in her path.

The sun was rising as the *Restoration* departed the shores of Istanbul. Dr. Petronevich and Nikolai were having their morning coffee on deck when Rosie and Harriet walked by.

"Please join us," the doctor said, pointing to the white plastic chairs.

Nikolai glanced around, waving his arm. "Why are you doing this? What have we done to deserve such special treatment on this beautiful ship?"

Rosie smiled at Nikolai. "It's quite simple. There once was a Jewish man who did something special for me." As Harriet interpreted, she held back tears.

While the men sipped their coffee, Rosie thought a moment. She knew the Operation Jabotinsky policy stated that the crew was not to proselytize the passengers. However, if someone asks, they were free to give their testimony. "The Russian Bibles in the passenger lounge are gifts that you may keep, so you can read his story," Harriet translated. "There is no language barrier when it comes to God's love."

"*Spasibo*," Dr. Petronevich said as he rose to make his way to the passenger lounge.

Laughter echoed from the Fiesta Deck as crew and passengers gathered for their farewell dinner. Everyone talked freely, and after dessert, Harriet led the passengers below to help pack their bags for departure.

Rosie joined the galley girls in the main galley for KP duty. Rosie shook her head as she tied her apron. "Who would have ever imagined that I would see Dr. Zhivago again?"

Tina loaded the dishwasher, then began rinsing the pots and pans. "Only God knows what happens after we sow seeds into a person's life."

"Even as far away as Siberia," Rosie said as she pulled her damp hair into a clip.

Tina handed a pot lid to Rosie. "We can only imagine what they are feeling tonight. Five days at sea, and tomorrow morning they will arrive in Israel."

Rosie scrubbed the lid, then stopped to wipe the beads of sweat from her forehead. "When I lived in Sweden, I knew I'd be returning to America in a year, but they are so brave to leave their homeland—forever."

Tina stopped rinsing. "Rosie, it took a lot of courage for you to leave your family to live in Sweden. And now, you have volunteered on this ship for fourteen months. Many would consider you the brave one." Tina reached out and gave Rosie a sweaty hug.

"Thanks, Tina, I needed that."

"But what I say is true, Rosie."

"Oh, no, I'm not referring to your words . . . I meant that I needed that *hug*."

Rosie went outside to cool off as the sun began to set on the Mediterranean Sea. She made her way toward the bow of the ship, gathered her skirt with one hand, held onto the rail with the other, and climbed the stairs.

"No sound of the engine up here, Resti—only gentle waves breaking against your bow."

Rosie held onto the bow's rail. She took a deep breath, pulled her right leg and then her left leg over, and then sat down. "If Urma can do this, then so can I." She glanced downward. "Now, Resti, don't make any wrong moves. I don't want to go headfirst into the water." She looked over at the life-buoy ring, but the *Restoration* continued moving steadily.

Rosie dangled her legs over the edge and looked toward the horizon. "Up and down, up and down, like a seesaw," Rosie chuckled. "This sure beats the roller-coaster ride you gave us off the gulf of Mexico." She patted the ship. "I'll never forget you, my friend. You've taught me more these past months than I could have ever learned by staying onshore." A lump gathered in her throat. "I've learned to trust God in ways I never knew possible . . . for the big and for the small miracles."

Amazingly, instead of tears, something welled up inside Rosie. "And, Resti, I have learned to trust you." She stood and shifted her weight until she found her balance. Then, without a second thought—she couldn't help herself—Rosie raised her arms toward heaven, looked toward the sky, and shouted, "I am Lady of the sea!"

Rosie was lost in time as she glided over smooth waters. The wind mangled her hair and the mist smudged her mascara, but she didn't care. It was just her, the ship, and the sea—until an unfriendly wave knocked against the portside.

"Oh!" Rosie screeched. She quickly bent over, grabbed the rail and sat back down. "Ugh, perhaps *you* are Lady of the sea after all," Rosie said as she fluffed her hair and arranged her skirt. Smiling, she climbed down the stairs and then strolled the deck as if it were just another evening at sea. She looked toward the bridge and caught a glimpse of Stuart with binoculars in hand.

He waved, as if to say, *I know the feeling, Rosie.*

Rosie waved back, as if to say, *this feeling will stay with me forever.*

48

Resti *was looking forward to peace and quiet in the Haifa port, but yet another obstacle faced them. She had heard how the ship* Exodus *had been treated when her cargo was brought into port. But that was forty years ago. Times had changed, hadn't they?*

Within minutes of the MS *Restoration*'s entering the Haifa harbor, an Israeli gunboat sped from the port and circled the World War II vessel. As two soldiers aimed their deck-mounted machine guns at the ship, another shouted instructions in Hebrew through a loudspeaker.

The captain of the MS *Restoration* responded over the ship's radio, "Please, speak to us in English."

Rosie grabbed the rail. "Do they think we are terrorists?"

Jesse touched her arm. "Rosie, calm down."

"Do they think we're pirates? What are they going to do?"

"Just calm down," her husband repeated, holding out his hand.

"Will they make us jump overboard? I don't have my life jacket!"

"Rosie, you must get hold of yourself."

Her mind raced as she gazed up at the man who'd brought her on this unpredictable journey. *Jesse's right. What's come over me?* Rosie asked herself, all the time wishing she didn't have to go to the bathroom. She didn't dare leave his side.

The ship, the crew, and their special passengers—the Russian Jews—had finally reached their destination. No more troubled waters. No more hurricanes. No more delays. On this hot July morning, they were home free—or so they thought.

Rosie looked at the crew, poised and ready to hit the deck. "Isn't this ironic? We've traveled halfway around the world, and this is the welcome we get."

"Stop your engine!" the soldier shouted.

Captain Alain immediately gave orders to the first engineer to halt the engine. Within seconds, they were dead in the water.

Rosie's stomach churned. She hung her head over the side of the ship and let it rip. After wiping her mouth with a hankie, she grabbed hold of Jesse's arm. She'd heard stories about people who'd experienced close calls. Her seventy-year-old father once told her about the time his ship almost went down in the China Sea during the war. "At that moment, my whole life passed before me," Talmage said.

Now, as the Israeli soldiers glared at the *Restoration* through their binoculars, Rosie wondered if this was her moment.

Quick, find your happy place, she told herself.

"I hope the stewards keep the passengers below," Jesse said. "If they see the guns, they might reconsider going ashore."

Rosie's mind raced. "They wouldn't do that—they've come too far!" She stared at the gunboat. "God, why is this happening?" she asked, feeling lightheaded. Then, like on a movie screen, her life passed before her.

What seemed like hours, she heard Jesse faintly calling her name in the background. "Rosie . . . Rosie, are you okay?"

The movie screen went dark, and there was Jesse, staring down at her.

"I'm fine now. I've just been to my *happy place*, and now I'm back."

"Everything's going to be fine," he told her. Rosie nodded, "Yes, I know."

She remembered that moments earlier, there had been an unexplained calamity below. The chief engineer had smelled engine fumes. Something was seriously wrong. "Fire down below! A cloth is on fire!" Bjorne yelled as he grabbed the nearest fire extinguisher and aimed it at the blaze. The captain gave orders to stop the engine, and within minutes after the fire had been extinguished, the engine again roared in victory and continued toward the harbor until the gunboat brought them to a screeching halt.

Captain Alain explained the fire to the soldiers over the radio, but they needed to investigate further.

Ten minutes later, the *Restoration*'s identification was cleared, guns were lowered, and the soldiers called for an Israeli pilot to come aboard. At Captain Alain's request, Stuart gathered the crew on deck.

"I'll explain what happened. When a ship enters any Israeli port, she must enter in order. The fire in the engine room took us out of the lineup for port entry, causing the Israelis great suspicion. They could have held us indefinitely, but because we have favor with God, they have allowed us to enter."

Still dizzy from the incident, Rosie whispered, "I'm grateful for favor, Lord. Now can you please take us to our safe harbor?"

After they docked, the Jewish Agency representatives came aboard, and after speaking with Captain Alain, the representatives welcomed the Russian Jews.

"You will be given a place to stay, food, and clothing, and the opportunity to learn the Hebrew language," they explained in English, with Harriet close by to interpret.

After bidding tearful farewells, the crew waved at the passengers as they made their way down the gangway.

"There they go. The Chosen Eight are walking toward their new lives," Tina said.

"May all their dreams come true," Rosie said.

Karina and her daughter glanced back and waved one last time. Dr. Petronevich, Yovita, and their daughters waved their last farewell. Then they were gone.

"Next year in Jerusalem," Rosie whispered as they turned the corner.

Tina placed her arm around Rosie. "We'll see them again, Rosie. If not in Israel, then someday in heaven."

The crew gathered in the troop mess for lunch. They could feel the absence of the passengers. "We will head for the Black Sea in a few days, and there will be many more passengers," Tina reminded them.

"We had them for only five days. Now they're gone, like the wind," Rosie said, moving her salad around her plate with a fork.

"But we have been an important part of their new life," Tina said.

The crew continued eating in silence.

But the silence was soon broken.

"Did you miss me?" Ellen asked Henrik as she entered the troop mess, followed by the remains of the Electric Eight.

"Of course, we didn't," Henrik smirked. "Where's the rest of the group?"

"Daniel flew to Sweden, and Dottie stayed in Athens—her boyfriend proposed marriage." Ellen smiled at Rosie. "I guess Stella Starlight's magic worked after all."

Ellen glanced around the room until she sighted her father standing next to his corner table.

"Welcome back, Ellen," Stuart said, smiling. Never knowing what to expect from his daughter, he waited for her response. Ellen walked over and gave him a hug. Tears filled his eyes. Embarrassed, Ellen reached in her pocket and pulled out a stained hankie and handed it to him. Rosie couldn't help but notice what was going on between father and daughter.

Ellen eventually made her way over to Rosie's table. "I can't believe I missed everyone."

"Well, I guess we missed you too," Henrik confessed.

"Would you like to sit with us?" Rosie asked.

"Thanks, but I need to talk with Dad."

Rosie watched Ellen return to Stuart's table. It was comforting to have the remains of the Electric Eight back onboard.

Rosie was finishing her pea soup when Ellen strolled over. "Can I sit down?" Ellen asked Rosie.

"Of course."

"I did a lot of thinking while I was relaxing at Dottie's villa."

Rosie put her fork down. "About what?"

"About my future."

"What about your future?"

"I don't have one."

"That's not true, Ellen."

"I should say I didn't have one, until I started praying."

Rosie choked on her coffee. "Oh?"

"Don't act so surprised," Ellen teased. "And after praying, I've decided to stay on the ship for the summer."

Rosie spilled coffee on her T-shirt. "That's great news! Does your dad know?"

"I just told him. He's thrilled, and Shelly's quite happy."

Rosie dipped her paper napkin in her glass of water, quickly wiping the brown smudge off her shirt.

"When does the ship sail?" Ellen asked.

"Hopefully, next week. Jesse and I are packed and ready to fly home.

"Are you flying to the states with Dad and Shelly?"

"We leave in three days," Rosie said, smiling. "Your dad's business in Seattle shouldn't take more than two days, then they'll return here for the following trip."

"Uh, one other thing, Eunice," Ellen said with a southern drawl.

Hearing Eunice's name brought back memories of the hilarious nights the girls had spent taping *The Plan for Your Future Show.*

"What's that, Gertrude?"

Ellen's eyes sparkled. "Gertrude is going to Bible school in the fall—in Sweden."

Rosie's eyes widened. "I do declare, I think that Eunice is feeling faint," she said in her ever-so-southern accent. "But she believes that it is one of the wisest choices Gertrude has ever made."

49

Resti's maiden voyage was a success, and one day she would be added to the list of prestigious mercy ships. And she would forever miss her California Lady.

The next morning the roar of the ship's engine awakened Rosie. She walked into the troop mess as the ship pulled away from the dock.

"What's going on, Torre?" Rosie asked. "Jesse and I have to get off the ship before it sails."

"Don't worry, we're not going anywhere. To save money, the *Restoration* has to anchor inside the breakers for a few days."

Rosie started wringing her hands. "How are we going to get to shore?"

"Stuart has scheduled a water taxi to pick up and deliver the four of you to the dock in an hour."

"I must finish packing," Rosie said, and walked out of the troop mess for the last time.

Shelly tapped on Rosie's cabin door. "The water taxi will arrive in thirty minutes to pick us up."

"Jesse has our luggage on deck," Rosie said. "I'm going to take one last trip to the bridge."

Rosie peered out of the windows of the bridge. She gently rubbed her hands on the freshly dusted woodwork as she looked out over the harbor. "I won't be cleaning you anymore, old girl, but I'm sure whoever takes my place will do a great job."

Rosie moved slowly down the stairs and then glanced one last time in their cabin. She patted their bed. "Everything's ready for the next volunteers to take residence."

Through the porthole she could hear the revving of the water taxi's engine, so she gathered her backpack and closed the cabin door. Tears warmed her cheeks as she walked down the dark, narrow hallway. As she fumbled in her pocket for a hankie she collided with Jeans.

"Jeans! I want to say good-bye. We're leaving on the water taxi in a few minutes."

"I'm going to miss you and Jesse, but I'll write," Jeans said.

"I wish you oceans of blessings on the ship and in Bible school," Rosie said. "I think we've all learned a lot while living on the *Restoration*."

Jeans looked over her shoulder, then spoke softly. "I know first-hand what living in such close quarters can do to a person."

Rosie waited for Jeans to continue.

"Out of loneliness I was drawn to someone that I normally wouldn't be interested in."

Rosie sighed. "I'm so glad you realized that Daniel wasn't your type."

"Oh, I'm not talking about Daniel! I knew he wasn't right for me from the start. After he shared his wild stories with me, I shared how God could change his life."

"And?"

Jeans shook her head. "He made it clear: he wasn't interested in religion."

"Religion is a bad word for most people," Rosie said.

"I told him it wasn't about religion; it's about having a personal relationship with the living God through his son, Jesus."

"And?"

Jeans frowned. "He was silent for a few seconds, then answered, *maybe some day, but not today.*"

"I'm sorry to hear that," Rosie replied.

"That's when he started hanging more with Ellen." Jeans hesitated, then continued, "That's when I became attracted to Henrik. He's so sweet and considerate, and he loves God."

Rosie didn't want to sound too much like a nosey-Rosie so she kept her remark short. "And?"

"After awhile I realized that there were no *sparks;* and he knew it too. Honestly, I believe Henrik has always liked Ellen from afar."

Rosie smiled. "Now, that would be quite a pair."

"Only time will tell," Jeans said. "Like I said, I'll write!"

Henrik offered his hand to Rosie at the superstructure door. "Right leg up, left leg up, and over."

"Up and over for the last time," Rosie said as she took hold of Henrik's hand.

Jesse seemed to be taking the departure like a real sailor, but Rosie's heart was heavy. She was leaving behind a crew who had become her family, and a ship she had grown to love.

Tina stood back, waiting until Rosie had finished giving her farewells to the the crew before she embraced her friend. "We will meet again," Tina said gently.

"Is that a promise?"

"Remember, we have a date in Istanbul and Sochi. And I'll keep you updated on the activities of the *Restoration*, if you know what I mean," Tina said, winking as she glanced over at Ellen and Henrik.

"Come on, Rosie!" Jesse yelled from the water taxi.

"Yeah, we're paying for taxi time," Stuart teased.

Looking down over the side of the ship, Rosie's heart started pounding. She had been dreading this moment. Visions of Deena clamoring down the side of the ship in Panama danced in her head.

"Be ready to catch me!" Rosie yelled to Jesse.

"If I can do it, so can you," Shelly said from the small taxi deck.

"Be careful where you place your feet. Now, up and over," Tina prompted.

Rosie glanced down to find a place to plant her right foot. "Wait! There's no ladder!" A large cargo net draped over the side of the ship was blowing back and forth in the wind.

"It doesn't matter, Lady Eunice, you can do it," Ellen prodded.

Rosie took a deep breath and then slowly climbed over the side. "Down, down, down, I go, and where I stop—"

Jesse took hold of her waist as she grabbed for his shoulders.

"There, you handled that like a tough sailor," Jesse said, hugging her.

As the taxi pulled away, Rosie held onto Jesse as she waved good-bye. And there was Ellen, waving back as she munched on leftover pizza.

Rosie's sight blurred. She looked up at Jesse. He, too, was having a hard time.

"Even tough sailors cry," he admitted as she wiped a tear from his cheek.

The hotel lobby felt oddly familiar. "I feel like we've been here before," Rosie told Shelly.

Jesse looked around the lobby. "This is the hotel where we stayed after Bible school graduation."

As they walked toward the elevator, they passed a large bay window that overlooked the Haifa harbor. Rosie stopped and pointed, "Look! There she is!"

Stuart and Jesse dropped the luggage and joined Rosie at the window.

"There she is, the *Restoration*, in all her glory," Jesse said.

"She looks small compared to the other ships in the harbor," Shelly said.

Rosie stared out the window and sighed, "She's a small ship with a big heart."

That evening they left the busy streets behind where cars, taxis and buses sped by, and walked along the wide, bustling walking streets where only people were allowed to stroll. They ate dinner at one of many outdoor cafés. A Russian Jew played a familiar folk song on his violin while children formed a circle and danced. As the Sabbath sun began to set, Orthodox Jews, dressed in black, made their way to nearby synagogues. Tourists mingled with the locals.

"Althought I can't wait to get home, I wish we could stay longer in Israel," Rosie said.

Jesse took Rosie's hand. "We'll come back again, I promise."

"Your husband is a man of his word," Shelly said, and then glanced at her watch. "We have a big day planned for tomorrow, so we're heading back to the hotel. We'll meet you in the morning at the hotel café at seven thirty sharp."

At ten o'clock, the streets were still crowded when Jesse and Rosie strolled toward Haifa's main boulevard. Jesse placed his hand on Rosie's shoulder to guide her through the busy intersection when, suddenly, police officers with Uzi rifles appeared. Policemen quickly moved in to block the street. Rosie's stomach knotted as Jesse grabbed her elbow.

"What's happening?" she asked.

"Maybe a bomb threat; we need to make our way back to the hotel—now."

"Which way should we go?"

"I'll figure something out—just hold on."

People scurried in all directions. Just as Jesse and Rosie turned into an alley, out of nowhere, a tall man in a dark coat darted in front of Jesse, and then turned right on a narrow, well-lit path.

"Let's turn here," Jesse said.

Rosie asked no questions, but quietly followed her husband's lead down the pathway until the tall man disappeared in front of their hotel.

Jesse released her elbow as they entered the hotel elevator. As soon as she caught her breath, the questions began.

"Who was that man?"

"I don't know."

"Why did you follow him?"

"I don't know; something inside told me that he knew the way back to our hotel," Jesse said, tapping his heart.

When they entered their room, Rosie collapsed on the bed. "The fear I experienced tonight was unbearable! We're blessed to live in a country that's safe from terrorism."

Jesse gazed out the window at the now-quiet streets below. "These people live in fear every day."

By the time they climbed into bed, the emotions of the evening had drained Rosie. Espresso or not, she would sleep soundly. She had no sooner closed her eyes when the warmth of Jesse's breath against the nape of her neck brought about a tingling sensation that she thought was nowhere to be found in her tired body.

"Hon, we've never done it in this hotel," he whispered.

She interrupted, "Don't give me that line! We stayed here before, remember?"

They laughed as they wrestled between the sheets.

Stuart was busy munching on fresh tomatoes and goat cheese when Jesse and Rosie joined them in the hotel café for breakfast.

"I was hoping Ellen would join us on our minitour, but she wanted to hang out with Jeans," Stuart said between sips of coffee.

"You'll get to spend time with her when we return," Shelly said. "Did you know that Jeans is going to Bible school next year?" Shelly asked Rosie.

"She told me a few days ago."

"Do you know that Ellen is going to Bible school too? That's an answer to my prayers," Stuart said, grinning.

"She told me yesterday."

"She realized that Daniel wasn't the romantic Viking she thought him to be—that's an answer to *my* prayers," Shelly added.

"She needed time off the ship in Greece to get her thoughts together. Now we can see why God didn't allow her to accept your offer," Stuart said.

"Besides, you were meant to be on that first trip," Shelly said.

Rosie smiled. "I think sometimes God tests us in order to check our motives."

Jesse looked at the hotel clock. "Well, my motive tells me that we better hit the road if we want to see all the sights that I've planned."

They were in their rental car and headed toward Jerusalem by nine o'clock. Stuart glanced in the backseat. "I hope you brought your swimsuits. We're going to swim in the Med and the Dead Sea."

Rosie had purposely hidden her one-piece black swimsuit at the bottom of their suitcase, but Jesse pulled it out. "Aren't you forgetting something, Rosie?" he had asked. She grabbed her swimsuit from his hand and thrust it into her backpack.

They lunched at a sidewalk café in the seaside town of Netanya, and afterward they strolled the walking street that led to the sea.

"The Med looks inviting, but we're short on time," Jesse said.

"That's okay, because tomorrow we'll swim in the Dead Sea," Stuart bellowed.

Jesse shook his head. "Stuart, you don't swim in the Dead Sea—you float. And a word of warning—some fatalities have occurred when people accidentally swallowed too much of the Dead Sea water."

"Yikes! I hope you can keep your mouth shut that long," Shelly said half-teasingly, half-seriously. Rosie shuddered at the thought.

Jesse drove south toward Jerusalem, playing the tour-guide role to the max. "These bare hills are now covered with houses, evidence of the growing number of people moving to Israel."

Jesse parked in a crowded lot across from the Jaffa Gate. Experienced tour guides talked loudly over the crowds, giving information about the old city before hurrying the pilgrims on to their next destination.

Rosie enjoyed the freedom to wander the streets at a slower pace. "I've been here before, but this city never fails to captivate me," she told Shelly. "I can feel electricity in the air as we walk the narrow streets that house Jews, Muslims, and Christians."

After spending time in the Upper Room, Jesse led them to the Wailing Wall. Rosie pulled her scrunchy skirt out of her backpack. "Why do we have to wear skirts?" Shelly asked.

Rosie yanked the skirt over her walking shorts. "It's one of the holy places, where a woman is not allowed to show her knees."

Jesse led Stuart toward the left section, and Rosie guided Shelly to the right. While they waited in line for a place on the wall, Rosie took a paper and pen from her backpack.

"What are you doing?"

"If you write your prayers and place them between the stones, they will be answered by Jehovah."

"Can I borrow your pen and a lot of paper?" Shelly asked.

Surrounded by women young and old from around the world, it was Rosie's turn to take her spot at the wall. She placed the paper between the stones and then prayed for her family, for the *Restoration*, for Operation Jabotinsky, for world peace, and especially for the peace of Jerusalem. This was Rosie's favorite place in Jerusalem. She could have tarried longer, but hundreds of pilgrims were waiting in line. She left, at peace with herself and with her God.

They arrived at the hotel late. "Let's get a good night's sleep, for tomorrow we shall swim—I mean float—in the Dead Sea," Stuart said, yawning.

The next morning as Jesse walked through the lobby, he found Rosie standing at the large bay window. He paused a minute, and then walked over and put his arm around her shoulder. "Rosie, it's time to close this chapter."

"I know. But isn't it ironic—it took us fourteen months to arrive at our destination, and tomorrow it will take only fourteen hours to fly home."

"Home to our family," Jesse added.

She smiled "Yes! Home to our family!"

Jesse continued his tour-guide role as they drove through the hills of Nazareth. "Israel's terrain is similar to California, a combination of barren deserts, rolling hills, flowing rivers, and a lovely sea."

"Thousands of trees have been planted by pilgrims who have journeyed here," Rosie added.

"The Israelis invented the drip system for their crops," Jesse said.

"I'm sure their Arab neighbors within her borders are appreciative," Stuart said.

"It's amazing what such a young country has accomplished since becoming a nation in 1948. They're intelligent, hardworking people with a vision for their land," Rosie said.

After lunching at McDonald's in Tiberius, Jesse said, "We won't have time to take a boat ride on the Galilee if we're going to make it to the Dead Sea."

Stuart gulped down his hamburger. "Then let's hit the road!"

Rosie looked out her window as they drove past tree-covered hills. "Something happens in my spirit the longer I stay here. This is truly God's country."

As trees gave way to desert, they spotted archeological digs taking place alongside the highway.

"Look at the sign!" Stuart said, pointing to a worn sign that read *Jericho* in English, Hebrew, and Arabic. "Let's go see the walls of Jericho!"

Israeli soldiers stood on one side of the road motioning cars to pull over to the right side of the road. Palestinian soldiers stood at attention on the opposite side.

"It seems that Jericho is in the middle of the West Bank cross fire," Jesse said as he pulled their car over.

Tension mounted as they waited at the checkpoint. Israeli soldiers pointed, giving tourists the choice to go through Jericho or to continue on the main highway. Every car stayed on the main road.

"Which way?" Jesse asked, looking over at Stuart.

Rosie was trying to overcome her reputation of backseat driver, but staring at the rifles slung over the soldiers' arms, she wanted to holler, *Stay on the main highway!*

Too late.

"Let's go to Jericho!" Stuart bellowed.

The moment Shelly whispered *yikes,* Rosie started praying. As they drove down the potholed streets, Rosie felt surreal, as if she were in a video documentary, except no one had a video camera. And if they had one, they wouldn't dare use it. *The last thing we need is to be accused of being American spies,* Rosie thought.

"This is no place to be unless you're a high-paid journalist," Shelly said softly.

"Well, I'll tell you right now—I am not cut out to be an international correspondent," Rosie said, glancing back at the main highway. Soldiers monitored every car on the road. Rosie only counted three, including their rental vehicle.

"Me either. I couldn't handle the stress," Shelly said, wringing her hands.

Rosie looked out the windows, trying to find another tourist car. "I bet they're wondering why four Americans are driving through a town as volatile as Jericho," Rosie mentioned to Jesse ever-so-sweetly.

"Yikes, can they tell that we're Americans?" Shelly asked.

Jesse's silence told Rosie what she suspected. He was concerned about their location. Israeli and Palestinian eyes were on them. He casually asked Rosie, "Do you have to go to the bathroom?"

"No, thank you," she answered politely.

"Is anyone thirsty?" he asked.

"I'll pass," Shelly said, trying to stop her voice from shaking.

Jesse drove onto the main highway, and as if nothing had happened, Stuart was talking again, which always made Rosie feel better. "I read in our American newspapers how certain Arab countries want to push Israel into the sea."

"There's a higher power protecting this small country. According to God's word, this land will one day be a land of peace," Jesse said with conviction.

"In the meantime, let's stay on the main highway," Rosie suggested.

The Dead Sea greeted them with 100+-degree temperatures. Jesse, Shelly, and Rosie sat in the shade of a large palm tree, sipping soft drinks, watching Stuart float, wearing his sunglasses and a closed-lip smile.

"I've never seen Stuart keep his mouth shut for so long," Shelly said, chuckling.

Jesse laughed. "I can't imagine Stuart putting himself in a place where he wasn't able to talk."

Rosie pulled her sunglasses below her eyes. "Look at him . . . I haven't seen him this relaxed in a long time."

Shelly smiled. "He's basking in the fulfillment of his dream—the *Restoration* is his dream come true."

Jesse wiped the beads of sweat from his forehead. "It's been a real journey of faith, and more challenging than any of us had anticipated."

"But Stuart wouldn't trade this experience for all the fish in Alaska," Shelly said, reaching for her backpack. "I think I'll join my husband."

Jesse smiled as he observed Stuart's arms and feet peeking above the salty surface. "This journey has caused his faith to grow. I swear his chest expanded twenty inches when Torre gave him the news that all the safety equipment had finally arrived."

Jesse picked up his backpack.

"Where are you going?" Rosie asked.

"I'm going to join my friend for a float," Jesse said, heading for the bathhouse. "Why don't you join us?"

Rosie reached for her soda. "Oh no, I'm staying right here under the palm tree."

Fourteen months of memories came rushing back as Rosie watched the three Americans float in the Dead Sea. The World War II ship had been named well. The old vessel had experienced a restoration back to her natural beauty. The first of many Russian Jews had been restored to their homeland. A father and daughter relationship showed signs of restoration. And the restoring of friendships continued.

Rosie recalled the inward struggles she went through to come this far. She would have never chosen to serve God on an old war vessel, but God had a better plan. "And to think, I almost missed this faith-building journey. I must remember to stay flexible in the years ahead."

A silver-haired woman in a one-piece floral turquoise swimsuit sitting on the bench next to her shouted, "Are you talking to me, young lady?"

Rosie hadn't realized anyone had overheard her. "Oh, no, ma'am, I was telling myself that I must stay flexible in my older age."

"That's right, sweetie. I stay flexible by swimming at the YMCA."

Rosie smiled at the woman, placed her soda can in the trash, dug in the bottom of her backpack for her swimsuit, and then made a quick change in the bathhouse. She walked to the water's edge, knowing that today she wouldn't need to swim. She would do what her father had taught her when she was a little girl. Today she would float.

Stuart reached for Shelly's hand that was resting on top of the water. "This is the best day ever," he said with his mouth half-opened.

Rosie held onto Jesse's hand. "This moment is dedicated to you, Captain Stuart," Jesse said.

Between clinched teeth, Rosie added, "And I dedicate this moment to you, Jesse, my traveling partner for life."

Then she looked upward through water-splashed sunglasses. "Lord, we dedicate this moment to you, for allowing us to be participators in prophecy."

"Here, here!" the other three Americans chimed.

As Rosie floated, she promised herself that, before the summer's end, she would sign up for swimming lessons at the local YMCA.

And the best was yet to come for the MS *Restoration*.

CPSIA information can be obtained
at www.ICGtesting.com
Printed in the USA
FFOW01n2010110314
4175FF